The Madam

Doug Booth

The Madam

For Linda,
As with all else I've written

The Madam

Part One

July 18, 6:30 PM
Atlanta, Georgia

The first set of knocks at the door was barely audible. Mercedes ignored them. No one had knocked at the door in a year. Not even the mailman knew anything about them and he cared even less.

Another set of taps followed seconds later with an impatient quality. She reflexively put down her little girl and, in a fleeting moment, allowed naïve curiosity to flout Manuel's repeated warnings against opening the door to strangers. The bright evening sun instantly scorched her skin that was still damp from the thick humidity of Atlanta's oppressive summer heat and she raised a hand to shield her eyes from the blinding glow. Neither man stepped back when she tilted her head to see their faces, answering the one who asked to speak with her husband.

They were chalky white, dressed in pale blue button-down shirts that were opened at the neck to show white crewneck undershirts. Their matching dark beige Dockers were buckled at their rounded waists, the requisite cuffs resting on oxblood-colored loafers with tassels. They were no different from thousands of other Georgia gentlemen and spoke with what she had recently learned was a Southern drawl, which made them unremarkable.

She hated the way people in her adopted hometown spoke: white women with a superior air and white men seemingly always ready to sleep. Then there were the blacks who had their own language she had absolutely no idea about. Her new world was not what she had expected, but, white or black, the eyes and the condescension were the same: She was a Mexican.

The men stared at her, one taller than his friend by several inches and heavier by a hundred pounds or more. He held a bright red prayer book against his blue shirt while his smaller companion stood with one hand by his side as he extended the other to Mercedes so she would reach out for the brochure. She didn't, nor did she say her husband was not at home.

"Ma'am, we do apologize for this interruption at the dinner hour. But with your kind permission we have such a joyous message of love to share with you and your husband, and an invitation to join our congregation this Sunday morning for fellowship and prayer."

She smiled, her expression showing that she understood none of what he had said. "No. I thank you. We are not interested to go. Good-bye."

The larger man smiled without seeing her, nodding sympathetically, looking past her as his partner casually glanced behind them.

"Señorita, perhaps we might have a word with the man of the house?"

The words were kind, the eyes were not, and she sensed too late they were not good men.

"I am sorry. I must go now. I thank you."

The powerful grip encircling most of her neck was paralyzing, causing her to kick and flail her arms involuntarily as he pushed her into the house, guiding her quickly and forcefully onto the floor. The second man walked in slowly, closing the door behind them, watching his friend turn her over face down before he grabbed at her chocolate brown ponytail and jerked her face away from them.

"Lady, this won't take long if you do what you're told. We won't hurt you or your kid as long as you don't do anything stupid. Comprende, lady?" He glanced at his partner, not letting go of her hair. "Bobby, you do the other rooms. I'll do in here, and don't forget the stuff in her purse." He pointed at the baby. "And lock up that screaming brat somewhere."

"Do not hurt my baby. Take all that you want. Please do not hurt my baby."

"We won't, lady, but you talk once more and I'll push your little Mexican head into the floor, comprende?"

"Sí. Yo comprendo. Gracias."

But she didn't. The one called Bobby had already picked up little Sofia, disappearing down the hall by the time Frankie stood, concentrating on the woman who lay sprawled at his feet. He gave her a long look, feeling a growing urgency at seeing the hem of her skirt that had ridden high over her white cotton panties that did little to conceal the soft flesh and contours of her buttocks.

"You stay exactly as you are. Don't move one inch," he threatened, "or I'll do something real bad to the kid."

He walked away from her, searching the room, eyeing her often, each time more aroused until Bobby returned. "There's no need to rush, Frankie. Her hubby won't be home anytime soon. If I'm not mistaken, I'd say a couple of months, September 30." He was watching Mercedes. "He's over in Iraq doing sniper shit according to the photo and calendar in the bedroom. Not too many red Xs between now and then."

"That so, lady? Your husband's gone off for a while?" She lay still. "Then let's do this right, Bobby. Go finish up, and take your time. I'll finish in here, and give me some time." He went to Mercedes, kneeling behind her. "You have any booze in here, lady?" She didn't answer. "Booze, liquor, vino… you got any vino in this shitbox house?"

"Sí, it is in the kitchen."

He pushed the her skirt up over her lower back, sliding a gruff hand under her panties, enjoying her youthful smoothness and her warmth as he groped uncaringly between her buttocks while his other hand heightened the sensation of his erection. She began crying softly, her rigid body trembling as she felt the tug at her zipper. She understood nothing he was saying. His hands at the hem of her skirt told her everything.

He tossed the skirt beside her, telling her to turn over and raise her hips, changing his mind when she was slow to react. He outweighed her by 150 pounds, he was hungry for her, and her panties came off in one fluid motion before he let her hips drop to the hardwood floor. He smelled them, inhaling deeply, tearing them apart before grabbing at her top as he stood, telling her to get naked before he got back. Then he left. When he returned the bottle of wine was open; his glass was half full. Mercedes was completely naked, sobbing, kneeling on the floor with her arms crossed over her breasts and her knees squeezed tightly together.

"What's your name?"

"Mercedes," she coughed.

"Well, Mercedes, seems like you won't' be waiting till Sunday for love and fellowship after all. Come over here, and stop all that crying. It's not the worst thing I could do to you. What's it been, eight, nine months? Hell, girl, you must be real hungry for some by now."

"Please do not do this."

"How old are you?" She didn't answer. "I asked how old you are."

"Twenty-three," she whispered, squeezing tears from her eyes, oblivious to her nakedness

He expelled a loud, satisfied sigh. At thirty-five he liked younger women and hated growing old.

"Now get up and get over here." He slapped an open palm on the glass-covered console table, waiting. "I said get up… and I want you up here with your legs nice and open so I can see what you've got for me."

She clambered onto the table, needing his help to balance on the narrow surface, letting him push apart her legs. When he pushed down the zipper of his pants she closed her eyes, waiting. She blocked him out, hearing only Manuel's tender whisper, knowing she would feel only his tender touch, desperately remembering the way they would always moan together from the same intimate pleasure as her bare chest began to glisten with her tears. She felt her legs easing farther apart, his hot, erratic breath between them as he tore at his shirt and pulled her into his face so her legs were draped over his shoulders, the coarse hair on his back already matted with sweat.

He stood, holding her knees away from the table, nodding his approval. He was completely naked and began sliding his hips against her thighs, his enormous and shapeless stomach pressing into her pulsating breasts as his hands slid under her buttocks to lift her and bring them closer together. He spoke slowly, in a whisper, so she would understand. The threat was clear. She nodded, moaning, wrapping her arms and legs tightly around him, letting herself be pulled from the table and held in his arms. She would be good, she agreed. She would be very good and do what he wanted for the sake of her little Sofia.

She was diminutive and weightless in his arms. Her moans were real, his thrusts urgent and rough. His hands groped freely, grabbing at her breasts, pulling and probing between her buttocks. She responded, helping him satiate a need as she ground herself closer to him. His skin was clammy, his breath hot, reeking of stale cigars. He said

9

nothing more, as though she wasn't there locked in his arms, unable to move, unable to resist, and when he finished he stood with his back against a wall, his erection deep inside her. She loved Manuel and she adored her daughter. When he pulled himself free he turned and stood her against the wall, letting his engorged penis prod and sign her heaving and wet abdomen. He smiled, enjoying the sensation.

"That was good, lady, wasn't it?"

He pinched her chin when she didn't answer, bringing her face to meet his.

"I said… that was good, wasn't it?"

"Yes, it was good."

"Now, do something nice for my big guy with those little hands of yours before I put him away, little lady."

"No comprendo."

He leaned in against her. "No comprendo. Then, let's go two-for-two, señorita. Do you understand that?"

Two

When the couple stepped from the cramped shower stall he was revitalized, she was silent and trembling. Frankie threw her a towel, telling her to towel herself slowly and turn full circle as she did, making the motion with his free hand.

He told her to bend forward as she dried her legs and to stretch out as she did her arms held over her head. He showed her how to open her legs and arch backward as she ran the towel across her breasts and stomach, and forward as she did her back as he stood behind her dripping onto the floor, helping his body react to her nakedness and clumsy ballet. When she was done he threw her a dry towel and faced her, fully erect with his legs slightly parted, his arms crossed behind his head. As she began he warned her about missing anything important.

When she was done he followed her into her bedroom and watched her dress in clean clothes. She was 5'2" and slim without being skinny and she was perfectly proportioned. Her breasts were firm, her nipples a slight shade darker than the pale golden hue of her skin. The hollow of her back curved into perfectly round and smooth buttocks, her dark pubic hair trimmed to almost nothing so he could see the delicate dark folds peeking from between caramel-colored lips.

When he was finished he told her to gather up his scattered clothes; then he told her to watch as he dressed.

When they joined Bobby, Sofia was playing with him on the sofa and giggling happily, squealing with delight when Mercedes swept her up to hug her protectively.

"I didn't hurt her, ma'am. I wouldn't do that."

"Never mind the brat, Bobby. What's the tally?"

"Not much, Frankie. Some gold jewelry, probably worth a grand on the street, a credit card and an ATM card. Don't think she'd have more than a few hundred in one and minimal on the other, being she's Mexican. Guess we'll find out. Guess she looks a lot richer than she is. Least you got some."

"Getting laid isn't much different from eating Chinese, Bobby. Wait five minutes and you're hungry again. Mind you, she wasn't half bad. Tell the truth, I think she had a good time. I wouldn't half mind spending the night." Mercedes stood huddled in the corner with her baby, struggling to understand. "You keeping anything from us, lady, like money or more jewelry?" She shook her head, not knowing.

"Dinero, lady, you got any more dinero?"

"No."

"I believe her, Frankie. Let's wrap them up and get out of here."

Frankie pointed to Mercedes who was clutching Sofia and speaking in sobbing whispers to Manuel.

"No. We got three more hours and we're a half-hour away. So what's the rush?"

Bobby shrugged. He had no answer that was good enough.

"You go call for some pizza and take the kid with you. This one fucks like a pro with the body of a teenager. She's a definite Ti-Fi without a mark on her. Who'd ever believe she's had a kid and there's no way Divine won't snap her up for an extra five," he sniggered, "once we get our money. She's perfect, Bobby. And the kid goes to Savannah for the usual ten. We've had a good day so far, so don't fucking spoil it for me."

"But she's a Combo. How can we be sure Divine won't screw us over?"

"She's been screwing us for twelve years. It's time we get what we deserve. We'll do this one different. After we eat, you get the camcorder from the van while I get the lady here ready for a dog and pony show. In the meantime order up an extra large and put it on her card."

Three

"It's dark, Bobby. Get the cam and bring the van around. Don't park out front, and don't hurry. We don't need anyone seeing us."

Bobby left through the front door with Sofia as though they were father and daughter. When he returned with the camera Frankie sent him again to the van and took Mercedes to the bedroom as though they were husband and wife.

"Take off your clothes, real slow, and lie on the bed. We're making a little home video, sort of a demo." He smiled. "And you'd better be good lady, as good as before, or we'll hurt your precious little Sofia real bad, then you. Understand?"

She was numb. She nodded instinctively, escaping in her mind to another place, not understanding at all what was happening, or why. What she understood was her daughter's name. She took off her clothes unemotionally as he studied her every move, stopping her when her hands tucked mechanically under the narrow band of her panties. He sat on the bed, telling her to turn around, to bend over, and to push out her butt before she pulled them off. They were words she hadn't heard before and she stood gazing blindly past him.

Impatient, he reached out, pushing her forward with one hand against her bare buttocks, pulling her into him with an

14

open hand across her lower belly from between the apex of her open legs. He told her to stay as she was while he stroked and kneaded her soft, bare skin, finally pulling the silky strands of her thong from between the fleshy mounds of her buttocks and pushing them to her ankles. Then he jerked them up with both hands, lifting her from the floor and told her to do it again, on her own, the same way, and the taping began.

He told her again to lie face down on the bed, then to roll over, and when she did he jerked her knees up and apart, staring at the reddened lips. She wanted to kill him; she wanted to see him die. Instead she turned her head, peering into the eyes of the man in the photograph, the man she knew would one day hunt and kill the men who had so quickly devastated and ruined their lives.

When the taping came to an end he made himself ready and leaned over her.

Four

July 19, 5.30 AM
Kou Senjaq, on the Iraq-Iran border

The blistering sun would not pierce the horizon for another thirty-seven minutes. The desert heat was already ninety-two degrees, by midday the forecasted 118° would be suffocating with a nine-mile southerly wind that would sear bared skin and do nothing to cool the superheated air rising from the sun-baked earth.

They were a squad apart, detached from others in the company as much by choice as by exclusion: an accepted anomaly worn as a badge of honor. His job was easy compared to the others. They resented him, yet he eliminated the most fanatical elements, the most ruthless and driven of the enemy, and for that they admired him, from a distance, in awe of the silent sniper who eradicated their worst threats. He worked in the dark and slept days when he wasn't killing cardboard insurgents or being jarred awake by the surround sound cacophony of a war that was not his.

Private First Class Manuel Del Fuego enlisted one year earlier at the age of twenty-four and was far from the youngest in the battalion. He wanted to make a difference. They all did, mostly in their own lives. They were all too young and indestructible, except those who had already died

16

in seven months of fighting to free anonymous men and women who hated them for a supposed high standard of living and the West's compulsion with ensuring freedom for the downtrodden of the world.

He snorted into the ground at the irony, crossing himself in silent prayer, praying for the family of the man whose face was centered in the crosshairs of his scope. The US Marine creed was: One shot, One Kill. A second later he fired the eightieth of eighty shots from the lethal M82 sniper rifle, ignoring the eyes of the eightieth man from eleven-hundred yards away. That very instant the mud-colored stucco wall behind the man transformed into a modernist fresco splattered in red.

The spotter slapped him on the shoulder, giving him the thumbs up. Juan Carlos had no family. He didn't want one, and he claimed the distinction of being the first Mexican gypsy and a direct descendant of the last ruling Mayan king. He was bohemian in every possible way. He cared about no one and nothing. He was 6'4", twenty-eight, dark inside and out with a slim, chiseled body. He spoke AAVE better than most American Blacks in the platoon or in the ghettos of any US city, and there wasn't a single Marine in the platoon he hadn't scoped at least once as he spit out Spanish in a blur with his middle finger stuck out to greet them.

Most of all he was Mexican, a Latino from Chiapas who even the Drill Sergeant called Spook behind his back. The only one to ever say the words to his face was a redneck army reservist from Alabama who learned the hard way that pissing off a Mayan gypsy Marine who never smiled or laughed was not a good thing. Even the biggest Marine kept his distance from JC. He possessed an aura they could see and smell. He didn't give a shit, pure and simple. They did, and his cold apathy towards all but the mission and his spotter spooked them.

Manuel closed his eyes, waiting for the thunderous roar

and crushing downdraft of the Huey helicopter that always seemed too far away after a kill. He hadn't thrown up since his first mission and now he thought of each one as target practice which would make the next mission that much better. He was good, one of the best in the squad, though he would never boast of exactly how good. He felt no pride in what he did, the only job he could find.

For Juan Carlos being in the Marines was self-serving part-time work, a necessary four-year interlude in a lucrative career he would soon reestablish once he returned to Miami in ten weeks, three days and counting. After Carmelita he cared about nothing else. All Manuel cared about was that Mercedes and Sofia were well and safe. And the Corps was the only way he could provide for them. He lay still, barely breathing, invisible to all but those who were coming for them, and he went to her as he did each time he survived a mission with a promise he would come home to his girls and give them a better life.

Five

July 18, 9:30 PM
Atlanta, Georgia

He told her before filming what he wanted her to do and say. Ejecting the cassette from the camcorder he left the room excitedly, not giving her a second thought. Mercedes lay on the bed and didn't move as she had been told. He wanted to review the scene on the small plasma screen in the living room before making her do her make-up, dress and pack a suitcase for herself and the girl. She was better than he hoped. She was a natural, Bobby agreed, as the duo ransacked her bedroom searching for the perfect outfit for Mercedes to wear while she sat naked in front of the photo by the bed.

Everything they selected was brand new, what she had bought for her husband's return from Iraq and their first special evening in nearly ten months. The ensemble was an emerald-on-midnight blue three-quarter bra with matching Rio panties and garters, a black cocktail dress, belted and décolleté with a bare back, and low-heeled patent leather pumps; the sensual result of five months of planning and budgeting.

"Get dressed, real slow, and do it real sexy. I want to watch you one last time. Then pack a bag for you and the kid, pronto."

"Where do we go? Where do you take us?"

"You'll see for yourself soon enough. The four of us are going for a ride." He reached into his rear pocket, smiling. "Bobby'll carry the bags, I'll carry the girl. I think she likes me."

The slim 8.5 inch stiletto blade shot from the mahogany handle in a blur, stopping Mercedes, the garter strap snapping against her hip, her eyes seething with hatred.

"I will kill you to even think about it."

He laughed. "It might be you'll think of killing yourself in a little bit, missy." He made a shooing motion with his free hand. "Keep going, nice and slow. You look great. She'll like you just fine."

When they stepped outside the deathly humidity of the afternoon had become pleasant nighttime air and the neighborhood was quiet. Anyone interested would see a family, however no one was interested. No one cared.

The van was clean, washed by constant summer rains, and Frankie made no effort to help her into the passenger seat as Bobby climbed in behind the wheel. The inside was also clean, though smelled of liquor and marijuana, she thought, and sex. Sofia was put on the seat behind Bobby and Frankie sat behind Mercedes. The ride would take thirty minutes and Sofia would sleep peacefully. She had seen her mother for the last time.

Mercedes spent the half-hour staring at her, wanting so much to hold her and kiss her, fearing the worst had not yet happened and that somehow she would never hold her again. She was told to see nothing, and she obeyed, giving her baby all her attention and well before the van arrived at its destination Frankie reached forward to wrap a dark cloth tightly across her eyes.

Bobby put his hand to the side of her head, preventing her from lifting the blindfold when Frankie climbed out and disappeared into the darkness behind them.

"Stay where you are and don't touch your head." Bobby warned, enunciating each word. "If you see where we are, he'll kill you, and your daughter. So, please, stay as you are."

"I can touch her?"

"Go ahead, and keep your head down. Understand?"

"Sí, yo comprendo."

"Frankie's not a nice man. We're friends and all, know what I mean? Still, he's not a nice guy. So don't piss him off."

"¿No comprendo lo que dice?" she said, not understanding.

"Don't fuck with him, lady. Do not make him angry with you, or he will hurt you and your little girl really bad."

"Why do you do this to us?"

He waited, as though thinking about the answer. "It's what we do, lady. We all do what we do to get by. Your problem is you're too pretty. That's why we followed you home. You're a pretty one. Bonita. Know what I mean? Frankie…he's got a good nose for women. He's never wrong. Shit, he must have a hundred pictures of you and the kid. He's wanted you for a while." He wanted to sound remorseful, being anything but. "Real stupid thing you did, opening the door. Hell, we probably would've left."

"You are not bad as he is. You can let us go, please." She gulped air, searching for moisture. "He is gone now. Please, I can go with my baby."

"I can't do that, lady. He'd kill me for sure. For thirty thousand plus ten for the kid he'd do me in a split second." He took a deep breath. "I'm sorry. I'm not that brave… and stay down."

Mercedes stopped listening, caressing her child for as long as she could.

Six

July 18, 6:00 PM
Atlanta, Georgia

She didn't mind. She knew everything would work out. What she cared about, all she thought about on her way home each day was that he might not come home. They had argued for hours that had turned into days, and he knew in his heart she was right. All the same, he was Latino and he didn't like it. She understood his feelings, but what were a few years of making beds and cleaning toilets if in the end little Sofia would grow up healthy and safe?

Four years and two months had passed since she first locked eyes on the young and very handsome chemical engineer in Veracruz on their way home from their studies in Mexico City; three years and two months since their wedding, May 05, el cinco de mayo, much to the frustration and disappointment of both families. To Mercedes he was gallant, brave and defiant, charming and bon vivant. To her parents he was dark and challenging, disrespectful and arrogant. He had taken their daughter from them and nothing good would ever come of it. El cinco de Mayo was one thing, naming their granddaughter after the invading French forces of 1862 was quite another.

Sofia Francesca was born nine months later, the day before an official envelope arrived from the US Department of Immigration. The letter was a long awaited answer to a dream thought to be lost. They loved Mexico, and leaving their families would be painful, but they wanted opportunity and streets paved in gold for Sofia. They had been told the chances were good, though midway through their second year together they had begun to give up hope of raising their daughter in America. Now they would and all Manny asked was that they not become lost in one of the faceless and stereotypical Southwest or Southeast Latino barrios. Hispanics and Latinos were becoming more outspoken and aggressive in their quest for linguistic and civil equality and he wanted no part of it. They were going to America, they would be Americans and they would speak English, which did not mean giving up who and what they were.

Those bright days seemed so long ago. Atlanta's social climate was cold with indifference. Not one of the middle class neighbors had welcomed them, nor would they and Manuel could not find work. Worse, their funds were dwindling as their debts mounted. The solution seemed desperate: four years with the USMC that would make him equal to the best and give his family the better life he and Mercedes had expected. One week later he enlisted and, after the initial testing, he left her for five months of intensive and grueling training on Parris Island and Quantico with rare weekends at home.

She was so proud of him at graduation. He was a US Marine and he looked the part. Then they went home for ten days, when he told her about Iraq, that he was shipping out for a nine-month tour and pride quickly turned into fear. That was seven months earlier and the fear had never left her, or his promise to return home.

Her work at the hotel was hard, more demeaning than she would ever admit to Manuel. The worst was waking Sofia so early each morning. She worked ten-hour days, and at the end of each day the other maids openly laughed at her the way the white women secretly laughed at them.

Manuel had made her a promise, but their life would not get better unless they acted as though it already had. She had a degree in art with a major in design and one day she would have her studio, he promised. Let them laugh because others laughed at them. She would not walk home wearing a maid's uniform from a three star hotel to be ridiculed by their neighbors. She would not disgrace herself that way, and she never did.

Each day at the end of her shift her drab black-on-white uniform came off and fresh lingerie went on with a proper skirt, a blouse and low-heeled pumps. They saw her change at the end of each day and laughed at her. She didn't care. She was doing so for him and to feel like a young, vibrant woman. She was beautiful, she was Latina. He always told her so and one day she would have the last laugh.

Sofia was waiting for her as she always did at daycare, not caring that mommy was coming for her. She was playing with her friends and making everyone happy, forgetting them when Mercedes picked her up and kissed her all over with wet smacking noises.

The heat was sweltering on the way home from the center. The torrential late-day rain hadn't come and they stopped for ice cream as they always did, which made going home Sofia's favorite part of the day, when her mommy told her all about her daddy who was the bravest hero in the Marines and that he would soon be home to love them. The men walking behind Mercedes had seen her many times over the past few days. Frank Randolph and Robert Baker were good at what they did. They were pros who had been in the business for twelve years without incident and Mercedes Del Fuego was not their first Acquisition.

Randolph was a rapist. Baker wasn't, which made him feel good about who he was. He was thirty, a high school dropout who believed in the afterlife. He also believed in the sanctity of single living, although he would often entertain at home after the last call as long as she was as drunk as she could be and had taxi money. He was a weasel of a man with thin hair, a gaunt face and a body deprived of any real shape.

He did his job with cold detachment, believing what he did was no better or worse than any other service industry, despite never having worked at a real job. Working with Frankie was all he knew. He had always followed Frankie's lead, had always followed orders, and always would, never giving thought to the human element. There was no going back. They knew too much about each other and Miss Divine knew that much more.

They had followed Mercedes to work each morning and had come home with her. They had been at the park with her and had done her groceries with her. Randolph knew quality at first glance and had often commented to Baker how good she would be. Latinas were always good, at least in bed. They were hot. They lived for it, and so did he.

They determined the mother and daughter arrived home each night at the same time, no one ever greeted them at the door and in the morning no one was there to say good-bye.

Seven

Frankie stared at the woman throughout the entire five minutes as she studied the video intently before replaying it, transfixed. She was like a bird of prey ready to swoop down on some child's unsuspecting pet, not realizing she was leaning closer to the screen. He had done well, again, and he would get his extra five grand this one time.

She would keep the tape for her private collection and wanted the girl brought to her as quickly as possible. Hearing Mercedes was as close as the main doors she could scarcely contain herself and Mercedes Del Fuego was duly purchased for thirty thousand dollars. She would never discover where they had taken her, or the irony that a few feet east of her new home, The Hotel Le Chic, Ellis Street became Freedom Parkway.

To the casual passer-by, Le Chic was a boutique hotel of obvious quality, a step above the dozens of other high-end hotels dotting the Midtown Quarter amongst exhibition halls, shops, commercial towers, restaurants and lesser hotels. The doors opened twelve years earlier and the occupancy rate seldom dropped below one hundred percent, save the week between Christmas and New Year's. The hotel was not known by any association, was not listed in any directory, was not on the web and the phone number was unlisted. Atlanta's most exclusive bordello was virtually unknown.

The Madam

The façade was old-Georgia amidst the steel and glass of surrounding modernity and the French-styled oak doors with plate glass inlay only opened electronically once the expected guest identified him or herself with a one-time numeric code given to them at the time of their reservation, which was confirmed with a bio-metric scan once inside. There was no doorman, no bellhop and each guest was expected to arrive by limousine, taxi, or on foot, surrendering his or her cell phone at the desk for the convenience of other guests.

Frankie reached into the vehicle, gripping Mercedes by the neck, jerking her onto the sidewalk. She saw nothing as she was dragged across fifteen feet of open space to the hotel's pink granite steps and heard nothing until he punched in the code and kicked at the brass panels at the bottom of the twin oak doors.

Bobby remained inert and expressionless, ignoring her, feeling nothing when she called out to him by name begging for help. He knew he was no better than Frankie. Together they had carried out dozens of home invasions and kidnappings across the Southeast, each time in a different city, each time in a different way. Terrorizing, stealing, fraying the nerves of innocent people was what he did and he did his job well.

Frankie had raped before, he always did, and he would rape again, though he never brutalized the women, Bobby justified. The first time he did attempt to intervene, until Frankie explained he was performing a pre-delivery inspection, the same as for any other household appliance. Miss Divine wanted quality, unblemished Acquisitions and how else were they going to ensure quality without first testing them. He was also told to never again cross the line, and he never did.

Rejects were out of the question, especially given the lucrative Disposals which were part of every Acquisition.

27

Of course, he harboured no delusion that one day Frankie would kill. Then the dynamics of what they were and what they did would change abruptly forever. Then, whether he was out of the room at the time or number two in line wouldn't matter. He never thought of Acquisitions after he left them because the money was good. Mercedes was far from the first woman they had sold to the hotel and she wouldn't be the last, however she was the first he had thought of as different. This time someone would not forget or forgive.

Perhaps the last one didn't have a family, as Frankie had told him, but this one did have a husband who would be truly pissed and would know how to hunt and kill. Bobby wasn't affected by what Mercedes said to him, rather how she sounded and what he saw in her deep brown eyes as she tried so desperately for one final glimpse of her daughter.

He turned away from her, cold with apprehension, shivering involuntarily and praying for unlikely salvation.

Eight

They would travel the 280 miles between midtown's Ellis Street NE and Savannah's River Street in six hours because being stopped by Georgia's finest wasn't an option with Sofia sleeping soundly in the backseat. Frankie had made certain she would sleep until noon, by which time she would be in Jacksonville, Florida. Unbeknownst to him, Tucker Richman had finalized the arrangements and the Hillmans were far too excited to sleep.

Tucker Richman, Attorney at Law, had not yet gone to bed when his phone rang at 11:00 PM, moments after Frankie and Bobby had left The Hotel Le Chic. When he did, some thirty minutes later, he did so with an unbalanced blend of cheap gin and soda that had become his loving and indispensable companion countless years earlier.

Roger and Marietta Hillman stayed up all night making plans, eager to pay Richman his twenty-five thousand dollar finder's fee in cash. He was finally bringing them a daughter. By noon they would be a family, as Frankie and Bobby began making their first of several ATM withdrawals from the Del Fuego accounts that would continue over the next several days.

Nine

July 19, 07.00 AM
Savannah, Georgia

Tucker Richman didn't appear as though he could afford the River Street address of the law firm Tucker and Associates, and he couldn't. His associates were gin and tonic, with tonic absent much of the time, and he was there because he had bought the building years earlier when he was still good at practicing law. At first, he refused to realize why that had changed. Now he couldn't remember all the reasons and didn't care.

He lived off rent from a restaurant whose owner did not want him as a patron and three other long-term tenants whose businesses he cared nothing about. He had no intern, no secretary or receptionist and his office hours were whenever he chose to press SEND on his cell. He worked by word of mouth, cash only, and prospective clients had to be referred. Walk-ins were never accepted and his land-based line was never answered. If you didn't know him, or someone who did, he wasn't interested.

His office was sloppy and dank with threadbare carpeting on uneven floors that creaked under the slightest weight, the smell of a cheap seaside motel with discolored and shapeless circa eighties furniture, and client files he hadn't touched in years piled high on his cigar-burnt desk.

Rows of ancient-looking law books lined water-stained walls, though they were old with neglect and the artificial aging that comes to everything influenced by ten-inch Cubans and carcinogenic pipe tobacco.

He was fifty-five, though a casual observer would believe seventy-five and seemingly ready to die after a long and miserable life. He was shapeless, bald and pathetic, abhorred by all women who thought of him as a troll and most Southern men who simply thought of him as someone not born there. He had no family or friends. His 5'6" frame had once been trim, now its pasty-white skin was bloated and his face was permanently scarred with patches and streaks of red and purple. His teeth and hands were yellowed from smoke and his eyes were dull, clouded over from excess.

He shaved on Mondays, his client day, the day he wore clean everything and brushed a previous week's worth of dust from his thick-soled shoes. He had one grey suit, one red tie with a tight permanent knot and changed his shirt when the need was apparent, which was usually by Thursday. This week the change came a day early.

He didn't like Frankie and never cared to know Bobby. Together they bothered him, so he told Bobby to fuck off and wait outside. They were scroungers, hunters, the worst of the worst, and lowest of the low. He despised them for what they were, when he really knew despising himself would be much easier.

Frankie always wanted more than he was worth: ten thousand for a day's work. He was aware of Frankie's perverse proclivity towards his pretty victims. The man enjoyed telling him about the mothers in graphic detail, as though reliving the moment, not that Richman ever relived the events vicariously. He didn't. He had no objection to renting a woman for twenty minutes of devoted affection, though he didn't like the idea of selling them and he thought the ten grand for the kids was excessive given the benefits. In any event, the deal was done: ten grand in twenties, and he wondered about Bobby's share, not that he cared.

The cute little dark-haired girl curled into a ball on a hard bench that served as a sofa and filing cabinet had no idea her mother was so far away, crying for her and knowing nothing while imagining the worst. Richman knew nothing about kids beyond their high marketability and he was unaccustomed to handling them other than pushing them into a car or dragging them out. He knew he would never be mistaken for a relative of such a pretty girl, even though at that hour there would be few curious Good Samaritans who might ask questions.

He ordered Bobby to carry her to his car, following at a distance with Frankie. When both men had gone he stayed, leaning against a wall with both hands in his pockets, looking out over the Savannah River with an unobtrusive black stub pinched into the corner of his mouth. He studied his Rolex, one of his two luxuries. By ten he would be twenty-five K richer and he was worth every penny.

The cold stub blew from his mouth unassisted, falling between his feet with a wet splat. He mashed it under foot before pushing himself away from the wall, turning as he spit dark brown tobacco flecks off his tongue. He never smoked or chewed stubs in the Mercedes, his other luxury that would do the seventy-five miles on the southbound I-95 to Saint Simons in one hour while the girl slept soundly in the back.

The Sea Islands were historical jewels of the Southeast and St. Simons Island was a quaint part of Georgia, where African slaves transported from the West Indies once found freedom and spoke a linguistic stew called Gullah.

Nestled in the shallow waters of the Intracoastal Waterway, the island was a peaceful and subdued Mecca for yachtsmen and the affluent. Richman knew the best place for seafood was on the scenic Torras Causeway where tables were seldom empty between noon and midnight during peak season, but at 10:00 AM only his car occupied the farthest spot in the parking lot.

Roger and Marietta Hillman were affluent, or so they appeared. He was a successful and ambitious senior engineer in a leading Jacksonville firm and until that morning she had worked as a receptionist at the same firm, giving up her job to become the loving and dutiful mother she'd been hoping to become for the past several months. They had everything and lacked nothing that could be paid for with credit or a second mortgage on their home that had financed a boat and beach house.

When not entertaining at their beautiful beachfront property in the St. Augustine Beach district, they entertained in an upscale ranch-style home in Jacksonville. They dined out often, they traveled twice yearly to Europe for the special je ne sais quoi flavor, to Quebec for what they thought was European flavor, or to Mexico because a charming, gold-toothed Mexican beach vendor once told Mrs. Hillman that she spoke good Spanish. She didn't. She suffixed English words with Os and As, spoke loudly and ended up paying more than anyone else.

They were both forty-nine and now had everything they wanted in life, except money and a room for Ana Jane who was coming to them so suddenly after being told by Richman that the delivery would take quite a while.

Ten

Tucker Richman waited several car lengths away, studying the blond couple in the red Corvette with the top down. He had seen them once before when they had come to his office to sign the adoption papers which he later destroyed.

He wasn't impressed by them, he never was. Anyone who would pay that much money for a kid that would eventually suck them dry deserved being screwed. And, as with previous clients, the Hillmans understood all pertinent documentation would accompany the child at the time of delivery.

Friend, fool or foe, twenty-five grand was big money and whose money didn't matter. He stepped from the sedan, shaking a pant leg and straightening his lapels before reaching in for the half-inch thick manila folder containing pertinent medical data, legal documentation and history on little Ana Juanita Vaquero, daughter of Juana and Diego Vaquero who perished tragically in a car accident some weeks earlier.

He was not one for formalities. Too many years and too many bottles of gin had gone by since he was last in a courtroom. Mr. Hillman struggled out from behind the wheel, grinning as though some obstetrician in pistachio green and a geeky paisley-colored cap with a stethoscope dangling from his neck had come from the delivery room to tell him it's a girl.

Neither man waited for Mrs. Hillman before the file changed hands and Tucker Richman unashamedly counted through the bundles of hundreds. All she wanted was the baby and when the counting was done Tucker Richman turned from them without a word, irritated by Mrs. Hillman walking in his shadow. When he reached the sedan he opened a rear door and stepped aside. Ana Juanita was sleeping peacefully under her cover as her new mother reached to sweep her gently into her arms. Until Mrs. Hillman stopped cold, gasping aloud with her eyes wide open, involuntarily clasping a hand over her mouth.

"My god, she's black!" She yelled to her husband. "Roger, she's black!"

Richman slammed the door. "Mrs. Hillman, she's not black. She's Mexican, what some folks call Latina."

"Roger, she's black. Mr. Richman we specifically asked for a white girl with blonde hair."

"Yes, I know, with blue eyes. The fact is, Mrs. Hillman, they're not easy to come by. We're not talking about used cars here. We're talking about little children who have lost their parents and need good homes. Blonde would have been better, I agree. But now you have a child to love and adore, a child who will love and adore you. Isn't that what you really want? Damn, Mrs. Hillman, even some of us Whites get darker than that in the summer."

"Roger?"

"Mr. Richman, I'm afraid this won't work out at all. The club, our friends and neighbours… how could be possibly explain a little dark girl?"

"Mr. Hillman, the very same way you'd explain anything else you've bought in the wrong color. It's done all the time. Mexican, Chinese or Black; what's the difference? At least you've got one. Most folks in your predicament don't." Richman leaned against the car, admiring his watch. They were mere feet from the well-patrolled causeway and he wanted to leave. "Mrs. Hillman you're forty-nine, topping fifty, and the kid's almost three. Even if she were white, who'd believe it's yours? So you tell your friends you paid twenty-five K for someone else's kid because you weren't eligible as fosters or adopters."

"I think we should cancel this adoption and let you get back to us when you have a child better suited to us."

"That's not going to happen, Mr. Hillman. I understand you think you have a dilemma, which you don't. However you will have if you don't take the kid."

"How exactly?"

Richman smiled, wiping the sweat from his brow with a handkerchief he tugged from his pants pocket. "You won't have a kid, and you won't have twenty-five grand. At least this way you've got something to show for your money." Richman pushed away from the front panel of the sedan. "Listen, do what you want. Leave the kid here, whatever. It's your kid and no sweat off my back. This thing I'm driving looks like a hundred others from a few hundred feet, not yours. Maybe you'd make it home, maybe not. All I know is you've got a kid and I'm leaving."

Roger Hillman put out his hand, grabbing at Richman's sleeve.

"I said I'm leaving, Mr. Hillman. Take your kid and be happy with her." He pointed behind Hillman, coughing a laugh. "Look where your car is, and take a gander at the corner of the building." He paused. "That's why you parked there and why I parked here, Mr. Hillman. They'd be at your home before dinner, and how would you explain that to your friends. Leave the kid, if you want. Do what you want with her, though my advice would be not to."

"We'll contact the authorities and explain."

"Explain what, that you bought a kid on the Black Market. Good luck, by the time you get out you'll both be in your seventies. Good day to both of you. Nice doing business." He circled the car, pausing with a grin before opening the door. "If it's any consolation at all, her mother was a hotel maid. Who knows, maybe it runs in the family."

Eleven

July 19, 10:00 PM
Midtown Atlanta

The blue waters of La Bahía de Campeche in the Gulf of Mexico were calm and as many people were bathing as were strolling, being lovers or becoming lovers, families building complicated fortresses whose parapets would soon crumple with the onslaught of the evening tide.

Her favorite time with him, a time when she could show him off and be proud of him, was when the hot sun was at its zenith and the warm waters of the bay lapped the shore lazily and mutely. He was 5'10" with wavy black hair, slender, always tanned and muscular. Best of all, he belonged to her. Her belly wasn't as flat as when they had met and she blamed him for the roundness with kisses every time he laughed at her, telling her she would never be slim again. It was their little boy, or little girl. They didn't know, and Manny loved her more than life with every rebuke.

She leaned into him, kissing him, playfully slapping away his hand that was pulling at the sensible bathing suit she so hated and cupping her breasts, not expecting the stinging smack that snapped her head into the unforgiving upper edge of the high-back wooden chair. The beach was gone and the sudden harshness of white light was blinding and startling.

In real time twenty-four hours had passed, though for Mercedes only a few minutes and she fought against the violent surge of dizziness and nausea. Her wrists, her knees and her ankles hurt terribly and she didn't know why. When she went to soothe them she couldn't and the pain worsened. Her mouth was dry with the sweet taste of raspberry on her lips, her knees were shackled far apart and she was naked.

Every nerve ending in her body told her she was cold as her mind struggled to seek comfort and refuge of the warm sun and his gentle embrace as incongruous pain, violence and absolute darkness invaded her entire being.

"Good evening, Monica. I hope you had a good sleep."

Mercedes' head swiveled rapidly in semi-circles, trying once more to free her hands. "Mi bebé, ¿donde está mi bebé?"

"Monica, stop struggling. You're hurting your wrists for no reason. Your kid's gone. She's far away, so be quiet and listen. What I have to say is very important and I won't repeat myself. So listen up."

"Me llamo Mercedes, no Mónica."

"Let's get something straight, right now, amiga. Your name is Monica, not Mónica, and Mercedes Del Fuego no longer exists."

"Where am I? Where is this place? Where is my baby?"

"This is your home, Monica. You are in The Hotel Le Chic, your place of employment."

"No. I work at the hotel. Quiero ver a mi bebé. Where is my Sofia?"

Miss Divine backed away from the chair, reaching for a decanter of Courvoisier VSOP, pouring herself a generous portion.

"Let's clear up a few things that will ease your adjustment period and help you fit in here, Monica. You will never see your baby again. She's gone, so forget her.

The best you can hope for is that she's alive and that has a lot do with you. You will be here for the next three to five years. If, after that, you've been a very good girl, a good employee, then you'll be released from your obligation and free to search for her. That's up to you. If you haven't been as good as you can be…well, that's another matter. " She put down the half-filled snifter. "I'm going to release the restraints now. Please stay seated when I do. There's absolutely no way out from here. Play nice and I'll answer your questions before I hand you over to Lucy for training. Don't, and that won't be so good."

Mercedes was sobbing, unconsciously massaging her chafed wrists. "Mi bebé, ¿donde está?"

Miss Divine was 5'10" with milk-white skin and shoulder-length blonde hair cut in layers which accentuated her long, narrow face and hollow cheeks. Her nose was aquiline, her thin lips glossed with bright red worked well with ice-blue eyes which seldom blinked. She was attractive, though certainly not beautiful, and she carried herself with confidence more than poise. She was wearing a crimson-on-cream silk baby doll tunic with beige satin pants and open-toed stiletto pumps, giving her a feminine yet commanding presence. When she leaned forward, Mercedes listened instinctively.

"Those are the last Spanish words you'll speak until you leave here and I'm not asking you. The language here is English, nothing else. Our clients at Le Chic are English-speaking Americans and I won't tell you twice."

Mercedes sat frozen with copious tears trickling from her chin into glistening rivulets across the bare skin of her torso that seemed even more golden under the harsh florescent lighting.

"Why do you do this to me and my baby?" She looked down, bringing her knees together. "Where are my clothes?"

"In your suite, though after tomorrow they'll be thrown out. You don't need them. For the next three years you will wear the clothes I give you, nothing else, or nothing at all. Lucy will explain everything in detail tomorrow."

Nothing she was hearing made sense to Mercedes whose heart was pounding to the point of rupturing.

"Why do you do this to me? Let me see my baby. Por favor, se lo ruego."

The impact of the woman's fist against the side of Mercedes' head was paralyzing, the surprising force twisting her torso against the squared arms of the heavy wooden chair.

"I told you, no Spanish. Believe me or not, Monica, eventually you will like being here."

"My Manuel, what will he do not to know where I am?" She pleaded, chokingly. "What will he do?"

"He'll try to find you for a while. He'll contact the police; he'll put your picture in the papers. Then, if he's not killed in Iraq, he'll eventually marry someone else and get on with his life."

"He will not die, and never will he stop to find me. Never."

"Yes, he will. They all do… each one of them. By the time my girls leave here the husbands have remarried and the children have adapted to their new families." She sipped from her glass. "You won't be any different. There are twelve of you here: ten working girls and two Prefects, two senior women who have earned my trust. The girl you're replacing left when you were brought in. She smiled when you screamed because she understood that soon you will like being here, like all the girls. Unfortunately, her obligation was up and she's gone. So it seems you've come along at the right time and, as I said, for three to five years. Three if you're good, five if you're not."

"I will not stay."

"Yes, you will. The bracelet on your wrist is my first gift to you. It's an electronic monitor which will alert us each time you come within several feet of the main doors. Lucy will explain what will happen to you, and her, if you do that. Only senior girls are allowed in the foyer area, those who know better. You won't have that privilege for a few years and by then you won't want to leave. This will be your home. When Alice left last night she was crying because she didn't want to go. Neither will you."

Mercedes brought a trembling hand to her lips, moistening them with her tongue and reawakening the flavor.

"That's mine also, Monica." she smiled widely. "Frankie was right. You're very beautiful. Some of our clients are women, women who can't be seen in certain situations publicly. That will be part of the training Lucy and I will help you with. Our guests pay dearly for our service. They expect the best, which is what we are, and I will be the one judge of how good you are. So don't ever disappoint me. Disappointment is the one other reason my girls leave, and not to search for a lost past. I promise you."

"Never will he forget me, or my baby. My husband will come for me. I do promise you."

"Come where, Monica? He won't know. We're invisible to the outside world, completely untouchable. No one in here knows where they are and no one outside knows what we do inside with the exception of a privileged few who pay well to maintain their secret and ours."

Miss Divine filled a second snifter and opened a small black, gold and red lacquered box in a Chinese motif. She handed Mercedes the cognac and opened her hand as a signal for the young woman to take the pill. Then she dimmed the lights.

Twelve

The next morning Mercedes woke alone, lazily stretching out naked, luxuriating under the cool touch of smooth satin sheets, feeling calm and at peace in the darkness as she tried to remember whatever she had forgotten. She was somewhere else; she was in love and reached out knowing he would not feel her touch.

She had no sense of time, no idea how long she had been laying before she eased the covers away from her and slipped both feet over the edge and into the carpet's plush softness. The darkness was absolute; her eyes were still too sleepy to focus. She called out his name, needing more than ever for him to know she loved him.

She stood too quickly, falling backward, thousands of minute flickering lights making her nauseous. She struggled clumsily to sit, waiting to push herself cautiously from the bed, balancing herself before unsteadily inching her way blindly away from the bed with her arms outstretched until she felt a wall and fell against it. She inhaled deep breaths, knowing something was wrong and telling herself not to fall.

She sidestepped one way, then the other, hand-painting the embossed wall with small overlapping circles until she felt the switch. The light went from dim to blinding and back to dim. She turned, bracing herself against the wall, scanning the room that was beautiful and elaborately designed with modern furniture in black and white, elegant and sophisticated, neither feminine nor masculine. There was no window, no television or radio, and no phone. The intercom by the king-size bed seemed to be a radio but wasn't. She had no idea what she must do, or when. There was no clock, no sense of time. She was alone and didn't know why or where.

She walked into the centre of the luxurious bedroom, wondering which of the French doors she should open first. Then she saw the suitcase resting on a stand between them, feeling her panic rise the longer she stared at the neatly packed contents. Her mind rushed to make sense of it all, calling his name as though he was nearby, needing him, and when the twin doors opened inward a cold blackness streaked through her body and she collapsed.

When Lucy walked unannounced into the bedroom she stared impassively at the naked girl whom she hadn't expected to see falling and huddling into herself, convulsing and crying so uncontrollably as though gulping in the unintelligible and hysterical words more than speaking them. She closed the doors behind her and when the worst of the hysteria was over she closed the distance between them, pulling Mercedes onto the edge of the bed. She put her arms around Mercedes, hugging her for several long and silent minutes, not speaking until Mercedes seemed alarmed at what was happening.

"Monica, I'm Lucy. I'm your trainer and your Anchor Girl."

Mercedes stared at her, dumbly, growing more uncomfortable with her nudity.

"¿Qué dices?"

"No. Don't ever speak Spanish again. Not ever." She let Mercedes pull away, crossing her legs and reclining on the bed as Mercedes curled into her own space on the other side. "You have a lot to learn and absorb, so if I speak too quickly you stop me. It's important for both of us that you understand."

There was no response.

"We let you miss breakfast. Miss Divine thought you'd be better off sleeping a while longer. She stayed with you last night. She stays with all of us every so often." Lucy smiled when Mercedes tucked in her shoulders. "Monica, very soon there won't be much you don't know about me or the rest of us girls and being naked in front of us or other people will be very natural for you. It is for all of us."

"Where is this place? Why have they brought us here?"

"Technically we're in a hotel, but it's actually a bordello and I have a lot to tell you so put on some clothes and I'll order you something to eat."

After her panties and bra Mercedes began dressing in a skirt and blouse she took from her suitcase until Lucy ordered her to stop. The hotel had a dress code and at that moment Mercedes' new life became much more apparent as she listened in horror to Lucy. The man called Frankie was right. She did want to kill herself.

"Your name is Monica. If you don't like it, no one cares. You're Monica, and you will be for three years, five if you mess up, or if you're good and want to stay. I'm Lucy. Who I was before doesn't matter and you'll never ask me or anyone else." She paused, letting Mercedes absorb as much as she could. "Soon you will decide for yourself what you are, Monica. Between you and me, we're high-priced whores. We sleep with men, and quite often with women. Very rich men and women. And we have to be good because if we're not we'll end up fucking drunks in some dirty place after they beat us, or we'll be raped by homeless men on the street," she paused, being serious, "and that's how you'll die... fucking a beggar. So you will be good." She forced a giggle. "Most of us prefer the women guests, which can be pretty cool. They're a lot more fun and not so one sided. They want us to enjoy as much as they do. Anyway, no one gets in before 3:00 PM and they must leave before 6:00 AM, even the women who always stay longer than the men. Some stay the whole fifteen hours. They like bathing with us and doing girl stuff like letting us do their hair. Mostly they like reserving pool time and waking up with us. Most men leave after a few hours and never use the pool, which is a great way to tan all-over and the one way we get to see daylight," she leaned closer to whisper, stroking Mercedes' hair, "not to mention talking without anyone hearing, even though they can watch us. Anyway, the pool is mandatory and we have to use the gym each day."

When breakfast came Mercedes ignored the tray, feeling as though she would vomit any moment.

"You will get used to being here," Lucy insisted. "Eventually your family will stop searching for you. Your husband will remarry and your daughter will grow up not knowing you. Sorry...that will happen and you're no one special. We've all been through it. I've been here for two years and my husband has already remarried. Miss Divine showed me the wedding announcement. My boy will be four next week and he doesn't even know I exist."

"You can run away. We can all run away."

"No, we can't. We're never given the codes for opening the doors and she'd know right away, wherever she is," she tapped her bracelet, "and she would kill our children, or worse."

"What is worse?"

"Our children being brought here, that's what. For some guests a pleated plaid skirt and pigtails isn't enough." Mercedes shook her head, showing her confusion. "There's another good reason, Monica. That's why each of us has an assigned Anchor Girl. We're responsible for each other and accountable to one another. If you did manage to get out, which is impossible, she would make me suffer because of you…and there's more. Don't ever get sick. She won't tolerate anything affecting your performance and, whatever you do, do not get pregnant. Dr. Dirty Fingers comes in once each month to examine us. We don't know his real name. We call him that because his exams are sort of extensive. Really, he's harmless…and pretty pathetic. She has something big on the old fart, but no one knows exactly what."

Mercedes' face twisted, her imagination subliminally filling in what she did not understand.

"It's not all bad. We eat well, we get Sundays off, and we get our hair and nails done every two weeks. Guests who fork out fifteen-hundred a pop for Courtesan Girls, more for Special Girls and a quarter-million for Preferred Girls don't want slobs fucking them. Brother Reamer's the hairdresser. He's a freaky ex-priest with a penchant for little boys. We don't know much about him either, except he doesn't like girls. He just likes to act and talk like one." Mercedes clutched her stomach as Lucy stood and went to the suitcase with the skirt and blouse. "This all goes in the garbage, Monica. By tomorrow you'll have all new stuff. It's one of the perks, along with make-up. Tonight you can use mine. We wear the best lingerie, something different every night. The costumes are stored somewhere else for special requests and, in case of unexpected visitors, we would all become the wives of executives on business trips. But that's never happened. That's why we have men's and women's overnight kits in our bathrooms and expensive men's clothes and shoes in our closets. What we don't have is television or radio. Our magazines and books are all about other places and times, and we don't have internet. The wall jacks are bogus, but we do have videos on Sundays… and each other. Pretty well all the girls are paired up."

"It is too fast for me, too fast. What is wall jack and bogus and this cay?"

Lucy pointed through the French doors to the small working desk in the salon.

"That thing on the wall, for the computer, doesn't work. It's completely bogus. On the other hand, that does work." She pointed to the mirror at the foot of the bed, "There's a camera behind the glass and the rooms are wired for sound. There are also cameras in your salon and bathroom. That's why she wants strictly English, so she can understand everything we say. Sometimes she watches when we're with guests. She especially likes watching girl-on-girl. You'll get used to them and soon you'll forget them altogether. K is a thousand. If you're good, a Preferred Girl, someone will pay 250 of them to get themselves off, to have sex with you whenever they want."

"This is not possible to be happening. I will find one way to kill me. I will not do these bad things. It is more than a sin. I will die first."

"They'll kill you if you don't, Monica. Or put you somewhere worse than here, and certainly they'll hurt your little girl. So get with the program. You still have a lot to learn and remember, so let's try to make our time together fun. I don't have a booking for tonight, which is very rare because I'm a Special Girl. You won't for about ten days, not until you're trained." She took Monica's hand. "So I can be with you all day, and all night… if you want me to."

Thirteen

July 21, 8:00 AM

Lucy lowered the receiver of the intercom into the cradle without speaking. There was no need. Her day had begun. She looked at Mercedes, pondering their night together, and felt sorry for the little Mexican. Lucy was certain she would be one of those who would soon disappear without warning, quietly during the night, replaced just as quickly, the way Alice hadn't come back from the fourth floor the morning after Monica was brought in.

The previous day had gone badly, which was expected. First days always went badly for new girls. By noon Mercedes had met the other eight girls and the Prefects; she had seen all areas with the exception of the fourth floor and was given a worksheet that brought her to tears at an intimate table setting in the hotel's quaintly seductive dining room. The agenda required that she indicate when she would be unavailable to guests, when she would then perform a week of hotel chores as a Duty Girl.

Mid-afternoon, at the outdoor patio pool, Lucy thought nothing of removing her satin robe and stretching out naked on a cushion-covered chaise-longue as Mercedes sat beside her, wrapped tightly in a borrowed silk robe, struggling between understanding Lucy's words and thinking of her Sofia and Manny. She would not survive.

She would be available by appointment everyday but Sunday and, when not with a guest, each day she would be expected to use the physical fitness centre, the pool, the spa and stay current with international news. Sundays would be her day off. The one day to retreat into her memories, dream of the future or enjoy the two indulgences the madam allowed on the only day she allowed them, and eventually most girls did.

There were three privileges for those who adapted and performed well: Sunday lounge privileges, boutique points, or becoming a Prefect after three years for those who no longer had a reason to care. More importantly, there were demerit day-points, recommended by Prefects and decided upon by Miss Divine to a maximum of seven hundred and thirty, an extra two years of service and one point beyond was as bad as being pregnant.

Every fourth week would be housekeeping week. Assigned Duty Girls would clean all the rooms and bedding each day. They would clean the common areas and toilets, cook meals for their peers and provide in-room à la carte to guests. They would wear housekeeping uniforms and be subservient to the others, including their own Anchor Girls.

The Prefects' sole responsibility was to observe the girls twenty-four-seven, maintain activity reports on each girl for Miss Divine and act as hostesses and receptionists. The status set them apart, they were special. They were no longer whores, no longer subservient to the whims of others. Even though they were still prisoners they were no longer one of the girls.

There were four floors. The main floor housed the reception area, a dining room and lounge, a fitness center with an indoor-outdoor pool and a limited spa, a fully equipped unisex hair salon and a boutique whose sole currency was points. The second and third floors each boasted six deluxe three-room suites accessible by stairs or a single elevator. The fourth floor had secure access and was the private domain of Miss Divine, talked about in guarded and casual whispers by girls who knew they could be summoned there at any time to service the madam's needs. The fourth floor was where they had all been taken the first night to be accepted or rejected by Miss Divine, though if there had ever been a rejection no one was the wiser.

Lucy leaned over and kissed her, waking her and wishing she hadn't Though each new girl eventually understood the need for closeness with one another, especially with their Anchor Girl, accepting that one day she would be gone, replaced by another. Alice had been taken from her too suddenly. She wanted and needed the tenderness and warmth they once shared, but Mercedes wasn't ready. As bad as the previous day was, the evening together was that much worse. During dinner Mercedes hadn't spoken a word and hadn't eaten until a Prefect noticed her full plate and threatened her with thirty demerit points: one month. Later, in Lucy's suite, she sat wedged into the corner of the sofa with her knees folded into her chest as Lucy prepared for their first evening together, the sweet scents of pears and apricots gradually wafting across to where Mercedes sat lost in her thoughts, oblivious to the sound of running water. The lighting around her dimmed, a pinkish warm glow radiating from the luxurious bathroom where Lucy stood leaning against the doorframe.

She liked the new girl and wanted them to be friends as well as each other's Anchor Girl. She called out softly to Mercedes once, then twice, going to her, taking her firmly by the hand. In the bathroom she slid her robe from her shoulders, climbing into the steaming white foam without insisting Mercedes follow.

The tub was deep, only Lucy's glistening bare shoulders showed. She held out a hand, smiling.

"I won't touch you, Monica, not yet, but remember what I told you about these rooms and what will happen if you don't adapt. The water feels so good. I promise I won't touch you."

Mercedes robe dropped and she reached down, bracing herself on the molded side of the tub as she crossed one leg over, then the other. Lucy turned her head away, activating the jets. The two women sat facing each other, Lucy smiling, Mercedes staring searchingly into her eyes as fragrant clouds of foam erupted around them.

"Monica, tomorrow night and Saturday you'll be with other girls because I'm booked, but if I finish early I can always come to get you, if you want. Next week we'll entertain my guests together. I'm limited to five because of my Special Girl status and two of them are women you'll have to be comfortable with, Monica. That means learning how. I'll be there to help you, but a week isn't much time to learn so why don't we start?"

Mercedes remained silent, completely still as Lucy's legs wrapped loosely around her waist and her arms encircled her curved shoulders, pulling her closer. When their lips pressed together she closed her eyes, hating herself. When Lucy kissed her again she resisted, pursing her lips.

There was a long and uneasy silence as Lucy pulled away from her, bringing up her cupped hands to wash away the foam from her own shoulders, then Mercedes' before wrapping her arms around her once more. The third time Mercedes responded by bringing up her hands, pressing them hesitantly into the wet smoothness of Lucy's sides. The sensation of their oiled bodies locked together in the heated water and the softness of Lucy's lips was strangely comforting. She hated herself for suddenly needing and wanting what was so unthinkable and when Lucy stood she followed.

The rest of the evening was difficult, not the lovemaking and closeness Lucy had wanted. She was there to train a novice, certain they were being watched. Even with air conditioning the room was warm and their still damp bodies glistened in the dim amber lighting. The bed was already turned down and Mercedes followed automatically as Lucy crawled into the center and lay on her side, patting the space beside her.

Mercedes had never felt another woman's hands on her breasts. She stayed inert, judging the sensation instead of resisting. Lucy's caresses were gentle and unhurried, her hands were warm, her breath hot as she pressed her parted lips into the soft flesh and kissed each erect nipple.

Mercedes closed her eyes, letting Manny arouse her as he became increasingly bold. He eased her legs gently apart, at first pressing firmly against her moist lips, the warmth of his hands penetrating into the recesses of the delicate folds. They were lovers lost in time. She loved how he touched her, caressed her, tantalized and aroused her. He was her man, her lover. She would always willingly give herself to him.

His hands never left her. His touch always gentle, moving as though gliding over her on a cushion of air, his soft lips leaving silent kisses from the rise and fall of her breasts to her scented aperture that he longed to titillate and explore the way she longed to be one with him. The slight pressure of his hands under her buttocks told her what he expected as she felt his hot breath between his hands that moved to clasp her thighs. Soon the precision and heat of his touch made her arch upward, gasping for air as she gripped his sides even more tightly, wanting more. She inhaled deeply. His scent was exotic and pungent. She wanted him on top of her, inside her. She needed to feel him as she engulfed him and closed herself around him.

"Monica, it's…"

Her eyes flashed open, her arms too tightly locked around Lucy to let her go. She screamed.

Now, hours later, she seemed so peaceful, lost in her dreams.

"Monica, wake up." She gave Mercedes a gentle nudge on the shoulder. "Get up. They won't call twice and missing breakfast is a demerit. Sit up. We have to talk."

She was naked, again, and beginning not to care. She turned slowly onto her side, raising herself onto an elbow and indifferent to Lucy seeing her breasts.

"I enjoyed last night, I really did, until you screamed. Monica, don't ever do anything so stupid again," she admonished. "Forget him. It's the best way. It's the only way. Believe me. If you don't, and you call out his name when you're with a guest, she'll make you suffer badly."

"I do understand what you say to me. You do not understand me. Never will I forget. Never will he forget. Last night in my head I was with him. He is always gentle with me."

Lucy smiled. "Is that a compliment, Monica? I hope so."

"No, it is no compliment. I wanted to say you were gentle with me, like he is."

"I miss Alice, very much. She was here for over three years, and she trained me like I'm training you. I loved her, and she loved me, the way we have to." She stroked Mercedes' hair. "What is in your head is private, Monica, but one day soon all that will change and you'll forget who you once were, like I have, like we all have. Soon you will have no idea who you once were and you won't care."

Mercedes leaned in closer, sneering. "I am Mercedes Del Fuego, my husband is Manuel Del Fuego and my baby is Sofia. He will come for us and one day I will have my gallery of art. What they will do to me in this place, he will not care. He will come for me and to kill them, to kill all of them. That is my Manuel. Never will I forget. I am his wife,

¿comprendes, chica?" She took Lucy by the wrist, squeezing hard, "¿comprendes lo que digo?"

"Yes, I understand, and I hope for your sake you're right. I had the same dream once, until he forgot me. Now, get up. Go to your suite and get dressed in your new clothes. Most of us wear slippers and robes to breakfast. I'll come with you, if you want me to."

Mercedes held out her hand. "I do want. Thank you."

"Thank you for what, Monica?"

"For being gentle with me, chica," she whispered.

Fourteen

The first seventy-two hours were behind her. They were late for breakfast, not absent, and were merely reprimanded without points. They spent the morning together in the gym and by the pool, talking privately without the anxiety of being heard. When Lucy left her matter-of-factly after lunch to prepare for her appointment, Mercedes went to her suite where she waited for one of the other girls to visit and train her.

The suitcase was gone, so were her clothes, taken by one of the Duty Girls. She sat on the sofa in her salon taking in the brightly lighted room, understanding another reason the girls were always at the pool, anywhere but windowless rooms, despite being spacious and designed for stylish comfort. She hissed. Designer fabrics and furnishings could never alter the reality of why she was there. Use of the freshly made bed and the bath was forbidden, verified by the Prefects each day after lunch and before check-in time, but she had no guest and the Prefect had already been in.

She had never seen so many beautiful clothes and shoes in one closet, in colors specifically chosen to complement her skin tone and body. There were evening dresses and lingerie for day and night. Silk teddies and chemises, long and short satin and silk robes and slip all hung for her and her dresser drawers were filled with embroidered bra and panty sets, thongs, garters, nylons and bikinis. The designer names were intended for work, including the pale blue mid-thigh silk shirtdress, which by any other description was a housekeeping frock, her Duty Girl outfit she would not need for another two weeks.

The bathroom was a mini spa in white marble and stainless steel. The jet bath was modern and deep with a contoured interior intended to provide guests with comfort as well as variety. The muted lighting was recessed and the music was controlled from the front desk according to each guest's preference. Two white fleecy robes hung on the clear shower stall wall with his and her overnight kits placed side by side on the vanity between two shallow sinks. A white leather and chrome director's chair sat in the corner opposite a stall framed with frosted glass for privacy.

She ran a bath, thinking of what she would wear according to the day code, when suddenly a thought struck her. She went to the bed and sat on the edge, briefly studying the single bedside table before opening the drawer. She snorted with disbelief, staring at the gold-embossed red jacket of the requisite hotel book, doubting whether anyone ever so much as opened the cover, and she wondered whether she would ever again believe in God. She slammed the drawer closed and strolled to the bathroom thinking God would need to seek her forgiveness for what He had allowed, more than her needing His. He would have to prove himself, she thought as she sank into the oil-coated water. She could never win. All she could do was play the game so she would not lose.

She wore a shimmering shirt-length espresso-colored slip with high-vented sides, a matching T-back thong and mid-thigh robe she left open, and three-inch stiletto slippers in a deep shade of bronze. She needed very little make-up and curled her hair to enhance its natural fullness. Then she stood in front of the mirror admiring her work. She was pleased, so would anyone else be.

When Mercedes opened the door to her suite she thought of Manny laying somewhere unseen, camouflaged in the dirt and rubble of Iraq, hiding from the enemy as he waited patiently for the precision kill. She was no different. She would hide from the enemy, camouflaged by subterfuge, and wait patiently for the kill. Monica closed the door, not Mercedes.

The Prefect was astonished by what she saw. Monica was unrecognizable, certainly one of the most beautiful girls at the hotel, if not the most beautiful. The message left with the Prefect for Miss Divine, whom she hadn't seen since their night together, was very clear: She would stay with Lucy and be trained by Lucy, not by anyone else, and she would not stay with anyone else. She would follow Lucy's instructions, follow her lead, and during the coming week she would help entertain Lucy's guests. Then she would be ready.

She left the Reception Desk compelling her body not to tremble and went to the patio pool where a few girls were either wading or sunning. She ignored them all, taking a towel from the rack, walking to the far corner where a single chaise-longue sat facing the sun. She knew most men preferred seeing women without obvious bikini lines. Manny did, and beautiful women hated having them. Her robe and slip fell away easily. She folded them neatly on a tiled patio table before kicking off her slippers. Manny would often let her take off her top to sun, never her bottoms, so before she could stop herself she pushed her thong to her ankles, her heart pumping hard, and lounged with her eyes closed to the world.

She would not be a whore. She would be the best, and very soon she would have Preferred Guests. She would be with one man instead of twenty, one woman instead of a second man. The girls often lost clients to new girls, if only for a while, or as twosomes. The hotel also wanted the girls to become Preferred, part of the lucrative Quarter-Million Club, and she would if Miss Divine allowed her to stay with Lucy. The other girls would understand.

The late afternoon sun was brilliant in a clear blue sky. A slight breeze made the air less humid, soothing against her skin, and she had to admit she felt good being naked. Already lost in her thoughts of Sofia and Manny, time had no meaning. She took a deep breath, wondering when she would know, wondering whether she would be punished or killed for what she was doing. She shrugged, not realizing she had. She wondered whether she would ever know time again, whether time would ever again seem important. Clocks and watches were not allowed. Intercoms told them where to be, and when. She had always hated watches, now she wanted one badly.

Her eyes blinked open, startled when her private world darkened with cool shade. The girl standing at the bottom of the lounge chair was dripping water and smiling at her.

"I talk with myself in my head, too, sometimes...actually, all the time. Hi, I'm Melanie. Let's break the ice." She sat beside Monica unabashedly in the nude, their skin touching as she turned towards the pool. "That's Jennifer, my Anchor Girl, and we want you to join us. Besides, it's way too hot to lie in the sun like this. See, even the others have jumped in."

Monica shook her head. "I thank you, Melanie. I am very okay here."

Melanie stood, stretching out her hand. "I'm nineteen and I've been here for six months. I remember my first week, so I know that's not true. You're not okay, and if you're wondering, we all like you already. Who cares about those stupid Prefects, the old bitches? It would be nice if you could like us too."

Monica studied every inch of her. She was blonde, petite and cute, her skin glistening with oil and water, eclipsing the sun in a way that outlined her body in a seraphic halo of golden yellow. They were the same height, though Melanie's body was childlike with small breasts and almost no curve to her hips or belly. She was completely smooth and perfectly tanned. She could pass easily for sixteen and, with her ponytail, seeing her in a pleated plaid skirt and white blouse while calling some pathetic and desperate old executive daddy was easy to imagine.

"I know. It's kind of freaky at first, being naked all the time. Soon you won't even notice. Sometimes I actually hate being dressed. Come on, it'll be fun talking with us. Lucy won't mind and they can't listen. Not knowing makes them nuts, but they want us nice and tanned for the guys, not that a tan matters much in the dark."

She knew snubbing them would be a mistake and she didn't want to alienate herself. If she had ever needed friends, now was the time. Monica gave in with a windy sigh, smiling and shaking her head. She took the girl's hand.

"It is not Lucy, Melanie. I am glad that everyone likes me. It is that you talk so fast. I will not understand everything."

"I'm a motor mouth, sorry."

"I do not know motor mouth." Monica smiled. "What I know is to run and to jump."

They disappeared into the deep end feet first, holding hands, Monica already certain her first purchase at the boutique would be a dictionary. The intercom sounded at 6:00, clearing the pool for dinner.

Fifteen

That evening she was told Miss Divine had agreed, with reservations, and Monica spent the evening alone with Manuel and Sofia where neither could be seen. The afternoon at the pool was fun, almost letting her forget. She had new friends, whom she would balance between love and hate. She would become the best, her status would be Preferred, which possibly meant taking two Preferred Guests from other girls who had worked hard for their own status and who might secretly hate her for what she would do.

She had no idea how long she'd been sleeping, playing with Sofia and loving Manuel. When the door opened at 2:00 AM Lucy stood silently at the foot of the bed, uncertain. Monica propped herself onto an elbow, sweeping back the covers, letting Lucy slide in beside her. The two women each draped an arm over the other's waist and kissed goodnight. The training neither girl wanted would wait. Manny was waiting with Sofia.

They woke as though they'd been best friends forever, embraced in each other's arms, their noses touching as though whispering inner-most thoughts. Though they weren't and Saturday was no different. She hadn't understood when they told her in the pool there were only two days at the hotel: workdays and Sundays. What she did understand was being held captive and her survival plan was near completion. By dinnertime on Saturday much had changed for Monica.

She spent the morning with Lucy and most of the girls in the gym and at the pool. Her afternoon was spent training without the slightest resistance, much differently from what Lucy had anticipated. In fact, Lucy was the one eventually reclining submissively. Monica liked all the girls except the Prefects, but she liked Lucy most. She was easy to be with, not demanding or imposing. She let Monica know what to do without preaching or threatening. When they trained her touch was gentle, soft, responding to Monica's involuntary gasps as much as her relaxed sighs.

She told Monica with a giggle she had always wanted a Latin lover, never once thinking a woman would be that lover and she wasn't disappointed. She was already beginning to forget Alice, the same way Monica would one day forget her when she, too, would go.

Lucy had an evening guest to prepare for and wouldn't be finished before two or 3:00 AM. Saturday evening after dinner Monica lay on her bed and remembered her one escape besides Lucy, her only way to endure the long months ahead until the day she knew would come, the day she would speak to him and he would answer.

Sixteen

She would say nothing derogatory or deprecating in supposed confidence about anyone. She would play the game. She would attend all three meals and would not get sick. She would be the best dressed and the best Duty Girl. Above all, she would earn the most points, the most respect. She would be one of them without becoming one of them, the one they would admire and emulate.

Sunday was her fifth day, the end of their week, when the intercom chimed for the Duty Girls and breakfast was optional. By noon the mercury soared well past a hundred with a heat index touching one-twenty and the low skies over Atlanta were stagnant, thunderous and black.

Sunday was the girls' day, their day to pretend they were like other women, their day to talk or play games, catch up on international news, knit or relax in the lounge and watch the latest videos on the hotel's one plasma screen. The Duty Girls would join them after the only dinner of the week that would include a single glass of wine. What they could not do was phone home, attend church, be with family or even look at photos of what was once a family. All they could do was remember past times and many had forgotten how.

No one cared about foreign issues and no one cared to talk. They wanted Cage and Bullock, or Bogart and Astair and paid for their choice with points. No points, no movies, which meant no lounge and Monica had no points. She lay in her bath remembering a story her father had once told her of an early American frontier family who hadn't locked their doors one night. The next morning, when the family woke and went outside to toil the land and meet with their neighbors, all was deathly quiet and they ran from door to door to see what the trouble might be, horrified at seeing how those neighbors had been slaughtered as they slept.

Looking toward the crest of the surrounding hills, scanning the seemingly endless ridge lined with red-skinned savages calmly mounted on tense ponies, the father gathered his family and ran to the safety of their modest home, certain they would soon be slaughtered. They waited in fear, the wife kneeling on the coarsely sawn floorboards, doing her best to calm her daughter, the husband telling his son the women were not to be taken.

There were hundreds of warriors with grim painted faces under feathered headdresses, their feathered spears pointed downward, she remembered her father telling her. They were deadly savages who would rape and plunder before going home to their own women and children. He had no way of fighting them off, no way to prevent them from bursting into his home and taking away his womenfolk and son. He took the clumsy six-shooter from the boy, leading him from the tiny slatted window and stood bravely at the ready, waiting for the door to open. He would be the last to fall.

The door did open, warily, and he pressed the long and slender barrel of the aging six-gun against his wife's pulsating temple, his long gun pressed into his young daughter's pounding chest. The chieftain's reaction was immediate. He stepped back, his empty and open palms extending outwards as a sign of peace, his painted face not fierce, but kind with worry for the woman and girl: the origin of the western handshake, a sign of peace. They meant no harm.

When the nervous frontiersman asked the chief why his family had not been slaughtered, the proud Indian replied: "Your hearth was the one not barred. You are the one who showed trust in us. Let us be friends. Let us share our knowledge and be as one, your family and ours as one."

Lucy had explained Monica's logic to the other girls, but that wasn't good enough for them. They had all chipped in points to pay her way and they wanted her there. No was not an option.

The twin French doors to her suite had no lock. There was no need for privacy when there were no secrets. They sneaked in, tiptoeing to the bathroom door before bursting through, the first few capturing the Kodak moment as Mercedes' wide-open mouth shrieked out a piercing noise and her gaping deep brown eyes seemed impossibly large behind an evanescent wall of white foam and scented water. By the time they dragged her from her cool bath and dressed her, ignoring her mild protests, they were laughing like giddy teenagers, each one scolding her for being silly with smacks on her bum that was already tingling and turning pink.

She hadn't yet been in the boutique. She saw no reason. She hadn't thought she would survive past Friday. At the time she'd seen no way out, she thought. Now she understood differently so she would selfishly share their knowledge and be part of their extended family. She would not think of her father again for a very long time.

The boutique had the appearance of a very small Duty Free shop, stocked each Friday with what the girls wanted most, or had asked for the previous week, subject to Miss Divine's approval. The cigarettes were stale, because smoking was not permitted with one exception, and all the processing-included film had past due expiry dates. The girls wanted perfumes, suntan lotion, beauty products, comb sets, barrettes, Paris Match and Elle for the pictures of current European styles and Belgian or Swiss chocolates.

Her account was opened and she owed twenty-five boutique points. She bought a soda and candy bar for the videos and saved the rest, very uncertain how many she would lose or earn on Monday night.

Sunday evening after dinner, after the Duty Girls joined them for the final video, the Prefects went to each one of them with an open lacquered box and a lighter. Monica was last and all eyes were upon her. She took one, lighting it the way the others did, drawing the sharp-tasting smoke into her mouth, feeling the increased heat of the glowing ember inside her cupped hand. She blew out the pungent smoke without inhaling, her mouth burning with yet another unfamiliar sensation as she gazed around the room. Proof perfect.

She was one of them, one of the Sisters of the Disowned. Soon after, or sometime later in the evening, or in the early morning, Manny seemed not to mind what she had done, happy to be with her, and little Sofia giggled happily in the arms of her mother.

Seventeen

Monday, July 24. Monica's day six began with a crushing headache and an overwhelming feeling of nauseous anxiety. Her indulgence with the girls the evening before hadn't made her sick, the evening ahead sickened her. She would be with a man who was not Manuel and she couldn't fathom the horror of such a reality. She lay in bed, her fingertips pressed hard against her throbbing temples with colored tears streaming down her flushed cheeks, silently begging his forgiveness. Sunday had been a ruse, as would all Sundays be until he came for her, as would all Mondays and she needed him to know.

Dying would be too easy. She would not leave Manuel and Sofia. She would fight, she would give him the time he needed and she would get them back. The weeknights were already fully booked for both of them, then she would be a Duty Girl and for the first time she was eager to clean toilets.

She ate breakfast, or gave the appearance she had. She was quiet at the pool and went through the motions in the gym. Then Brother Reamer arrived mid-afternoon on special assignment to make her ready: the prelude to the end of her day. They all understood what she was going through. A week earlier she'd been a loving mother, an anxious wife, and in a matter of moments she would become a fully-fledged member of the Atlanta sex trade.

The week, the days, the hours had all gone too quickly. At nine-ten Monday evening she sat quietly waiting with Lucy, terrified, wondering how the girl could be so calm, so unmoved, and thinking she could one day be as calm and unmoved scared Monica all the more. She wondered about him, the man, and how he would act, smell and talk.

Lucy described him as tall, not quite six feet, slim, reasonably handsome with silver hair, not grey, clean shaven and middle-aged. She thought he was most likely married to a woman he had been with for too long. Boredom had probably set in and she had begun loving the luxuries he provided more than him. He wanted and needed more than she was willing to give. He wanted his youth back, the excitement of their early years she had forgotten. Now he paid a quarter million as a Preferred Guest for anytime privileges with Dree, occasionally requesting doubles and Miss Divine was the one woman he hadn't been with. The truth was: Lucy knew absolutely nothing about the man.

She was his second favorite when Dree was unavailable. He was known as William. Who he was when he wasn't a guest didn't matter. He was well-spoken, gentle and not too kinky. All the girls liked him; each one having done her best to become his Preferred Girl. He was always telling them how he enjoyed being with each one, though the reality was he enjoyed how each one responded differently to him, how each one dressed or undressed for him, how they used their bodies for him. He loved the competition between the girls, each one striving to outdo the other, and he loved how Miss Divine regularly brought in new talent.

He had been told when booking his reservation there would be a new girl in training with Lucy, unless he objected. He didn't. He never did as part of his preferred status and long-standing membership. Trainees were particularly arousing to him, especially the younger ones like Melanie.

Before their guests arrived the girls were either in the lounge or their suites, as though waiting for husbands or girlfriends to come home from a hard day's work at the office. Lucy and Monica were doing precisely that, sitting together on a black velveteen settee, waiting for the doors to open into the salon. When they did, there was no polite knock.

Lucy wore Romanesque mauve chiffon baby dolls with dark blue velvet and rhinestone ribbons at her waist and under her breasts; for Monica she had suggested a full-length silk robe with a shawl collar, long sleeves, and a wrap-tie waist. Underneath she wore matching silk panties with snap-away ribbons.

Lucy helped her stand, tugging slightly at Monica's wrist, indicating for her to stay. She went to William, wrapping her arms around his neck and pressing her cheek against his as she would a close friend or father before slipping his jacket over his shoulders. She took his hand in hers and led him to Monica who stood motionless, her eyes locked with Lucy's.

He remembered the first evening she'd been training with Jennifer, thinking if Monica was half as good he would stay the night. He was not remotely what Monica had imagined. All day she remembered how Frankie had breathed on her, the wet skin of his protruding belly, his soft arms pushing her into the mattress and pillow and against the wall. His foul breath had suffocated her as his gruff hands fumbled between her thighs to find her opening for his half-ready polla.

This man was a caballero, a real gentleman. He stood tall and straight, his shirt was pure white, his tie the color of her robe. His slacks had razor sharp creases and his shoes shone in the dim light of the room. He looked mid-fifties and was probably late-forties. His face was smooth and tanned with only faint lines, his hands were smooth with manicured nails and his grip was neither loose nor tight. His voice was clear and even, he was completely at ease, completely at home. He carried himself as any important or confident man would. He was a man in full control of himself and others, the primary reason Miss Divine forbade contact with the outside world. The girls were never to know who these men or women were in daily life. They paid exorbitant sums and in return they expected complete anonymity, even from each other. Guests were discouraged from leaving or arriving at the same time and the hotel went to great lengths to make arrivals and departures as convenient as possible.

Their true identities were known to Miss Divine alone and supposedly limited information on file was held in absolute confidence, her guarantee to them, a surety she knew not to breach. The Hotel Le Chic was more than a bordello of the highest order. It was a private club of the rich and the powerful, well-placed and high-ranking men and women who were not to be toyed with.

Lucy poured a double Glenmorangie on the rocks from a mini bar service which Carol, the other Duty Girl, had wheeled in earlier. She poured soda water for herself and Monica. Unlike time spent with female guests, evenings with most men began with polite and cursory conversation. They were pragmatic by day and by night, most preferring not to waste time getting down to business. Any subsequent conversations would be time-filling adjuncts between sessions.

William was different. He spoke with the girls to the extent that doing so was proper and he always smuggled in contraband chocolates, lipstick or nail polish. He treated them as ladies, each one his mistress rather than women who earned the right not to be discarded by fucking five or six different men each week. He was a favorite. He knew

70

their names, likes and dislikes, and how each one reacted differently to his touch. He never called them honey, dear or sweetheart and never did anything unless by mutual consent. He never forced them or hurt them, though the girls never refused a request because they all wanted to be his Preferred Girl, to be his mistress.

His numerous visits each week were so much a part of his life, he thought nothing of them. He never explained himself on the home front; such men never did, nor were explanations expected. He was unhappy with her and she was happy without him. Theirs was a perfect marriage away from home and not so perfect at home.

She remained faithful because she had no choice and she let him wander into the arms of others because she had nothing else to offer him. His affairs were her fault. She had driven him away and his occasional sortie had become his occasional night at home, which had become fine with both of them.

He poured the second drink himself and left the two girls to undress in the bathroom and luxuriate under the steamy water hissing from the oversized rainhead. He liked Monica very much. He liked her skin color, the way her hair was pulled into a tight bun. He liked the way her robe opened when she sat, how she crossed her legs, enticing him, commanding his attention. He would enjoy her very much. He'd never been with a Latina, though first he would enjoy Lucy's charms as was expected and proper.

He was unhurried. Apart from enjoying the different girls, he enjoyed their different suites. He walked in on Lucy and Monica, leaning against the doorframe to watch the girls lather and rinse each, Lucy toweling Mercedes, rubbing her skin pink before reaching for a dry towel and leaning forward to wriggle her instructions.

He stepped into the bathroom, letting them pass by, and took a shower. By the time he rejoined them Lucy had already pulled back the thick white duvet and was lying on her side in the middle of the Swedish-styled king-size bed, speaking in a low voice with Monica who was lounging on the settee.

He dropped the fleecy robe to the floor so naturally, so completely uninhibited, Monica felt as though she was sitting watching from another dimension as a man climbed into bed with his wife or girlfriend, raising one knee, then the other, joining Lucy who stretched out both arms to pull him in closer.

He wasn't athletic. He was either fortunate or worked out at least a little, Monica thought, hoping foolishly she would be forgotten as he tossed the foil onto the carpet and snapped the latex in place. Kneeling between Lucy's legs he gently raised her hips, slipping his hands under her buttocks to lift and position her. Monica's mouth went dry, her heart pounding. She'd never seen a man penetrate a woman, as mesmerized by the sight of him hovering over Lucy as she was terrified of the moment when she would join them.

His arms were slightly bent at the elbows, his back arched from his shoulders to his buttocks that tightened with each thrust. Under him, Lucy squirmed and raised her knees, squeezing them into his sides, meeting him, her arms locked together by her hands at his waist.

Monica wasn't shocked. She had been through too much. She was more intrigued by a man who could simply walk into a room, remove his clothes, and have sex with a woman he barely knew in front of another who was a complete stranger. They said nothing to one another. There were no endearments, no tender whispers, no tiny shrieks brought on by mischievous pinches. He had paid for her and she was giving him what was taken from her and bartered for so many boutique points.

They rolled, and Lucy sat upright with her arms behind her head, smiling as though she was enjoying herself. His hands were on her hips, guiding her. She was beautiful, Monica thought, watching Lucy press her hands against his chest, raising her buttocks ever so slightly as she gyrated and pivoted around his hips.

Lucy suddenly arched exactly as she had shown Monica, grinding into him, intent, focused on the here and now as though no one else in the world mattered. William's entire body strained to resist, giving in, his arms falling loosely to his side as Lucy waddled backward until she was sitting on his knees, reaching for a second foil.

Lucy revitalized her guest in moments, slipping on the mandatory latex before turning away from him and grabbing his ankles as Monica watched transfixed, her mind a complete blank. She had gone through all the positions and techniques with Lucy during their mornings and afternoons together, doing things with Lucy she would only ever have thought to do with Manuel, and more, confused by her body's spontaneous reaction and mixed emotions.

The training and Lucy had been surreal. The man on the bed with Lucy was not. He was very real, not strapped on, and she couldn't help but stare as Lucy expertly dressed his discolored penis in latex. He was leering directly at her as she struggled to swallow, her chest palpitating. She was excited watching them, fearing what would come next. He was asking her if she liked watching, if she had ever watched a man and woman together, assuring her he would be gentle with her, that she would like being with him.

Finally the two bodies lay on the bed breathing heavily, Lucy's hands clamped over her heaving breasts as William lay on his side facing away from Monica, lightly massaging Lucy's belly. Monica knew the moment had come, in a bizarre place where time no longer existed. She wondered how he would feel, how much she would hate his touch, whether she could even walk to the bed. Hating herself was not the issue. She already did for what she had done to her family.

The couple sat, Lucy moving behind William to massage his shoulders and smiling at Monica, asking her to take off her robe and run another bath. Her loosened robe fell to the floor as she stood and she focused hard to walk away nonchalantly in sheer panties, knowing both sets of eyes were following her. The clear water was steaming and her skin moistened quickly from the vapor permeating the room as she waited for the moment William and Lucy would join her. When they did, they slid in, wincing at first, then sighing with the intensity of the deep therapeutic heat, both gazing at Monica. She had never taken off her panties in front of another man. Frankie had brutally ripped them from her body, and she hated William savoring every inch and movement as she pushed them to her ankles and kicked them away.

She stepped into the space between them as discreetly as she could so he would see less of her and Lucy more, avoiding his eyes and wanting desperately to cry or scream as she faced away from him. Lucy was first to touch her, leaning forward with her cupped hands opening to let the water cascade across Monica's breasts before kissing them as William watched quietly excited.

Lucy reclined sensually, facing them, her legs together. She helped Monica straddle her, bringing their faces together. Monica knew to kiss her. She knew what Lucy enjoyed and stretched out flat, letting Lucy feel the full weight of her body as their mouths lightly pressed together. The kiss lingered, Lucy feeling every beat of Monica's pounding heart. She was terrified, barely able to swallow as her warms tears trickled onto Lucy's face.

The movement behind her was gradual. The touch of his fingers gentle as he parted her legs, kneading and probing the soft flesh between her buttocks, making small deliberate circles against the soft folds of her lips until she opened and he strummed the delicate petals between as he would a magical harp until she stiffened and her body shuddered.

Lucy didn't let her go. Feeling the swell of warm water as William moved behind them, she clasped Monica's tear-drenched face between her hands, staring deep into her terrified eyes as William moved slowly, his hands pressing against her hips. He liked her, deciding he would stay the night. He went into her easily, as slowly as he could manage, enjoying the eroticism of two women lying under him and the sensation of someone new. She was crying and somehow the emotion made the moment more special.

Lucy pressed her lips harder against Monica's, wrapping her arms tightly around her. She seldom looked into a man's eyes and never kissed their mouths. This time she did. His eyes were fixated at his juncture with Monica, his lips pursed together, his face grimacing with effort. His quickening motion rocked the girl's unresponsive body against her own until, without warning, his face twisted and he arched backward, pushing Monica forward with a violent thrust before resuming a slower rhythm, not wanting to pull away from her.

Manuel always stayed inside her, loving her, his arms wrapped tightly around her or traveling across the contours of her body with tender caresses, kissing her. She loved how he felt inside her and beside her. She would always love him, she would always be his. She always wanted more of him, though sometimes all they could do was laugh and agree maybe not.

He felt exactly how she remembered, how he smelled. She knew every inch of his body. She smiled at Lucy, feeling Manuel reawaken inside her.

Part Two

September 29, 11:55 PM
Mosul, Iraq

They had been laying in the saline-impregnated soil for eighteen hours. Pressed into the ground, they listened intently, constantly searching through the twenty-power spot scope and across 104° desert air to the home made from stacked layers of dried clay.

Their only distraction was eating something that had the appearance of toothpaste and tasted like shit, then washing away the taste with heated water that tasted like piss from a one-liter bottle. If they spoke at all they did so in muted whispers. After nine months of long days and longer nights together they sensed each other's every move and thought. Speaking was unnecessary. Best of all: they were going home.

The night air was stale, heavy with humidity and rancid with the smell of humus and clay mixed with the stench of heated animal excrement. The moonlit village stood alone amidst a barren terrain and nothing moved, not even the lone, rag-covered Al-Qaeda insurgent who stared out at them from his humble rooftop terrace three thousand feet to the east, shadowed in the green of night vision scopes. The pale smoke billowing from his mouth enveloped him like a gloomy shroud.

The Madam

The M82 was built for Marines, by Marines: the ultimate weapon for men like them. Before leaving base camp they had tossed for the kill which was Manny's. As spotter, Juan Carlos was the one to see the single bullet burst into the man's face, snapping his head sideways, propelling him violently upward into the night air, killing him instantly.

His hundredth kill, his hundredth round with no misses, and Manny thought nothing more about it. He no longer prayed for the men he killed, or for himself. Not praying made the job easier, impersonal.

Juan Carlos slapped him on the shoulder, hardly raising his hand, saying nothing, his right eye pressed tightly against his scope's rubber eye-piece. What mattered at the moment was the retrieval, getting the hell out. Waiting before the kill was easy for them. Waiting for the Huey was the difficult part and this night was particularly so. Their last night had come, their final mission completed, the last time either man would dive headfirst into a chopper wondering if they were in someone's scope, the last time Juan Carlos would stay directly behind Manuel as they ran with a purpose. The last night was no time to let him take one in the back.

Manuel had lived up to the USMC creed: One shot, one kill. The target in rags that evening smoking a cheroot was his hundredth, his last kill, and had died with smoke still in his throat. Manuel was going home. Shy of forty-eight hours he would be in Atlanta, loving his girls for a full month before reporting. Juan Carlos would be in Miami, loving girls who weren't his.

He hadn't spoken with Mercedes in over three months, though he had managed on a few rare occasions to leave her hurried messages, telling her how much he loved them, and how much he missed them. The practice was allowed, but discouraged. They wanted his full attention on the kill, whether emotionless cardboard or heartless flesh.

Just as many weeks had gone by since her last letter, he supposed because he was never in one place more than a day or two. None of that mattered. In two days she would be waiting for him at Hartsfield-Jackson International with his little Sofia in her arms. He was going home and all he wanted was to get out alive.

The Madam

Nineteen

Juan Carlos was going with him. They had become each other's salvation: the black sheep of the herd left alone and ignored. The next morning at base camp the sniper section leader took the M82s first, then the scopes and radios before signing them out, congratulating each of them on their separate kills and walking away.

In Germany he was another faceless grunt boarding a military transport with his backpack bulging with dolls, teddy bears and gifts for Mercedes he hoped would fit. He was afraid she wouldn't recognize him. The desert sun and the guilt of his first few kills had aged him and his eyes had darkened from too many desert nights. He hadn't smiled in months. Being with JC there had never been any need.

The flight lasted eight hours and everyone smoked... a recent habit he would have to explain. She would smell it. She hated secondhand smoke as much as she hated beards. They were both dirty and he would do neither one as long as he wanted to touch her. He shaved in-flight and chewed as much gum as he could until his jaws ached. The smell of his uniform he could easily blame on Juan Carlos.

Concourse C was an obstacle course of civilian backpacks, crying babies and worried travelers rushing to catch the next flight out. JC despised them all, particularly the size eighteens with weakened hips and weaker knees making them list to one side with pained grimaces. Their

79

look-alike husbands, who hadn't seen their sagging balls in years and seemed to be propelled forward by the oscillating momentum of uncontrolled and downward hanging bellies, were equally offensive. Most of them carried Styrofoam boxes filled with what had made them that way in the first place, the only future their fat and knock-kneed bratty offspring could possibly envision.

The young kids were unmanageable brats, the shit-makers worse than mortars. The absolute worst was the applauding, as though Manny had "one hundred kills" stamped on his forehead, JC with "ninety five" etched into his. They had been warned of the effusive attention from a grateful nation, and told to take it in stride. No way.

An airline courtesy cart came from behind, swerving into oncoming civilian passengers because the driver knew from experience the twin hulks in computer-generated desert colors would not step aside. An old-timer sitting on the rear bench facing them tipped his USMC cap in a salute. Manuel returned the gesture, Juan Carlos grimaced.

The man was leaning into his cane, the buttons of his bright yellow shirt straining under the maximum recommended load to contain a fully spherical belly, thus preventing any further sagging between spindly and bowed legs that were partially covered by red polyester walking shorts and white knee-length socks. He'd been told by his Drill Sergeant four years earlier that Marines never stopped being Marines. Now he wondered when they stopped looking like one.

They parted at the train. Manuel was headed for the Baggage Terminal, JC had no baggage. There was nothing about the Marines he wanted, including his cap. What he wanted was his life back, and he got out at B Terminal to wait for the flight that would get him there.

"Been fun, bro. Nine months of shit, but it's been fun. You saved my life that night, hombre. I never did say gracias, so gracias."

What else was there to say? The job was done. They were separating. One was being transferred, the other was getting out.

"You ever need me, hombre, you make certain you find me. JC, Miami. In the worst of the worst places, hombre. That's where you'll find me. Or call this number, probably safer for a little pussy like you. Take it, hombre, and don't you ever forget. You call; I come, simple as that."

"I won't forget, JC. I won't forget."

"Don't say something you don't fucking mean. I mean for anything, hombre. You need help servicing your little lady, you come find me." He smiled, putting his arms around Manuel, hugging him hard in front of the other passengers. "At least you give her a big kiss for me, amigo, a real big one like this one, from a real man." He kissed Manny hard on the mouth, slapped his cheek even harder and jumped out onto the platform "You remember hombre. JC, Miami." He yelled. "I love you, man, I'll never forget all our special nights together. I love you, man."

The lady eyeing Manuel tilted her head, feigning surprise, covering her wide smile with pale fingers accented in deep red. She was stunning, and he could think of nothing else to say.

He shrugged his shoulders. "Medical leave, ma'am. Shell shock; it's very sad."

Twenty

She was not there for him. At first he stood off to the side, avoiding the tangled mess of careless bodies searching through thousands of pieces of non-military-issue luggage that all looked alike. He scanned the first row. Then he balanced on the narrow stainless steel edge of an emptied carousel, searching each serpentine row of waving relatives face by face, head by head. She wasn't there. She should have been in the first row, waving Sofia's little arms and whispering "daddy's home," but she wasn't and suddenly he didn't like what he was feeling. He phoned home and got the same message he heard in Germany when he'd called with precise details of his arrival, the same English message he recorded for her before shipping out. He called again and pressed END.

The north end of the baggage claim was devoid of human existence other than a lone porter redirecting several passengers whose luggage had been lost, not remotely close to sounding empathetic. The airport was the largest in the world. What did they expect?

Like any other street in Atlanta's dinnertime suburbia, the avenue sparsely lined with trees and modest homes was abandoned as he took in everything and nothing from the rear window of the cab. His neighbors who had not already gone to favorite eating haunts had begun backyard barbeques and the air outside his home was thick with the heavy smell of slow-cooking beef. Very few of them would come out until the sun had set and that was still a few hours away. When he stepped out he saw no yellow ribbons decorating the single family cottage to welcome him home and no beautiful Mercedes at the door waving Sofia's little arms.

The slightly overgrown grass was burnt, the flowers along the narrow walkway were wilted and the windows were dust-covered. The doorbell still didn't work. He knocked loudly countless times, stopping briefly to peer through the front windows. The lights inside were on during daylight hours. He didn't knock again, crashing the door wide open with enough energy to cause an instant rebound and he kicked out a second time, staring disbelievingly at the maelstrom of envelopes and junk mail settling across the floor. He already knew calling her name was pointless. She wouldn't hear. She had not been for a very long time. He did anyway, screaming.

Her skirt and blouse lay on the floor near the hallway, something she would never have done. When he picked them up he saw her torn white panties and reached for them, tucking them into his hip pocket. She had made the bed, yet the bedspread was disheveled and one pillow was on the floor. The other was stained in an all too familiar pattern and lay in the middle of the bed. The shower stall door hadn't been closed and two dried towels lay in a crumpled heap on the ceramic floor. His suitcases were still on the closet floor, hers were gone.

He didn't panic, nor would he. He'd been trained too well and had seen too much. He was a US Marine, a sniper, the best of the best and not to be fucked with. The pizza box lay on the kitchen floor, open and empty. There were no dishes, two glasses and two empty red wine bottles standing side by side in the sink, something that always caused her to wrinkle her forehead and say a simple, "no hazlo como así cariño. Gracias." She loved scolding him, and he loved teasing her.

She was telling him something, and not that she hated red wine or empty bottles in her sink. His entire body went cold imagining what the two men had done to her, and when. There was no longer any point checking the door for forced entry. The first priorities were notifying the police, searching through the other rooms without touching anything, sorting the mail in chronological order which would at least tell him when.

The red light on the phone had not stopped flashing since his first message to her. He saved them and dialled 9-1-1, answering the operator's first question with information he knew was already showing on her screen. He gave his East Point address and name, and after a long pause the operator asked if he was alone. Yes, he was. So what? His wife and daughter were gone, kidnapped. He needed someone there ASAP. How did he know they were kidnapped, the woman asked? He responded by telling her to send a car, repeating ASAP. Then he hung up to wait.

He heard them first, turning slowly, seeing the guns before their faces. They were positioned on either side of the door he hadn't closed. He remained perfectly still, his every nerve ending pulsating. He wasn't afraid, they were.

"Stay the fuck where you are, drop to the floor and spread. Do the drill, boy."

"I live here. My name is Manuel Del Fuego. I'm a corporal in the US Marines, home from Iraq. My family's been kidnapped and I don't drop to the floor for fucking anyone, asshole. I put them there. You want to come in and try me, you white-faced fuck?"

"Don't be a smart ass, boy. You drop to the fucking floor. Do it, now!"

"Don't be a fuck up, and don't fuck with me. When was the last time you heard of anyone leaving their shit at the door and breaking into a house wearing a USMC uniform, fool?" He walked towards the door with his palms facing outward. "I'm unarmed, not that it matters much, and I just called 9-1-1." He ignored them, kneeling on one knee to begin gathering the mail. "Don't trip on your way in, if you can manage. And close the door."

"One of them called in for verification, the other stepped in behind Manuel.

"Show your ID, right now, nice and easy."

"You think that makes a difference, you standing behind me with that gun in your hand? It doesn't." He threw his chin out in the direction of an end table. "That's my ID, right there."

The cop walked to the picture frame, happy for a reason to step away. He signaled his partner with a nod and a thumbs-up.

"How long have you been gone?"

"Nine months."

"How do you know she didn't take off with some other guy?"

"I know." He emptied the cluster of mail on the sofa. "She was kidnapped and raped by two men several weeks ago."

The cops exchanged curious glances.

"How do you know that? You assigned to Intel?"

He ignored them. "Her clothes were on the floor. She never does that, and her underwear was torn. The bed is made with a stained pillow in the middle, a stain that could only be made one way and the thick shit smeared all over the table was put there the same way. Two towels are on the bathroom floor, dry, with that dirty laundry smell. There's one pizza box with chewed crusts on the bottom and the lid, and two bottles of wine in the sink. The crusts are covered with fuzzy blue and white shit and the wine bottles are bone dry."

"So, you're a detective now?"

"She hates fast food, especially pizza. She hates red wine and she would never put them in the sink. Do I have to mention the mail?"

"What about the door?"

"I kicked it in. I didn't have my key. Got a problem?"

"They teach you that over there?"

"Not just that, amigo."

"Military wives running away happen all the time. Guys coming home all messed up with all sorts of fucking battle syndromes."

"Do I look fucked up to you, or you?" He glared at both of them. "They probably left the lights on intentionally. No one would notice during the day, just a night. Not that anyone around here would notice or give a good shit."

"You touch anything?"

"Yes, her skirt and blouse, the phone and the mail, nothing else."

"You said her underwear was torn."

"That's what I said. You snoop around if you want. You won't see anything I haven't."

They nodded. "We have people who are good at this. If there's something to find, they will."

"Then get them here, now."

One of the cops called it in as Manuel showed the other the evidence he'd alluded to. Five minutes later the second cop joined them.

"It's been a busy day for us. I spoke with some detectives." The cop paused. "Listen, because there's no sign of a struggle or murder, and it's been a while, they probably won't be here for a few hours." He turned to his partner. "We stay till they get here. So who goes for coffee?"

There was no sign of violence, just that his wife had been raped. Manuel ignored them, resisting the urge to beat in their superior faces with their own batons, knowing full well he'd enjoy unfair advantage. Instead he went to the living room to sort the mail, making separate piles for junk, bills and his eleven letters to Mercedes. They'd taken her sometime during mid-July.

Twenty-One

The detective arrived at midnight. She spoke privately with the uniforms and toured the home for ten minutes before going to Manuel.

"My name is Samantha Peachtree, Mr. Del Fuego. I'm sorry you came home to such a terrible situation. Is there anything you can tell me that you haven't already told the officers?"

"They took her in the middle of July, after they raped her. There's nothing left in our bank account where there should be a few thousand dollars. The last withdrawal was yesterday, so they must have known when I was coming home. Her credit card's maxed out as well with three separate ATM withdrawals between July 19th and the 23rd in Macon, Atlanta and Birmingham, ten thousand, total, plus the three grand in the account. Thing is, they left enough in the account for all the pre-paid stuff, probably to keep the account from being overdrawn and closed. The bank's fraud department is working on it. They're sending me papers to sign."

"Her passport's gone?"

"Yes, along with her banking cards, her citizenship papers, her green card and some jewelry. We've been here for only a few years. She worked at the Holiday Hotel. I couldn't get work, so I signed up."

"You may have trouble with the bank. They'll want

proof your wife wasn't the one who made the ATM withdrawals. That could take a while." She paused. "Mr. Del Fuego, nine months is a long time, and I understand you were gone for several months before that." She seemed instantly embarrassed. "I saw the stain. How can you be sure she hasn't run away with your daughter? Do you know anyone who might have run away with her, the husband of a friend, a neighbor, a boyfriend?"

"We have no friends, detective. Imagine that. You see how lovely she is. She is even more beautiful on the inside and she doesn't have one friend in this new country of ours." He picked up the blue bottle, snickering. "See, I even drink American vodka. Three nights ago I killed a man. I shot him in the face from a thousand meters, over a thousand yards. I killed him for your president and your country that will never accept us. Because I couldn't find a job in my field I had to kill a hundred men. What does that make me?"

"You were a sniper?"

"I am a sniper, señora," he corrected. "What I was before isn't important." He took another sip. "We had such dreams for ourselves and our Sofia, our daughter. Our neighbors have never spoken to us, not once. Don't you find it strange they would call the police because they saw me breaking into my own home, yet not when those men took my wife and child? They didn't even recognize me. I've been here for six hours with police cars in the front and no one's phoned or knocked on the door to ask about us, to see if we're okay."

"You're in Atlanta, sir, not some little town in Vermont. If you wanted good neighbors you should have gone there, or to Miami to be with your own kind."

Manuel finished the glass and poured another, slouching. "Mercedes wanted that, but I didn't want our new neighbors thinking we were two more fence-jumping

Mexicans sneaking in to find work in a hotel or a field. I'm a chemical engineer and we're legal, which doesn't make a bit of difference. All they see is Mexican."

"We're not all like that. Some of us see life differently, in a better way."

"Thank you for the insight detective. But my family is more important to me than one-sided rhetoric. What will you do to bring her back?"

"Everything we can, Mr. Del Fuego. We'll start with the pillow and towels to test them for a DNA match, and the bottles for prints. We'll canvass the neighborhood, though I doubt that will produce much. We'll involve the media, though, please understand, that's all short term. By this time tomorrow you'll be old news. We'll check the airlines, bus terminals, local taxi services and women's centers." She faced him directly. "And what will you do?"

"I will find her if it takes my lifetime, or my life. I will find her."

"Please understand, sir. If your wife has been kidnapped, apart from her apparent rape, both her and your daughter could be thousands of miles from here, possibly not even in the country. You can't possibly hope to find them on your own, without resources. Forgive me for saying so. However you must realize Western women as attractive as your wife are very sought after in other countries, so are young girls. They could be anywhere by now, including the Pacific Rim, any one of a dozen Arab countries, or Mexico for all we know. Please don't go down a road to disappointment...or worse."

"There is nothing worse, detective, and I do have resources...my training. I can see what others do not or cannot, I can decipher visual and aural information and react. It's all about life and death, mine or theirs. In this case it's my wife's life, so I will go down that road starting right now and for however long it takes."

"There is a possibility she may already be dead, perhaps both of them. You have to be prepared for such an eventuality."

He checked his watch. "The longer we talk about doing nothing, the less we will do. Take what you need and find my wife."

"Sir, there was no underwear with your wife's clothes. The officers told me you mentioned they were torn. Where are they?"

"I know what I told them, detective. They're in my pocket and that's exactly where they're staying. No one gets them. You want them that bad, go get a court order, then try to find them. You've got all the DNA samples you need, not to mention all the shit on the table."

She stood, seeming indifferent. "When do you report for duty?"

"In thirty days. In the meantime I'll be in the Crucible, ma'am." He ignored the openly inquisitive expression. "I will stay in close communication with you, Detective. Count on it."

Twenty-Two

He stood through the night, pacing his home, not caring about sleep that would have escaped him, thankful the cops had taken every possible piece of evidence. Phoning Mexico to tell her parents and his that Mercedes had been kidnapped, raped and possibly killed or sold was excruciating. His mother hadn't listened at first, calling everyone to the phone, crying with joy, so happy her son had come home alive and safe from Iraq.

When she finally understood the words she screamed uncontrollably and his father grabbed for the receiver. He listened intently, wiping away his tears, ending the call with a promise not to call the Catalina family until his son had spoken with them. He argued that he and his wife should join him in Atlanta as soon as possible, to be with him and help him. Manuel refused as gently as he could without suggesting they could do nothing to help.

He remained still throughout the entire conversation with Mercedes' father, paralyzed and emotionally drained as he listened to hysterical sobbing and accusations as they struggled to understand what he was telling them. He made them a promise: He would find her. He would find them, the men responsible, and he would kill each one. On his life, he would kill each one.

They were simple people in Veracruz with no contacts and no means to help. He knew that, and her brothers' bravado was real to the young men alone who were still in their teens. Mercedes and Sofia had been missing for ten weeks and the Catalinas were right to say what they did. He should have been there for them, protecting their daughter and granddaughter instead of fighting a war that wasn't his. His was an engineer, not a soldier. He should never have taken them from Mexico to a country that would never be their home, a country that would never accept them. He hung up when the line went dead and by morning the vodka was finished.

The Sunday news gave him thirty seconds without an on-air interview; the interim anchor for Date Line gave his story twice that long on Monday and the Atlanta area newspapers ran the story on the second page alongside a two-column article on falling house prices that carried over from the front page. He took out a month-long ad in the personals with their photograph and personal data, posting a reward for information which the police had asked him not to do. Then he went to the hotel to speak with the manager.

Had he heard the news report the night before? Yes. Had he tried calling their home several times to ask why Mercedes had not been reporting for duty? Yes. Then why was there no such message, and why was her final check dated July 21? Why did he not report one of his staff missing to the police? The man understood any answer would be the wrong one.

"I know why, hombre." Manuel reached over the desk, easily pulling the man from his seat by his collar with one hand, their faces an inch apart. "You could have saved her, cobarde. It happened on her way home from cleaning your stinking toilets, but you did nothing." The other hand came up, holding the crumpled check. "Open your mouth, Señor Manager, very wide, or I will break every tooth in your miserable head."

He left the man sweating profusely, afraid to take the

envelope from his mouth that was making him gag, making him appear much smaller and less important than he had thought of himself moments earlier. Day two was coming to an end and he had no idea what he was about to endure would make the USMC Crucible seem easy. The final fifty-four hours of grueling field endurance tests intended to separate Marines from those who merely think they have what it takes. By the dinner hour he hadn't eaten, nor did he bother replacing the cap on the half-empty bottle of Skyy. All he could do was stare at the empty bed he knew he would never again sleep in.

When he ordered the pizza he specifically requested that Jason make the delivery. He expected a pimple-faced teenager wearing a ridiculous hat and shirt combo to knock at the door, surprised to see an older black man dressed in Dockers and a polo shirt. Yes, his name was Jason. He needed the money, sure enough, but not badly enough to wear the silly red shirt and the sillier yellow hat. His speech wasn't canned. He just knew to expect the question from each new customer. Yes, he remembered the house, and the man who answered the door that night. He wasn't big. He was out of shape, and white, like he'd lived in Alaska all his life. He was a local boy, no doubt about it, late twenties, maybe early thirties, and cheap, real cheap. He paid by card and didn't tip, which was strange. White folks always tipped, even the poor ones, the brothers never did and Latinos went to their own places.

He remembered the man was about five-seven or eight with red hair, but not bright red, and he dressed like all the rest of them, like a salesman in one of those blue denims the white folk like so much, and a tee-shirt. There could have been a car, he couldn't remember. What he did remember was the crucifix which was silver or stainless steel and real big. No, sir, there've been no cops poking around the restaurant asking questions.

Jason took the photograph, visibly saddened, shaking his head from side to side, feeling the sorrow of the desperate man in front of him. As much as Manuel insisted, Jason refused the tip, shaking the young man's hand, wishing him luck in finding his wife and child. He hadn't prayed since his wife had left him in her sleep years earlier, he said. There wasn't much need for prayer in his life, but he would pray for Mercedes and Sofia and would look out for them every day.

Jason had no words of advice that would matter. What he did say was: "Don't lose faith in yourself, son. I heard on the news you're a Marine, so be one. Stand tall. Do yourself proud. Don't know where you'll find her, but she won't be in a bottle. Don't know what else I can say, other than if you need to talk you can call me. You call me whenever you want, and I'll come over to listen."

The next morning, day three, the unopened pizza was cold, the bottle was half full and he was stiff from sleeping on the two-cushion sofa. He had no funds in his account, he was thirteen thousand in debt and the bank hadn't returned his call. All that was left until his next paycheck was a modest investment they had begun for Sofia's education, which would pretty well cover the monthly prepaid bills.

The '96 Impala was the best he could afford with enough left over for a month's supply of gas, if nothing broke down, and by 5:00 PM he had color-copied over a thousand prints of his two girls from the same print he'd given Jason. By six he had stamped his name and cell number on the back of each one, by seven the pizza was finished and so was the booze. When he woke at four nothing had changed.

By day ten he had given out all one thousand prints and no one had called. By day twenty he had given out a thousand more, the phone hadn't rung once, and much of what Jason had said still lingered hauntingly in his mind.

He was driven, which was fine, but he was a Marine first and foremost. That said it all. He had already let them down by not telling them. He had ten days left before reporting for duty, ten days to remember who and what he was. He was a Marine, damn straight he was, and it was time to remember that, time to remember the code, to focus on the kill, time to smash the bottle, recapture himself and be the man Mercedes married.

He was ordered to report to Fort Bennings on the thirtieth. Instead he would report on the twenty-first as a new man and a new Manuel Del Fuego. Jason was right. He wouldn't find her in a bottle. The dingy room was purple, the lighting dim except for the workstation. The guy hunched over the counter was huge with "Twenty-Six" scrawled into his left arm and "Mother Fuckers" scrawled into his right. Manuel put him at seventy.

Manuel couldn't think of anything else to say. "So are you twenty-six or a mother fucker?"

The man snorted, grimacing. "I sniped out twenty-six VC mother fuckers back in Nam in '69. You got a fucking problem with that, señorita? You even old enough to know what the fuck I'm talking about?"

"I did a hundred in Iraq, mostly headshots. The last one was three weeks ago."

"Seems to me like you're more of an army girl, missy."

"I'm a fucking US Marine, asshole, with zero misses."

The human gorilla smiled. "Back down, son. I'm just having some fun. I can spot a Marine a mile away. Most of us, we don't ever change. Most guys coming in here these days are freaks, or young girls wanting their little titties and asses fucked up with dye, which isn't the worst way to make a living. Dancers are the best, though." He grinned, widely. "Sometimes I work them for free...sort of."

"Sorry, I don't have little titties and I don't dance. But I do need this done PDQ. I report back in fifteen hours and I can't be bleeding all over the fucking place."

The man dragged a catalogue over the counter. "Choose what you want."

"I already know what I want, hombre, and don't frigging cripple me. I've got three more years to serve."

"Don't worry, Pedro. I've been doing this awhile. I'm getting pretty good at it." The man pushed himself from the counter. When the time came for Manuel to stretch out his arms, he asked. "Are you sure about this? This shit don't come off so easy and it'll hurt like a bitch both times. Mine took two weeks."

"I'm sure, muchacho. I don't have two weeks. Do like I said: On this arm: Mi cariño, vengo, and do it facing me. On this arm: One Day, One Shot, in red, and do it facing away."

"Why facing away?"

"So the fuckers will see it when I kill them."

The man's eyes squinted into narrow slits. "Don't tell me shit I don't need to know...and you should know that's not the creed."

"When I came home three weeks ago my family was gone. My wife and my daughter were both gone, kidnapped. My wife was raped and the cops aren't doing squat. Believe me. One day one shot is all I'll need. ¿Comprendes, amigo?"

The man took a loud and deep breath. "Si, hombre, comprendo. Buena suerte compadre, y vayas con Dios. The right arm is on the house."

Twenty-Three

The man was right. His arms hurt like a bitch and still did Sunday morning when he arrived at the Fort Benning Military Reserve at 0845. He was listed for a meeting with Master Sergeant Dwayne Bishops at 0900 hours.

He had first met Bishops before shipping out; the protocol of military chain of command and neither one remembered the other. He had left a message the day before with Lance Corporal Jennings, Bishops' right hand, insisting it was imperative he meet with the sergeant ASAP. Bishops called within the half-hour for what he thought would be a brief conversation ending with a curt order. Sixty minutes later, his pad filled with illegible bullet notes, he hung up and leaned into his seat before pressing down on the intercom that connected him with Jennings, telling the subordinate to bring him the complete up-to-date file on Corporal Del Fuego.

He spent the rest of the afternoon on the phone gathering pertinent data from several other sources and by seven PM his meeting with the Platoon Commander Billings ended.

"You stirred up a whole whack of shit, corporal. My day was already interesting enough. I really didn't need the shit bomb you dropped on me yesterday."

"Sir, yes, sir," Manuel looked straight ahead.

"Save that for the Drill Sergeant, Del Fuego. Sit down, and tell me where you think this is going."

Manuel took the closest straight-back chair mechanically, sitting with his fingers interlaced, doing his best to ignore the stinging heat under his shirt sleeves.

"I need to find my family, sir, like I said, and I can't do it part time, sir. I need to do things right, to find them, sir."

"How do you plan to accomplish that? This is one big country, Del Fuego."

"I'll start with nursery schools, hotels, day care places, funeral homes, women's centers, that kind of thing … and the hospitals," he cleared his throat, "and the streets at night. I was speaking with this tattoo guy. He gave me some good information, sir."

"Like what, corporal?"

"Like where to go and when, how to talk with them, how to act with them, sir."

"I told you to save that 'sir' shit for the Drill Sergeant. How will talking with hookers help you, corporal? That's a pretty far stretch."

"Don't know, sir. Sorry, sir. Maybe someone could have seen her. Maybe she's …."

Bishops took over. "I had a conversation with some lady cop in Atlanta, a Lieutenant Peachtree. She's under the impression Mrs. Del Fuego might not be stateside, that perhaps she's been taken out of the country."

"I don't believe that. Each time I've spoken with her she puts me off and has nothing to tell me. In my opinion, sir, she's not working the case."

"And the reason for your opinion is what, corporal?"

"I guess it's a social thing. You know, what's been going on in the news about Latinos, all that militia shit along the border, throwing them in jail for three months before deporting them."

The sergeant leaned forward. "You think because you're Mexican your file's been lost somewhere?"

"Something like that, sir. It wouldn't be the first time."

Bishops was pleased by the lack of resentment and the dispassion in his voice. Keeping a clear head was the difference between life and death for a sniper, success or failure. Snipers never had a choice. Staying calm and focused when others could not was elemental to the creed.

"What if your wife was taken overseas? What then?"

"Then I'll go overseas, sir. I'll do whatever it takes to find her."

"You did good work in Iraq, Del Fuego. You took out some pretty significant targets and managed to pick yourself up a Commendation Medal and a Bronze Star for putting yourself between enemy fire and a Corporal Martínez."

"That report's a little exaggerated, sir. JC was spotting for me that night. Enemy fire got the side of his leg just as the retrieval guys were coming in for us. He was limping a little and I gave him a push. The guys in the Huey took care of things pretty fast."

"That's not your squad leader's version. He had a list of good things to say about you. Hell, even your Drill Sergeant had good things to say about you. That alone should be worth some sort of medal."

"Thank you, sir. Still, it wasn't much. It's not like I took the bullet for him. I just covered his ass a little, sir."

"Del Fuego, snipers are a separate breed. What keeps them alive is focus, concentration, not letting anything get in the way of the kill. Long story short, this situation has compromised your safety and the safety of your platoon. You come back to us this way and it's a matter of time before you fuck up and get yourself or someone else killed. So, this is how it'll play." Bishops stood, walking around to the front of his empty desk, facing Manuel with his arms folded tightly across his chest. "Del Fuego, this comes directly from Colonel Billings, Platoon Commander. You're a good man, a good Marine. We like what we see in your file. It's a very good beginning to what can be a fine career.

You have potential. You've gone from PFC to Corporal, and that's fine, but it's not good enough and you know it. So far you've taken the easier road. We want you thinking about officer training, not quitting, and because of that we have no intention of giving you an honorable discharge so you can go off to some half-ass civilian job and get shit-faced at night because things aren't going your way. You've got ten months, son, ten months to find your family and bring them home. However, you will report here one weekend each month and for two weeks during the sixth month. We don't want you getting sloppy. You'll be on full pay, of course, but your enlistment will be lengthened by those ten months. Are you good with all this?"

"Yes sir. Thank you, sir."

"Ten months, Corporal, and don't get lost. Catch my drift?"

"That won't happen, sir. They've already been gone three months. Ten more is a long time, even longer for them, sir."

"For them, yes, maybe not for you. Either way, Corporal, September first next year you get your ass back here, ready and fit for duty. Before you leave the base you'll report to the officer in charge at personnel. He's expecting you. He'll do the paperwork, and Corporal, we don't need everyone and his brother knowing about this. It's a one-time exception. Understood?"

"Yes, sir, thank you." Manuel stood, surprised to see Bishops' open hand extended. "September first, I'll be here, sir."

"See that you are, Corporal, and see that you find those young ladies of yours and bring them home. Don't let them down, or the Corps. Dismissed."

Twenty-Four

October 22, 8:00 PM

Monica never ate breakfast on Sundays. She valued the time alone. At the beginning she spent the prized morning with Lucy, cuddled into a spoon shape, but those times became less frequent and she missed waking up with one special person, able to be themselves.

William began regular visits, rarely missing a Saturday and often stayed through to the six AM deadline. By the end of the first week with Monica and Lucy he requested that she become his Preferred Girl, though he continued arranging for Lucy, and sometimes Melanie, to join them. Some nights he played the aroused voyeur as the girls tickled and teased each other, other times he was the submissive neophyte doing what he was told, and sometimes he took center stage.

Her mornings in the gym had begun sculpting her already well-toned body, her tan lines had disappeared completely and her body was completely smooth, which was the most exciting to him. He visited with her often, arriving earlier and leaving later, taking up most of her time from the beginning, and when she wasn't with William she was with Cynthia who, like William, was unable to get enough of her.

She accomplished in one week what most of the girls could not achieve in a year and was immediately unavailable to other guests. She was exclusive. She had two paying guests instead of five, ten or twenty, and was a favorite amongst the girls.

At first she had worried about Dree and how she would feel losing William, but her plan had worked well. Dree had kept her Preferred Girl rank with a guest who had been requesting an upgrade from his Special Guest status and that vacancy was filled with another guest of the Courtesan Girls which allowed Miss Divine to consider several new memberships applications.

Monica also had Lucy. They had become lovers, each other's confidante, and each other's escape. She liked when Lucy could work with her, which meant they could wake up together, especially on Sundays, but not the fourth day of her third month.

Miss Divine had called to say she would be at the hotel in the evening to meet with her. The madam's Sunday visits were rare events and Monica spent the entire afternoon with Lucy luxuriating in warm scented water choosing not to think about the fourth floor suite, forgoing Gregory Peck and wondering if she'd ever again see her favorite Despierta América and El Gordo y la Flaca.

She would. She dreamed of him every night and thought of him every moment of the day. He had been home for three weeks and she could scarcely imagine the pain and confusion he was going through. Still, she knew her man. He would forgive her for what she had done, for the pain she was causing him. She also knew he would find her one day soon and together they would find Sofia.

She didn't mind the marijuana. Like the other girls, she was anxious for her once-a-week gateway to freedom. She never dreamed of William or Cynthia. That space was for Manuel, Sofia, and increasingly, Lucy. He would have to take Lucy with them when he came for her. She loved Lucy and would not leave her. She did not like wine; it made her head ache. The little rolled reefer with twisted ends didn't and she took another deep breath. When the Prefect called out her name, breaking the euphoria, she stood matter-of-factly, kissed Lucy on the cheek and sauntered from the lounge, stopping at the Reception Desk where the Prefect gave her the one-time access card to the fourth floor.

Only one person had permanent access to the fourth floor and Miss Divine rarely visited the hotel during daytime hours. She came in the dark most times, and left in the dark, rotating the girls through her private suite as she saw fit. Monica had not been with her since her initiation, though she knew she would be from then on if the meeting went well and she had no doubt the evening would go very well. The alternative was not an option, neither was the vault.

The private and secure suite covered the entire floor and was Miss Divine's retreat as much as her office and boudoir. The large room smelled of pears, other nights the scent might be of apricots or raspberries, or apples, or more synthetic aromas such as lavender or vanilla. There was nothing Miss Divine didn't know about her girls. She made a point to discover and explore each personality. From behind tinted glass she studied what turned them on, she overheard pet peeves from the corners of each suite, and in her own private world she had made each one her on-demand lover. The lights were low and the madam was lounging across her silk-covered settee, wearing red satin and black mesh baby dolls with a red thong that did nothing to diminish her authority.

She was sipping wine as the elevator doors parted; toying with the satin bow intended to draw attention to the swell of her breasts.

"Come in, Monica. I'm anxious to speak with you. How

are you getting along?"

"Very well, Miss Divine, thank you for asking."

"Pour yourself a glass of wine, Monica, and come sit beside me."

"Wine will make me sick, Miss Divine. I am sorry."

"Of course, I should have known. How stupid of me. Then why don't you light up. I'm sure that won't make you sick. They're in the drawer under the bar, and bring me one." She crossed one leg over the other, leaning to one side, consciously moving a hand lightly along a bare thigh. "I'm very pleased with you, Monica. At first I thought you'd be trouble. I see I was wrong. William is very happy with you, very happy, and Cynthia's ecstatic, which makes me ecstatic."

"Thank you. I like both of them very much, Miss Divine."

"They like you, which is more important. Sit, and put your legs over me."

Monica's sheer lace pleated slip with a baby doll open front separated, showing her matching pale-yellow panties. Miss Divine ran her hands along her satin-smooth brown skin, luxuriating in the sensation.

"It's been three months, Monica."

"And four days."

"Yes, and four days. I have some news for you: some good, some not so good."

"You are not happy with me?"

"Yes, I am. You have guaranteed me 500K for the next year. I'm very happy with that, though at first I didn't think so. You've proved me wrong."

"What is the news you have for me?"

Miss Divine smiled warmly, pressing her fingers gently into Monica's thighs. "You know you'll be out one day, free to go, because you have no idea where you are. And that's precisely why it's so important that you not know. If you ever do discover where you are, Monica, I will kill you and I will kill your little Sofia. Our clientele's privacy must be protected at all costs. Do you understand?"

"Yes, Miss Divine. This I have understood from the first day."

"Good. Then, I'll give you the good news first. Your daughter is fine. She's very happy. She's being well cared for by her new family."

"Do you have a picture, can I see her?"

"No, you can't. Be satisfied that she's doing very well adapting. I made a point of checking on her, to make certain she's happy and safe, and she is."

"Christmas is not far. I want to buy her a teddy bear. Can I do that?"

"Put through your request at the boutique. I'll approve it and if you maintain I'll make sure your daughter gets her gift. I really do want to know you're happy here."

"Thank you. I know. It will make her so happy. She likes teddy bears so much and she could not take one when we left. Thank you."

"Now I have some bad news for you, but the last thing I want is to spoil our evening."

"Tell it to me. I am ready."

"It's about your husband. I'm afraid you won't like what I have to say."

Monica waited, expecting the worst. "He is not dead. This I know."

"No, not yet, though he's trying hard. He's been shipped off to Iraq. He volunteered for another tour. I told you, Monica. I told you this would happen."

"It cannot be true. He would not give up to search for me and our daughter."

"It is true, Monica. He shipped out on Friday. He'll be gone again for nine months. One way or another they leave. Ask Lucy. It always happens. Men are pricks, Monica. It's what they think about and what they care about: getting their rocks off." Monica didn't understand. "Getting their rocks off, getting laid. It's all she wrote, girl, end of story. So much for you and your precious little daughter. He's left you, and her. Some brave Marine and husband he turned out to be."

Monica inhaled deeply, taking in as much of the cannabis as she could. She chose not to respond to her keeper. She knew what to do, what was expected of her and she lay back thinking of the man who would save her.

"Tell me, Monica, what do you think of your man, now?" Miss Divine drew a deep breath. "At least you have William and Cynthia, and now Lucy of course."

"As much as I love Lucy, and want to love you, he will come for me. This I know."

"I'm glad you love Lucy, and I hope one day soon you do love me. I'd like to be with you more often. But don't count on him, Monica. He hasn't tried very hard. He put your picture in the paper for a couple of days, big spender. I actually passed by your cute little house to see your hero," she lied. "Want to know what I saw?"

"Yes, I do."

"A FOR SALE sign covered over with Sold. He sold your home Monica."

As the reality of what she was hearing sank in, Monica's eyes glazed over. She reached to one side, dropping the cinder-tipped weed into an ashtray. Miss Divine shifted under her legs, gathering her hair into a ponytail and pulled her closer.

"All the girls have felt the emotions you're feeling right now, Monica. You'll get over him, believe me. When you leave here in a couple of years you'll feel as though he never existed. One day you may even resent him for what he's done, or hasn't done. They're all the same. Take away their pussy and it's the first thing they go sniffing for. But, hey, that's what keeps me in business," she paused, pressing her lips into Monica's, lingering, "and you're what keeps them coming back."

They kissed again.

"I will be the best."

"You're a strange one. You still think he's coming for you, yet you want to be the best. I think you already are the best." She lounged back, pulling Monica over her. "I wouldn't stop searching for you."

"This I know."

"I enjoyed seeing you with Cynthia the last time you were with her. The two of you together was a real turn-on, very hot. It's easy to see why she wants you to herself. I think if not for William she'd be here every day with you."

"I do think so, too. I like her. She is nice to me."

"I want you to do with me exactly what you did with her, Monica. Don't do anything differently."

Monica leaned forward bracing herself on the arms of the settee as she stood. Hovering over Miss Divine, she let her breasts wispily caress her guardian's face, reacting with a guttural moan as she felt one hand press gently, deeply into the soft flesh of her bare buttocks, exploring intimately. She tugged at the delicate fabric of her own baby dolls, letting the woman under her draw her nipples in between her lips one at time, sucking tenderly, titillating them with her tongue and hot breath, making them erect and herself aroused. Within moments her panties and top lay on the floor and she felt the heat of Miss Divine's rapid strokes between her open legs, their mouths locked tightly together, their tongues urgently exploring.

The suite's motif was modern, done in black and amber with steel-trimmed furniture and brightly colored ceramic accessory pieces. In contrast, the feminine en suite sitting room and bedroom were done in dreamy pastel pinks and greens, the bed crowded with brightly colored cushions over rows of puffed-up pillows on a thick eggshell-colored quilted duvet.

Neither woman wanted to interrupt the moment. Cynthia was mid-thirties, slimmer than Miss Divine with a deep brunette bowl cut, and shorter by three or four inches with unblemished skin that was several shades darker. Monica had not remembered how her boss looked that first night so many weeks earlier. Cynthia wasn't drop-dead gorgeous, she was pretty. Her breasts were small, her stomach was naturally flat and Monica had told her that her buttocks were perfect because they were.

Monica ran to the bed, sitting naked in the pillows and watching Miss Divine tug at the loosely tied ribbons of her panties, letting them fall to between her feet before pulling at the bow and arching her back to let the black and red satin and silk fall from her shoulders. Her body was toned and hard. She was sensual in her own way, indefinable, with a strangely masculine quality that seemed natural and belied her forty-two years. She was strangely sexy, though just as strangely not. Most men would think of her as attractive, though as far as anyone knew she had never been with one. Most women would think of her as an overbearing dyke. The girls all did.

Her baby dolls were incongruous, overly feminine to Monica who thought she should have worn a full-length halter gown or slip. Her breasts were firm and perfectly shaped other than a slight slope, fuller than Cynthia's or Lucy's, crowned with nipples barely visible in the dim light. Monica had learned to go with the flow, determined to always act turned-on, never to be turned-on. Her determination had saved her, had quickly made her a Preferred Girl with only two guests.

Miss Divine crawled onto the bottom half of the king size bed on all fours, stopping when Monica told her to. "Monica, forget who I am for tonight. Enjoy me. Let me enjoy you. I think you'll see I'm a good lover."

"Miss…"

"No, no Miss…Divine. Call me Divine whenever we're together like this."

"Yes, Divine. I will."

Monica moved behind her, pushing Divine's calves apart, pushing a ripple of flesh from each ankle to the center of Divine's buttocks, her hands spread wide, her thumbs probing the warm and fragile inner walls in concentric circles, making Divine react in a slow rocking motion. Monica moved to one side, keeping one hand centered on the open cleft, her thumb working gently as she reached down and brought her other hand first up the inside of one quivering thigh, then the other before burying her thumb deep into Divine's moist epicenter. The polished tip of her determined forefinger worked in unison for the desired affect and moments later Divine's entire body shuddered, Monica feeling the intense affects herself and working all the harder to heighten both their responses as she watched the woman's back arch downward.

Monica brought the other hand to the crevice between Divine's buttocks, wet with her lover's natural dew, letting her long chocolate brown hair cascade and drag over the firm white mounds as she inhaled deeply and kissed the warm, slippery flesh. Her tongue darted in and out, probing, tasting, pleasing Divine with an erotica the madam had never before experienced. She wanted more, but her legs gave out and her body collapsed, her groans muffled by the moistened duvet.

Her body glistened. Her heart was racing with anticipation. She had thought the evening would be more of the usual stuff: the usual kissing, licking and caressing. She was wrong. Monica had changed all that.

Monica eased herself over the palpitating form, forgetting who she was. She enjoyed the slippery sensation of Divine's wet skin between her legs and against her own wet lips as she rocked intently to and fro over Divine's buttocks and lightly into the downward curve of her back, letting her soft dark hair drape teasingly over the side of Divine's sculptured and taut face.

Monica leaned forward, her arms straight, her pelvis saddled in the small of Divine's back, letting the hard tips of her breasts draw invisible etchings into the other's shoulders. Then one arm moved and Divine felt the slightest pressure as Monica shifted before coming to rest on her elbows, reaching to kiss Divine first on one cheek as she let the delirious woman inhale the scent of her own arousal. Then she reached to kiss the other cheek as she brought up her other hand, again letting Divine inhale deeply, asking her which one she liked best and telling her if she chose the second she would have to turn over and lay perfectly still.

Divine barely managed to roll onto her side even with Monica pulling at her waist. Monica looked at her, closing her eyelids with kisses, making soothing cooing sounds as she stroked Divine's hollowed cheeks and crossed one leg slowly over her heaving stomach. She wiggled backward, her arms straight out to the sides, letting the cool wetness of her bare lips trace a scented trail from Divine's breasts to the apexes of her twisting legs.

Her lover tried pushing her back mere inches, feeling Monica resisting, feeling her raise ever so slightly, taking Divine's hands in hers and guiding them to her hips as she leaned forward again to kiss her face first on one side, then the other, gasping at the urgency of Divine's probing fingers.

"I am not finished with you, Divine. Is that all that you want, my little bare pussy?" She ran a finger along Divine's lips. "Do you like the taste?" She moaned. "So do I, but if I turn it will be over so soon. Do you want me to turn so that you can kiss me there, and smell me? Would you like me to turn so that we can kiss and taste each other?"

Her eyes stayed closed. "Yes, I do." Monica yelped at the suddenness of the hand closing against her delicate folds, squeezing. "No, no I don't, not now."

"I will not turn, Divine. I want you to close your eyes. To be surprised is always the best."

She kissed Divine's chin, leaving another glossy smear. She slid back, feeling the pressure on her buttocks reluctantly surrender to her hips, then to her waist. She cupped one breast in her hands, squeezing ever so gently, pressing kisses onto the unyielding flesh. She flicked the nipple with her tongue, waiting, gently drawing the new thimble-shaped hardness into her mouth.

As she sat, most of her weight bearing down on Divine, she cupped as much as she could of each breast into the warm palms of her hands, kneading them, pinching each nipple as hard as she dared between her thumbs and each of her fingers in turn. She leaned forward, kissing one before bringing both hands together to fully cup the other. She whispered how beautiful Divine's breasts were, how sensitive, as she watched the pale pink areola change shape once again, more erect than before, as though begging Monica to take it in her mouth and tease it.

Monica sat straight, letting Divine reach up to clutch her breasts and play with her nipples, pinching and plucking them as she gyrated to the rhythm of Divine's hands, feeling her buttocks and labia open slightly and close against Divine's belly.

She was sensitive, eager to be satiated. She wanted to dig her nails into the hard flesh of his shoulders, waiting for the final explosion, the final thrust when she would wrap her arms tightly around him and grind herself into him, wanting more. She pulled his hands away, resting them at her side so that she could turn.

Divine's legs spread wide as Monica turned, wanting her to see. Monica placed her open hands at the top of Divine's thighs, bringing one after the other in a light continuous motion over Divine's responsive labia, stopping teasingly to pluck the dark pink lips apart or to agitate the glistening tip until Divine's body arched and shuddered as her legs flailed involuntarily for the umpteenth time in less than an hour.

Monica slid forward along Divine's parted legs, grasping her ankles and wedging herself into the open space. Her own legs parted in a wide V, feeling the hardness of the other's hips against her own. She leaned to one side, raising her torso, pulling herself slightly forward to lower her mouth over Divine's left foot, kissing each painted toe before leaving a trail of deliberate kisses and nips along the inside of the thigh as she inched her way back, waiting a breath or two before working her way teasingly along the other thigh to the painted and curled toes.

Divine raised her knees, urging Monica backwards, delighted when the young woman grabbed them, kissing her from the knees downward, pausing to make her lover shudder once more before working her way enticingly up the other quivering leg. Her legs were streaked with bronze lip gloss, her lips and thighs soaked with the pungent and arousing fluid coating Monica's mouth and cheeks.

Monica's mouth tingled from the effort, the bitter-sweet unguent felt cool as it began to dry. She stayed as she was breathing deeply, aware how open she was to the other's most intimate touch, wondering at the movement behind her and the rustling sound of silk cushions on satin. She felt warm hands press into the very tops of her toned thighs, pushing upward and outward, bursts of hot breath giving way to the madam's probing tongue. Monica placed her hands on Divine's hips, easing herself gently backward.

She was soaking, they both were. She enjoyed it, she

would always enjoy it. They were one: the sensations, their scents melding together, their urgent moaning. She loved him inside her, penetrating her slowly, teasingly, always careful not to hurt her, filling her completely before rocking her with gentle rhythms, so slowly, so expertly bringing them both to a crescendo.

She closed her eyes dreamily, swaying her hips in sync with the twirling motion and purring pulsations inside her, feeling her lips folding and unfolding with each deepening thrust. Divine adjusted the silicon member for maximum affect, craning her neck to spread Monica's sticky wetness into the open crevice of the already glistening curves of her buttocks, pressing urgently into the delicate center at the very instant Monica's fingers found the tiny nodule deep inside her.

Fevered jolts shot through both of them, neither wanting to stop, their slippery bodies convulsing, shuddering as one. Divine's arms dropped to her side before she was able to wrap them around Monica's hips to pull her closer, the bodies pressed tightly together. Monica nestled her head sideways against Divine's heated and slippery thighs, intoxicated by the sexual aroma, unaware her buttocks and hips were still squirming to the whirring sensation inside her.

"I can't remember when I ever felt this good, Monica."

"Thank you, Divine."

"I'm exhausted. You weren't trying to kill me, were you?"

"No, I was not. How could I finish, if I killed you?"

She raised her hips, reaching behind her to gently pull out the indifferent phallus with an in-out motion before teasingly sliding the purple tip upwards towards the small of her back.

"That is so sexy to watch, Monica."

She wanted to ask where Monica had learned to make

love like that, knowing what they had shared wasn't love, also knowing the answer. She pulled Monica backward, raising her face to kiss the still open and reddened petals, feeling a pressure under her legs asking her to lift them.

"Are you hurting in your pussy?"

"My pussy's fine."

Monica kissed her there. "I know she is fine. I can see she is happy."

"She's very happy. Is yours?"

Monica wiggled her response, her fingers fluttering across Divine's swollen labia, plucking them gently apart, working her tongue soothingly between them with tiny droplets of their combined erogenous juices. Divine winced at the initial touch, jerking her legs, tensing until the sensation became soothing. She liked Monica seeing her naked with her legs open and she liked the sensation of the girl's probing tongue. She was good, too good to lose.

"I hurt you."

"Yes, in a very nice way. One more second and I think I would have lost my mind. I think you might have broken something down there."

"I will kiss her better when I finish. It is your other little button inside that I want for you one more time."

"When you did that I thought I would explode. I've never been touched inside before, not that way. My head's spinning."

Monica giggled. "You did explode, on me. Now you will explode again." The toy went in easily on low as Monica twirled it in one hand. "Tell me when I touch you there. You must tell me because I cannot see it like this little one, and do not stop what you are doing to me."

"I'll tell you."

Lying over Divine, feeling her hot breath and smelling her arousal, she felt her own excitement, her own arousal. Monica wasn't in a hurry to please. She wanted perfection.

She wanted Divine to remember the evening above any other. She had always wondered how she would feel being with another woman. Lucy had said the same to her. She liked the closeness and the smells, the tastes and the texture of Lucy's skin and hair, and wondered whether one day she would miss that newly discovered part of her.

Divine whimpered and her body stiffened. Monica's hand that held the exaggerated silicone member stayed perfectly still as the other increased the speed and pulled at Divine's lips as much as she could as a prelude to teasing the exposed reddened tip with her tongue.

She was holding him in her hands. He was pleasing her, he always would. He was her man, her caballero who would come for her. He had been in a brutal war. He knew about torture. He understood survival. He would understand this. She could feel his fingers inside her, probing, wanting to go deeper, wanting to please her, wanting to be one with her. She could feel his hot breath and hear his muffled groans. He loved her and adored her.

Divine screamed, not expecting the violent spasm that racked and twisted her body into the dampened duvet. She was trembling, breathing hard, her body drenched in sweat and trying to catch her breath, her nails still digging hard into Monica's soft flesh. Neither woman moved. The evening was over and Monica counted to three hundred, what she thought was five minutes, before crawling over and away from Divine. She had been still for fifteen minutes. Sitting at the edge of the bed, depleted and dehydrated, she studied the nude body, thinking how easy killing her would be.

She had spent the entire evening making passionate love with him without feeling passion for her. She felt nothing. She did what was expected of her, unlike being with Cynthia. Cynthia had a heart she had come to neglect and was learning to rediscover. The woman lying naked on the bed had no heart. She had no soul, no expression. Her eyes were closed, streaked with blue and green, her pale red lips pursed together as though in deep thought. Her hair was tangled and wet, plastered against lipstick-smeared cheeks in blonde patches and she seemed not to be breathing. The swell of her breasts and the concaved curve of her belly rose imperceptibly. Her legs were slightly parted, her thighs coated with a pungent glaze and the essence of her femininity at their apex seemed clinical and discolored against her cream-colored skin.

Monica smiled, imagining a name tag dangling from one of the painted toes, though even in sleep the immobile form was the intimidating Miss Divine, in full control and menacing from some faraway nether world, and killing her would not save Sofia. Manuel would do that and her evening guaranteed he would have the time he needed.

She felt dirty and she ached. Her skin was smudged with make-up and smelled rancid with caking body fluids that earlier had been his and her aphrodisiac. She hoped Lucy was waiting for her. They always kissed each other before sleeping or before leaving each other's room for the day, and she wanted to kiss her now.

She leaned over the foot of the bed as far as she could without touching it, her hands on her knees.

"Buenas noches, puta," she said, softly. "Ahora soñaré con mi marido. I will dream of him every night until he comes here to kill you, whore."

The time was 12:45.

Twenty-Five

Monica stepped into the elevator dragging her baby dolls in one hand and her crumpled panties in the other. There were no guests and the other girls would either be sleeping or playing in their rooms. Perhaps the Prefect on duty would see her, perhaps not. Supposedly there was no camera in the elevator, but no one really knew. She pressed three with barely enough time to take a deep breath before the doors opened.

Lucy was waiting for her, flipping through a hairstyle magazine she had bought earlier for a hundred points, circling possibilities for her nine o'clock appointment with Brother Reamer. When Monica walked in the magazine flew into the air and Lucy ran over to hug her. "Yuk, you stink," she said, recoiling with her hands held out. "What did she do to you? You look as though you've been fucking a freaking army." She saw the familiar reaction, feigning frustration. "Freaking, it means fucking, sort of. It's an expression, little girl, like no freaking way. Understand?"

"She did fuck an army, and the army did win very well."

"Sometimes I don't know about you, little girl. But you still stink. I want you in the bathroom right now. I'll give you a bath. You remind me of my dog on a wet day."

Monica pulled away. "I hate you, Lucy, more than very much."

"So did my dog when I washed her. Now go."

Monica let herself be pulled reluctantly, making Lucy work at it. She jumped in, not waiting for the tub to fill, cupping her hands under the stainless steel faucet to splash the hot water onto her face. She scrubbed briskly with the palms of her hands, stopping for an instant to tell Lucy she wanted toothpaste and her brush.

"Wash my hair first, Lucy. Please. I do smell like a dog." Mercedes glanced up, grinning mischievously and whispering, "One that is blonde."

"Is she as good as me?"

Monica giggled, twisting sideways. "You say first."

"No, you say first."

"We will both say. One... two... three," and they whispered a loud "lousy!"

"Did she say anything when you left?"

"No, she did not. She was sleeping, I made her very tired."

Lucy whistled. "Get out of here." She put her hand on Monica's shoulder to stop her from standing. "Did she give you extra points? She always gives points. I think it's a hundred for each orgasm."

"You are joking with me, amiga. If you are talking the truth, then I am very rich."

Lucy slipped in behind her. "How rich, stinky?"

"One night, maybe soon, I will show you and you, too, will sleep so well."

"I'm jealous of the old cow."

"Do not be. Her skin is rough like a carpet with no wool."

"You mean threadbare."

"Maybe I do. She does not use creams. This does not make a woman," she splashed the water between her legs, cupping her breasts, squeezing, "or these. "She does not know what it is to be a real woman. Ay! Stop, you are putting soap inside my eyes. Be careful."

"Has anyone ever spanked you for carrying on so?"

"Yes, he did, very often, even when I did not carry anything."

Lucy shook her head, pulling the flex-link hose out from the side of the tub, flooding the thick suds from Monica's head and face. "I think I should."

"What?"

Lucy lathered Monica's body with liquid soap with one hand, hosing her with the other. "I said, I think I should spank you."

The Madam

Twenty-Six

Christopher Brandon and Warner Stevens shared a single commonality: neither one was aware of the other. Brother Reamer was at the hotel every other Thursday and knew nothing of Doctor Dirty Fingers who did his examinations on the last Friday of every month. Dirty Fingers knew nothing and didn't pry. He didn't want to know anything, secure in knowing his past was behind him as long as he kept his mouth shut.

The same held true for Brother Reamer. He was as safe as Miss Divine wanted him to be. She knew his weakness and his past. He had an appetite for young boys and, just as Dirty Fingers enjoyed seeing young women dressed as little girls, Reamer liked to see young men dressed as little boys.

The girls didn't know him as Christopher. They called him Brother Reamer because he wore a solid silver choker around his neck on the rare days he wore black, giving him an ecclesiastical air. Most times he wore blouson silk shirts, tight-fitting linen pants and knee-high nylons with imported Italian slippers. He was never seen without his signature silk scarf and his lingerie was always the latest in European design.

On October 23rd he wore four shades of blue, from dark to pale, from his shoes to his scarf: the epitome of elegant effeminateness and the girls never ceased doing their best to distract him, the Prefects included. They were twelve of the most beautiful women in Atlanta, though to Brother Reamer he was the most beautiful. His highlighted blond hair was swept into a tight knot, his eyes were a brilliant Mediterranean blue put in each morning, his fake horn-rimmed glasses were a daily perplexity, and his white-tipped, French-manicured nails were all the whiter against his tanning-bed glow that was more orange than golden.

The girls went in pairs, one Anchor Girl washing the other's hair while Reamer cut and styled another couple, occasionally streaking or dying, which took more time and caused him to hyperventilate in a way particular to his social genus.

Lucy didn't wait for the intercom wake-up call. She was crossing over from straight cherry blonde to crimped vixen red, and she was anxious. Monica had threatened to leave her if she did, but after the little spanking that had led to a sleep-inducing massage she drifted into her private world murmuring that her Lucy would always be beautiful, no matter what, and that she would never leave her. She would never be alone and many more months would pass before Monica would hear Lucy's response.

That was then. Now she was scolding Lucy for sitting in front of Reamer in her panties and bra, again, and Lucy stuck out her tongue, again. She was gorgeous, in keeping with the hotel's business plan. The clientele wanted and deserved newness and Miss Divine demanded constant change, forbidding stagnation and disappointment. Monica was next, succumbing at the very last moment to Lucy's suggestion that she say good-bye to her massive head of chocolate brown hair and hello to a much shorter French triple braid, threatening Brother Reamer not to ruin her satin robe or he wouldn't need to worry about his next little man-boy.

They scurried to the pool when they were done for the girls' hair fashion parade day, one of their few precious distractions. Nothing ever changed outwardly, though Monica knew each girl had her private dream, her own reason to be set free after three years, her own reason not to accumulate demerit points. There was no animosity or jealousy between them. They were a tight-knit sisterhood and she was happy her plan hadn't hurt Dree. There was camaraderie and mutual caring because each one knew one day she would be set free to recapture her life and never see the others again.

No one spoke of the inevitable day. As much as each girl dreamed of being set free, freedom was what each one secretly feared: the unknown. Each one had seen her predecessor sitting in the other large wooden chair bolted to the concrete floor of the vault the night of her kidnapping. Monica saw Alice as Melanie had seen Deborah Wilkins the previous January, as Kelly saw Cindy Stevens the previous April. All had been shackled, sedated and carried out blindfolded by the rapist.

Still, each one prayed for the day she would be set free to die one way or another. That's what they believed, save one.

Twenty-Seven

Late Wednesday night Miss Divine came through the main doors in a silent flurry, seemingly flustered. She first checked to see whether the young woman was in the lounge before going to the dimly lit reception area to review the evening's guest roster with the Prefect on duty. Though she wasn't flustered, she was excited, aroused by the expectation of the evening she had waited for all day, as much as the previous evening had excited her when she happened to see Amanda for the second time.

Brenda was the only girl not engaged with a guest, sitting in the lounge, content that Miss Divine wanted her company for the evening. She was wearing her prettiest and sexiest outfit: a high-neck with bare-back velveteen slip in midnight blue that covered none off her exquisite legs.

She was as tall as Miss Divine, over six feet with her wrap-around stilettos, twenty-five, athletic with fine features, bright hazel eyes, long straight platinum hair swept to one side and her deep plum lip gloss sparkled on full pouty lips. She belonged on a catwalk, or graduating in the top five percentile of her Pre- Med class. Now she was a whore-for-points with no family, just Carol and the other girls, and she had long since forgotten such dreams.

When the madam stepped into the lounge a second time Brenda knew to call her Divine. She eased away from the sofa, smiling as she pirouetted with her arms in the air. The

124

color was Divine's favorite and Brenda was one of her favorite and senior girls. She had been at the hotel for three years and two months and knew how to please her frequent lover. She had made herself stunning for the evening ahead and needed Divine to say so, which she did while unabashedly devouring every inch as the snug outfit traveled higher over Brenda's bare curves.

They kissed as soon as the elevator doors closed, Divine slouching against a wall, exhausted from a day that had taken its toll. Once inside the fourth-floor suite Brenda went directly into the bathroom to run a bath, leaving Divine in her bedroom to undress. When the older woman came in she was naked, toking on one reefer, holding another out to Brenda.

"It's been an absolute bitch of a day, darling."

"Step into the bath and lay back. The water will soothe you."

"I know. I can't wait. God, your body is so fabulous."

"Do you want me to join you?"

"No. Stay there and turn for me so I can see those little cheeks of yours. I adore every inch of you." Divine stared at her, absorbing every detail. "Who wouldn't like that? Shit you're gorgeous."

"I wanted to be for you." The tip of Brenda's reefer glowed bright. "I'll get some wine for us and get the bed ready. Is there Burgundy for me?"

Divine nodded. "But don't undress. I want to watch you."

"I won't."

"And don't be too long or you might have to wake me. Call me when you're ready."

"You might enjoy me waking you." Brenda paused, reaching for the ashtray.

"When you're finished with the bed get us one more each of these. I really have to forget my day so I can enjoy you as much as I want to. Put the wine by the bed. I'll join you in a minute."

Brenda pulled at the duvet, scattered the pillows around the base of the bed, and put the glasses half-filled with white and deep burgundy on the night table with two twisted cigarettes between them. Divine stepped out wrapped in a towel, combing her wet hair in straight downward strokes as she padded with a casual slowness across to where Brenda had taken off her deep blue suede shoes and now sat with her legs crossed on the side of the bed.

Divine moaned with appreciation at seeing long, perfectly shaped legs transition into the smooth, flawless curves of Brenda's buttocks as she leaned to one side.

Brenda smiled demurely, leaning forward. She knew Divine. "You're an ass-man, Divine, and very incorrigible."

"The last thing I want to be is a man. The first thing I want is my hands all over your sweet ass." Brenda giggled, wriggling from the bed and reaching for the hem of her slip that had ridden to her hips. "No. First let's have some wine and a few tokes while you tell me about your day. We have all night together." Divine passed her the comb. "Be a sweetie and take this to the vanity in the bathroom for me while I light up."

Brenda took her time strolling, wondering what she could possibly say that would interest a woman like Divine. She lived in a three-room suite without windows. Her outside world consisted of a pristine patio pool walled on two sides by windowless brick walls of adjacent office buildings and on a third by a tall privacy screen put in place to hide them from the windows of distant high-rise apartment towers and hotels. She never saw through the mirrored main doors and, even though she was senior, she had no reason to know or care what the date or day was other than Sunday when she would spend the day with

Carol.

She found Divine sitting on the settee in a loosely tied silk robe, patting the upholstered arm beside her with one hand, holding out a lit reefer with the other. "It's too early for bed?"

Divine ignored the question. "Sit here, and take your slip off, slowly. I want to see those beautiful tits. Then I want to see the rest of you."

"They are beautiful, Divine. Thank you. I love the feeling when you touch them."

Brenda brought up her hands, pressing against the substantial curves under the sensual fabric, reaching behind to free the clasp at her neck. The front fell away and she shifted her weight slightly forward, taking the sides and pushing the tiny outfit to her ankles.

Divine passed Brenda the cannabis and her wine, letting her robe fall open as she leaned forward. She reached out, toking with one hand as the other traveled timelessly across the young woman's well-defined back and the curves of her buttocks, tugging at the strings as she stood.

Her panties came off easily and Brenda raised a foot to the settee as she toked and sipped her Bordeaux, letting Divine absorb what she could see before Brenda eased herself over Divine's thighs so that their breasts pressed together. The cannabis was taking affect, made all the more euphoric and potent by the Rohypnol-tainted wine.

Divine took her glass and reefer, placing them on the side table, locking Brenda into a passionate kiss. They held their bodies tightly together, twisting until their arms and legs were firmly entwined. They slid onto the carpeted floor, not caring. Divine loved the feel and odor of the young woman's body. She was gorgeous. She was not as lithe or nimble as Monica, yet she was as ready to please. They all were because eventually they all came to love her.

Now Divine wanted to please, to be a good lover. She

eased herself over Brenda's body, her face poised over two beautiful full breasts, her hands free to explore and titillate. She made cooing sounds as she kissed Brenda's lips, moaning as she cupped and kissed her breasts, not hurrying. Then she raised her knees from the floor and turned, taking time to luxuriate and lose herself in Brenda's calm cool breaths between her own warm thighs.

In response she trailed kisses between the soft warm arch of Brenda's thighs before rolling the willing girl onto her front, massaging and exploring the soft firm flesh of her buttocks while kissing every inch as the girl's relaxed breathing became shallow and she drifted into a peaceful sleep.

Twenty-Eight

Thursday morning Miss Divine hurried from the hotel moments before six, no different from any other successful business woman leaving for an early morning appointment, not stopping as she called out to the Prefect that she would return later the same evening. She disappeared instantly behind the mirrored doors, her heels clacking on the pink granite steps before taking her into her other world.

At breakfast Carol worried her friend had slept through the wake-up call and went to her suite because being with Miss Divine the evening before was never an acceptable excuse to be late. When she didn't return Monica and Melanie went to find her, holding each other instinctively at seeing the young girl curled into her knees, sobbing plaintively in the center of the bed that hadn't been slept in.

Melanie ran directly to the closet, stepping into the empty space. They would never see Brenda again.

Twenty-Nine

Anyone chancing to notice the ornately paned windows would see an expressionless woman gazing down or across to them. She was in her private place, her secret place, where no one had ever been invited. She had no one to invite. She had no friends, she had no lover and her co-workers were excluded by virtue of her compulsive need for privacy and escapism from a male-oriented workplace. She would never be part of the boys' club. So screw the arrogant bastards. She didn't need them.

They were no better than her pig of a father who had crept into her room so many nights throughout her pre-teens and teens to touch her in ways she hadn't understood until it was too late. All those precious years lost, when she should have dreamt of becoming a beautiful ballerina or played dress-up as an elegant lady in her mother's clothes. Lost to a mother who preferred not seeing the truth, a mother who never saw a scared young girl curled into the corner of her bed each night waiting for him to sneak into the darkness and pull her away from the wall.

Now she was worth millions, money she would never spend. She had the best of everything money could buy, yet she was alone with no one to share either of her two secret lives. She owned two city condos. She slept in one and maintained the other for convenient appearance. She had two European roadsters and she owned two city wardrobes that would tempt most women to cheat on their husbands. She could buy two of anything she wanted for either of her two equally callous and calculating personas, never once thinking there might be a third woman imprisoned between the two she had come to know so well.

Her suite at the hotel was her third residence. She was a wealthy whore who had a day job in which she excelled. She performed better than any of them, she had since the day she graduated, and they hated her for her success instead of embracing her as one of their own. That resentment festered into the genesis of her rebirth and the creation of the most unknown and most lucrative brothel in Atlanta.

Tuesday evening Miss Divine sat on the contoured and cushioned bench under the tinted bay windows of her eighth-floor luxury condo in Atlanta's Atlantic Station, the city's marvelous new and shining centerpiece. She was part of it, intently watching upwardly mobile couples sipping Pernod with water, or hopeful singles eyeing other hopeful singles as they nursed whatever overpriced premium drink they thought was au courant or in vogue that week, which rarely tasted better than the bar brands they actually could afford.

In her own eyes she wasn't beautiful, not an elegant lady because no one ever told her beauty radiates from within. So what good was all the money? She would never be the true definition of femininity, although anyone seeing her sitting in her tiny alcove wearing ultra-low-rise faux-suede beige boot jeans and a winter white plunging bra top cami would certainly allow her the benefit of the doubt.

The young women seated in the bistro settings lining the avenue were all stylish, all wearing the latest fashions from the surrounding high-end designer boutiques, like the one a few days earlier where she first saw the girl she would call Amanda trying on dresses and skirts. The men were no less trendy, some excessively so, imagining themselves as sophisticated and debonair beyond their realities.

Drab and gawkily dressed Neanderthal tourists and passers-by from the North and West were sporadic blurred images crossing her high-powered lens, each time frustrating her, disorienting her, causing her to turn away and refocus in the hope Amanda would still be there. She enjoyed watching the women, particularly during the spring and summer months when styles were always more daring and alluring. The street below was the premier feature of her condo she had never dared to capitalize on beyond intruding on their privacy, wanting them and fantasizing. Her fear of rejection far outweighed the fear that one day a lover might discover the truth.

Amanda was different. Miss Divine was instantly attracted to the girl in the store, seeing her sitting alone, so innocent and so vulnerable. The temptation was overwhelming, the culmination of so many nights at home in bed alone, fantasizing. This evening would be different. She would do more than fantasize. She pulled on dark brown suede boots and a matching fleece-lined suede hoodie jacket; she checked her hair, then she crossed the pedestrian avenue and walked onto the open patio of the café-terrace knowing where she would sit, ordering a Chardonnay from an irritated waiter as she pulled out a chair herself.

She changed tables before her wine arrived, frustrating the man even more, but she was sitting closer to the attractive young brunette whose life was already irreversibly preordained to change; completely unaware the attractive blonde woman smiling at her from a few tables away would effect that change within forty-eight hours. Miss Divine harbored no misgivings that the impulse was reckless, driven by the need to be with someone for one night who wanted her, who would say things to her out of desire and heated passion, not from fear of a wooden chair or demerit points. She stood with her drink in her hand, forcing herself. What did she have to lose?

"Hi, I'm normally not this forward, but I'm from Alabama on vacation and really don't feel good sitting by myself. I suppose I'm feeling like the loser of the evening, not that I'm interested in anything or anyone at the moment."

The young woman smiled at her, nodding her understanding. "Then I'm loser number two. Please, do sit down. I know what you mean. Even when we're not interested we feel as though somebody else should be, in us. My name's Rachel."

"Hi, Rachel, I'm Beverly," she smiled, knowing a one-night stand wouldn't care.

"Hi, Beverly, so how long are you in town?"

"One more week, and now that I've seen this place I'm changing my hotel. I'm over on the north side, off Virginia and, really, it's not so great."

"And not the best place for a lady alone, but you'll love being here. It's all so new and very much the in place. You'll have something different to do each night."

"Are you here most nights, Rachel?"

"I come when I can find the time. One bedroom apartments can get pretty claustrophobic at times, especially with the days getting shorter, but I work shifts and sometimes it's so hard waking up, like tomorrow."

"You don't look like a shift worker. Don't they always wear sloppy blue things with boots and have dirty finger nails? You're so lovely."

Rachel laughed the way young women do, enjoying the compliment. "No, I'm a customer rep with American. All this week I have early duty: 6:00 AM. It's tough, especially on my social life. When I get up all the guys in town are sleeping, and when I get home their working. Most times when things start picking up here I'm already in bed alone or studying."

"Still, the job sounds ideal for a young woman, meeting different people all the time. And what about those hunky pilots huh?"

"It is a great job Beverly, except at that hour I'm the only one for passengers to blame for everything that goes wrong and pilots aren't what you think. The so-called top guns are more like rusty pistols. The only reason I'm doing it is to become a flight attendant, but with all the cutbacks going on, who knows?"

A few minutes later Rachel glanced at her watch, though not to get away from Beverly. Her expression was real.

"Don't tell me you're leaving so soon." Rachel nodded, scrunching her face into smile. "Can you stay for one more, my treat?"

"Beverly I'd love to, but I'll have to go after I finish this one. Four-thirty comes fast."

"Then let's both finish up. I'd feel too conspicuous, especially after sitting here with you. Could you perhaps suggest a good restaurant for a late dinner?"

"I know a few great places between here and where I live, if you like Italian or French."

"Just as long as it's not southern-fried I'll eat anything. I may not be far from home, but I am on vacation."

"That's so true, and you're a guest to the city. May I add your bill to mine?"

"No you may not. I'm adding yours to mine and I want no arguments. Have you eaten?"

"Yes, I have… sorry. Perhaps we might see each other again."

"Is there a chance you'll be here tomorrow, not that I want to impose."

"Unfortunately not until the weekend, I have to study for the exams."

Miss Divine tilted her head, showing her curiosity. "I caught that earlier, what subject?"

"It's nothing earth shaking. Flight Attendant training, but it takes up a lot of time. Most of them tell me it's not worth the long hours, low pay, bidding for routes, that type of thing. Guess I'm a sucker for punishment."

"So maybe I'll see you on the weekend. I'm kicking myself for not coming to this place sooner. I would have enjoyed your company and I promise if I do see you over the weekend and you're with a handsome young man, I'll just say hi and keep walking."

Rachel nodded graciously as the woman in front of her took the leather folder from the waiter, enclosing three tens before waving him off.

"Let's go see about those restaurants, and thank you. You're very kind."

"That's when it's the most fun, Rachel. Let's go."

She could have said how nice it would have been to see her again, or offered her phone or cell number, or said it's a date, or any number of things, but she didn't and Miss Divine wanted her so badly.

She was well acquainted with the Italian restaurant. The women parted company at the entrance, Miss Divine holding Rachel's hand for as long as she could. When Amanda left her she went in quickly, ordering and telling the waiter she wouldn't be but a few moments and that he should bring her wine in the meantime. Then she left. In the time she was gone she saw Amanda go into her condo building, noted the address, checked the entrance of the underground garage and called a very argumentative Frankie with instructions to meet her later that evening, alone. She had identified a suitable Acquisition.

He did as directed, by which time she knew everything about the girl she'd followed home. Frankie had the pertinent information he needed, which included a close-up photo taken from her condo window and instructions to acquire the girl and deliver her to The Hotel Le Chic Thursday evening at precisely 10:00 PM: a serious departure from standard procedure. He wasn't amused. Even though she had specific and unalterable requirements regarding the acquisition of girls, she had never before requested a specific, pre-selected girl. And how in the hell were they supposed to track her in a frigging airport, he wanted to know?

She didn't care. She wanted Amanda and would have her one way or the other, though midway through a dinner of tasteless linguini and poor white wine she realized the consequence of what she had done. There was no room at the hotel for eleven girls, meaning that somewhere not far away another young woman would never know of the desperate fate she had escaped.

Thirty

Frankie and Bobby were her personal marionettes, no different from Brandon and Stevens. They were her Acquisitions and Disposal team and very much in her debt. They kept their mouths shut, not having to suppose what would happen if they didn't and she never worried about the unlikely eventuality. What they did on their own time was their business and as long as she was never implicated their extracurricular activities would remain their business.

She wanted no involvement beyond knowing the children's names. This time there would be no child's name, though she would pay a premium, an extra ten, the maximum compensation she was willing to extend for a No-Line or Ti-Fi. She needed them as much they needed her. Her strength was in guarding the secret

Early Wednesday morning the men were at Rachel Wright's apartment for a trial run, trailing her to the airport, then to her work station where they lingered uneasily, reconnoitering the environment. Before pulling out from the open-air parking they circled her late model BMW, appraising the value at five grand worth of parts. They returned at 2:00 PM to follow her home, after which Frankie contacted Miss Divine insisting he wouldn't go through with the Acquisition for a meager ten grand bonus. The girl would cost an extra fifteen, end of discussion. The risk was too great, and the response was anticipated. Thursday would be twenty-year old Rachel Wright's last day as a Customer Relations Representative at Jackson-Hartsfield. The two-man Acquisition team was stationed outside the girl's apartment and at the exit from the garage well before dawn.

She would leave her one bedroom apartment early that morning for the last time, leaving her young life behind. The plan was simple. She would be carjacked and anaesthetized in her garage as she arrived home in broad daylight eleven hours later, giving them more time to work and less time to store her. Then they would drive her to where Frankie would have parked his van and Bobby would stay with her, watching her sleep, while Frankie returned to the apartment to remove her papers and as much clothing and jewelry as he could manage. By late evening most of her car would be itemized, shelved as reconditioned or authentic parts and by the end of business Friday her bank account would be overdrawn. By Monday her credit cards would be maxed out with multiple cash advances.

Appearing nervous throughout the day as they rotated their watch posts between concourses was easy. They were nervous. That Miss Divine agreed to increase the no-child compensation from ten to fifteen grand didn't seem like much of a good deal throughout most of the day as they played disgruntled passengers with cells stuck to their ears, keeping each other apprised of her actions, alternating their positions with empty suitcases trailing behind them. But they were good at their profession and when she left the terminal at 2:50 PM they left with her.

Traffic on the downtown portion of the I-75 was never easy, either white-knuckle fast or frustratingly slow. At four o'clock most afternoons the latter usually prevailed and Thursday was no exception, though for Frankie and Bobby the drive was easy.

She had no idea, and like most urban dwellers she was complacent about her city's dark side. She believed most people were good and honest, thinking bad things happened to careless people, and didn't think to prevent a vehicle with stolen out-of-state plates she didn't recognize from following her into the garage before the time-delay door came down.

They turned in the opposite direction and she thought nothing of it, complacency degrading to carelessness as she cut the motor and stepped out without surveying the immediate proximity of her vehicle or the empty garage. When Bobby passed in front of her, tipping the brim of his straw fedora while saying "hello neighbor," wishing her a good day as he continued walking, she returned the greeting, distracted briefly while clicking the remote.

The chloroform-laced hanky closed over her mouth and nose with such speed and inescapable suffocating pressure she didn't realize she'd been lifted from the floor in the same motion that yanked her backward, arching her back to minimize the effect of her frantic kicking. She went limp quickly, her excited breathing accelerating the process, and Frankie wasted no time throwing her unceremoniously onto the backseat of her car.

The Acquisition took three minutes by the time Frankie tailgated Bobby's car into daylight. By four-fifteen she was lying face-up in the cargo compartment of the van, her face covered with the damp hanky, her small wrists bound with a tie wrap while Frankie was at the apartment by four-forty filling two suitcases, one of which he would leave at the hotel. She had good taste in clothes, excellent taste in wine. He stayed a half-hour longer enjoying a bottle of '89 Bordeaux with extra old cheddar and imported biscuits, putting the empty bottle in the suitcase with another he would enjoy later in the van with the girl who was no longer Rachel Wright.

He took the stairway to the side entrance, walking a
block to her car. The chop shop was on the other side of
town where Bobby would meet him at 8:00, giving him
ninety minutes with her while Bobby went for something to
eat. He was hungry; he had no immediate interest in the
pretty perks of their success as Frankie called them.
Anyway, with Frankie there would always be another one.

Miss Divine arrived at the hotel at 8:00, at 9:55 she
instructed the Prefect on duty to disarm the video
surveillance system from the main control panel behind the
Reception Desk and to check the condition of the pool
water. She was not to return to the desk until ten past the
hour at which time she would reactivate the cameras at the
main entrance and elevator entrances.

At 10:01 Frankie and Bobby came through the doors
whisking the gagged and blindfolded woman through the
lobby to the elevator as though she weighed nothing at all,
her feet scarcely touching the ground. They knew precisely
where to go and what to do. Once inside the fourth-floor
suite they went directly to the twin French doors at the far
end of the salon, pulling at the twin handles with their free
hands before twisting the girl around while Miss Divine
punched the confidential code into the panel on the ten-inch
steel and concrete door.

They needed no further instruction. The routine was
second nature and always went smoothly. The girl gave up
straining to talk. They were ignoring her. Only when the
blindfold came off and she saw another young woman
strapped into a wooden chair, disheveled platinum hair
hanging in damp strands, her unfocused eyes staring into
space, did her own eyes open wide with terror. She twisted
and kicked in vain, her feet still off the ground. She had no
hope. Within moments she was securely shackled to the
wide arms and base of another high-back wooden chair, the
vicious attack jerking her head sideways, slamming it

against the frame of the chair, stunning her into silence until she saw the syringe squirt liquid into the air.

Realizing who held the syringe she screamed in hysterical, wordless tones. Her head crashed against the back of the chair a second time, Miss Divine shaking the sting from her open palm before sliding the syringe smoothly into a straining blue vein. She instructed the men to leave immediately with emphatic instructions to go directly to the disposal destination and not stop for any reason. Frankie could wait for whatever playtime he wanted with Brenda until they arrived.

The young woman being unshackled wore a sheer black tank top with a black bra and a red ultra mini skirt with four-inch red stilettos. She was limp, though an easy cargo for Frankie who heaved her over a shoulder, jostling her once for a comfortable fit. He took the fifty grand in hundreds under Bobby's watchful eyes with one hand while securing her in place with the other hand as far under her tight-fitting skirt as he could manage, half listening to Miss Divine. She would not need another Acquisition before late March unless specifically requested, or unless the girl was absolutely spectacular.

Disposals were an easy ten grand extra, and always guaranteed: one girl in, one girl out. This time they decided on New Orleans at the corner of Baronne and Julia streets in the heart of the Warehouse District, 420 miles from the last person who would ever love her. If she were fortunate she would find St. Pat's and have one day of sympathy and confusion before learning about her new life on the street with pimps, hookers, low-life johns, drug addicts, dirty needles and dirtier cops who would certainly coerce her into the backseats of cruisers or darkened alleyways. Brenda didn't know she would never see Carol again. She didn't care; neither did she know to be afraid. The cocaine had already absorbed into her body and the next hit was fast becoming the most important part of her day.

She had no name or identity to set her apart other than the one that wasn't her own, no past to remember or future to dream about. She would never become the doctor she once wanted to be, she would never parade along a catwalk and would never again see her parents. She would spend the rest of her life as she had spent the last three years: For Sale by Owner.

By the time Warner Stevens was buzzed through the main doors of The Hotel Le Chic Friday morning the process had already begun for the most recent addition to the French Quarter's overcrowded and derelict nighttime citizenry, without the blessings of St. Pat's priest. She would be known to the police by midnight and either ignored by the post-Katrina hires on the force or coerced with double entendre and promises of seeing her again by those who weren't so new.

By the dawning of another day she'd be one of them. She would walk and she would talk like the rest of them, with no Anchor Girl to worry over her or love her. By Sunday morning services at St. Pat's she wouldn't care about or remember the pious male parishioners she would have serviced at curbside for a twenty and a beer the night before, or the potato farmers from Idaho who would think her asking about their rubbers would mean rain was in the forecast.

She now had one need, one friend, and she would do anything for any price to get it.

Thirty-One

Miss Divine would release Amanda from the chair at 10:00 PM Friday to begin her training. She would awaken to her first visit with Doctor Dirty Fingers. The origin of the name had been passed down over the years to each new recruit who invariably agreed the appellation was well-suited to a doctor who had put Melanie last on his list of ten patients since first examining her. She was the youngest, looking much younger than her years, especially the way she kept herself smooth, the way he liked them. In fact he never had enough quality time with her.

The AMA and several police departments across the Southeast knew more about the good doctor than he remembered about medicine. The list of offences was long. His degrees and accreditations were defunct, taken from him without much defiance or defense on his part. His amassed wealth had petered to nothing, disbursed to equally conscientious lawyers or parents who saw more merit in taking the man's money than seeing him do jail time for molesting their daughters and robbing innocent young girls of youthful purity.

Without Miss Divine he was by all accounts, including his own, destitute, entirely in her debt. He was sixty-two without family or friends, with no practice other than his monthly visits to the hotel and a handful of backroom abortions each year that usually took longer than necessary with sedated young girls who seemed not to mind the absence of a registered nurse.

When not at the hotel he spent his long days taking photographs and longer evenings printing out hard copies of real schoolgirls playing in short pleated skirts with white shirts hanging out as they pulled up their white knee socks, unabashedly swung each other around or played tug of war with their red or tartan neckties, always hoping for that next perfect shot.

Lucy was always more forgiving, taking her examination in stride, whereas Melanie teased him with promises of wearing something special for him and she didn't mind that his cell camera was a frequent part of his routine as she and the other girls lay in the stirrups of the portable folding table.

For Monica he was a necessary evil she tolerated, a defilement worse than any other and she stayed as fully dressed as she could each time. She told him his breath smelled of liquor and cigars. His tongue had a grayish hue and his jagged teeth barely passed his stained gums. His clammy, liver-spotted hands sprouted yellowed fingers with thick nails crammed at their chewed corners with a white flaky fungus which made her insist that he wash his hands and wear gloves before touching her during the first and subsequent examinations.

He insisted that working with gloves gave less accurate results, but no, and Mercedes insisted Lucy do the same from then on unless she wanted to find another Anchor Girl and soon all the girls followed suit. He would also discontinue the photo ops or she'd put out one of his leaky, blurred eyes. She was a Preferred Girl and he would regret doing anything more than taking a swab. What she didn't say was who preferred her.

On any Halloween he would pass as a made-up goblin or gnome. Any other night of the year he was a 5'5" hunchback troll with a reddish-white pot marked face sprinkled liberally with tiny black tips of fatty plugs he'd never squeezed out, embedded into the loose skin as permanent features that varied only in diameter. His yellowed white hair was greased into a ducktail of sorts that would make Brother Reamer retch with disgust. His eyebrows were the same in color, trimmed short. His eyes were dark, sunken above a blistered nose covered with sores that seemed impossible to blow or touch without some sort of fluid oozing or squirting from under its putty-like and porous surface.

The Prefects were exempt from the monthly ritual unless they wanted the examination and neither woman saw the need. One had been at the hotel for seven years, the other for six. Genevieve was twenty eight, Stephanie twenty-six, and both were quite content with their supervisory duties. They enjoyed automatic points with no demerits, save expulsion; they each had the largest suite on their respective floors, and had either forgotten the outside world or were afraid of it.

They only had each other, on a needs basis, terrified of not being loved or needed by Miss Divine. They would do anything for her, together or separately, and that's what set them apart: They were Prefects, not to be trusted, and Sunday was the one day that fact was partly forgotten by the others.

Thirty-Two

Monica's ordeal with Dirty Fingers was over by eleven, including her second bath of the day and a cleansing douche that would expunge any residue he might have transferred into or onto her from his discolored gloves. She checked her bath and toilet water for any foreign matter, like the loose ends of his hardened cuticles, the fine particles of his finger fungus, wiry black hairs that grew indiscriminately from his wrists to his fingertips or anything airborne that might have escaped his mouth or his nose.

At one point during the examination he had disappeared between her legs, continuing his probe. She felt the rough skin of one distorted ear scratch the inside of her thigh as she heard as much as she felt the aromatic scent emanating from her being sucked into his dirty snout as his fingers pushed their way into her. When the exam was finished she snapped her legs shut like a trap, making a smacking sound before springing from the table and ignoring his canned remarks about her health as she stormed out knowing he understood nothing she said.

William was expected at 3:15 and when she discovered he would leave by six she didn't mind being double-booked with Cynthia for the evening. She was delighted. Saturday would be a day off, another reason Courtesan Girls tried so hard to become Preferred or Special.

William did leave at six, kissing her on the cheek as he

146

might kiss his daughter, if he had one, or his wife, if she would ever think to let him come that close. Mercedes almost never thought of him. She had no reason. He was what he was, though at times he did cross her mind unexpectedly.

As her suite was being freshened by one of the Duty Girls she took her third bath of the day, soaking in scented oils, suddenly thinking of him, wondering where he'd be going and what he would be doing. She had no doubt he was someone important, someone influential. He didn't walk, he swaggered without pretension and didn't merely speak, he articulated. He did more than listen, he absorbed information as his mind processed and filed the data. He was that and more. He was gentle, a true gentleman, a caballero, and whatever his reasons were for being a guest of the hotel did not detract from her image of him. She saw in his eyes and heard in his voice that he was honest, unaffected by success, secure, confident, and Mercedes was all the more curious that he would pay a quarter-million dollars ostensibly for the pleasure of her companionship.

She might never know. Most times they began their sessions with a deep bath, quietly luxuriating or eventually giving him release. Then she would massage him and he would slip away from her and she would sit on her settee until he woke, when he would call her and she would go.

Sometimes his energy seemed boundless and they would both fall into a deep sleep after sending Lucy and Melanie to their respective suites, William feeling satiated, Monica feeling nothing at all. Other times he wanted her to himself and she would lay quietly by his side, each one an enigma to the other to be forgotten when he left.

She couldn't help wondering if he ever thought of her as more than a young female body that was always a phone call away. She wondered whether he was friends with Cynthia, Mercedes' other enigma who vied for her time.

When she wasn't with one she was booked with the other, though client-couples were not allowed. This was the first time she would be with both of them on the same day within hours of each other.

Cynthia almost always wanted to go to the pool. She was proud of her body; she loved other women seeing her au naturel. She loved the cool pristine water flowing over and between the curves of her body as she swam or frolicked with the girls in the summer, how her every curve and crevasse was caressed with warm water in the autumn and winter. The erotic freedom surpassed any Caribbean beach and was much more exhilarating.

Officially the pool area was available to guests strictly on a reserved basis and limited to a few hours in order to respect their privacy and protect their identities. The hotel went to great effort to accommodate everyone, particularly Preferred Guests, and Cynthia was not accustomed to being refused.

Monica's first time with Lucy, then with Lucy and William together, were traumatic. She remembered wanting to die, though she never faltered in her decision to give Manuel time, succeeding in achieving what she recognized as survival. What did change in those three months was Lucy showing her that being together was a refuge as much as loving, if love between them would ever happen, and she felt the same about Cynthia: She was a refuge against what she would otherwise live through over the coming years.

At times playful, at times eager, Cynthia was never disappointed and Friday evening was no exception. During the week she would arrive in two-piece suits. Saturdays she might arrive in linen slacks and a sheer blouse, ultra miniskirts and tank tops or jeans and a tee-shirt, not surprising anyone one rainy Saturday when she arrived wearing a three-quarter flared rubber raincoat, rubber boots, a matching rain hat and nothing else. She was 5'6"with the same skin tone as Monica, slightly smaller breasts, and she got as much out of Monica running her fingers through her hair as anything else. She especially enjoyed stripping. Her entire body was a sexual nerve ending, the slightest touch set her off, always wanting more and never satiated. She enjoyed toys and occasionally other girls. She had no preference; she liked them all, Monica being the clear favorite since their first encounter.

Friday evening she came through the doors beaming as though she hadn't seen Monica in weeks and not two days. Cynthia hurried to her, kissing her as though they were lovers reunited, wrapping her arms around her, hugging her tightly before holding her away to appreciate what she was seeing.

"You're a vision, Monica, an absolute vision. I couldn't wait to see you."

"You are lovely also, Cynthia. You are so pretty tonight. I do love your dress."

"This thing?" She gave herself a casual once-over knowing she looked fantastic. "Just something I threw on at the last minute. Do you like the way it fits me?"

Monica nodded, smiling approvingly as she sat on the sofa. The dress was designer, brand new, and within a few hundred dollars Monica could imagine the price. The knee-length prune-colored coat dress had three large buttons, no belt, flap pockets and allowed ample exposure of her pushed-up breasts and shimmering nylon-covered thighs. Cynthia undid the three buttons slowly, placing one foot on the brocade ottoman so the dress would open to show Monica more of her legs and the feathered ribbons at the clasps of her garters, teasingly pulling apart the edges of the silk-lined dress, letting it drape behind her.

Her foot came down and she stood there akimbo, her legs wide apart, shrugging the dress to the floor. The deep-blue balconet bra sparkled with embroidered rosettes and deep-ruby beads, her matching V-string panties an eye-catching centerpiece to the embroidered sides of her garter belt and the sheer stockings that left no more than a hand-width of bare flesh.

Monica's amber satin bustier and panty set was equally arousing, evoking the intended response as she lounged into the sofa, watching Cynthia perform as first one hand, then the other, went behind her to unclasp her bra. She tugged at one strap, then the other before cupping her breasts in both hands to pull away first one side, then the other, slowly baring one breast, then the other. She let the bra fall, bringing up both arms in an embrace, hugging and caressing herself, enclosing her breasts in small hands, kneading the small firm mounds until they began to peak.

She sat on the ottoman facing Monica, bringing one foot straight up as she reached forward easily pulling away the low-heeled patent leather pump, doing the other in a slow, easy motion, stretching her legs taut and pressing her painted toes into the plush carpet. The clasp of one garter snapped away, falling between her thighs and she leaned slightly to one side freeing the clasp from under her. She felt it tap lightly at her bare hip as she began rolling the delicate legging to her knee, leaning forward as she pushed downward to her ankle and over the foot she raised from the carpet. She brought her hands to the top of her thighs, squeezing the soft flesh of each leg into narrow and undulating folds, mesmerized by the responsiveness of the tiny embroidered triangle between them.

Monica put out her hand for Cynthia to stop, kneeling in front of her. She ran her hands lightly along the bare and silky surfaces of Cynthia's open legs before taking the top clasp between her fingers, gently prying the clips apart, leaning into her and pulling even more gently at Cynthia's bare hip with open hands to search for the clasp hidden beneath her.

Cynthia raised her leg and Monica pulled the stocking away, tossing it blindly over the other. She draped one of Cynthia's legs over her shoulder, then the other, reaching forward to wrap her arms around the woman, releasing the narrow elastic band, tossing the garter behind her. She delved intently under the breathless woman's firm cheeks, making Cynthia raise her hips as she felt Monica grasp her panties and pull them tauntingly to her ankles before freeing the flimsy fabric.

They were face to face, relaxed and unashamed. Cynthia reached behind Monica, undoing her bustier hook by hook, held in place by their bodies until Monica stood to push her panties to her ankles in one fluid motion, letting Cynthia help her step out of them.

"Let's go to the pool, just like this, Monica. How sexy would that be?"

"Miss Divine would not like that very much, Cynthia. Why do we not wear our robes and take them off soon after the doors?"

She pressed her face into Monica's lower belly, leaving behind bright purple lips.

"Deal, let's go, because if I stay here one minute more I'll change my mind. You are so hot. Girl, in my next life I'm coming back as a Latina lesbian whore. Screw this frigging corporate life. Next time I'll make my fortune doing what I like doing most."

Monica stumbled over the stockings and lingerie and onto the sofa, stunned by her own reaction. Her face flushed deep pink with shock. Cynthia sprinted forward, still on her knees, reaching out, placing her hands firmly at Monica's waist.

"No, Monica. I didn't mean you're a whore. Jesus, no. Without you I don't know how I'd get through my week now that I know you. It's not what I meant to say. I've always thought of you as a beautiful, sexy lover, my companion. You're a friend to me. I have no one else, Monica. There is no one else but you. I need you. Please, I need you. Forgive me. I didn't mean what I said. I meant you're a gorgeous and great lover. Some women I've been with thought they were good because they were lesbians, but it's not true. There are just as many hopeless dykes as useless dicks."

"I do forgive you, Cynthia. I know that you did not mean to say such a thing, but for one moment I did believe I was a whore, when I try very hard not to be. I am the one who is sorry. Please, you must forgive me because I made you feel so bad."

"You've never made me feel badly, Monica. You make me feel alive. Sometimes my life is a bag of shit, a real fucked up mess I jumped into because I believed my father when he told me our family wasn't wealthy enough and my family duty was to take over when he retired, which he did, the old fart. At least you get to leave here whenever you want. I can't leave what I am."

Monica twisted her head quizzically and Cynthia thought she understood. She let her tongue peek out from between her lips as she blew air to approximate what she wanted to convey as she wiggled her ass.

"That's right…fart. He hates that I'm not married with bratty kids and a husband who would undoubtedly screw around. What he hates most is not having grand kids, which is his tough luck. I can't even imagine anything that big and dirty screaming its way through this tight little thing." She kissed Monica's knees. "Monica I am so sorry… truly. If you want me to go, I will. No one will know and I'll wait a few weeks before coming to you again. Then, if you still don't forgive me, I'll stop coming. I'll never come here again and I'll tell Miss Divine I've found the girl of my dreams, which I have… and she's you."

"Yes, Cynthia, I do want you to stay. Besides the pool is

ready for us and I know that you love being there so much."
She bent forward, kissing the top of Cynthia's head. "So do
I and I do forgive you. Let us forgive each other. I do not
want to miss you."

"That makes me so happy." Cynthia stood, wiping her
eyes. "Then let's get out of here, after you give me a big
hug."

Monica pushed herself from the sofa and into her open
arms, their cheeks coming together as she palmed Cynthia's
hips unemotionally, transmitting a silent message for which
she had no words. A mutual, unspoken curiosity had grown
over the previous months between the women. Now
Cynthia had either broken or reinforced the barrier, though
in the awkwardness of the moment neither woman was
certain which of the two had happened.

To-date they had made what was desperate love to one
and fatalistic escapism to the other. They spoke about travel
and art, each amazed by the other's command of the
subjects, spending hours talking about hairstyles and
fashion when they weren't romping in the pool together or
with the other girls. The conversations had been safe and
noncommittal, now any such topic would seem trite and
banal, a clumsy obstacle to overcome irrespective of tight
embraces and gentle kisses.

Miss Divine had a number of Golden Rules which the
girls adhered to on pain of dismissal, demerit points, or
worse, which was synonymic with disposal. No one was
ever to disturb a girl when she was entertaining a guest, and
no one did unless they were invited to the party. Alone on
the rooftop patio the quiet sound was easy listening music
Monica had earlier selected to soothe her guest and the
lighting came from the swirling colored waters of the spas
and pool that was a comfortable eighty-five degrees.
Instinctively neither woman had any desire to imitate their
usual playful, amorous antics. The mood was already set for

simply luxuriating in the much hotter spas.

The first was very shallow, designed for intimacy, where Cynthia lay quietly gazing at the starlit sky and Monica stared down, letting herself drift beyond the stratum of colored mist covering her. Occasionally they eased into the shoulder-deep spa alone or together for an aggressive and unforgiving full body massage, clinging to the rounded edge with folded arms, moaning quietly in concert with the music and the relentless indelicate probing of forceful jets. Other times they clung silently to one another, letting the turbulence sway and rock them. By midnight they had barely spoken a word until Cynthia suggested ending the evening with a fast dip in the pool.

Coming out they were scarcely able to climb the wide concrete steps to the deck, cringing and rubbing warmth into their bodies against the tingling shroud of cooler night air as they searched the darkness for the robes they left at the doors, shrieking as they ran.

Once again in her suite Monica felt strangely empowered. Cynthia was paying the hotel a quarter-million dollars to be with her; so was Bill. That was true power. She knew Cynthia would spend the night. She usually stayed until check-out time and the sudden shock wave that had threatened their evening and relationship had subsided.

"Cynthia I do hope very much that you can stay tonight. Sometimes to wake up alone is very bad. Also, I do forgive you for what you said in my room. Please stay," she paused, not taking her eyes from the woman directly in front of her, "because if you do not I am afraid you will not come to see me and I would not like that."

"Or me, Monica. You're right. I wouldn't like not seeing you and I will never say anything so stupid again. I didn't mean what I said. I promise." She brought a hand to Monica's cheek. "I loved our evening together, until the pool. That woke me up more than a little. Now I don't feel at all tired."

"I am glad you are not, but I think you will be soon."

Thirty-Three

Cynthia was soon sleeping like a baby until the intercom
sounded at 5:30 AM. She was gone by six. Miss Divine left
at 8:15 after briefly spending time with Monica to give her
curt instructions for the day.

They all knew they wouldn't see Brenda again, the
second girl taken from the hotel in less than four months.
She had been a good girl with very few demerit points and
Miss Divine had kept her word to terminate her obligation
within a few weeks of her three years. She was doing fine
and so would Monica in due course.

A new girl was already in-house, who would take over
from Brenda. Her name was Amanda and her training
would begin immediately. She would be Carol's Anchor
Girl and Monica would train her in conjunction with one of
the Prefects due to Carol's Saturday guest schedule and her
Duty Girl responsibilities the following week.

Amanda was in her suite, groggy from her night with
Miss Divine who saw no need for further explanation. The
evening had been difficult, requiring more than the usual
glass of wine and roofies in a desperate effort to set the
mood. The second glass had made her unresponsive, unable
to stop crying, which completely changed the dynamics of
the evening Miss Divine had waited for so anxiously. She
would be back that evening for a few hours and wanted
Amanda turned around, making Monica understand she

156

would tolerate neither defiance nor failure.

That Brenda was gone gave Monica as much hope as doubt. The thought of one day leaving gave them all strength, what they doubted and secretly feared was what would happen when they did leave. Carol was sitting on the edge of Amanda's bed when Monica walked in alone, reliving the heart-wrenching emotions of the first morning Lucy had walked into her suite and stared at her on the floor. She took the deepest breath she could, searching her mind for comforting words. There was none. She certainly wouldn't be the last girl brought in. More would come and she wondered when she would begin losing track of time as Lucy and all the others had done.

She left them alone, padding to the suitcase by the French doors of the walk-in closet, hearing Carol explain to Amanda that her clothes would be replaced with beautiful silk and satin lounge wear and haute couture dresses for intimate dining with the more elite clientele.

The girl didn't stop crying, ignoring or not seeing Monica as she walked passed them into the bathroom to pour a bath. She asked Carol repeatedly where she was, disbelieving and terrified when she was told none of the girls knew. She would be there for three years, after which she would be allowed to leave, and even then they wouldn't know. She'd been brought in to replace Brenda who left with no idea of where she had spent three lost years of her life, wherever she was. More importantly, she got out. That's what counted, because she played by the rules and was the best she could be with the guests and other girls. The alternative wasn't good. Miss Divine was not a woman to challenge.

"And you must not open your mouth to say bad things. There are wires in the rooms and cameras behind the mirrors. Maybe now they are listening, so you must do what we are saying Amanda."

"My name is Rachel, not Amanda."

"Monica is not my name, Carol is not Carol, and you are Amanda. Carol is your Anchor Girl and if you are bad Carol will be hurt for what you do, and you. You are her Anchor Girl and you will be together very often. Now take off your robe. I have made a bath for you. You will feel better."

"I don't want a bath. I want to leave. Get me out of here."

Amanda tried standing, pushed back by both of them.

"Amanda, Carol is a very nice girl. We are all very nice girls and we will all be kind to you and help you, but you must not do what will hurt us. We are ten girls, we have no one else."

"She's right, Amanda. There is no way you can leave here, not as long as that thing is on your wrist. You'd set off an alarm before getting anywhere near the doors and you don't want that ever to happen. So please do what Monica says and take off your robe. If you want, Monica will join you in the bath."

"What? No, no way!" Her mouth stayed open.

"Sorry, it's part of your training. Today or tomorrow, so get used to the idea. There will be times when our lady guests will want to visit with you and you'll have to know how to please them. It's what we do, all of us."

"So you're all lesbians?"

Monica answered. "No. We are not lesbians or whores and you must not believe that or your time here will be difficult, also for Carol. You will be with men and with women. They are all very special and important. You will learn in your training time how to be with them. You will learn very much in so little time, but you must learn and we will all help you. Now take off your robe and go into the bathroom. We will both go with you, but we will only talk."

"No, I can't do it. I'm not like that."

"It is also what I said, Amanda. But Lucy did teach me

one thing that I will teach to you. You can do it," she smiled, "and maybe soon you will like it. You will see. It makes us like special sisters. We are very close."

"Miss Divine is coming here tonight expressly for you, Amanda." Carol added. "Don't make her angry by disappointing her or us. If you don't do what we say we'll be punished and so will you. Believe us. You don't want that to happen."

"I thought she was so nice the first time I saw her, at the bar."

Monica leaned in, whispering. "Which bar?"

"One of the bars at the Atlantic Station where I live. She sat with me the other night. She invited me to dinner, but I said no. I had exams."

"Maybe you should have said yes," said Carol. "She might have done you and left you alone. You were in the wrong place at the wrong time. Usually they bring us in differently."

She looked at Carol. "At first I thought they were taking me somewhere to rape me and that they'd let me go. Instead, when he finished what he was doing to me, they brought me here."

"The big one raped you?" She shook her head, spreading her hands across her wet face.

"The big one's raped all of us, not the little guy." Carol stood, exchanging glances with Monica. "That was the worst part, Amanda. The rest isn't so bad once you realize and accept you're here for three years. Even Miss Divine isn't so bad if you're good with her, which you won't be if you don't let us help you. From today Monica will spend most of next week training you without guests. Then you'll be with me the following week for the rest of your training with actual guests. I suppose you've been with men before."

Amanda retched violently, clutching her stomach and mouth. Her eyes were open wide with panic and disbelief as she jumped from the bed and rushed toward the sound of running water. Monica and Carol followed quietly behind.

Thirty-Four

October 28, 4:00 PM
Miami, Florida

The ten-minute drive from the MacArthur Causeway slowed to thirty with heavy Saturday beach traffic, blasé local pedestrians and nervous out-of-place neutered tourists in sloppy cargo pants, oversized tee-shirts and pink or blue rubber flip-flops. Without exception they were clownish and anemic alongside beautiful young Cuban and Mexican chicas and the macho muchachos who ignored them.

Low riding tight-fitting white jeans and pastel-colored drawstring pants with glittering thong ties riding over brown or tanned Latin hips that left nothing to the imagination did nothing to make him forget Mercedes. Neither did tanned and bare midriffs, or well-filled laced bras worn under open boleros, or cotton tank tops that were white-on-white or white under white. He hated himself for being there, hating Juan Carlos even more for not living in Chicago or New York. Instead he was in the heart of the Art Deco District one block north of La Calle Ocho at the center of Little Havana ,and if he hadn't cared about the scenery along the 600 miles from Atlanta. He cared about what he was seeing now.

But they didn't care about him, not in a '96 Impala that spelled out "poor working man" in blue jeans and a USMC sweatshirt which they probably thought wasn't his. The cars around him were imported German or Italian convertibles that spelled out money, good times and a one-night chance for some lucky bottle-blonde with perfectly reworked tits who believed or hoped the man in one of those extended-payment rides might really love her. He stood out.

He didn't see them, he saw only her, as vividly as though she was standing there with them, taunting him. He once hated when other men would stare at her. He knew what they were thinking and would scold her for being too sexy, feeling her soft palm press against his cheek as she asked how she could possibly be too sexy for him, her eyes glistening when he would drop his shoulders in defeat.

She loved that he was jealous, knowing all the while he enjoyed how other men were envious of him. He was proud of her. He loved how she was always so sexy for him, making him feel like a man, her caballero, her hero who had fought another man's war so she could be brutally raped at home before being kidnapped and possibly killed. And his little Sofia, his little baby girl he hadn't seen in almost a year.

The good times are what he struggled to remember, each night in his living room waiting for sleep to overtake him, ultimately revisiting his first night at home, his thoughts turning to dreams and waking in a cold sweat, calling out her name. Dreams were his penance for deserting her. He hadn't been in their bedroom since the first night. He hadn't touched her clothes or touched Sofia's favorite Poochie the Bear, nor had he ever cleaned the visible memory from the table.

But he did keep Mercedes' torn white panties and carried them with him. If long sleepless nights were his penance, her torn panties were his secret pennant and the simple words shadowed by the healing scars on his arm were his raison d'être: One Day, One Shot. He climbed from the car swearing an oath not to fail her. One day soon he would find her and someone would die for what they had done, for what they were doing.

"Te prometo, cariño, te prometo," he whispered.

The man was leaning on the hood of the bright yellow Corvette Z06 parked three feet behind the Impala. He was disgusted, waiting with his arms crossed, speaking in low tones with the beautiful woman at his side, oblivious to the three teenage girls on the sidewalk who were admiring his car and Gerald Genta watch. They could see something serious was about to happen. The handsome Latino with the expensive car was visibly angry and the ordinary woman who must be his mother was way put out.

"Where did you get this piece of Midwest shit, hombre, and what are you thinking to park it in front of my home?"

Manuel turned his head for a moment, his hands working at the key in the door. His eyed the woman first, then the somber-faced man. The girls on the sidewalk were touching each other's arms giddily, one of them talking into a cell phone, probably telling a friend to hurry while Manuel casually eyed the man up and down. He said nothing, giving all his attention to the woman who returned his smile from eyes as black as coals. The man noticed.

"This is my sister, hombre," the man said. "Do you want her? She will be a better ride for you than this piece of shit and she will make just as much noise."

The woman's beautiful eyes, black as only a Latina's can be, opened wide with shock, bringing an open hand against the side of the man's face before making a fist, pounding his unmoving chest several times.

Manuel stood his ground. "You look like a fag, hombre, and why are you polishing a car you cannot afford with your ass in those fancy pants?"

The man stood straight, making the woman beside him suddenly seem so much smaller.

"Screw you, hombre. I have seen your ass enough times. It is a girl's ass, smooth and tight. Sometimes it was hard for me not to take you."

The woman punched him again, turning to the young girls on the sidewalk with a glare.

"What took you so long, amigo? Did this piece of shit fail you somewhere again?"

Manuel shook his head. "I know now why I was so nervous when we slept together, hombre. Eres una chica muy bellísima, muchacha, in your little white designer panties and your sexy white blouse. I think I want to kiss you."

"Screw you, hombre. I can still beat your ass."

"Not dressed like that you cannot, hombre, not unless I let you." The man in front of him grabbed Manuel at the shoulders, waiting an instant before bringing him in close, hugging him. "I did not think I would see you so soon, JC."

"I told you, amigo. When you call, I will come. What matters is that you called, not the city we are in." Juan Carlos turned his attention to the woman. "Amigo, this is Carmelita, my cousin. She made herself pretty for you so at least pretend as though you appreciate her hard work. Normally she is very ugly, hombre, and you are not much better. You look like shit."

Manuel's expression showed pure shock, taking Carmella's extended hand in his and kissing it. "Con mucho gusto, Carmelita. I am so sorry to meet you this way. Perhaps one day you will see me the way I once was. Also, please forgive my rudeness. I have come with empty hands. I was expecting to meet JC alone, as he deserves to be for never mentioning you to me."

"The pleasure is mine to finally meet you, Manny. My ignorant cousin talks about you each day. I feel already as though you are a cousin to me also," she glared at Juan Carlos, "and a better one than this stupid man. Come inside.

I see that I must feed you."

"Come, amigo. We will go inside where tacos and cold beer are waiting for us. It is the only thing she can cook in her pitiful restaurant. That is why she is so old and still without a husband and children."

"I have only seen one other woman as beautiful, Carmelita, the reason I am here. But the beer does sound very good and I can taste your delicious tacos already. My mouth is watering with expectation."

"Then why do we not go in, Manny, and leave this idiot to flirt with the children who seem so enthralled with his stupid ways?"

She took his arm, Juan Carlos trailing behind as he gave each girl on the sidewalk a smile and a full-figure appraisal they seemed to enjoy. Once inside Carmelita spoke with Manuel directly and briefly before leaving the men to talk.

"Manny, I have heard such a little part of your story and have cried myself to sleep each night thinking of your Mercedes and Sofia. You are our guest and you will stay as long as you want. Do not argue with me. Now I will leave you alone to talk for as long as you need. I will join you for dinner," she smacked her cousin, "one that I will prepare myself, especially for you. I want to hear everything about your precious family the way my stupid cousin has not stopped talking about you."

"Gracias, Carmelita. I would like that very much. I will do my best to let you know them as I do."

She kissed his cheek, reaching for a linen napkin on an adjoining table as she hurried away. JC and Manuel drank their beers, studying each other for long moments, neither one feeling the strain of silence. They had spent so many endless hours together, waiting for the right moment was not difficult for either one.

"Amigo, you made me believe that you had no family."
JC shrugged his shoulders noncommittally. "Are there more

of you for me to meet?"

"No. She is alone to plague me and more than enough for even me to handle."

"JC, I took a while. I do not know why. Perhaps I thought I could find her on my own, but I cannot. I have done everything I can think of, but nothing is working. I need help to do this thing." Juan Carlos emptied his bottle, saying nothing. "I got myself a special leave, go figure, for ten months, with full pay. It is not much time, hombre. Already I have wasted four weeks. So far I have not done shit to find them." Juan Carlos cracked open his second beer. "The cops are useless, dumb as shit and have not done squat to help me, not a fucking thing. She was raped, JC, a couple of times. I puke each time I see the stains and God knows what they did with our little Sofia. The cops are useless shit. They have done nothing. Are you going to say something or just sit there gawking at me like a fucking shrink."

JC flashed a smile that disappeared in an instant. He put down his lime-corked bottle.

"I am royally pissed with you, hombre, supremely pissed. Big time. I told you. Do you not remember? I told you to call me whenever you would need me and you waited a full fucking month. You saved my life over there… and this is how you repay me. She has been gone more than three months and you…"

"People say things, hombre. I thought…."

"Do not talk bullshit to me. We lay in our piss together, hombre. We shit and blew farts inches from each other and now you are telling me this bullshit. Tell me what you have done, hombre, from the beginning and do not leave out one word."

Juan Carlos sat waiting, saying nothing. He was the same JC: dark and foreboding, introverted and secretive, no different from the man who had laid in the dust and dirt spotting for him as he focused not to miss the breathing target.

"After I left you at the airport I thought she would be there, waiting. She was not and I went home expecting all sorts of yellow ribbons and shit and there was nothing so I kicked in the door. I saw her clothes on the floor, I saw some other stuff and before I knew it some cops were at the door telling me to hit the floor." He took a sip of his beer. "I told them to fuck themselves and they started poking around, not doing shit. Later a detective came by, useless as teats on a bull, hombre, and she started asking stupid questions about my Mercedes. She said she might have been shipped out somewhere, that she might not be here, stateside." He bit into the taco and emptied his beer. "So, what have I done? Is that not what you really want to know? Fuck all is what I have done. I have been to women's centers, hotels and motels; I have met all of Atlanta's working girls and have put posters on telephone poles and city trees in the parks. I have been to hospitals, funeral homes, fire houses, office buildings and I have posted information on the web. I tried posting info at the airport, the MARTA stations and bus stations until transit cops and security stopped me and the city called me to say that I was to stop placing posters on city property. I did the newspapers a month ago, and that got me fucking zip."

Juan Carlos said nothing. The glib exterior Manuel had expected wasn't there, neither was any indication JC would say anything anytime soon.

"Now I just walk the streets all day, talking to as many people as I can, giving them photographs of my girls. I cannot sleep, and when I do I wake up screaming. I cannot even go into our bedroom because of what I saw there."

"Saw what?"

"It was one of the places she was raped, JC... in our own fucking bed."

"She was raped, hombre…where doesn't matter. Get rid of the thing and the detective might have been right. Mercedes may not be here, or Sofia for that matter and people do not give a shit. Show them a photograph and they will throw it in the can. That is not the way you will find her."

"So what do I do? What the hell do I do?"

"First you will let me think for a while and Carmelita will show you to your room. We will talk later, at dinner." He smiled half-heartedly. "We will bring her home, Manny. I know this, and so do you. You were always a better Marine than me, but no one ever got left behind and neither will your girls. I swear to you on my miserable life that you saved. Now give me some space and let me think."

Thirty-Five

When she came to dinner Carmelita was a vision sent by the gods for few mortals to see. Even Juan Carlos stepped back to take a breath.

"I told you, hombre, she is anxious for a husband. She would appreciate anything you can do to help her, as would I. It would remove her weight from my shoulders. You can see for yourself, she is a heavy load."

The restaurant was one of the most frequented on the Drive, owned by Carmella Martínez who wasn't yet twenty-two. Her cousin loved her deeply and she loved him as much. They were alone in the world and when he came home to her with stories of his nine months in Iraq she had cried thinking how she might have lost the stupid fool. He had never written to her, thinking one day he might not be there to read her letters. Then there was the man, the man with no face, the man with no body to hug or to feel, with no voice to hear: the man who had saved his life, the man who was now sitting at her table waiting for her to join them.

He stood. "Gracias Carmelita, thank you for inviting me here. I do not deserve your kind hospitality."

"Stop such talk, right now. I think of you as my family. Sit, please. We are private here. No one will hear us. What I must say to you is very easy for me. You saved what is most important to me. Even if you had not I would feel the

169

same way. I will do whatever I can to help you. Without question I will help you and Juan Carlos do what you must so that one day I will meet your Mercedes and hold little Sofia in my arms, and I will. When it is time for me to leave you will tell me, but right now we will eat and you will tell me everything about them. And you," she glanced over to Juan Carlos for the first time since Manuel had pulled out her chair, "my cousin, you will be quiet and eat what I have served you, tonto."

The dinner was a six-course Mexican feast with superb California wine. Manuel cried and laughed throughout his story and Carmelita laughed and cried with him as Juan Carlos sat quietly, absorbing every word. He knew speaking with Carmella was Manny's time, his therapy, without which he would be no good to himself or to his wife. His Genta watch showed eleven when they finished. Carmella knew what was about to be said, and she knew to leave, snapping her fingers as she stood to order her men cognacs. Manuel stood with her, thanking her for listening to his babble. She answered him with a tight hug, assuring him they would find Mercedes and Sofia. He was family and one day very soon Mercedes and Sofia would be with them.

"I made some calls, hombre. Listen to me. I got you a job." JC put up his hand. "Hear what I have to say, hombre. It makes sense, even if you do not think so." He moved an envelope across the table. "First, here's fifteen grand, get rid of the bank debt. If those tontos de mierda do not believe what you are saying they will find out soon enough. Only then will you repay me, but not before we find them. Second, you will sell your house right away. Screw the market. You need rest and you cannot live where sleep is impossible. You also know you will never return your wife to her nightmare. Third, you will contact this man. He owns a taxi company in Atlanta."

"I am already on full…"

"¡Cállate¡, chico. Let me talk. What you have done so far is done, finished. We begin again. You must take the job because you will see and hear things that are not yours to see and hear at this moment. Also, when you find Mercedes she will probably not be with your daughter, she will be with the ones who have done this horrible thing and you will need money, amigo, to deal with them properly, more money than a grunt earns. That is something we will plan together when the times comes, which I hope will be soon and you will not wait to call me or you will see my darker side, amigo, not this pleasant one. You saved my life and do not think to say once more that you did not. You did and I owe you, which does not matter. Over there, in all that shit, you were like a brother to me. Now I will be a brother to you." He smiled, showing a row of faultless white teeth. "The fact that I tried to kill you with my cousin's cooking is beside the point." He downed his cognac, snapping his fingers for another. "Manny, you will find these people and when you do we will take care of business together, like always."

"I have become a burden to you, JC."

"I was once a much heavier burden. That copter took a while to come for us, amigo."

"No sé que decir. Gracias."

"Say nothing, nor will you thank me when I help you kill them, which will be my pleasure. But that will take money, amigo, and not for me. So take the job and the envelope. Remember, Manny, before you get into any shit you call me. Like I said, I will come, and if you do not believe me you can vete a la chingada right now."

Manny nodded. There was nothing to say. "Her birthday is on Tuesday."

"You will be in Atlanta by then, driving. That is the best way for you to celebrate her young life, amigo. I will tell Carmelita and together we will think of Mercedes, though I have no doubt she will cry all day and pretend to hate me for making you leave. I want you gone by tomorrow, early. As much as Carmelita will despise me, I want you in a taxi by Monday, muchacho. Do not disappoint me. The men who have done this to you and your family travel in different places and times than you do, this I know. To find them you must be in those places and those times. The tattoo man who told you about the street whores, he was right about what he said. Become part of the dark world. That is where you will find them, in the dark, not here and not in the daylight."

Thirty-Six

Manuel left late Sunday morning, the front seat of his car piled high with home-cooked meals for a week, a concession Carmella insisted upon when told Manuel would not be staying longer. JC had been right. She hated him.

In front of the restaurant she unclipped and pulled away her favorite gold cross from her neck, draping the pendant onto Manuel's. She kissed his cheek and told him she wanted it to be his first gift to Mercedes when he found her, punching him when he tried to refuse, walking away before he could see her tears. Juan Carlos held out his hand, pulling Manuel in to him, grasping his shoulders with firm assurance.

"We are brothers, Manny. The only way you get rid of me is with more of Carmelita's cooking. You are stuck with me, hermano, and I will lose no time preparing for the kill. I will be ready when you are. Count on me."

"Gracias."

"Say that one more time and you will not need this piece of shit for the drive home. I will kick your Latino ass to Atlanta or the angels will guide you. Now get out of here. You insult me with this poor excuse for a car." They embraced again. "Vaya con dios, mi amigo, mi hermano. Vaya con dios."

"I will find her, JC, I will. I needed to be here. I am glad that I came to hear your stern words and to speak with

Carmelita, to hear a woman's voice and her wisdom. Tell her that she will see my Mercedes and my Sofia, that I will wear her gift until I can put it safely on my wife's neck. I will call you, amigo. You will know as soon as anything happens."

"Don't, and I will call you. Worse, I will have Carmelita call. Do not let her down, amigo. Do not let Mercedes down. You know what they are like when they are pissed with us." He smiled, pursing his lips. "Now get out of here before I have you towed."

Thirty-Seven

The house was sold by week's end and he'd driven the drunk and the weary from the hustle and bustle of downtown streets into the doldrums of Atlanta's lethargic suburbia four of the five nights. He didn't on Tuesday night because he was the one too drunk to drive.

He had advised the dispatcher he wouldn't be reporting for his shift and the reason was readily understood. He would celebrate Mercedes' twenty-fourth birthday, eating alone with only their photographs for company, though perhaps if he'd seen the daily headline he would have stayed sober long enough to call Rachel Wright's parents in San Antonio.

He knew what to expect, what the future held for him, for them as a couple. He would be strong for her, and for himself. She would need his strength. He poured one more, thinking of the happy day he would kill anyone who had touched her, or was touching her.

SECOND ATLANTA WOMAN REPORTED MISSING IN THREE MONTHS: POLICE STUMPED
AIRLINE OFFERS $10,000 REWARD FOR INFORMATION
LEADING TO SAFE RETURN OF TWENTY-YEAR-OLD RACHEL WRIGHT

By Wednesday the crushing stupor evaporated, by Thursday he rented a one-room furnished apartment downtown and by Friday he destroyed whatever impersonal furnishings he hadn't given to the charitable mission.

Wherever they would live next, she would see nothing of her past, no tangible memory of that horrific night, absolutely nothing to remind her. She would have a new beginning; he just didn't know when that would be. He began to know their names and where they stood, some offered him a backseat freebie for each customer he brought them, most of them taking her photograph and promising they would call. He started recognizing the jaded faces of the cops behind the tinted windows of their parked cars, and the city's pitiful and weather-worn indigent population who spent their days sitting cross-legged with their arms reaching upward and their nights curled onto concrete mattresses. They covered their emaciated bodies with cardboard blankets, their gaunt heads resting on the soiled and tattered fabric of their sleeves or pushed up against concrete steps at odd and disturbing angles.

By mid-afternoon Saturday he knew he would have to do more. He worked a ten-hour shift that left him too much time to lay awake in cramped quarters, letting his thoughts fester. His only diversion was despising an enemy, a target he could only imagine, a bad situation contravening everything he knew about the art of killing. War was impassive, not personal, particularly his type of war, one-on-one, and was as much about not being killed as being killed. He had eliminated one hundred men with extreme patience and even more extreme precision, men he didn't hate and never thought about. Now he couldn't stop thinking about the men he would kill and that made him dangerous to himself, not to the enemy.

Monday's shift began at ten; his second shift would take him through to two AM every day until he found her. The fourth weekend of each month would be at Fort Bennings, his free weekend mornings he would spend at the dojo for intensive training with the sensei. He was a trained Marine, not some office chair jockey hobbling around with a brown or black belt to keep his pants from falling. He found the best in Atlanta. His free afternoons would be at the gun club.

Thirty-Eight

Carol's first week passed quickly, not so for Amanda, which did nothing to slow the arrival of her inevitable second Monday. Monica did her best not to terrorize the girl during their first session. She did exactly with Amanda what Lucy had done with her, letting Amanda cry herself asleep after their unhurried bath when Monica spoke gently, searching hard for the right words. And all the girls did their best to make her feel she was one of them, which was precisely the problem. Her second evening with Miss Divine was a catastrophe. She was rigid and unresponsive, making their time together uneasy and physically clumsy. She had forgotten or shut from her mind everything Monica had shown her, for which she spent the evening and early hours of the morning naked and cold, deprived of light and sound, shackled to a wooden chair in the stark, steel interior of the vault as Miss Divine slept dreamily between warm satin sheets.

She had not stopped crying throughout most of the week. She ate nothing; certain she would throw up during her times with Monica and quickly became a topic of conversation. She spent her first Sunday alone in her suite with the lights off; she hadn't stepped foot in the pool and her time at the gym was spent sitting idly on the equipment. Not until Thursday did she begin responding to Monica's whisper-like kisses and increasingly thorough probing.

Only then did Lucy join them, though Amanda was still sullen and distant.

By the second Saturday evening the other girls were trying hard not to have their sympathy wane because they had all gone through the same process of fear, denial and disbelieving what was happening to them as their minds searched futilely for ways to escape. But there was no escape, not even when their minds inevitably drifted towards darker solutions.

Amanda had surpassed any of the other girls in her number of demerit points and many of them had made a significant sacrifice when combining their points to offset the imbalance, allowing her to enjoy lounge rights the next day. She would have to be a premier performer in order to reimburse the debt and not extend her obligation to the hotel, a fundamental realty she was oblivious to. She would have to repay them, which meant working and being good at what she did. Not accepting the generosity meant being ostracized by the girls. She was floundering in an inescapable catch - 22 and the worst was yet to befall her. Miss Divine had given her a second chance after a beating that left her naked body bruised and stinging. Though, despite wanting the girl so badly she could taste her, there would be no third chance.

Monica had slept with her the first night. Her other nights were lonesome and sleepless. Carol gave her space, hoping eventually Amanda would become more than an Anchor Girl and Monica's assignment didn't include leaving Lucy alone or not joining her after their respective guests went home to their wives or husbands. Miss Divine understood the closed sisterhood that excluded her and the need for the girls to form special bonds, as she understood the importance of not imposing on that intimacy for reasons beyond her own satisfaction.

Saturday was a watershed day for Amanda. She spent

the morning in her suite reciting answers to Monica's questions as though reading a script, amazing her tutor, making her believe for the first time there might be a chance for Amanda to make up her points and complete her obligation in three years. At lunch Carol was happy, relieved to see Amanda sitting with Lucy and Monica, albeit quietly. After lunch Amanda went to her suite where she changed into a bikini, strangely bothered by excessively large tan lines from her previous suit made all the worse by a three-sided curly ridge of light brown hair.

By the time she walked out onto the patio, the deck and pool were abandoned. The girls were preparing for scheduled guests who would begin arriving by late afternoon, or relaxing in their suites, something Amanda didn't know as she dropped her robe and stepped into the warm water in her thong and matching triangles that did little to cover the soft white of her small breasts.

She stood for a moment in the shallow end before moving deeper, her hands rising with the depth, swirling the water around her. Nearing the deep end she kicked her way to the rounded edge, pulling herself around the perimeter hand over hand until her feet touched bottom in waist-high water. The rooftop breeze felt cool against her bare skin as she spun in dizzying concentric circles. When she stopped she tugged at the strings of her bottoms and stared at the thick mound of hair Monica had discussed with her. She would get rid of it, she decided adamantly. She would ask for Carol's or Monica's help because she didn't know. Besides, all she had for the pool was the thong, which seemed to have a fur trim. She would be ridiculous to the other girls and without a thong her pubic curls would be clump of seaweed clinging to her legs. She tossed her top onto the deck, held her breath and fell backwards.

She had been at the hotel nine days, intimate with a woman five times in ways her few boyfriends could only have hoped for. She didn't want to die. She didn't want to be found on a dark street with needle marks in her discolored arms. She couldn't remember when she had last thought of her parents, but she wanted to see them again. She loved them deeply, remembering their worried expressions when she told them she was moving from San Antonio to Atlanta, and for what reason. She didn't want them to see her that way, dead from ruin. Not ever. Worse, that they would never see her again.

They were all she had. She had no current boyfriend and she hadn't thought of her work since her kidnapping and rape, unaware she was very much in their hearts and thoughts. When she climbed to the deck she padded to the first row of lounge chairs, dropping the micro-fiber triangles by the patio table before picking up a towel and rubbing herself as briskly as she could before reaching for the two little plastic bottles.

She spread the SPF 15 over her buttocks and breasts, warming the goose bump-covered skin, using the thirty for the rest of her body, her first positive step towards building her point value. She lay on her front, forgetting her nudity, cradling her head atop folded arms as she let the pale glow of a low autumn sun warm and soothe her until uncertain thoughts became pleasant dreams.

The gentle voice waking her was Monica's, draping her in a thick fleecy robe and calling her name as softly as she could, not wanting to startle her. Darkness had taken over from daylight, the air had cooled and dinner was being served for the girls who were not already with guests.

"You must come inside, Amanda. It is too cold to be outside like this. You cannot become sick. It would be very bad for you. How long have you been outside this way?"

"Most of the afternoon, I guess. You were right Monica. All those things you told me last week, you were right. I was dreaming of my mom and dad when you woke me. I do want them to see me again. Not seeing them for three years is better than never seeing them again."

"Yes, you are right to think so. Then you will still be so young and so beautiful." She pulled away the robe as Amanda tried awkwardly to roll onto her side and sit, helping her to stand and enshrouding her in one motion. "My guest will be here very soon, but the girls have put together many boutique points for you to be with us tomorrow at the movies. Please come. We would like this very much. They want to know you like them."

She nodded. "Yes, I will. I will also use the gym and if it's not too cold I'll come outside again to even my tan," she parted the robe ever so slightly, "without this."

Monica giggled, nodding. "Come. Carol has made a nice hot dinner for you."

Amanda wasn't certain. "I'm terrified about Monday, about what will happen."

"What will happen on Monday will happen for three years, but not every day if you are very smart. Do not count the days and your time will go faster. Soon you will forget the days and you will be surprised when you hear that it is Christmas or Easter. Also, you will be with Carol who will take care of you. She will not let any bad things happen to you."

"Are you afraid anymore, Monica?"

"Yes, I am very afraid, all the time, of one thing."

"What is that?"

"I am afraid of what he will think when he comes to find me, that he will think I am a whore."

"After all this time, you still believe he will?"

"No, Amanda. I know that he will, and never do I doubt him. I know that at this moment when you and I are talking that he is searching for me. This I do know. He will never stop. He would die first. He is my man."

Amanda frowned. "I have no man. I wish I did."

"You do. You have mine, and you must never repeat these words, ¿comprendes?

"Sí, mi hermana. Comprendo lo que dices. Gracias."

Monica recoiled, shocked at hearing such a young American woman answering her in her own tongue. "¿Lo hablas, chica?"

Amanda nodded. "Sí, claro. Ven conmigo, mi hermana. With you and Carol helping me, I will get through this. I have no one but my parents, and I want to see them again. That is all that I want. I will do what I must to survive. I have already seen the wrong side of Miss Divine and I believe that if she were to know we can speak together like this she would kill one of us. We should keep that from her, from all of them, and you should believe in your man secretly. I will also believe in him, but keep our secret for your own well-being. I do not know what speaking this way will give us, when we can. I do know she cannot take it away from us."

Monica was shocked at the revelation. Amanda was fluent. Now the question was one of deceiving Lucy, the same Lucy who had loved her for three months and who had protected her by showing her the way. She didn't like the deception. She loved Lucy in a special way and this would be a critical and unforgivable contravention of their mutual faith and trust. But Amanda was right. What they shared could not be taken from them and Mercedes decided right then to do anything that would give her an edge.

Thirty-Nine

The girls in the restaurant saw the smiles and greeted them with quiet approval. A full contingent of happy girls made each one's life more livable. No one wanted the Prefects or Miss Divine in a foul mood. The meals at the hotel were always different, each girl lending a different flavor, though when Monica's time came to delight their taste buds a greater need for ice water was generally expected.

Carol's meal was excellent and Amanda devoured it as quickly as good manners allowed, however what followed the warming beef broth was mostly fruits and vegetables mixed with marinated julienne strips of Angus beef and dessert was a vanilla moose that was light enough to float away. Not quite enough for someone who had barely eaten over the past week.

She was uncertain whether or not asking for seconds was permitted. She had never seen the girls eat more than one serving and she didn't want to incur more demerit points, so she simply asked Carol how long she would have to wait before once again eating her fantastic Asian stir-fry. When Carol's face lit up with the compliment, Amanda added that it would be a terrible waste if any was left to throw out and her Anchor Girl agreed, disappearing into the kitchen.

The day Brenda left to rekindle her lost life seemed like ancient history. Carol thought of her often, though she was

ecstatic Amanda was coming around. Her Duty Girl
assignment would end Sunday after dinner and what could
or would happen then made her very nervous. They all went
through the uncertainty twice, each one as a new and a
current girl: the unease of the second week when current
girls wondered if they would have special friends or merely
Anchor Girls, the new girls wondering if they still wanted
to die.

Amanda awoke in the dark alone Sunday morning with
no intention of going without breakfast. She was still
famished. She was alone in the restaurant and the first one
in the health club, after which she was the first at the pool
after going to the boutique to enquire as to whether she
would have enough left over after her purchase to join the
girls in the lounge. Yes, she would, and now she couldn't
wait for Monica or Carol.

She wanted to be first in the pool; partly for the time
alone, partly to meet however many girls came out one at a
time. She found the unfamiliar sensation of cool morning
air and the warm invasive water against her complete
bareness somehow sensual, not knowing whether to feel
embarrassed or guilty. What surprised her was when nine
girls came out onto the deck at the same time, ignoring her,
particularly Carol and Monica. She would have thought
Monica, at least, would not have turned her back on her and
she waded slowly into the chest-high water.

The girls dropped their robes facing away from her. For
Amanda, not watching them was strangely difficult. They
were compelling. They were all beautiful and she somehow
liked seeing the girls who took their time turning to face her
with the precision of a chorus line, looking down at her,
Amanda feeling disappointed by Monica and Carol. Then
she saw the wide, bright smiles as they broke formation and
charged at her, screaming as they became airborne, their
screams turning to loud gurgles and spitting as the calm

water burst into hectic life amidst a wall of flailing arms.

She was one of them. She did her best to defend her position, jumping up and down, splashing erratically, mostly with her eyes closed, but there was no contest. She lost. Worse, she was surrounded and they were closing in, splashing. Then the splashing stopped and they all just stood there, shoulder deep, bedraggled and scary with their scraggly, matted hair and running mascara. Each girl hugged her, lifting her from the floor of the pool, kissing her on the cheek. Carol was the last, not kissing her, rather wiping her tears and for the next hour they were just young women talking and waiting for the November sun to warm the deck. It didn't, so they left the pool and squeezed into the percolating spas without stopping their chatter.

That afternoon no one cared, the lounge taking on the appearance of a lazy retreat for pampered women or an esthetician's spa. The order of the day was fleece for everyone except the Duty Girls, styled in shorts or drawstrings with comfy tops or brushed cotton sleep shirts with fleece-lined pom-pom booties. The Prefect on duty wore a linen pant suit, looking more like a stern den mother than a twenty-eight-year-old woman who would have given up her reefer to join them as folded toilet tissue separated delicate toes and freshly painted nails fanned the air.

By the time Carol joined them after dinner, they were talked out and Amanda was a little more subdued than the others, which didn't matter. The day could not have gone better for her and by the end of her evening, which ended somewhat early for her, she knew she had done what was right. She would not count the days, she would not stop thinking of her parents and she would believe as deeply as Monica that one day she would be free. She would play the part for as long as need be and if something eventually happened with Carol she either wouldn't mind or perhaps she might enjoy it.

The Madam

She doubted very much that she could ever be a Preferred Girl. She wasn't like Monica, or Daphne who had been at Le Chic only a few months longer than Brenda. The two were different. Their inherent allure and exotic personalities were who and what they were, not what they had become. Amanda knew she was attractive, despite having worn sweats to bed every night since she could remember and her smallest panties to-date had been sensible briefs that came six to a box. She would never have thought to go anywhere without a bra or dark camisole and the balls of her feet still ached from wearing the new patent stilettos Miss Divine had given her.

She was the quintessential girl next door, her daddy's little girl and she had a lot to learn. At one time she had thought to save herself for marriage, though eventually she came to understand the need for compromise with twenty-first century would-be husbands or live-ins. Soon after that she came to understand that compromise meant getting laid one night and being alone the next, or very soon after, and she began to be alone more often, adopting a laisser-faire attitude about finding her dream man who didn't wear gold wings on his self-inflating chest.

Monday she awoke to the buzzing of the intercom, still dressed in her drawstrings and hoodie, reaching blindly for the glowing red off button with as little effort as possible. She didn't remember going to bed the night before, or flopping face down onto the duvet, or how she got there. Her body tingled and her mind, although seeming clear, was not letting her remember.

She lay there, opening and closing one eye before trying to open the other. Her mouth tasted horrible, her tongue was dry and her clothes smelled slightly smoky. She was alone, a soft guttural groan emanating from her throat as she taxed every dormant muscle in a strained effort, pushing herself backwards onto the floor and upright; strenuously reaching her arms upward and almost falling as her head swirled and her legs wobbled. Instead, she stumbled against the wall at the very moment Carol knocked and walked in.

"Good morning, dopey. Hey, you do know there's a timer switch for the lights?"

"No, I didn't. I don't."

"No one expects you to bounce off the walls every morning. How's your head, kind of light?"

Amanda rushed forward, crossing the bed gracelessly on all fours, holding her mouth as she rushed as directly as she could to the open French doors. When she came out wiping her mouth along her arm, Carol was sitting on the edge of the bed looking guilty.

"Did I help you, or make things worse? It might have happened anyway. Don't you think?"

Amanda answered by crawling onto the bed, reaching for a pillow and swinging against Carol's head, mimicking her words in a smiling whine. Carol retaliated immediately, grabbing her own pillow, and the fight was on. Within seconds they were wrestling, each locked so tightly onto the other to gain an advantage they looked like a modernist sculpture.

Neither girl conceded defeat, breathing hard. On the count of three they rolled away from each other and stared at the ceiling, saying nothing.

Carol waited a few moments before becoming serious. "It's Monday, Amanda. You can do what you want until noon: the spa, the pool, whatever. Then we'll have lunch together and talk about whatever you want to talk about. After that we'll start getting ready and that depends on what you want to do." She felt for Amanda's hand. "He'll be here about five-thirty, which won't give you much time. He likes panties and bras with garters. He's really nice. They all are because if they're not they can't come back or they have to pay a fine which has never happened. Anyway, the first time with a new girl they usually prefer watching us together before joining in. Usually they want the new girl second unless you want me to tell him differently." The response was a tighter grip. "Okay, so he'll be with me first, then you, or both of us."

"Carol I can't believe this is happening. Tonight I'll be with a man I don't even know."

"Think of it as a game, Amanda. Listen, most of us are married with children, or were. You're different, so was Brenda. So what? How many guys do most girls have in three years? It's the twenty-first century. Listen, if you're good enough to attain Special Girl status you'll be with fewer guys than anyone of them on the outside, and if you make Preferred Girl you'll be a nun compared to most high school girls. Monica's told me you shouldn't worry, and I believe her. So you haven't done this much, so what? At the beginning let your mind go somewhere else, with someone else, the man of your dreams or a bad date. After a few sessions they'll want more, but until then they're just as happy with something new."

"When I get out, I'll still be a prostitute."

Carol bounced quickly onto an elbow. "That is something you will never say, not ever again. You're saying we're all whores and we're not. So get that straight, right now. We do what we do because we have to. Understand that! Because we can't be sure what will happen if we don't, including someone like Frankie dragging our children in here for some freak who likes that shit. Do you understand, Amanda? Don't ever say that again. Don't even think the word."

"Carol I'm sorry. I won't, but when I get out I'll still have to tell some guy what I've done."

"What you were forced to do, Amanda. And why would you tell anyone or want to tell anyone? When you do get out in three years you'll have a very different impression of men and a very different understanding of women. So don't dwell on the bad, or sell the good short. Believe me, in three years you'll be an entirely different person and not a bad one."

"What is he like, this one tonight?"

"He's in his forties, a little on the round side, clumsy, clean and bald. He likes doing doggie because it's easier for him. Or with us on top because the other way would be premeditated murder, manslaughter at best. That way he can let us do all the work while he plays with the twins," Amanda crunched her brow, "our titties. He loves titties. He won't stay long, a couple of hours. Tonight I think he'll watch us a while, maybe doing his own thing, so to speak. Then he'll do me, you, and when he's done he'll take a shower, have a drink while we're having our shower and he'll leave."

"My God, Carol, my body feels like a block of ice. I can hardly breathe."

"This afternoon, if you want, we can spend some time together. I can ask the Duty Girls to do your suite last. Monica said you'll be okay, like the rest of us, but if you want we can get an early start to help set the tone." She shrugged. "It's up to you. I was a wife and mother before I ever thought I could be attracted to girls."

"We'll make love?"

"No, we won't. If something happens as we go along over time, that's fine. We'd be good together, but I don't want anything you don't. It'll be strictly instructional, "she giggled, "a refresher course.""

"Then what?"

"Then we get ready. We do our hair, our make-up, we choose our clothes, we wait, and we hope he's not late. Late always means they stay longer."

Amanda nodded, feeling Carol's light touch on her forearm. "Does he do anything bad, anything weird?"

"No. He's strictly in and out, but some do, mostly mild stuff." She chuckled. "Sometimes he gets excited and it's more out than in, never anything weird."

Amanda turned her head, inhaling deeply. "What time is class?"

Forty

November 11 was Veteran's Day, a military flag-waving day, his first weekend to report to Fort Bennings and Bishops wanted to see him first. The meeting was brief, the purpose being to see the Marine they had left on a long leash. They wanted assurances they hadn't made a mistake, to be sure he was still of sound mind and body. He was and he minded not at all when asked to roll up his sleeve.

He hadn't tasted liquor in seventy-two hours. He promised himself the three days prior to each Checkpoint Del Fuego would be vodka-free, not even his usual two. He knew what to expect, or at least suspected they would want to check him out.

Bishops asked all the right questions, presupposing the answers and giving the poker-faced corporal enough encouragement to be realistic and not patronizing. Manuel had earlier been instructed to report to Bishops directly with any pertinent information regarding any significant event, whether good or bad. He hadn't called. Enough said for the moment.

The military was having an increasingly difficult time in Iraq, specifically due to the lack of expert snipers. Fewer recruits were enlisting and the commandant of the Marine Corps concurred with the other three Joint Chiefs of Staff that recalling seasoned troops rather than re-institute a national conscription program would be more effective, marine snipers included. The decision was ad hoc, which Washington believed involved fewer immediate repercussions, though primarily the question was one of expediency and effectiveness, not necessarily about cost and certainly not about politics. Simply put, less time would be required to retrain, ship out and deploy those troops who had already served in Iraq, especially those who had volunteered for possible future tours or had taken on Reserve Status. The young face remained stoic. His dark eyes betrayed him.

"You're good, son. You're not going anywhere, at least not for another year. Even then, when you find your girls, you'll probably be posted stateside. I don't see the brass separating you from them again. Of course, that would be your decision. Like I said, you do what you have to until then. In the meantime you make damn sure you keep coming back to us and if you need..."

"Sir, I'm fine, sir. Thank you."

Bishops nodded, his chin pressed into his fists. "Make sure you stay that way. We need men like you. Stateside, when this is all said and done, there'll be a place for you. We," he paused, "I want to keep up-dated on what's going on."

"Sir, yes, sir, I will."

"That's good, because I want to meet your girls one day." He reached for a file, flipping the pages for no reason. "Del Fuego, this Juan Carlos Martínez, you ever see him? When you were over there you saved his ass. He ever get back in touch to say thanks or buy you a beer?"

"Sir, no, sir. We had our beers in Germany, sir, and I've been kind of busy the last little while. I haven't done much socializing. Besides, being over there wasn't exactly a party. Suppose most guys just want to forget and get on with life. You need him for the recall, sir?"

"No. He wasn't one of the volunteers. Officially he's

done, but we sure would like him for another eight or nine months."

"He was good, sir, very good."

"That's why we want him, son. Any idea where we can find him? None of this information seems worth shit. He's effectively disappeared and we're always kind of curious about where the good ones go. I'd hate to think some smooth talker in Washington took him from us. Do you have any idea where he might be?"

"Sir, no, sir, but if he ever does call I'll let him know."

"Thank you, corporal." Bishops' lips pursed into a grin. "The wife wants to know if you're alright for the rest of the year."

"Beg your pardon, sir?"

"The wife makes great Thanksgiving turkey and Christmas is even better. She knows more about what's going on around here than I do. She doesn't think your being alone on family days is a positive thing and the kids don't get home very often."

He didn't know what to say. "Thank you, sir, and thank Señora Bishops. I just wouldn't feel good being with you and your wife, enjoying myself while my wife is not. The worst so far was her birthday, a couple of weeks ago. I had a bad time, but I got over it, sir. I can't let that happen again. I can't afford to fuck up, sir. Excuse me, sir."

"I'm a Master Sergeant in the Marine Corps, Corporal, not a nun. Don't apologize for being determined and there'll be enough for another plate if you change your mind later on."

"I'll remember, sir, and please thank your wife. Is that all, sir?"

"That's all, corporal. Just remember the invite and the up-dates. Dismissed."

Forty-One

Thanksgiving was never important to them. No one had ever invited them into their homes and they never knew anyone they could invite, even though Mercedes knew nothing at all about turkeys. Anyway, she once argued in her inimitable way that all they had to be thankful for was each other and their daughter. What do turkeys have to do with that, she had asked him? Pointing out that her dress size was four, not sixteen, as he was wisely content to sit there and listen.

He chuckled, thinking back to the day as he dialed Juan Carlos' cell. He hadn't been completely honest with Bishops, certain JC would never agree to another tour. He was out and he was staying out, though he listened intently to what Manuel was saying without comment before he passed the phone to Carmella who did her best to lure him to her home for a good Mexican meal.

Juan Carlos took the receiver when he felt Manuel had endured enough, a split second before Manuel heard the loud smack through the phone. "She is rough with me, hombre. My life here is miserable. Perhaps I should go back, if only for the good food. What do you think?"

Manuel laughed at hearing Carmella in the background. "I think that you should find another one like her and marry her."

"You are not a good friend, amigo, to wish me a life in

hell. As punishment you will join us at Christmas. Being here will be good for you, and for me."

"Gracias, amigo, y le doy gracias a Carmelita igualmente, but I must stay here and continue what I am doing."

"People do not need taxis at Christmas, amigo. At New Year's, yes, after they have tried so hard to forget the last one. How can anyone celebrate what has not yet happened? Locos, they drink to forget what has happened in the past. That is when you must your work, and not become one of them. Tolerating them will be bad enough, so we will expect you on Saturday, the 23rd, or you will be responsible for her broken heart. Or, more sadly, my broken head. We will have time to talk and by then six more weeks will have passed."

"I will think about it, JC. Tell Carmelita that I will think about it."

"You will come, amigo. Remember your training, Manny. When you remain focused for too long, you become unfocused. You must not let that happen. So you will come and you will be with us."

Manuel took a moment. Juan Carlos was right. Without focus there was no kill. "Tell Carmelita I will come, JC, if she does not mind my intrusion. I will bring the wine."

"It is a restaurant, amigo. If you bring anything, bring make-up and diet pills. Hasta luego hombre, y cuídate. Adiós."

Forty-Two

December 25
Atlanta, Georgia

Amanda survived her first evening with Carol's guest. A week later she got through the evening with her own first guest, by which time she had begun accepting her transition. She had made amends with Miss Divine, though all her lost points had yet to be reinstated. By Christmas she had repaid the girls, leaving very little in her account to spend on Carol's gift and credit wasn't generally considered a good thing. Such a debt was tantamount to demerit points which could conceivably become days added to their obligation, which wasn't an option for the girls, most times.

Their vacation week had come, the one week of the year they could do as they wished. For the Duty Girls the week was doubly good. Each girl was expected to do their own cleaning and help keep the common areas clean. They would prepare their own meals and would be allowed a glass of wine with dinner each evening.

Doctor Dirty Fingers did his exams one week earlier on Friday the 22nd, the hotel closed for business at 6:00 AM Saturday and Brother Reamer was told not to arrive before noon. By dinnertime the girls were still dressed in slips, sleep shirts, silk boxers and bras, or satin camisoles and thongs in a moving tapestry of every color imaginable as they moved and squirmed around and between each other like giddy teenagers at a sleepover.

Some girls and the Prefects drank their dinner wine. Others wanted to save theirs for after dinner when they would change into long silky robes before tearing at boxes of decorations to dress the tall Douglas fir in the lounge. Or such was the plan until they heard about the brandy-spiked eggnog. The evening wouldn't make them forget that their husbands would spend Christmas with new wives or girlfriends or that their children would open gifts from mothers who could never love them as much. But for one night they could put aside how they were forgotten and be with the one they loved.

Sunday was a do-nothing day for the girls who had already wrapped their gifts. They watched the requisite Scrooge, The Grinch Who Stole Christmas and Miracle on Thirty-Fourth Street, which prompted comments from Monica that were far more entertaining than the movie. Sunday evening after their dinner and wine they had a choice: toke up or drink eggnog, not both. That would be allowed the following week with champagne. But they all knew now there would be more eggnog the following morning so they toked, and soon no one cared that little Timmy would soon walk like all the other little boys.

Christmas morning there was no intercom, nor would there be throughout the week, which didn't stop the five couples from jumping out of bed with smiles, doing the minimum morning ritual and rushing to the lobby to see if they were the first. Jennifer and Melanie were, followed by Katrina and Kelly. Amanda and Carol came last at the behest of the Prefects, somewhat more tired than the others and pouring out apologies because no one could open their gifts until they were all around the tree with hot toddies or eggnog.

Each girl bought their Anchor Girl the most special gift

and each one got a second gift from Santa Claus who had picked her name a few weeks earlier. And there was always a third gift, from Mrs. Santa Claus, who was always somewhere else Christmas morning and throughout the week. The gifts were extravagant: beautiful gowns, slippers and lingerie for the New Year's Eve party, when she would still be away plying herself with SPF 30 on a Caribbean beach.

One gift at a time was opened, sometimes slowly, accompanied by purrs and moans of the girls who wanted to open their own gifts, or with lightning-fast speed, heedless of the beautiful wrappings. Either way, the remainder of the day was spent admiring all the gifts.

Together they were the essence of Christmas. Nowhere in the outside materialistic world could Christmas mean more. What they shared was the quintessential interpretation of a holy day for some, a holiday for others, though none of the girls was conscious of the significance. For them Christmas was pleasing those who now meant most to them.

They didn't care that each point spent pleasing a special friend, or someone who may have done something nice for them, meant a possible lack of points to counter future demerits and all that sacrifice entailed. They were enjoying Christmas: the one week of the year Prefects didn't judge them, report or condemn them, one of two days of the year Prefects actually served them, unless someone got too close to the main doors.

Dinner was served by the Prefects. They had spent the day preparing the feast in a kitchen equipped with every convenience, including locks, a feast served in a dining room that had every luxury including plastic cutlery, dancing and table-to-table gossip between courses. New Year's was a week away, everyone unanimously agreeing not to spend the evening listening to scratchy sounds of once-upon-a-time crooners or newer wannabes who thought they were suave or cool sounding, older than their years with a repertoire originally recorded decades before they were born.

The girls wanted something different, particularly since they had a willing teacher and the vote for Latin rhythm was unanimous.

Jacksonville, Florida.

The Hillman's Christmas was a sight to behold. The sloping roof and façade of their elaborate Jacksonville home glowed in bright reds and whites, flickering in greens and blues, the tree inside their home judged best overall in the gated community by the Home Owner's Committee.

The white and blue lights lining the gunwale and cockpit of their blue-hulled 360 Cigarette, and the matching miniature white tree with blue lights that flickered even when they weren't aboard, were judged to be the best once again by the assiduous Harbor Committee at the annual Christmas Party. Of more importance was the annual charity drive to help underprivileged children have a happier Christmas and a boat ride. Christmas Eve at its best, no doubt, if not for a little one who didn't know Christmas, left alone to sleep in the dark with fading remnants of simple memories to make her feel safe.

Little Ana Juanita saw none of the merriment, nor did she hear tidings of peace and good will. She didn't know what Christmas was. She was not yet three, yet she knew what dark was and she knew what it meant to be alone in the dark. She'd been in the dark for close to six months, her little space lit by a narrow band of light at the bottom of the locked door, but this day was different, a stranger had come during the night. It was Christmas morning.

This day Anna Jane would come upstairs, open her gifts

and play with her new dolls. She would have dinner with mommy and daddy and wear new pajamas. Then they would leave her and she would know darkness again, holding her dolls as she wondered in a childlike way whatever happened to her favorite Poochie the Bear who had always been with her.

Her Christmas day lasted from ten until noon, and what could she possibly know or care about an upcoming New Year's celebration at The Harbor Club? Nothing. Worse, the one gift she would have wanted, from the one who loved her most, another favorite teddy bear she would have kept for years to sleep with and talk with, now lay orphaned in the open street gutters of downtown Atlanta.

Miami, Florida.

Concentrating on the road required an extra effort. He wondered what they would talk about for three days when he wanted to be in Atlanta searching for her. Juan Carlos had been right, of course. Still, knowing the truth didn't make being there any easier. Miami in December was no less distracting to the males of the specie than any other month: short leather skirts replacing white linen or cotton skirts, stilettos or knee-high boots replacing rubber flip flops and thin tee- shirts or bare midriffs becoming décolleté sweaters or sheer chiffon blouses with color-coded bras worn to be seen and appreciated.

The locals had stopped going to the beach by the end of September. The white sand and cooler blue waters left to the hedonistic French and Germans who could be faithfully counted upon to discard the matching tops to their brazen Rio, Brazilian and thong bottoms. Miami was a sexy place for those with someone, a winterlude scene to delight American men and disgust American women who weren't Latina. Alone, he was in another sexually charged beach town that made him all the lonelier.

He shook his head at seeing the man removing the orange cones from the space in front of the restaurant. Rare indeed were the occasions for even the closest to Juan Carlos to witness his bright smile. Manuel remembered how, when they first met, he wondered whether the unsmiling mask was practiced or inherent. Strangely, the man's exterior was neither, simply Juan Carlos: a man sometimes somber, though never despondent, always pleasant, though never engaging and never out of control. He was measured and calculating. He knew most friendships were transient because familiarity breeds contempt that is not transient, and for that he never sought to be anyone's friend. He was a loner who believed friendships long or short were needlessly labor intensive, though Manuel saw him in a different light. He was dark, yes, but friend didn't begin to describe him.

JC never told jokes and never laughed with those who did. More often he would laugh at those who did. He bowed deeply, waving Manuel into the spot, dressed more like Don Juan than Juan Carlos, complete with boots, black leather pants and a black silk shirt with billowy sleeves.

"You have the biggest cojones, hombre."

"Bigger than yours, chico."

"You made yourself pretty for me once again, I see. Eres muy guapo, muchacho."

"And I see you dressed for Carmelita. She is waiting for us. We will move this thing later. She has been running around like a mother hen all morning. I am afraid you are in for a bad few days. She will not let you be." He put out his hand to stop Manuel as they reached the open doors of the restaurant, turning, swinging one arm around his guest's shoulder. "It is good to see you again, hombre, very good. Thank you for coming." He slapped Manuel's shoulder. "I needed to see how you are doing. So far I am pleased.

Come. The old cow is waiting for us."

"You are a good friend, JC, to be concerned about me. But you would be a happier friend if you had such a beautiful young cow grazing in your pasture."

Manuel suddenly blushed deep crimson.

"What would any woman want with such a puny and ill-mannered man, Manny? He has nothing to offer a girl more than his dull wit and big ego."

"Buenos días, Carmelita y Feliz Navidad. I did not mean to…"

She pushed Juan Carlos away, punching him, wrapping her arms around Manuel.

"All I heard was beautiful and young. ¡Ay! It is so nice to have a man around who knows how to talk properly in the company of a woman."

"I am a bit out of practice, Carmelita." He gave her the dozen red roses. "I am doing my best."

"Gracias, Manuel." She kissed his cheek. "Look, Juan Carlos, such lovely flowers." She ignored the rolling eyes. "Come, Manny, take my arm. You are so handsome. First, you will refresh yourself and change, and we will go to the beach for lunch." She turned to Juan Carlos. "You may join us if you wish, cousin. I have made a special basket for you Manny. Not one that will spoil your dinner. Anyway, you are too skinny to me. Eating a few good meals will not hurt you."

Later Juan Carlos carried the large wicker basket and voluminous wool blanket easily, trailing leisurely behind as Manuel and Carmella walked arm in arm to the ocean. Her soft voice was as musical and soothing as her wide smile and dark enchanting eyes were piercing and sincere. She talked with him about the sound of white crashing waves, the brilliant blue of the ocean and the feel of the cool sand under her feet. The light wind played with her hair, her gypsy skirt fluttering gently against her legs, the pink and red ribbons of her peasant blouse teasing one another.

She wanted the day to be his and she would devote every moment to him. Sunday would be one of her busiest days of the year and Juan Carlos could wait until then to be with his friend, to say whatever he wanted or needed to say. This was her time with Manuel and she had made very clear to her cousin how important the day was to her.

Manny shook his head. She couldn't possibly have prepared their lunch, he insisted, touching his crystal glass against hers. Such an elaborate, delicious feast must have been created by an angel from heaven. She glared at JC, snubbing him, telling him to hold her glass as she stood. Manuel sprang to his feet, extending his arm to help her. She took her glass, bending slightly to allow her cousin to fill it, telling Manuel to do the same before pulling him away.

JC watched them stroll arm in arm once again to the eroding edge of the miniature cliff of dry sand lined with white foam as he topped off his own crystal goblet, propping himself onto an elbow, so proud of his beautiful Carmelita and happy for his friend. She wanted his visit with them to be perfect, a pleasant memory to see him through the difficult times ahead. She wanted to know everything about Mercedes and little Sofia, hanging on his every word, not breaking the mood with questions, every so often squeezing his arm or rubbing his back with silent reassurance.

By the time they returned Juan Carlos had repacked the basket. The sun was setting and Manuel's jacket draped loosely over Carmella's shoulders. As they came closer he stood with discreet agility, acknowledging them with a casual nod, walking ahead of them without speaking. He knew Manny would have done the same for him.

Manuel let the space between them widen. When he held the door to the private rear entrance for Carmella, JC was nowhere to be seen. She hugged him, her coal-colored eyes glistening, not daring to speak. She smiled weakly, patted his chest with one hand and walked away.

He was tired. He wanted to do the unthinkable, to excuse himself from dinner. Instead he trained in his room as quietly as he could, taxing every muscle, taking a shower that was steaming hot, turning slow circles until his reddened skin prickled with deep, penetrating heat. Throwing the chrome lever from red to blue he spread his arms across the cubicle, bracing himself against the paralyzing jets of frigid water that numbed him until he trembled with cold.

Talking and remembering had been good for Manuel and Carmella understood his frequent lapses into silence. They hadn't spoken together since October and he had surprised himself with how much more he had to tell her. He would apologize at dinner for being so self-centered, not thinking to ask about her.

"Do not bother, muchacho. Her story is a very sad one. You will only make her cry and we will have no choice but to listen to her wet noises all evening."

"You love her with your life, hombre; a blind man would see that. Why did you never tell me of her?"

"I have to love her, Manny. If I do not, who will? You have seen her, amigo. This is not an easy thing to look at. Can you blame me for not telling you?"

"One day she will be gone, taken by another and you will know the pain of missing someone so badly," he sipped his vodka, "though I feel sorry for the man who must pass through you to win her. The battle will not be an easy one."

"It is my one wish, amigo. She weighs me down."

He took another sip. "JC your beautiful cousin brings out the worst in people. I am afraid my stories got the best of me today. Lo siento, amigo. Forgive me."

He dismissed the lament. "She is a woman, amigo. That

is what they do best. They bring out the worst in all of us. They are like leeches." He grinned. "And as with the mysteries beneath the sea, we are wise not to touch the most beautiful of them, or the ugliest. So we are left with what is in the middle unless we want to be stung."

Too late Juan Carlos felt the warmth of slender hands and arms wrap around his neck from behind, sneering at Manuel who wasn't holding in his laughter as Carmella pressed her cheek against his.

"I will sting you this very moment you sad, pathetic man, unless you tell me I am one of the most beautiful." She kissed him. "I know you love me very much, cousin." Her eyes sparkled, much happier than a few hours earlier. "You tell me each day with your silly ways and with your eyes."

"Hombre, you led me into a trap."

"No. No hice tal cosa, JC. Lo juro. I swear I did not."

"Let go of me, woman. People will believe I have reached blindly into an under-stocked aquarium with nothing left to pull out but what they see clinging to me."

"And what is that, cousin, a beautiful mermaid?" She winked at Manuel.

"Perhaps in your eyes, chica, in ours more like a well-fed seahorse without a comfortable saddle to mount. What do you think, amigo?"

She pinched his arm hard, twisting her fingers as Manuel stood to pull her chair from the table. He opened his arms in a narrow V to hug her as she came towards him, whispering a thank-you into her ear before raising one of her hands into the air and steering her into a slow pirouette to the applause of all those around them.

She had instructed the mariachis to stay away from their table and Juan Carlos had been told the evening was to be happy and gay, which had left him with a hopeless grimace on his face and his open hands in the air. She had gone out of her way to be beautiful. Her brilliant red satin gown was slightly longer than knee-length, fanning out below the knees in a series of ruffled edges. She had bought if for New Year's. Her neck was bare. No jewelry could make her lovelier and her hair was pulled into a tight Spanish bun, held in place with a hard leather barrette and two lacquered wooden pins. Her perfectly shaped earlobes refracted ruby-red darts of light from delicate studs that matched the high-gloss of her nails and the center-piece of her single diamond ring.

Manuel guided her chair closer to the table and both men sat, saying nothing as Carmella's maître d' poured the French Champagne, explaining the wine was compliments of Señor Del Fuego. He ignored her pursed lips and furrowed brow with a faint smile, waiting for the maître d' to back away before he stood. Juan Carlos was visibly pleased his friend was being silently and severely scolded for the gesture.

"A toast, Juan Carlos, to the most beautiful woman in Miami and, I daresay, the whole of Florida."

JC stood, raising his glass. "Sí, amigo, our little seahorse is indeed the loveliest of mermaids. I stand corrected." They drank, admiring eyes watching them from every corner as Carmella brought open palms to very flushed cheeks. "Amigo, please sit." Juan Carlos' voice rose perceptibly. "For the last week I have endured much in relation to your visit. I have been told what to do, what to say and what not to say or do. Quite frankly, it has all left me very confused, though I would endure the agony a hundred times over to have you here with us. Having said all that, I believe my mermaid of a cousin would let me do this." He paused, sweeping his glass in a wide arc across the restaurant as each of the fifty patrons in the restaurant stood holding their own raised glasses along with all the restaurant staff. "A toast my friend, to Mercedes and Sofia. We will find them,

amigo. I swear to you… and we will bring them home safely."
*

Buying Christmas gifts for Mercedes had been difficult enough, trying to be different each time, especially when she imposed severe budget constraints. Buying for a 6'4" ex-Marine with an attitude and a beautiful woman whom he'd met just once before was something else entirely. At least the welcome task had taken his mind off his own narrow concerns.

Carmella made Monday morning special in her private corner of the restaurant overlooking the ocean and after breakfast she invited them into her private sitting room decorated with a colorful spectrum of Mexican and American Christmas decorations. She wanted them to be first, the men insisting ladies first. JC had bought her an eighteen carat gold bracelet, and when she read the inscription she made sounds impossible for men to make. She passed the bracelet proudly to Manuel and reached over to hug her cousin who finally had to sit her down. Manuel sat on the floor nursing his hot tequila toddy, not quite certain how well he had done.

The lacquered black box with her initials engraved into the lid was sensual to the touch and she first looked at Juan Carlos who shrugged with obvious sincerity before she turned to Manny who sat beside her expectantly. Inside, resting on pure white silk was an elegant barrette of deep black obsidian bordered with a thin silver ridge that matched the sleek silver pins resting along the top and bottom edges. In the center of the barrette was a single red ruby.

The gift was extravagant. She smiled, not daring to open her mouth. Juan Carlos' inhaled whistle spoke for her. She leaned over and kissed him, saying simply: "I have never seen anything so lovely. I will wear your gift at New

Year's, Manny, with my new black dress. It will be perfect."

"You are the perfect one, Carmelita. Without you it is nothing."

Juan Carlos cleared his throat, suggesting more tequila. "Hombre, I had no help from anyone in buying you a gift." He grinned at her. "It is not something I have done since I was a young boy in Chiapas, when I would buy nothing gifts for my not yet murdered father." He passed over the heavy envelope. "I hope you will understand, hombre."

Manuel opened the envelope, smiling at both of them as he pulled out the thin brass plaque wrapped in tissue paper. Carmella held out her hand, inspecting the engraved square before staring questioningly at her cousin.

"It is a very handsome plaque, Manny. I am certain you will enjoy doing something with it." She turned again to Juan Carlos with a familiar and deprecating expression.

"I believe so, Carmelita. Not all things are as we see them at first. JC, I have never had as good a friend as you, no one who has understood me. We have been through much together. I am not one for being close to people, yet I feel as though I am with family. Yesterday was good for me. Gracias." He slid the large green and red glittering package across the carpet. "Feliz Navidad, hermano."

The paper peeled away slowly, JC focusing on the large box. "Hombre es demasiado, honestamente." He slowly extracted the polished mahogany humidor preset to seventy percent from its protective casing. The inscription read: Para siempre, MDF. He beamed as he opened the lid. "Carmelita you told him of my favorite brand."

She leaned over. "Manny this is too much. It is a work of art... and what is this little package."

JC tore at the wrapping. "Manny, you show me up, amigo. There is but one way to thank you."

He caressed the cool titanium skin of the triple-jet

butane lighter between his fingers, reaching with the other hand for two of the eight-inch Cubans.

"¡Ay, no! You will not smoke these filthy things in my home, Juan Carlos." She took the cigars from him, returning them to the humidor before standing. She gave each of them a stern reprimand, reaching behind for her gifts to them. "First you will open these, you will both kiss me, and then you will go to smoke these dirty smelling things on the patio. ¿Comprendes? mi querido primo."

JC feigned disappointment, pretending he could sulk. "Then we would both miss you, cousin. Here, we can enjoy your company as well as these fine Montecristos."

"I am not listening to you, silly man." She passed each one a meticulously wrapped little box. "Has anyone noticed my glass is empty? What has happened to those handsome and gallant caballeros from last night, or was I dreaming that such men can still exist?" Her dark eyes spoke volumes to Juan Carlos. "Do you expect our guest to go?"

"Hombre, do you wonder why I am still unmarried. Can you imagine this chatter all your life?" He paused, suddenly realizing. "Manny, forgive me. Sometimes I talk too quickly."

Manuel shook off the innocent remark. "I care for both of you deeply, as will my Mercedes when you meet her, and Sofia will think of you as her aunt and uncle. Until then you must not make yourself uncomfortable trying to please me or placate me. I am fine, very fine, because of you. Carmelita you are a sister to me. JC you are a brother. Let that be enough. I could never ask for more. I am truly blessed."

"I agree hombre. That is enough, please, before you turn her black eyes red again. We feel as you do. Remember my promise." He rolled onto his knees, standing with gymnastic litheness, listening to the silence behind him as he walked to the wet bar. When he returned Carmella was quietly holding Manuel's hands.

JC's Santos 100 Chronograph was a man's watch. She sat like an anxious little girl as he opened the box, smiling as he told her someone important from Cartier must have seen him at the beach and immediately ordered a special edition that would celebrate real men. He reached over effortlessly, lifting her from the floor despite her feeble protests, hugging her before he plopped her unceremoniously onto the carpet in front of Manuel who waited for her nod to open his gift.

He stared in awe at the ceramic and steel Hublot Big Bang with its thick black rubber strap and Kevlar fittings. Then he stared at her.

"There were many things I wanted you to have, Manny, so many things I know you deserve. This is what I thought a man such as you would need to help make the best use of his time. Did I choose well?"

"Carmelita we have known each other for so little…"

"Do not say such silly things, Manny. You begin to remind me of another stupid man." She lifted herself a little off the floor, turning to JC. "We are family, the three of us, and soon our family will be much bigger. You saved my cousin, Manny, though sometimes I think I should not love you as much as I do for doing that." She gasped, searching Juan Carlos' bright eyes for the deep hurt. "I did not mean that Juanito. You know that I did not."

"Chica, how can you not love me? I know that you do. Who would not love such a man?"

"Get out of here both of you, and take your dirty Cuban sticks with you, after you help me up." They each took a hand. "Both of you be here by one for lunch on the beach. Now, go. Get out of here. I have things to do."
*

Both men sat side-saddle on the white PVC banister overlooking the ocean, letting trails of rich blue smoke drift from their open mouths between sips of Jalisco tequila and the best American vodka.

"We did well, amigo. My cousin is a lady of taste. Also, thank you for treating her so well and making me look so bad."

Manuel laughed. "You will never be anything but wonderful to her, hombre. You treat her like the jewel that she is. If you ever stop I will beat you severely."

"So you do dream, amigo, and in color. That is good." He filled his glass, reaching for the blue bottle to refill Manuel's. "I have more than a plaque for you, Manny. What I have I could not give to you in front Carmelita."

"I need nothing more from you, JC. I will treasure your plaque always."

"Cállate, chico. Do not talk to me like I am a fucking girl who will never see you again, or it is Carmelita who will never see you again because I will bury you right here in the fucking sand for the crabs to eat." A man appeared as though on cue and left immediately. "This is my gift to you, amigo. Feliz Navidad."

The black velvet ribbon around the cherry wood box was thick, difficult to undo. JC pulled a stiletto from his hip pocket, helping his friend with a single flick.

"JC what is this?"

Juan Carlos laughed heartily. "Merry Christmas, hombre, and you know very well. So put it in your hands where it belongs. Caress it as you would a beautiful woman. Both are dangerous."

The beautiful black masterpiece didn't gleam in the noonday sun: a 9mm 92FS Vertec Beretta with infrared tracking that would kill a man easily at a hundred and fifty feet.

"JC, no sé que decir. This is really too much."

"Listen to me, mi amigo. This gun will kill your worst enemy." He reached under his leather jacket. "And this is how he will die if you miss, though I know you will not. I will be there with you, Manny. I swear to you. You call my cousin your sister, as I will one day call Mercedes my sister and Sofia my niece. Now, do we smoke these perfect cigars or do we continue to speak like old women?" He paused, inhaling deeply. "Turn it to the other side, hombre. Turn the gun over."

Manuel did, smiling as he read the brief inscription before replacing the beautiful weapon into its snug resting place. Then he embraced his friend. "One shot is all that I will need. The kill is a given."

"Manny you saved my life. I would have been shit on a stick out there without you. I will never forget what you did, even if you do. You are a great Marine hombre, one of the best; still you are a novice in the dark affairs of our city streets. I am not. If I do not help you, you will fail. I will cover your back and you will cover mine, as always." JC drew in the heated blue smoke, blowing it out between his lips in a perfect stream. "Besides, if I do not help your sorry ass our beautiful mermaid will make my life a living hell."

Manuel chortled. "Thank you, JC, and one day my Mercedes and our little Sofia will thank you."

Juan Carlos took a deep breath, shrugging. "For the little they know. You will take this thing we will do to your grave. Do you understand me, hombre? The only ones to ever know will be the ones who see the red dot too late, or see the pleasure in your eyes as you end their miserable lives. Mercedes will know that she was lost and that you found her, nothing more. If you do not already know, amigo, we are going to war. So be ready for the day. It is not far away. I can smell it."

Forty-Three

December 31
Atlanta, Georgia

The gym equipment remained pushed against the wall. By the end of the week the girls were humming or singing passable renditions of Monica's favorite Latin songs, slipping, colliding or bouncing off each other before finally swaying their hips as they glided along each other's arms and around each other's bodies like pros.

Genevieve and Stephanie watched from the sidelines, feigning indifference. They lived with the same restrictions as the other girls, but only had each other. They wore monitors, though were able to leave the hotel anytime they wished, albeit only once, and the first girl to arrive at the end of her three-year obligation would be given the choice to leave or to stay on with Prefect status. Both women had made the conscious choice years earlier, convinced they had nowhere to go.

Genevieve's husband was killed in a car accident towards the end of her obligation and she had no idea where to begin to find a child who'd be better off without her. Stephanie's husband remarried within her first year at the hotel and her son would have had no recollection of her after the three years that had turned into six or seven.

They had no access to the fourth floor, though they did

have perks which included street clothes rather than closets lined with lingerie. They were allowed a glass of wine with every dinner; they had DVD and CD players in suites free of cameras and mikes, or so they were told, and they could watch the girls whenever they felt the need as Prefects or for pleasure. What they couldn't do was fraternize with the girls. What they could not have were friends.

They were never each other's Anchor Girl. Genevieve had been a Prefect for almost two years when Stephanie was given the choice to stay or go and she had already seen more than a dozen girls leave the hotel to recapture their lives. In fact, she had never seen them leave. They simply weren't there one morning. She never thought of them. She hardly remembered them and never thought of leaving, though she knew as well as Stephanie the day would come when they would be told to leave and the thought terrified them.

They could leave anytime, they simply didn't want to. They knew the bracelets weren't the deterrent keeping the girls from running through the doors. They were afraid for their children, their families, though Genevieve and Stephanie wanted to stay. The fact Miss Divine had reviewed their files with them at the time of their decision, reminding them of their children and their parents, was moot. They needed to stay.

Neither woman could remember the last time Miss Divine invited her to the fourth floor for an evening because the madam preferred younger, newer girls and Genevieve's time alone with Stephanie was often strained by the endless demands of their opposite schedules. When they did have time together their romance lacked the heated energy of youth.

On Sundays, or occasions like Christmas and New Year's that were so special to everyone else, they acted more like co-workers in front of the girls, seeming distant from one another. They weren't lovers or friends. There was no girlish intimacy. They were simply there for each other when needed, not unlike the hotel's numerous guests who would think nothing of calling either woman to reserve a suite with a girl. They had signed away their remaining youth with the carelessness of distorted reasoning, seized by the subliminal fear of retribution that had been such an integral part of them for such a long part of their young lives, not realizing how deep sadness emanated from both of them to be perceived by all as stoic indifference.

Christmas had not changed for them. Secretly, Genevieve wanted to learn to dance with Monica, she got perfume. Stephanie secretly wanted to jump into the pool with Melanie and splash around like a carefree young woman, she got perfume.

Monica worked from 8:00 AM, minute beads of sweat masking her determined face by noon. She was in charge, issuing each girl implicit instructions as the Prefects looked on. The pantry was the one place in the hotel with real knives of every description and, New Year's or not, they were the only ones with access to the potential weapons, though the two women were displaced by majority rule, content to sit and watch. The Prefects should have prepared the New Year's feast, but most Americans were as capable of cooking Latin dishes as they were of dancing to Latin rhythms. Monica had one proviso: her bath would be ready for her by 6:00 PM.

When six o'clock arrived she was ready for a deep, steaming, expunging soak... alone. She was exhausted. Lucy came in at seven, lovely in her emerald green chiffon slip dress and green patent leather three-inch pumps. Seeing Monica she fell onto the bed. Had she ever thought to question how she had transmuted from the loving mother and wife she once was to loving Alice, that all faded. Monica was absolutely stellar, the epiphany instantaneous:

she loved Monica.

The liquid Mediterranean blue of Monica's silk gown muted into pale green that sharpened to a retro green without distinct borders. The gown was parted in the center from her blue-green stilettos along the smooth, bare contours of her parted legs to the cinched waistband styled as a feminine cummerbund. There was no top to the loosely flowing gown other than two widening Mediterranean blue bands that concealed none of her trim contours from her waist to her otherwise uncovered breasts.

She pulled the dress apart at her waist, showing Lucy the front panel of the most elaborately embroidered blue-on-green satin panties either woman had ever seen. If nothing else, Miss Divine had good taste. Not to be outdone, Lucy pulled slowly at the bias cut of her hem until her open hand had traveled across the miniature clasp that pulled at the laced edging of her nylons. They hugged each other and left. The restaurant and lounge had converted to a nightclub atmosphere, complete with Christmas and New Year's decorations, champagne, music and the most beautiful women in the entire Southeast. No one cared about the one missing element: The evening wasn't about men.

Melanie was impish in her white baby doll mid-thigh dress with ice-blue trim accentuating the swell of her little breasts with an empire waist and wide shoulder straps. Her low-heeled, close-toed pumps were deep blue with white trim and her single piece of jewelry was a sapphire-blue nugget suspended at the center of a crystal and faux-pearl choker. The other girls were equally stunning, each one strutting from one end of the lounge to the other as they swished and swirled their hems to loud applause as Monica laid out her avocado and shrimp tortilla hors d'oeuvres for those who wouldn't want her burritos stuffed with lamb and black beans. No one was allowed in the kitchen as she put the final touches to their dinner, except Genevieve who would later serve the feast with Stephanie under Monica's watchful eye.

Miss Divine had given Mercedes free reign including serving the girls her special frosted margarita. Some girls wanted the avocado and chicken soup, thinking the combo would be easier to manage than the hot and spicy beef and vegetable. The first entrée was a glazed mélange of cauliflowers, carrots and red peppers seasoned lightly with vinaigrette, the second was a mixture of black beans, lentils and fresh fruit served in baked shells, leaving them all to wonder how she had ever gotten away with a size four dress.

The main course was marinated grilled salmon smothered in smoked jalapeño chili accompanied with fresh tomatoes, green onion slices and lime, which required a lengthy half-hour of wine and chatter before dessert was served: a mouthwatering cocktail of blended frozen fruits served with Mexican meringues mini-cakes sprinkled with chocolate. Coffee was refused by all, until everyone understood it wasn't regular coffee, and after dinner they danced to exhaustion, each one creating a personal flair as Genevieve and Stephanie went about the business of cleaning up after the partiers, occasionally checking in on them.

The restaurant was reset for breakfast by ten and Genevieve wanted to call it a day, though she couldn't until the last girl decided she had danced enough. She really wanted to dance with Monica, knowing she couldn't do that either. The years before had been much different. At New Year's and Christmas the girls had never done anything more than lounge around, toke up and drink champagne. This year no one toked. Instead they danced; laughing like any other young women would in a dance club that was not a whorehouse.

What was different was Monica, and how the girls had taken to her. She would complete her obligation in thirty months, during which time nine other girls would leave. Monica would be the tenth, and she wondered how things would change for the worse when that finally happened. She also wondered secretly whether Miss Divine had thought of the potential dangers, or whether she had already decided on the timing and a suitable replacement Prefect.

Genevieve knew she was better than Stephanie. Despite being a few years older, she was in better shape. She used the gym, the pool when the girls were working, and watched what she ate. Stephanie didn't, and since becoming a Prefect, even though she was no less attractive, she had become sedentary. She hadn't once been with a guest and preferred solitude to being with Genevieve.

Genevieve had once been a Preferred Girl, not Stephanie, and that had to mean something. She still had special requests from guests, hers to accept or refuse, though most often she refused. She knew each guest she entertained meant points not credited to the girl who lost the reservation, more time potentially added to her obligation.

In two and a half years she'd be thirty, Monica would be twenty-six and there was always a chance her husband wouldn't want her. He was Mexican after all, a macho asshole who'd think more about how he looked in tight pants than he would about his woman. Or maybe he'd be killed in a mortar attack. Everyone knew he went again to Iraq after giving up searching for her.

She watched Monica as often as she could during the evening as she danced with each of the nine girls, bumping and grinding, twisting and turning, mostly with Lucy, and Genevieve could not imagine anyone abandoning her. But he had, and she had no chance of finding her daughter. Frankie and Bobby were good at what they did, so maybe Mercedes would want to stay on as a Prefect, if not become one sooner, and then perhaps she could have more in her life than merely watching Monica on a plasma screen with William and Cynthia. Why not? Though she doubted sooner would be a viable option. Miss Divine would never give her up prematurely as a Preferred Girl. Simply put: she was too good for business.

Lucy hadn't sat all evening, and she seemed so much happier than the year before with Alice. There was definitely something between them and she began paying closer attention to Monica to see whether the sentiment was mutual. Genevieve had been thinking of Lucy as well. She'd be gone by July or August. Miss Divine rarely altered the obligation dates beyond a month or two. She smiled inwardly, seeing Monica dance so gaily with her hands gripping the sides of her gown that fluttered around her knees and thighs. Genevieve knew she could easily be part of any new girl's training, so why not with Monica's new Anchor Girl? With Lucy gone she would have a perfect opportunity to know Monica better.

Often the music changed from an electrically charged Latin beat to soft rhythms that soothed their souls, even though they had no idea what was being sung and no one noticed Amanda softly whispering the words as she danced with the evening's unofficial hostess, not even Lucy.

"Mónica," she whispered, "te doy gracias."

"Thank you for what, Amanda. I have done nothing."

"I know now I will become a Preferred Girl. One or two men will be easily explained to any man who wants me." She giggled. "And I do not think explaining a girl will be very difficult."

"Perhaps you will explain, perhaps not. You are not yet married to anyone, whoever he will be, and right now you owe him nothing. It is not the same for me, but I think you are right."

"Thank you for wearing my bracelet. Did Lucy mind

very much?"

"Lucy did not mind at all. She thinks it is very beautiful. I think so also, but not necessary, amiga."

"Yes. Without your help being here would have been much harder for me, without your advice I would be a Courtesan girl instead of a Special Girl. Now I will be a Preferred Girl with less history to hide than someone after a few Spring Breaks."

"Es verdad chica, and if he does not like that you have had one or two lovers he will have missed someone very pretty and special in his life."

"Thank you. I suppose I will find out in two years and ten months."

Monica smiled, noncommittally. "How is it with Carol? You seem good together."

"We are becoming good friends, like you and Lucy. Are you sure she did not mind the bracelet?"

"She did not, nor did I mind the scarf she gave to Daphne. They have been here the longest and know each other so well," she glanced over Amanda's shoulder, "besides, I think she wants to dance with you again. Maybe I should be the one who is jealous."
*

Atlanta newspapers did not publish on the Sunday and Manuel was busy not being busy on the Saturday to see the headlines. His regimen hadn't changed. His mornings were spent at the dojo, his afternoons at the gun club. With the Berretta he polished all week, and the laser tracking ability, his accuracy went from the usual 99.9 -100 to a constant one hundred and he made a mental note to boast about that the following evening when he would call JC and Carmella to wish them Happy New Year.

She had sobbed quietly when he left the previous Tuesday morning and he barely had room in his trunk for all the meals she made for him. JC had hugged him and walked away, telling him it was better for two old women to say their good-byes alone, hearing nothing at the time from Manuel but feeling his cousin's fist punch into his shoulder. There was no way Manuel could repay them for what they were doing to help him.

Sunday the clubs were closed and, despite the extra business and the certainty of alcohol-induced exaggerated tips, the other drivers had no qualms letting Manuel do their shifts. The night was a time for family, for the Rose Bowl on Monday with beers and burritos for pre-game, followed by double servings of gravy-laced turkeys stuffed with potatoes and bread, canned peas swimming in the same gravy and fluffy white dumplings that had little chance of getting cold. Then mom's hot apple pie lovingly made by someone else's mother at the bakery, without coffee, but with more beers, potato chips, dip and perhaps a smack across her face for any of the kitchen club who might suggest to an intense fan the sagacity of a sober driver getting him home.

The newspaper spent the day on the passenger seat under piles of non-glossy photocopies of his two favorite ladies. He picked it up near ten, after the last of the Johnnie Come Lately revelers left his cab.

SAN ANTONIO PARENTS TO WELCOME IN THE NEW YEAR ALONE
MISSING DAUGHTER STILL NOT FOUND
ATLANTA POLICE NOT HOPEFUL; NOT HELPFUL, SAY PARENTS

The reporter went on to explain the airline had upped the reward from ten to twenty-thousand, and the friends she had never known she had, who had not given up the hope of finding her, had planned a midnight vigil for New Year's Eve. And, still, the Atlanta police had done virtually nothing to find yet another young Atlanta woman who had disappeared without any change in character or behavioral patterns.

Rachel Wright was a pretty girl, too young to disappear without a reason. She had a career, an employer that wanted and needed her; her parents loved her, wanted her safe at home, and her friends loved her and missed her. What else could a young woman want? She had everything going for her. He wanted to believe Mercedes and the Wright girl were kidnapped by the same people, which would mean there could be other abductions and eventually someone would make a mistake. People simply didn't disappear just as their lives were beginning.

He wore the Beretta every hour of the day, meticulously soaping and softening the rich leather contours of the holster as he ate Carmella's meals according to the dates she had labeled on the plastic containers so that, when needed, the weapon would transfer into his hand smoothly: a fluid and instinctive motion. He pressed an open hand against the holster, letting the leather absorb the heat. Then he reached for his phone and dialed 411. The state was Texas, the city was San Antonio and, yes, he would like the call put through. The phone rang twice.

"Good evening."

"Mr. Wright, my name is Manuel Del Fuego. I apologize for interrupting your evening, sir."

"Is this about my daughter?"

"Not directly sir. Though I believe your daughter Rachel was kidnapped by the same people who kidnapped my wife in July."

"My daughter was taken from us in October. What's the correlation?"

"I don't know, sir, but I do know it's nothing good."

"Why are you calling me now?"

"Sir?"

"Your wife was taken in July. My daughter was front page news in October."

"Sir, I was out of town during the last week and the thirty-first was Mercedes' birthday. I got drunk, sir." Wright said nothing. "It was not a weak moment for me, sir. The calm before the storm, I believe you say. If I had known I would have called immediately. I swear."

"Do the police concur with your thinking, Mr. Del Fuego?"

"Sir?"

"Do the police believe there is a link between your wife and our daughter?"

"The police haven't been much help, sir. It's been six months. They've even stopped me from posting pictures. I believe she's alive, sir. And I believe your daughter is alive. I also know that one day I will find my wife, and my daughter."

"Your daughter, also?"

"Yes sir."

"It's been two months, Mr. Del Fuego."

"Yes sir, and six for me. Time doesn't matter, I will find her."

"Rachel is in our thoughts constantly. What you're saying is false hope, Mr. Del Fuego. If the police are unable to locate her, even though I believe they have other more important cases in their minds, how can you?"

"Because nothing is more important to me, and how is not important, sir. What should be important to you is that I will find them."

"You don't believe they might have been taken offshore?"

"No, sir, I do not, but if I'm wrong I will find those who did. I am not alone, sir."

"I don't follow your meaning."

"You don't have to, sir. People are helping. That's all."

"Family, I suppose."

"Who they are doesn't matter. What does is that I can do the same for your daughter." Manuel paused. "It's better than nothing, sir. Anything is better than nothing and that's all we have to lose. All I need is the best photograph you have of your daughter, the sooner the better." There was a silence, again, and Manuel began feeling as though he was begging to save the man's daughter. "Sir, my name is Manuel Del Fuego, I live in Atlanta, I drive a taxi part time, but I'm a full time Marine on special leave. You can call Master Sergeant Bishops at Fort Bennings. The number's in the book, sir. He'll verify, sir. This is all on the up and up, sir."

"You're a Marine driving a taxi."

"Yes sir, with a purpose."

"And what is that, Mr. Del Fuego?"

"Sir, call Sergeant Bishops. If what I'm saying was good enough for him it should be good enough for you. "Manuel paused. "Whether you do or not, when I find my wife I know I will find your daughter and bring her home to you. Or you'll know what's happened to her. I am certain of it, sir."

"I will do that, Mr. Del Fuego, first thing tomorrow morning."

"I understand."

"How may I get in touch with you?"

"Just e-mail me the image of your daughter, sir. I'll do the rest and I promise to keep in touch."

"I will speak with your sergeant, Mr. Del Fuego, as a matter of 21st century prudence, you understand."

"Thank you, sir. I will wish you Happy New Year when your daughter is found."

The phone went dead.

*

By four PM New Year's Day the reply came, followed by

dozens of family photos.

"Thank you, Corporal Del Fuego. Please help us find our daughter. Let us know whatever you need. Sergeant Bishops told me at length that if anyone can do it, sir, you can, The Marines at Fort Bennings have great faith in you, he told me, and so do we. I regret having doubted you. May God be beside you in your quest and please let us know your wife Mercedes and your daughter, if you would care to forward a photo. Seeing them will help us through this difficult time, as we hope our photos may help you remember happier times. God bless you for caring Corporal Del Fuego. You are in our thoughts."

Part Three

January 02,
Atlanta, Georgia

Samantha Peachtree was all business all the time. She had no husband, no one wanted her as a girlfriend because she was a hard-ass cop who worked cases 24/7, she never backed down and she had no idea how to say thank-you, I'm sorry or I need backup. Most times she was an unparalleled bitch who acted more like a man than the men under her command, sometimes dressing with a feminine touch that seemed incongruous, most times not.

The men and women of the downtown precinct called her Sam when they were with her, or within earshot of anyone they didn't know, the old-timers called her Sammy. Alone or in a bar the men had their own particular favorite, the women who thought she might be a dyke had another. She never wore silk, preferring micro-fiber tops with pantsuits and low-heeled pumps, though there was no doubt amongst them that she was a bitch with no sense of humor, no life and no feeling. The men generally agreed she'd be good lay, and she probably would be, for whoever could survive her cold exterior long enough to penetrate her frigid corridor in search of a warmer interior. Though none was willing to volunteer, fearing there would be no warm interior, just more ice and an inexplicable case of frostbite he'd have to explain to his wife.

She had left Homicide at Division several months earlier to join Missing Persons, making some cops happy and others unhappy, knowing in advance she would make Captain inside twelve months, not thinking the promotion would be as early as the second day of the New Year. The men in her squad congratulated her with matter-of-fact handshakes, the women with glossy smiles of varying widths that disappeared quickly as Samantha Peachtree walked away.

She had no family, no friends and no reason to be at home when she could be at the office in full control. She worked hard, she was hard, and she cared little for small talk or extending her simulated sympathies to victims she felt no sympathy for; something she regularly did without compassion or compunction. She might have been an excellent mortician or executioner. She wasn't. She was a cop, a bitch with a gun who lacked humanity.

To some, her sixteen years of service were unblemished with several citations to her credit. She had killed five men, a woman and one teenager who thought he was cool, indestructible, and better at throwing a knife than she was at discharging her Glock. He was wrong. He was the last one, and she still might have been assigned to Homicide if the IAD hadn't walked in on her as she was including the shooting to her colorful scrapbook of the other six.

The Police Commissioner had intervened unexpectedly on her behalf, the end result being a transfer to Missing Persons with an eventual promotion to Captain as a quiet reward for excellent past service once the bad press was forgotten. The then incumbent Captain had been asked as a favor to the commissioner to delay his pending retirement as a means to that end. He did, not bothering to ask why. He'd been a good cop for thirty-nine years and like most big city cops he could smell bullshit before he stepped in it. He loved his wife and his grandson, sufficient incentive to be a team player. He saw no good reason to get in the way.

Thanks to a certain friend in Miami Manuel knew about the Atlanta politics and he knew about the seventeen-year-old boy who had been shot twice when a warning shot and a suspended sentence would have sufficed for the crime of trying to defend his younger brother against arrest. He was also aware of a young girl kidnapped from her condo at the Atlantic Station and that no life existed inside Samantha Peachtree.

Her voice was never colored with inflection and he had seen first-hand how her manner of speaking to those around her was commanding, her seemingly casual choice of words intended to expertly restrain potentially uncomfortable dialogue in concert with a stiff, unyielding and androgynous body language. She was all work and no play and he wondered indifferently as he sat in front of her how she had come to be that way. The several occasions he'd spoken with her were brief encounters at best, often confrontational, and not once did she offer any words of encouragement or comfort he could cling to, never anything different.

He knew his wife and daughter had become unimportant, if not downgraded to forgotten files in a brown box identified with a felt pen scribbling that would only differentiate them from other boxed victims by last name, initials and the effective date of official indifference. He decided to ignore the still fresh black lettering on the door as his uniformed escort stepped back.

"I don't have much time, Corporal. I'm understaffed this week and I've already told you I'll call whenever we know something. So far we don't."

"I know that. All I'm doing is making sure they're not being forgotten."

"They're not being forgotten, Corporal. The case is

active. How can I make you understand that?"

He ignored her. "I spoke with Rachel Wright's father the other day. Any chance the kidnappings are related?"

Her recovery would have appeared seamless to most others, not so to a man who had spent so many months focusing on unsuspecting faces.

"Corporal, I'd hate to think you're planning to interfere with an ongoing investigation."

"I wouldn't think of it, but then it's only been six months." He paused. "Mr. Wright doesn't seem to believe you're doing much either."

"I won't discuss the Wright case with you, suffice it to say we're searching for her car and we're working with the banks. She's a probable runaway and will show up eventually. Most of the prissy ones do. Your wife is another matter. For your wife not to be found after six months she either doesn't want to be found or she's outside the US. Let's remember there was no sign of forcible entry at your home, except for you kicking in the door. And if not for your flight coupons and the fact we spoke with the cabbie that brought you home you'd still be a prime suspect."

"Meaning?"

"Meaning we're overworked, understaffed, and the case is active. We're stretched to the limit. Your file is one of a few dozen others we're working and I have nothing more to tell you. When I do, I'll call you. I can't be more specific. You just have to believe we're doing our best."

"Perhaps, Detective, there is help out there that isn't yet apparent to you because you're not searching in the right places. And you haven't answered me about the Wright girl. Is there any chance the two cases are connected?"

"No."

"Why wouldn't they be? If she was just kidnapped, wouldn't someone already be asking for the twenty grand from the airline?"

"Not when the ransom or street value is much higher."

Manuel paled. "Street value... and you're sitting in here like a fucking secretary." He stood, heedless of his chair toppling over.

"Corporal..."

"Screw you."

"Get out of here, Corporal. Your time's up and next time why don't we do this on the phone? In fact, I will be assigning your wife's case to another detective tomorrow." She stood, walking to the door. "Of course, you can always go over my head to the commissioner or the mayor, but ultimately nothing will happen any faster."

"Sounds to me like you've already spoken with the mayor and the commissioner, detective. I don't see what I would gain by speaking with your buddies." He smiled, inches from her face. "No, Señora, we will continue what we are doing. We will find her. You can count on it, and when we do there will be shit to pay."

"What is that supposed to mean? Who do you mean, we?"

He had said enough. Manuel walked away from her, not bothering to answer.

Forty-Five

Little Ana Juanita Vaquero had never had a birthday, or a birthday party, neither had Anna Jane Hillman whose birthday Tucker Richman had selected and her new parents had forgotten.

Little Sofia Francesca's birthday was not forgotten. Her father set the barren dinner table for one, he propped his girls' photograph against the blue vodka bottle and let Poochie the Bear lay on his side, believing his Sofia would somehow understand she would never be forgotten. He promised himself not to exceed his usual two doubles as a few miles away Sofia's mother fought against her tears, fearing demerit points. She hadn't been allowed to order birthday candles from the boutique, the bear at Christmas had been enough. Instead she saved a cupcake from dinner and let three wooden matches burn to the vanilla coating as she and Lucy looked on quietly, waiting for the tiny orange flames to sizzle and flicker out.

Little Sofia had no candles to blow out. She no longer had memories of a beautiful and caring mommy who danced with her every day and rocked her to sleep every night with lullabies and gentle touches, let alone her daddy whom she had forgotten half her young life ago. She now saw perfectly in the dark, though the door did open for breakfasts and dinners. Marietta Hillman had found another receptionist position within a few weeks of Ana Jane's arrival and the only other time the downstairs door opened was when she got home before he did, when she would quickly clean up after the girl's necessary mishaps with soap and water. Most often she would find the girl huddled in the corner of her small mattress, squeezed into the corner wall with one doll in her lap and the other in her arms. One doll had a hard and pink plastic face with coarse blonde hair and cheap cotton clothes; the other was chocolate brown with black woolly hair, round white eyes and no clothes.

She had learned on her own to pull the string at each doll's neck, deciding for herself that one was called mommy and the other daddy, though she didn't understand when they asked her to love them, to play with them or to feed them because they were hungry. Neither did Marietta Hillman when Anna Jane began to mimic the same words with a disconcerting mechanical quality.

On February 05, when her daughter asked her for love, she dropped the soiled linen and ran out screaming into the stairway of a loveless house where a few short months earlier she and her husband had been ecstatic about the arrival of their daughter. Though their joy had instantly turned to paranoia that someone would soon discover their little dark secret.

They had been unprepared for Richman's phone call and even less prepared for a dark-skinned daughter. Their first solution was to renovate a room they'd been using for storage, a room with no window that was far enough away from their living area to give them peace and normality for as long as they had her, or so they had thought. But Anna Jane's constant whimpering had worsened with each uncaring slap or shake that her limited faculties interpreted as horrific pain each time she refused to eat food that turned cold on the way to her room, and within a week Roger Hillman had explained to his neighbors that he had bought the drywall to build an add-on to their storage in the basement.

They had to find a way to regain their lives. Richman had acted on their behalf once before and could do so again. Cost was no issue they decided. Whatever the cost they would get rid of her. That was the key.

Forty-Six

Wednesday, April 04
Fernandina Beach, Florida

Miss Divine listened to the cryptic message at 12:55 PM. By one o'clock she had spoken with Stephanie, advising the Prefect she would arrive at the hotel by 10:00 PM to spend the evening with Daphne. Frankie's second call was to Tucker Richman who coughed tainted spittle into the mouthpiece as he listened to the abridged details of his unexpected good fortune. Frankie and Bobby had hit pay dirt. She was perfect, and so were her twin boys.

Jacksonville was one of America's little known jewels and those who lived there valued what set them apart. Status quo was as integral a part of their laid-back lives as their slowly changing neon skyline and forty miles to the north was an even better kept secret: Fernandina Beach. Certainly not Spring Break's best destination for nubile young women on the hunt for short-term love and affection, or their eager male counterparts who were ready and willing to give them what they wanted most. However Frankie and Bobby saw other qualities in the quiet town. The people were unsuspecting to the point of naiveté and the area attracted either young families or those who preferred a more tranquil oceanfront setting over groups of rowdy college kids and their beer-induced antics.

Miss Divine wanted young and beautiful women for herself and for the hotel. There was no preferred marital status. Each of the three customary types had unique advantages and unique designations. Singles, Ti-Fis, were the most difficult to acquire and train. They were also less profitable for Frankie and Bobby. Childless married women, No-Lines, although easier Acquisitions than Ti-Fis, were also less profitable for the team, albeit more cost-effective for the hotel. Combos of young mothers and children were actually the ideal candidates, particularly for Frankie and Bobby who were then able to market the children.

They were the easiest of the three types to acquire, as long as they weren't marred by the ravages of childbirth and this one had seemed not to be. Hence Frankie's requisite pre-delivery inspection. Tight-Fit, No-Line, or Combo, when it came to the inspection they were all the same to Frankie who spent the better part of an hour Monday morning studying her body through binoculars and a zoom lens while Bobby distracted her husband with banal vacation parlance.

Richard Templeton was the name, Dick to his friends. The handshake was firm without being too firm and the wife was Valerie, The Val. They'd been vacationing for ten days. The food was mediocre at best, not quite up to Boston's finer establishments. The beach house was somewhat dank, though reasonably comfortable. Next year they would certainly do Miami or Daytona, where the action was, if the wife's mom could take the young guys.

The place was a little slow, but Jacksonville was too far away to do every day just for the sake of being at the ocean. The wife enjoyed the beach with the young guys. They did the picnic thing every day, what with the time it would take to get ready for lunch in town and the line-ups. Though, certainly, cost wasn't a factor, not that the restaurants weren't all overpriced for uninspired local fare.

He did eighteen holes every afternoon. He couldn't take the sun all day, not like the wife. Though she was top notch for a mother of two young guys, a perfect ten, he boasted, as good as the day they'd met. He had the same confirmed tee off times for Wednesday through Friday. If Bobby wanted to join him he didn't see that there would be a problem, though rentals were rentals, after all. Having one's own equipment was optimum, particularly if one could afford carbon clubs. They'd be returning home Saturday, early, and would drive the thousand miles straight through for dinner with the in-laws on Sunday.

Bobby wanted to kick him in the balls, and he wanted to kick The Val in the balls, not at all certain he and Frankie had made the right choice. Frankie had enjoyed watching her long range Monday and Tuesday, as Bobby followed The Dick each afternoon to verify he would be gone and for how long, imagining precisely how she was going to feel squirming underneath him.

The boys were two-years-old; she was twenty-three, twenty-four tops. She was flawless in her sensible two-piece bikinis, lightly tanned, and the fact she was a spoiled Boston bitch, catered to by a self-centered dickhead husband who was about to get a second chance at life, wouldn't matter. The duo had no doubt Miss Divine would like her. The woman was the mirrored likeness of Brenda whom he knew Miss Divine had reluctantly disposed of to make room for Amanda. The preppy arrogance Frankie had described to her was a non-issue. Miss Divine had a way of adjusting attitudes that differed from her own.

They did their drinking early on Tuesday because Wednesday would be a long, demanding workday. They were a safe distance from the beach house early that morning, monitoring her every step. Frankie waited before calling the madam and the lawyer, wanting to be certain of the Acquisition. The husband would leave at one o'clock and wouldn't return until six. He would do his eighteen holes, have a few drinks with the members of his foursome and take thirty minutes to find his car and drive back.

Happily, the afternoon began exactly that way with a friendly kiss on a tilted SPF coated cheek before he hurried to the family car. Frankie shook his head, holding the binoculars tightly to his eyes as he told Bobby with a snicker all she needed was a good servicing by someone who knew what he was doing. He was anxious. He'd been thinking about doing her since Monday morning.

Miss Divine usually didn't mind him enjoying her girls before he delivered them, as long as he didn't damage them, interfere with their initiations or their ability to immediately interact with hotel guests, even though she was furious about what he had done with Amanda. He remembered Brenda. He remembered how she fought with him the first two or three times in the rear of the van, which made waiting for this one all the more painful, though he did promise Bobby he would wait until her dual spawn were dropped off in Savannah.

Richman assured them all would be in order by 4:00 PM, that he would have their twenty thousand in the usual hundreds. He wasn't about to complain about the short notice, not with a net profit of fifty-five thousand. He had previously explained to the prospective parents how twins were virtually impossible to obtain and, when they were, there would be a premium to pay because not separating the children would deprive another needy family of their right to love a child. The additional cost hadn't been a problem, and still wasn't when he had called the excited couple Monday evening.

Bobby took his time strolling along the beach while Frankie spent the half-hour reversing his van into the private drive on the opposite side of the house, sitting unobtrusively on a small dune behind her as Bobby came closer. By 1:30 she hadn't moved from her place a few yards in front of her beach house when Bobby approached her diagonally from the shoreline, pocketing his cell phone as Frankie approached from behind, working with a speed and agility that belied his middle years and several excesses.

His hand clamped over her nose and mouth like a vice, Bobby sat across her ankles, pinning her down. She was unconscious in seconds, after which carrying her atop the plastic and chrome beach gurney to the beach-level entrance and loading her into the vehicle through a private side door was a simple matter.

Bobby retrieved her boys as she lay sleeping on a thin foam-filled mattress. Frankie took what he could from the house, including most of her clothes, a suitcase for the boys, her purse, three bottles of chilled Riesling and they were gone, turning onto the I-95 at two PM sharp. The twins needed nothing more than mild sedatives to put them out for the duration that would allow them to wake mildly disoriented in a nice new home with loving parents and brand new toys. They would never see their mother again, caring nothing about her as they were carried from the van and deposited into the back of Tucker Richman's still-running Mercedes at three-fifty.

By the time Bobby turned onto the I-95 from the 16 the young woman's bikini lay crumpled at her side. Frankie dragged her limp body towards him, pulling her slender calves onto his shoulders, raising her buttocks from the floor of the cargo compartment as he positioned himself to crush his open mouth rudely against her. He wasn't hurrying, there was no need. She'd be out for another thirty minutes, enough time for a second round after a glass of fine white wine. They had the best job in the world, he repeatedly told Bobby. They each pulled in over a hundred

K in tax-free dollars a year with cost-free loving and several months' vacation time. Bobby always agreed, mostly with a nod, though he never opted for the love: one less thing he would have to account for one day, which is not to say he didn't mind seeing as much as he could.

With rush hour traffic they would be in Atlanta well before eleven, allowing an hour for a relaxed dinner in Macon and some time out for a few requisite banking transactions.

Forty-Seven

By the time Richard Templeton arrived at the beach house, impressed with himself and ready to boast of his near-perfect 94, his sons were in the loving arms of a new father and mother and his wife lay naked under a blanket in Frankie's van in the half-lit parking lot of a licensed diner off the I-75. The hour passed quickly, though they had each gone out once to check on her. He never wasted time trying to convince his friend and associate to fully enjoy the fruits of their labors, shrugging indifferently as he left Bobby to finish his meal and pay the bill.

She was stable, sleeping peacefully, and she stayed that way until her banking was done for her and they were once again en route to Atlanta. At first her eyelids fluttered, her speech slurred mutterings. She had forgotten seeing Frankie on top of her. He was quick to react with more chloroform, her struggle to throw him off lasting mere seconds. Now she began understanding how her body ached, that she was naked and the rest flowed easily into her consciousness.

He was a large man, much more powerful than her. Still, she was 5'10" and dressing her would be difficult. He leaned forward from between her legs, folding one rear seat into the floor, then the other, telling her to stretch out. He had selected the clothes she would wear for her first meeting with Miss Divine who liked seeing her girls coming in with dresses and proper shoes.

He felt her hands pushing at him, her voice growing louder, more coherent. He brought his open hands quickly over her breasts, squeezing hard before easing back and driving them into her stomach.

"Shut that mouth of yours, Val, or I'll throw your ass onto the frigging highway and that won't do much for this lovely naked body. Now, shut the fuck up."

He brought his hands to between the juncture of her thighs, working his thumbs roughly against the soft folds and into the moistened crevice. She twisted with loud, strained groans as his probe deepened. "Just one more Val, and then we'll be out of your hair," he chortled, "no pun intended. Then we'll get you dressed and ready. Just once more, promise."

Her head remained motionless, staring at the roof as he hunched over her, working intently at his buckle, working his pants past his knees. He pulled off his polo shirt, lowering his torso over her with one hand as he guided himself into her with the other, reminding her in a whisper that he had her children. Of course, he wouldn't mind a little resistance to make the moment more memorable, but too much would land her naked ass on the asphalt, he reminded her, which wouldn't be good for anyone at seventy-five miles per hour, particularly the two kids and Mr. Templeton. When they finished he relaxed, telling her to pull herself up, telling Bobby to pass him some hand wipes which he tossed onto the seam of her tightly closed legs.

"We still have a couple of hours. So here's what you're going to do. First, you'll clean yourself, completely. Second, you'll get dressed and you'll take one of these." He let the gel tab roll in his open palm.

"And if you're a good girl you may have some chance of seeing your big Dick." His mouth curved into a smile, his eyes remained emotionless. "It's a mild sedative, Val. When we take you out we can't have you screaming, that wouldn't be good. And we can't have you falling in front of the lady who's waiting so anxiously to meet you."

"We don't have much money. He won't be able to pay a ransom. We're ordinary people." She left the package untouched. "Let me out right here with my clothes, you can blindfold me. You'll have time to get away. I have no idea who you are. I couldn't tell the police anything."

He smiled the same way again. "Not even how good I am? I'm disappointed, Val. Now wash up. And don't be shy, start down there. It's not like we aren't already good friends, and I will be blindfolding you."

When she didn't move he wasn't inclined to tell her again. He grabbed her ankles before she could react, sprawling all of her 5'10" frame onto the bed with one violent jerk. When he finished doing her front for her he rolled her over, twisting one leg over the other, pulling her off the mattress by her waist. Her white buttocks were inches from his face and he gave each one a malicious slap before cleaning her along the back of her legs and working his way up.

When he finished at her shoulders he sank to his knees, studying her pensively. She stayed as she was, waiting on all fours. He sensed this one was different. Of the dozens of girls he had acquisitioned and initiated for Miss Divine over the years this one hadn't cried or begged him to stop, though he believed a man of smaller stature, like Bobby, would still be fighting with her. He put his shoed foot against her hip, pushed her into the plastic side panel and told her to sit. When she did he threw the remaining wipes into her open lap.

She told him it wasn't too late. He told her to wipe her face, to put on her make-up and comb her hair into a ponytail. She brought her knees together, stretching her legs across the width of the van, telling him as she wiped her face clean that she wasn't afraid. He told her to get dressed, panties first, after she took her sedative. She did, with a million questions flooding her mind.

She thought he was old enough to be her father, and big didn't mean fast. Pulling on her panties was hard enough with him watching, pulling on her skirt and doing the zipper was almost impossible with the motion of the vehicle. Finally he handed her a pale yellow bra after what seemed like an eternity, absorbing every minute detail as she brought together the front clasps, her breasts suddenly more exotic, more enticing than seeing her in a prudish bikini top.

He reached for the third wine bottle, filling two plastic glasses, calling out to Bobby to tell him when they were at the city limits. She believed him when he told her the wine would help her over the next several hours, and she knew one glass wouldn't prevent her from getting away. If anything, being relaxed would help her. Her mouth was bone dry, her flat stomach concaved from not eating more than a garden salad at noon.

He said there would be time for a couple of glasses, so why not enjoy? He slouched, trying to get comfortable. He was right. Why not? She took the glass, asking for her blouse when he clinked his plastic glass against hers. Instead he threw it recklessly over the front passenger seat, asking her only once, convinced she would react with horror. When she simply said "no" in a calm, flat voice he didn't press. In any event, he was well-acquainted with Miss Divine's sexual proclivity and knew she would rebuke or penalize him for the few moments of a particular pleasure.

She took a single sip from her second glass as the vehicle slowed to a stop at the first red light in ninety miles and Bobby spoke with the indifference of a taxi driver dropping off a customer. They would arrive in ten minutes and he tossed her the blouse, telling her to step away as

Frankie twisted on the floor, bringing the rear seats to their passenger position.

She thought Frankie telling her to climb into the seat behind his friend was good. She tried focusing on what she saw through the clear windshield as Frankie clambered into the seat beside her, passing her a pair of low-heeled pumps. She'd never been to Atlanta and the few street names she saw meant nothing, though she would do her best to memorize them, to concentrate and remember the most recent. Then everything went black and the air burst from her lungs for a second time. She felt an arm encircle her shoulders, the heat from his expansive free hand groping an unresponsive breast.

She heard him talking, but he wasn't speaking to her. He was saying something about being just past ten, about being too early and not ending what was an enjoyable evening. She smelled his closeness. He didn't smell like Richard, yet part of the pungent scent emanating from his heated skin was her. He had done nothing to clean himself and she wanted to vomit. She felt tired, her effort to stay alert and ready to run draining her energy. His hand freed her breast, probing between her legs that she parted at his first touch to give him better access so that he wouldn't punch her again. She would need all her energy, all her strength to escape, to scream and beg anyone for help at the top of her lungs.

She sensed the vehicle was slowing, coming to a stop. There was no talking, though she could hear Bobby twisting in his seat and Frankie had stopped massaging the cotton V of her panties and her inner thighs. Her time had come, she thought. Her hands were untied, so were her legs and she was much younger than either of them.

A phone chimed once, nothing was said and the driver's door opened. Then more darkness and the sound of Frankie's calm breathing. She listened for footsteps, hearing nothing. Frankie's arm was draped loosely around her as she listened for his or her door open, raising her head as much as she dared to search from under the blindfold for a doorknob or inlaid toggle.

Before she could focus Frankie pushed her head downward, grabbing at her hair, jerking her sideways at the very moment she heard his door open. Then she felt the cool night air, suddenly too confused to think of running.

She thought it strange that she tripped without falling on what must have been steps as they grabbed her arms and ran up. She was flying, her feet barely touching the ground. She thought of her children, images racing across her mind and she thought of Richard. She wanted to scream out with horrific fear, but Frankie had heard her loud intake of air and clamped a hand firmly over her mouth.

The Madam

Forty-Eight

Richard Templeton married his wife out of need, a decision not borne of guilt or the pragmatism of assuaging any societal reaction to his or her sexual indiscretions. Nor was the decision borne of his insatiable desire to possess her. That was never an issue. He knew he wasn't her first and her previous life didn't bother him. Although she was adamant he would never know how many of his predecessors were able to boast of their weak conquests, or who they were, no matter how many times he broached the subject

In terms the other girls at her private and preppy school would often use and unanimously agree with, she had been a spoiled, neglected girl turned slut who performed more rites of passage than the average chieftain of the tribes she had studied throughout her studies in Comparative Anthropology. Now all he wanted was to have her back. What he didn't want or need was to explain to the head of his Boston law firm what might have happened, or probably did happen, to his only daughter. When he dialed the unlisted number he was drunk. The cops had taken cursory notes, leaving with practiced regrets and vague promises he knew were empty. That left him crying, which made him even more pathetic under the scalding flow of unending questions and accusations from her father.

He had fucked up big time and didn't have to be told not

to come home without her. In addition, he was to consider himself outsourced until her safe return. What had he been thinking to leave his daughter and his grandchildren alone? Better yet, what had he, Beverly Turnbull, been thinking to let his one daughter marry such a complete and useless asshole, not to mention a barely mediocre lawyer who had little likelihood of achieving anything beyond marginally acceptable billing hours?

He would arrange appropriate double accommodations in Jacksonville for Turnbull and his wife, at the waterfront. Then he would step aside and let others take control. The phone went dead in time to allow the outraged old man to weep in the privacy and comfort of his younger wife's trembling arms. As much as she loved her errant daughter, she loved her husband more. She was twenty years younger than the youthful Grecian Formula-tinted and irascible Turnbull, twenty years older than their promiscuous daughter, and she had heard all the stories from the gossipy wives of the men indebted to her husband. She was his first wife. He was her second husband, something he'd always held against himself for not having the courage to stand before hundreds and tell the priest exactly why the happy couple should not then be joined in holy matrimony. He had always loved her and always would.

She had been an intern in the firm, the other man an important client who'd been in the right place at the right time to soothe and comfort a confused young woman. When, all too late, Turnbull did find the courage, he did so at the cost of the firm's largest client and her reputation.

Years later the general consensus was: Like mother, like daughter, and very few thought differently. The mother was a cheat and the daughter was a Happy Hour whore, a 5 à 7 buffet, which didn't mean half price on drinks before going home to a haggard woman in a one-size-fits-all house dress and screaming brats. Except in Louisiana and Alabama where she would be a one night Dip and Soak and a fairly good one at that.

His wife's past had never mattered and was never a topic of conversation. He loved her, he loved his grandchildren and tolerated his daughter, and she understood because she did as well. So what had Val finally done, she wondered, to make a mess of her life this time?

Beverly Turnbull would pull out all the stops and spare no expense to find their grandsons and daughter. He would pull in all favors owed to him and would put himself in the debt of those who could help him in any concrete way. Then he would file a civil action against his daughter for custody of the twins, confident they would soon be found well and safe. What he and his wife could not know, was that their lives were forever altered. They would soon see their daughter one last time, though not the kids who knew only to love those who held them the closest as the old man cried.

Forty-Nine

The twins did feel love, interpreted by their undeveloped minds as warmth, comfort and safety without knowing what those words meant. Feeling the love was enough. Charles and Louise Belmont were in their early thirties, successful in business and they loved their new boys whose first party was planned for Easter. The entire family would attend and little Charles junior along with his brother Luke would lack for nothing, even though they wouldn't know the difference.

Unknown to the boys they had been delivered unto heaven, into the arms of young unselfish parents who would cherish and nurture them. They had been reborn into a better life which hadn't yet begun as their previous mother was escorted unceremoniously onto the fourth floor of The Hotel Le Chic.

When the blindfold came off The Val involuntarily expelled a burst of gas at seeing the gagged girl strapped into one of two wooden chairs, her reddened face wet with dark tears from eyes too desperate to be afraid. At first she resisted their attempt to restrain her in the other chair until Frankie's compelling fist to the side of her head encouraged her. She sat frozen, letting them strap her body to the smooth wood, increasingly horrified by the face of the increasingly oblivious Daphne. She watched, mesmerized, as the needle slid into Daphne's tanned arm, thinking she would be next, not realizing her mouth had completely dried.

Frankie was pleased with himself. "I did say you would be pleasantly surprised."

"I normally like my girls here for twenty-four hours, to make sure."

"We might have lost this one if we had waited." He looked at Daphne. "It's no big deal. Give her a double shot. By the time we drop her off in Memphis she'll be fine. She won't know it's not tomorrow."

Miss Divine nodded. She plunged the syringe into the vial, squirting a fine stream into the air before jabbing Daphne's arm a second time, stepping away indifferently, waiting for the drug to take effect. Daphne struggled to keep her head straight; fighting the euphoria she somehow knew was a bad thing. She was going home. She thought so, but how could she go home like this. Leaving was not supposed to be like this. Leaving was supposed to be a good thing, a happy thing, but it wasn't. She hurt, like the first night.

Was that really three years ago? Or had she been sleeping, lost in her dreams of all the other girls, the filthy old man, the queer and the men who paid for the privilege of fucking her? She was supposed to spend the evening with Miss Divine, instead she was being hurt. Why? She was a Preferred Girl. She might even have stayed if Miss Divine had asked her.

Did she have a home and a husband? Would he recognize or remember her? Would she know him, and what was his name? For so long she had believed he wouldn't forget her, that he would always love her and she forgot when he had begun not to matter. She felt the strain at the nape of her neck as her head dropped heavily onto her chest. She was so tired, doing her best to focus, to stay awake. She could not go home dressed this way. She was dressed like a cheap whore. She had no money to buy nice clothes to wear for him, and she knew he wouldn't understand. Ben. Thinking of his name seemed so odd after so long. Ben. He would never understand.

Valerie looked from Daphne to the floor in disbelief, watching the curtain of water trickle unevenly over the edge of the chair and splash into a radiating pool of liquid yellow light as the girl humped over beside her seemed to stop breathing. The big man was angry, swearing, telling the other one to untie her, to put her on the floor. Valerie's heart was on the verge of exploding as she watched Bobby drag Daphne from the chair, sprawling her face down on the floor and pulling up her skirt as he pushed apart her legs.

The men spoke, the big one sounding upset. He lifted her at the waist while the other pulled off her wet underwear with a single motion before taking the towel from the other woman. He wiped her legs and inner thighs, reaching under her to lift her before swiping the towel blatantly between her open buttocks.

Valerie couldn't turn her head or close her eyes to the woman lying exposed at her feet as the two men argued about the soiled skirt with the woman who finally left the room as the big one ripped the skirt from the limp body. The force twisted Daphne onto her back. Valerie gasped.

Frankie glared at her. "Haven't seen a pussy quite so clean before?" He chuckled. "Don't worry, Val. In a few days you'll be just as squeaky and you'll be walking around with your ass just as bare and loving every moment." He grinned at his friend. "And if I had a spare fifteen hundred I'd be here myself for a little more of both."

He took the towel from Bobby, throwing it onto Daphne's chair, both men turning towards Miss Divine's voice, shrugging. They grabbed Daphne by the ankles and wrists, tugging off her knit top, letting her body sag at the middle as they carried her from the vault onto Miss Divine's settee where they dressed her in a another skirt and

The Madam

V-neck sweater.

Fifty

"That was Daphne. She's going home, lucky girl. The reason we drugged her was quite simply that we cannot have her knowing where she's spent the last three years. It's sort of a secret. Anyway, by this time tomorrow she'll be in Memphis with her family, if that's what she wants, or if her husband still wants her. Either way, she'll be okay. I take care of my girls."

"I'm not one of your girls. Where are my children? What have you done with them?"

"They're safe. They're with another family, they've been adopted. You'll never see them again, though you will see your husband if he wants you." She began preparing a syringe with a different vial. "This will help you relax, let you sleep a few hours. When the affects wear off I'll tell you about the hotel, me, and what I expect of you over the next three years."

"You don't think I'm staying here for three years? Are you fucking insane?" Valerie strained against her restraints. "Get me the fuck out of these."

Her face went instantly numb, so that she didn't feel the second punch or the thin line of blood crossing from her upper lip to her chin.

"My girls don't swear, not ever, and if you ever do you'll forfeit a month's worth of points."

"You're brave with me tied here. Do that when I'm

standing and things won't be quite the same."

"No, it would be worse," she paused, "for you. And if you ever speak to me like that again I'll break your nose. This will be much better and easier if you relax. Make a fist." Valerie stayed still, her breathing labored. "Make a fist. I need a vein, and I won't ask you again. So unless you want to be a pin cushion, make a fist." She did. "Frankie was right, you do closely resemble Brenda." She leaned forward, tearing quickly at the buttons of Valerie's blouse before slowly undoing the clasp of her bra and kissing a horrified Valerie on the lips, pausing with a satisfied smile, kissing both her breasts. "Nice, very nice, but let's wait until tomorrow to enjoy each other. You'll be more into it by then. In the meantime I think you should sleep. You have a busy week ahead of you, learning the hotel business, and I'm sure you'll do well. If you're anything like Brenda, and I hope you are, you'll do very well. You'll be a Preferred Girl in no time."

Fifty-One

Thursday night Miss Divine arrived at the hotel after eight, excited about introducing another girl to the hotel. New girls were exciting; special occasions when she would dress with particular care, taking the time to select what she thought each girl might like to see her wearing.

This one definitely liked the good life. She was a pampered stay-at-home mom with perfect hair and expensive tastes who spent more time at the spa than in the kitchen. She was a prom queen who would never think of wearing thongs, short skirts or a teddy, and who would always close the bathroom door.

Her husband would never quite meet her always changing expectations and never stop trying as she wasted her life dreaming of that special Prince Charming who didn't take her to the prom because everyone knew she was a prissy stuck-up bitch who wouldn't drop her pants without a contract. She probably referred to her breasts as boobies or chest, her buttocks as her derrière or seat, and her vagina as her girl or down there, but strictly on those occasions when 'her friend' came to visit.

All that would change. They all changed eventually. Brenda did, and so would this one. She would miss Brenda, though she hadn't been wrong about Amanda who was working out beyond all expectations. Having Cassandra with her would be like having Brenda again and she planned to be at the hotel most of the week to play a major role in her training, perhaps with Amanda.

She knew Brenda enjoyed being invited for an evening on the fourth floor and so would Cassandra. Miss Divine had never worn the black-on-red silk wrap dress with a shirt collar, a décolleté front and flared skirt that tied at her waist with a wide matching ribbon and she was anxious for the girl to see what she wore underneath. She seldom wore garters unless the occasion and the dress called for them. She was sexy and feminine. She felt sexy and feminine and she wanted Cassandra to see her the way Brenda had always enjoyed seeing her as she undressed so deliberately, so seductively, knowing exactly when Brenda would take over.

She had no one special for whom to buy Christmas gifts and her girls never did for her. She had no one to celebrate birthdays or anniversaries with, New Year's was unusually spent finalizing year-end reports and Mother's Day was a page in her agenda. She had been with only one man in her life, still twisting and struggling under his familiar weight every night in her troubled dreams. She hated him the most, enough to kill him over and over again if he hadn't died so mysteriously when she was still so young. All others ranked an indistinguishable second.

She had thought many times recently, as she sat alone studying young couples strolling or sitting at one of the string of cafés below her bay windows that she might like to adopt. She would simply tell Frankie and Bobby ahead of time and they would do the rest, knowing full-well she never would, never could. Apart from creating an unnecessary link to the hotel, she was too old to tolerate the smells and the noises, the costs and the invasion of her privacy. Not to mention what a kid would do to her beautiful condo.

That's what made her first evening with each new girl so

special, her compensation for everything she had forsaken in life. She had her favorites. There would always be someone special for her to enjoy as girls continued to come and go. Currently Monica and Amanda topped the list. Melanie was her least favorite, increasingly testing her patience with her little girl thing that was so good for business.

The previous night she waited for the sedative to take affect before undressing Valerie and letting her sit on her toilet. She did the same as she prepared to leave early the next morning. After securing Valerie into the chair, kissing her and repeating the injection, she closed the young woman into the darkened vault after telling her to expect one more injection that evening, that she would remain naked until that time, although she could scream if screaming would make her feel better.

Valerie stared at her bare breasts and open legs, trying hard to recognize the smallest rational thought. There was none, but there was an instant total darkness that frightened her and she did scream, transitioning into her own darkness that dispelled the fear of the other and brought her well-being. As suddenly, there was a blinding light and searing pain.

"Good evening, Cassandra." She didn't answer because she wasn't Cassandra and she didn't want to open her eyes. She didn't want the well-being to disappear into the light. "Good evening, Cassandra. I hope I didn't give ..."

"No, my name is Valerie."

"Was... your name was Valerie. Now you're Cassandra. You are definitely a Cassandra." Miss Divine understood the silence. "I'm giving you one more little jab, the last one. It won't make you sleep like the others, just relax you, take the edge off." She smiled. "When I'm done you can bathe and dress into something appropriate before we have a glass of wine and some dinner. We have a lot to talk about. I have so much to tell you and I'm sure you must be very curious about what's going on. Make a fist."

Cassandra glanced at her wrist, then up questioningly.

"It's a monitor, Cassandra. Something that lets me know if you're going somewhere you're not supposed to be, like being too close to the main doors."

"I'm a prisoner?" She tried the restraints. "I told you, we have no money. My family won't be able to pay you anything."

"I don't want money." Miss Divine slid the syringe into the firm flesh of Cassandra's forearm. "I want you, Cassandra. Really, you're all I want. So why don't we get you out of this horrible chair and into a bath? Stand up. Remember, I don't repeat myself."

Cassandra stood, shakily, puzzled at how she was letting the woman take her hand. She was moving, gliding, her lips moistened with the sweet taste of raspberry. In a few fleeting moments the scented warmth of titillating and piquant water enveloped her as she let herself sink into the soft white clouds. She brought up her cupped hands, letting the warm water splash over her face. The heat felt good and she did it again. She had to feel and to think. She had to look and she had to see.

She couldn't remember how she had come to be there. She remembered the beach, the man in the truck and the girl. She remembered the girl in the other chair and what they did to her. She knew why she was naked, her mind told her, and why the woman standing at the door was stripping and eyeing at her that way. She could taste the woman's lip gloss, she could remember the woman's hands pressing against her bare chest, but not when.

She watched the dress open and float to the floor, focusing her eyes on Miss Divine's midriff. She was afraid. She was afraid to watch and more afraid to speak. Her heart was beating in a way unfamiliar to her, in a way she couldn't fathom. She had never watched a woman undressing, not even at the athletic club where she changed in private. Yet she couldn't help herself.

She saw the embroidered bra fall and the woman's hands cover her bare breasts, squeezing the tips. Her hands came away and she raised a shoed foot to the contoured edge of the bath, not caring at all that her underwear did nothing to cover her front as she began unclasping her stockings. She was close. She did one, then the other, pushing each one to her knees before turning to sit on the edge to kick off her shoes and peel her nylons effortlessly away from her raised legs. Then she leaned forward, pretending to brush the nylons away from the bath.

Miss Divine knew full well Cassandra's eyes were glued to her.

The Val never thought of the male body as anything exciting or arousing, even though she'd been under more of them than any ten other girls at her school, and being with a woman, even kissing a girlfriend for a thrill, had never crossed her mind. Her husband was no jock. The only balls he ever thought about were in his golf bag, which was just as well; the only men she ever thought about, when she wasn't at the club or the spa, were her twin boys.

She never thought about women, not that way, and didn't understand the male need to ogle young naked women squirming on dirty blankets or performing clumsy acrobatics on filthy poles when one was no different from the others. She certainly didn't understand any woman who would willingly expose herself to unclean strangers who saw them as no more than public vaginas, or let themselves be fondled by drunken men for a few dollars. Yet now she was naked in a bath, inches from a woman whose buttocks were completely bare except for two red strings.

The woman was talking softly as she caressed her own body dreamily with both hands. Just before she stopped

Cassandra heard a low guttural sound, a deep, seductive purr. Moments later, her breathing under control, the woman swung one foot into the far side of the bath, placing the other so that Cassandra was between her with no alternative but to acknowledge what was about to happen.

"Take them off Cassandra, so I can get in there with you."

She scarcely took note of other women at the beach, apart from comparing bathing suits, now a woman was an inch from her face, telling her to take off her underwear.

"Take them off, Cassandra. You have to start some time." She paused. "And don't be surprised if you like it. All the other girls here do, with me and with each other." She squatted, sinking into the water, letting her breasts slide over Cassandra's face as she reached for her hands and brought them to the strings of her thong as she stood. "See, it's not so hard. Now, pull." She did, with her eyes closed tight, feeling Miss Divine wriggle free of the designer panties, and when her eyes opened she gasped. "I'll take that as a compliment, and now I want you to touch me." Cassandra didn't move, her hands clutching the limp red and black triangle. "Touch me or kiss me, Cassandra. It's your choice."

"I have to go to the bathroom."

"You are in the bathroom. Touch me."

"I have to use the toilet."

"Fine, use the toilet, after you touch me." Cassandra brought up a hand, her forefinger extended, looking away as her fingertip pressed into the crease between the top of Miss Divine's thigh and her lips. "Not quite what I had in mind, Cassandra. Put a hand against one of my ankles, now." She hesitated, finally and slowly doing as she was told. "Now come up against the inside of my leg until you reach my pussy and do it with a little pressure. When you get there, press harder. There's nothing to it. Believe me, in a few days you'll be a pro."

Cassandra did as she was instructed, the madam forgiving her slowness as her unsure hand came closer to the soft and sensitive flesh. It was all Miss Divine could do to stand as the edge of the young woman's warm palm touched ever so lightly against her delicate folds. She drew a deep breath, putting her own open hand over Cassandra's, pressing harder as she moved a quivering leg to one side, balancing herself with her other hand against the back of Cassandra's head as she began to tremble.

Cassandra wanted to vomit, knowing she would if she didn't get out of the bath and away from the vile woman. "I touched you. Now can I to go to the bathroom?"

Miss Divine took a deep breath, composing herself, nodding her head. "Okay, go. But hurry. We have all night and I want to enjoy every minute with you."

Cassandra clambered out and dried herself facing away. She padded to the toilet, sitting in full view of the woman who watched her every move. She had no physical need, though she did have a need and she waited as long as possible before flushing to conceal the quiet ruse. She reached toward the dispenser, opening her legs enough to ease her hand between her thighs, pressing for no reason, twisting her body to flush again.

She didn't feel drugged or sleepy. She felt at peace, carefree, perhaps a little drunk, she thought, in a time and place that had no meaning. She'd been taken from her children; she'd been raped, drugged, left in the dark and forced to fondle the labia of a woman she didn't know.

As she stood, purposefully, all that mattered was regaining her life. She wasn't avoiding Miss Divine's alluring smile as she sat calmly on the toilet wrapped in the towel, she was focused on the floor, the crumpled dress and the matching black and red ceramic vases on the green-marble glass shelving. Then intently on the woman who showed no surprise at seeing her smile; she was ready, for whatever might happen. She was at peace, she was thinking clearly. She could escape. She was young. The pathetic old whore in the bath wasn't. She could easily sprint to the elevator door. She was certain she could.

"I'm sorry. You're right, it wasn't that bad. But I've only ever touched myself there. Touching you was strange, that's all."

"I know it's strange at first, but it's very natural. Everyone likes these things."

"I might need a while. You'll have to be patient with me."

"I'll be very patient, Cassandra, and very good to you. You'll see. I'll be very good to you."

"Do you want me with you now?"

"Yes, I do, then we'll have dinner with a few glasses of wine and by tomorrow you'll be an entirely different person."

Cassandra smiled timidly, pivoting as though wondering where to put her towel, wasting no time crashing one vase through the three glass shelves without any effort before hurling that one, then the second, directly at Miss Divine's head, missing her both times by a few inches. The whirlwind of flying glass and ceramic happened in a hectic fleeting moment as she tugged away her towel, threw it haphazardly onto the shard-covered floor and reached to grab the silk dress as she ran into the suite's main room.

The mirrored elevator door was ornate and obvious, time standing still as she pushed her thumb hard and repeatedly into the brass disc. All that mattered was getting out, getting away. Her heart was pounding, her temples were throbbing. She had completely forgotten she was naked when she chanced to twirl in a tight half-circle, driven by natural instinct and fear. In an instant she forgot all else, including her twin sons as the jagged glass knife pushed through her larynx, making her final scream a blood-tinted gurgle.

Fifty-Two

Daphne had been in Memphis a little over eighteen hours. Very likely she was afraid, hungry, and if she hadn't managed to find adequate shelter she was very likely cold. All Miss Divine had given her were new ankle socks and boots, a short skirt and a snug-fitting top that would make her a tempting property to any pimp or give her the best chance of earning twenties for each ten-minute drive by.

She had spent the entire drive blindfolded, curled-up with her head angled onto the floor, her hands bound behind her. She felt her body rock freely with every change of motion, mindless of time or space, scarcely aware the pain had gone. She tried listening, wondering why they were laughing. Then she stopped swaying and they stopped laughing. She wanted to talk, but she didn't know what to say; then she thought she was alone. Again she tried listening, engulfed by grim silence until the rear doors swung open and the chill of pre-dawn hours rushed in to make her shiver, kicking out when firm hands grabbed her ankles. The grip tightened, twisting her onto her front, dragging her backward from wrists that burned from the sudden jolt.

Bent over the floor of the van she felt his hands press against her thighs, stopping at her buttocks. He told her to stand, pulling her from the waist. She did, and when she collapsed he laughed. She felt his arms wrap around her chest, her bare legs coming away from the wetness of the dank city street, gasping when her ankles clashed with the sidewalk.

Again he told her to stand and she tried, afraid she would fall, feeling a rough hand grope cruelly at one of her breasts while the other tore away her blindfold and she couldn't understand why it was still dark, not seeing the one who held her. She saw the other one in the vehicle's front seat looking away and thought she recognized him. She called to him, hearing laughter from behind as she was jerked around and pushed against the brick wall. She felt his hands press hard against her breasts, then not, then again as he told her to take one step forward. She did, and slumped back, not bothered by the dull pain of her head clashing with the wall.

She was staring at the sidewalk and didn't see him, just his hands, then he was gone and she was alone: the fragile centerpiece of a long city block and suddenly not so certain life was worth living. By the time she took her first step the two men had passed the city limits and wouldn't think of her again for several months, though she would never think of them and eventually she would forget Miss Divine and the other girls. But that was not now, when what she wanted and needed most was to cry and wonder what she had done wrong.

Constantly being on the hunt for ideal recruits wasn't easy work, constantly going one better while restricted to searching for women who were beautiful, young and sexy. Not an easy feat by any means in a country where the average dress size was sixteen and the definition of vanity was being able to squeeze into a size fourteen before the nightly all-you-can-eat ritual that had made them sixteen in the first place.

Working with Richman was no easier. Everybody wanted white, blond and clean kids who were free of visible defects and unfavorable attributes. Though, increasingly, half of any beach, shopping center or park was anything but that. The Mexican's kid was a tough sell and Richman wouldn't accept another one. The adoptive parents were still bitching, going as far as to call Richman suggesting a reasonable buyback or an exchange, which was out of the question.

Bobby was younger by several years, single, in average shape for his age and still preferred picking up what he needed for the night at the local bars he'd been frequenting for years. He was also contemplating a career change, which Frankie was not about to let happen.

Frankie was overweight and chain smoked, he was divorced and losing his hair everywhere but where he wanted to. He thought of himself as a necessary element of the hospitality and entertainment industries with a particular talent for scouting and auditioning newcomers.

He trusted Bobby implicitly and couldn't imagine not having him to rely on. In fact, he would never let that happen. There would be no career change. He had dropped Bobby off at the bar in time for Happy Hour and continued home where he would have a few drinks, watch a few of his favorite home videos on fast forward and sleep through to the next morning. That was the plan, until the cell chimed at 12:20 AM and he answered. That was the arrangement: When she called, he answered, and he would do as he was told. He could think, say, or do anything he wanted or needed to make himself feel however he needed to feel, as long as he did what he was told, which meant being outside the hotel with Bobby at precisely 02:00 AM and waiting for her second call. He would also ID the van as an appliance repair vehicle. Never mind why.

Fifty-Three

He punched in his six-digit code. He ignored Stephanie on his way through the lobby and walked directly to the open doors of the elevator. The girls shared the same opinion of him, the Prefects included, and he knew not to bother with her. When the doors opened she was standing facing Frankie and Bobby from the middle of the suite, dressed in a bath robe and holding an empty wine glass.

"She's in the vault."

"Who is?"

"The bitch you brought me last night. I need for you to get her out of here tonight. She didn't work out."

"What do you mean she didn't work out? Just shoot her up a few more times and tell her what you tell all the others, that you'll let some guy play pin the tail on the donkey with her kids. Last night you couldn't wait for us to leave. So what happened?"

"She almost killed me this evening."

"And?"

"And she's in the vault. So just get her out of here."

Bobby was the closest, the first to see the body on the floor between the wooden chairs with the dagger-size shard protruding from her throat. He stopped so abruptly that Frankie crashed into him, propelling him forward, causing him to stumble and two-step over the naked corpse. He had always known the day would come, though he thought

Frankie would be the one who would kill an Acquisition, not Miss Divine, and now they were complicit. He was complicit, their careers catapulted to a whole different level.

"You must be kidding."

"Do I look like I'm kidding?" she retorted. "Does that look like I'm kidding?"

"What are we supposed to do with it?"

"Do what you're paid to do. After that you can do whatever you want, if you're so inclined."

"She must have pissed you off big time."

"I told you. She tried to kill me and damn near succeeded." Miss Divine stood behind them in the doorway, talking to their backs. "Just get her out of here. Take her to Jacksonville and make her into a rape-murder victim."

"That's four hundred miles. You want us to drive with a fucking corpse for six hours. Are you crazy? We wouldn't be there before nine, maybe nine-thirty. Then what do we do with her?"

"That's not my problem."

"It is now. Our arrangement is to bring them in alive and take them out alive. This is a whole new game." He kneeled by the still-warm body. "But consider it done for twenty-five thousand without an Acquisition."

"No, you'll take the usual ten."

Bobby turned. "He said twenty-five, and if you say ten once more we'll make it fucking fifty. We're talking murder here."

"It was self-defense."

"Then phone the cops and tell them. I'm sure they'll understand, especially when they see this little chamber of horrors."

She glared at him, saying nothing until Frankie stood. "Fine...twenty-five. Now get her the hell out and bring me someone who doesn't have a stick up her ass."

"How do we get her out? Stephanie's in the lobby."

"There's only one guest in the hotel. She'll call me when he leaves, which is usually about now. Then she'll go to bed. It's a perk, like getting off work early. When she does I'll deactivate the lobby and entrance surveillance cameras and you can load her after you're certain the street's clear. In the meantime get her into the elevator so we don't waste time."

"When do you want her replacement delivered?"

"Yesterday would have been good instead of this bitch, but not before next month and make sure as hell she's not from anywhere around here. It's time you started extending your geography. Start crossing the Mississippi or head north. The last two you brought in were front page news. It's a complication I don't need and neither do you."

Frankie nodded. "That means increased expenses. We're Georgia boys. We know the Southeast, so the fee schedule's moved up to thirty for a Combo and forty when we bag a No-Line or Ti-Fi."

She ignored Frankie's base vocabulary. "Twenty-five, tops, irrespective of the kids. That's not my problem. In fact, you should be bringing in more Amandas and Brendas. People forget faster when kids aren't involved. So let's say the next few won't be mothers or wives, at least not mothers."

He chuckled. "So we ask them if they have kids before we bag them. Good thinking."

"I'm sure you'll be able to tell fast enough. It wouldn't be the first time you've left one behind."

"That doesn't work for me. Ti-Fis are harder to track, with less profit," he lied, "and we'll have to be in a different town every day. We'll decide who comes in. We haven't let you down before so don't start bitching now because this one didn't want to get you off." He took a breath. "We'll drop the No-Lines and Ti-Fis to thirty-five K and that's

270

final."

Her silence sealed the deal. She needed to change her philosophy. Younger girls were impressionable, more easily intimidated. They had younger parents and would be as easily manipulated by threats against their parents as anyone else would be by their children. As long as they were young and weren't scarred with telling lines Frankie's designations didn't matter.

Valerie's head came slightly away from the floor as Frankie extracted the glass blade using a paper towel, surprised by the depth of the wound and the force Miss Divine would have used to embed it, thinking hell hath no fury as he walked into the bathroom to flush away the sticky paper. When he came out she was at the intercom with the neatly banded stack of newly minted hundreds. He glanced at his watch. The final guest had gone and all three watched the screen as Stephanie checked the main doors, dimmed the lights and climbed the stairs to her second-floor suite where they saw her open the door and walk in paying no attention to the lens.

Frankie's knowledge of Jacksonville was sufficient to know he couldn't dispose of a body in broad daylight. The chances of being seen or photographed were too great. He would drive Bobby home, drive to his home for a few hours' sleep, leave for the coast before the rush hour and Miss Divine would be none the wiser.

Saturday's Jacksonville press would headline a young woman's nude body found after midnight in the center lane of the I-95, ahead of the 351-C exit by a driver who saw the disfigured body too late. The coroner would determine that the cause of death was a fatal stab wound that had perforated her larynx within the previous forty-eight hours and that she was sexually assaulted prior to her death. He would report that she impacted the roadway at a high rate of speed and that the driver who was unable to avoid her was

271

neither DUI or otherwise negligent. He presumed.

The reality was that the family had no comment for the press at the time Nor would they, insisted Beverly Turnbull. He met the driver of the car who had felt compelled to be there and shook his hand compassionately. Then, at the request of the coroner, he was taken without his wife to see his daughter, not expecting his body would weaken with sudden age as he gazed transfixed at the young woman resting on a cold steel slab, horrifically mutilated and broken.

His wife would never see her daughter again, though he felt in his heart that however much and for however long she might imagine the truth and hate him for his well-intentioned deprivation, the reality and subsequent nightmares that would haunt her forever would be that much worse.

He did not extend that empathy borne of love to Richard Templeton.

Fifty-Four

Easter Sunday, April 08
Atlanta, GA

Rare were the occasions when Miss Divine stayed over on a Saturday, even rarer when she slept alone, but Saturday was the girls' busiest day of the week and the hotel was fully booked.

Miss Divine didn't give much thought to sparing Monica's feelings, nor her reaction, despite wanting deeper relationships with the girls, more genuine and longer lasting than the time needed to reach their physical crescendos. She housed and fed them, asking nothing in return but their commitment to maintain the uniquely high standard and unparalleled quality of service that was synonymous with The Hotel Le Chic, allowing her to keep them in a very comfortable, stress-free environment for the term of their obligation. Unless or until they broke the rules.

That almost never happened because they loved her. They were well-behaved girls, faithful to one another, and for that reason she never worried them by announcing a departure date in advance of a new girl's arrival, which was usually within forty-eight hours of any disposal and such was her quandary. Cassandra didn't work out and the girls were expecting to meet Daphne's replacement. She had already told Monica to assist Dree with her training.

"Come in, Monica. Sit beside me, please. I know it's early, but I'm having a glass of wine. I have tequila for you. Why don't you pour yourself one and bring each of us a cigarette. There are some things I…not very pleasant things." Monica went to the wet bar, pouring herself a tequila and soda she wouldn't drink, taking two reefers from the humidor. When she turned Miss Divine was straightening her robe. "I didn't call you here for intimacy, Monica, but if you would like to stay after we're finished perhaps a night together would be good for both of us."

"What is wrong Miss Divine? Is this about my family or Daphne?"

"No, it's not your daughter. She's fine and so is Daphne. I assure you." She sipped her wine, put down her glass and took Monica's hands in hers. "Monica, you do know I maintain contact from a distance with our families, the girls' families, so when they leave I know where to send them, or whether there is a reason not to."

"I know. You told me my husband went to Iraq."

"Yes, he did, and was killed in action the day before yesterday. He would have come home to the States in a month or two. I'm very sorry."

"If my husband was dead, I would know already in my dreams and in my heart. He is not dead." Her hands were trembling. "He is not dead."

"I'm very sorry, Monica. He is. If you want you can have tomorrow off as well. You can even stay here with me. I can cancel William's reservation. I'll tell him you're not well. He'll understand."

Monica gulped the tequila and coughed, wiping her mouth with her hand. Miss Divine lit both reefers and passed her one.

"I have not seen my husband for fifteen months, and before that for only two weeks. Sometimes I think I forget how he looks, then I sleep, and when I wake up I remember again how handsome he is. I believe you are telling me what you think is the truth," she lied, "but if my husband was dead I would know this. He is not dead."

Miss Divine patted her hand. "It's that kind of devotion that will get you through the next two years. Do you believe it, Monica? You have been with us for eight months."

"And twenty-one days. Yes, I do believe it."

"I am very pleased with you, and when your time comes to leave I will miss you very much. Unfortunately, then you will think of this evening and remember what I have told you."

"May I go? I want to be by myself. I would not be good with you today. I am sorry."

"Yes, you may go…in a moment." She reached for her glass, taking a sip before inhaling the reefer. "You all know we brought in a girl to replace Daphne." Monica sipped her tequila and nodded. "Well, she's gone. I had to send her away. Friday evening Frankie and Bobby took her to where she could find her family. She didn't work out. I had great hopes for her, like I do for you. Unfortunately, she disappointed me and I sent her away."

"And she does not know of the hotel?"

"No, she does not. However, I am very unhappy with the men. They have made my life extremely complicated. As a result Dree has no Anchor Girl, or a special friend. I had to pay twice for the same girl and I still have one less of you to accommodate the guests."

"What are you saying?"

"I'm saying, for the time being, for a short while until I can find a suitable replacement for Daphne, I've asked Genevieve to help out."

"But she is a Prefect."

"Yes, she is, but she has agreed to help on two conditions."

"This is not my business, Miss Divine. This is between

you and her."

"It is your business, Monica. She agreed on the conditions that she would entertain Preferred Guests… and be with you. She would be your Anchor Girl, Lucy would be with Dree and Stephanie doesn't care either way. Genevieve tells me she's just as happy being alone. Actually I told Genevieve about your husband and the first thing she asked was whether you could become a Prefect before the end of your obligation." Miss Divine smiled. "I told her maybe."

"What will Stephanie do?"

"Confidentially, do you know what that means?" She paused, waiting for the answer. "Confidentially, I believe Stephanie wants to leave us, and perhaps it's time she does when someone is ready to take her place. Perhaps that someone could be you."

"I do know Genevieve likes me very much, but never will I hurt Lucy in such a way. Dree will understand this and if the Preferred Guest is William never will he agree to change from me. I am his Preferred Girl and I am very special to Cynthia also. I am important for them and for the hotel, no?"

Indeed, and the madam was trumped. She was also deadly furious. "You're right. I certainly would do nothing to upset William or Cynthia."

"May I go now?"

"Yes, please do." Her face was expressionless. "And don't expect Genevieve to be very happy. Remember, she is a Prefect. Now get out of here."

Fifty-Five

James Burton was the CEO and president of Quantum Communications, the most successful advertising firm in the Southeast. Although his elite residence towered distinctively over all other high-rise properties in downtown Atlanta, an address known to his private secretary and very few others, he was a man of very refined and simple tastes. He never traveled, he worked unjustifiably long hours, he never vacationed and he adored his wife. Though he hadn't loved her or been in love with her for years. At first he refused to believe the reality. Then he did, and for the longest time he endured a painful struggle to accept and understand their lives would never again be the same.

The evening of their tenth wedding anniversary so many years ago had begun with long stemmed roses, endless kisses and indecent proposals as he lay across their bed and watched her dress in the slinkiest evening gown he could find. She was petite, stunningly attractive with an inherent sensuality she wore as a radiant glow, and she was his. Both the evening and the hour were indelibly etched into his memory because seeing her every day since was a constant reminder.

Their friends eventually drifted away as inconspicuously as they could, becoming distant business associates. Their mischievous banter and laughter became predictable pleasantries and pleasant smiles, once heated passion towards each other cooled to friendly compassion and they both secretly wished she had died in the crash.

Doris Burton enjoyed the best of care, a constant homecare companion who never tired of her company, and a wheelchair that had been her prison for over twelve years. She thought of him every moment he was away and she loved him as much as she despised him for seeing her that way whenever he was with her.

She understood. She knew the truth and she understood, though she would never think to broach the subject. He had told her moments after the Chief of Staff delivered the callous news that she would never walk again that he would never leave her and he never did. He had been by her side through her worst times that first year of painful, failed attempts at rehabilitation, quietly blaming himself. So what had she to complain about? He was the one who continued to suffer the most and if seeking solace in the arms of another brought him comfort how could she mind?

The Madam

Fifty-Six

The mandatory two weeks at Fort Bennings were as grueling as he could make them. A time of mental and physical cleansing, and he was happy Sergeant Bishops wasn't calling him in for an update. He had five months left and nothing to report. The Marines didn't take failure lightly. Failing was never an option and Bishops had already made that clear to him. Manuel was to bring his girls home and so far he had achieved no measurable advance toward that objective.

He knew he was failing Mercedes, feeling as though he was letting down the Corps and not living up to JC's expectations. The longer he took the less chance he had of finding them. His one salvation was Juan Carlos who stood firm in his belief that she would be found, and in his oath to help kill those who were hurting her. The single joy in his life was Carmella who called him weekly, refusing to let him succumb to the grip of defeat and depression.

She made him promise that he would eat properly and not drink too much. She reminded him of her favorite stories about Mercedes and Sofia and how all of them would be together soon, in Miami, at the beach, and how they would watch Sofia playing in the sand and splashing in the waves. She let him talk for the most part, never faltering, not until she hung up, thankful most times her cousin was nowhere near.

When Manuel arrived home Sunday evening the red light was flashing. The single message was from Juan Carlos, that he was to phone at any hour. JC was aware of Manuel's conversation with Rachel Wright's father and although he didn't like that his friend had identified himself, and that Wright had spoken with Bishops, he merely insisted in his inimitable and quiet way that Manuel never repeat the error. The faux-pas was tantamount to wearing fire engine red camouflage in Iraq during the day or lighting a campfire at night in the desert, he said, to wait for the perfect kill shot he would never feel. Point taken.

There was a kidnapping in Florida on the twenty-seventh, a woman in her twenties and her sons. A Valerie Templeton had gone missing for two days before turning up dead and naked on the I-95. That wasn't all. Her boys were still missing, but almost a year to the day another woman, Cindy Stevens, went missing in Charlotte with her year-old daughter, and three months before that a woman called Deborah Wilkins disappeared from Tallahassee with her young daughter. All of them including Mercedes were taken within a radius of 300 miles. Some bad shit was going on, and that's about all the cops were doing about it.

"Atlanta is the key, hombre. That's five chicas in fifteen months, all within a one-day drive. Could be a cult thing, some fucked-up religious freak, or could be independent operations: Sell the women, sell the kids. Sorry hombre, but whatever they are we are going to find them and I will bet my cousin's fat nalgas it will not be long."

"My friend, despite the fact that Carmelita has a perfect ass, and I hate you for making me talk of her that way, you always seem so certain of our success."

JC chuckled. "You cannot get away from me, and my thick-skinned cousin has adopted you. She will give you no rest if you try. Hombre, listen to me. They were all young, they all had children except for Wright, and they were all white except for Mercedes. There is a piece of the puzzle we are missing, a piece that is not yet clear to us, which will come. And believe me, when the missing piece does become clear we will find Mercedes and what is happening to her is nothing to what we will do to them. You have a few eager friends, hombre, and not just me and my cow of a cousin."

"Without you, JC, I would never find them. Without Carmelita I would go to bed drunk each night."

"We do not dream through our drunken stupors, amigo, and sometimes that is a good thing. Not so for you who must dream. ¿Comprendes lo que digo?"

"Yes, I do. You're a good friend. You both are."

"No, I am not, because I must tell you that Carmelita expects you here for her Cinco de Mayo celebration to poison you with her cooking, and if you do not come I will drive her to Atlanta myself and give her my gun. She will not aim for your head, hombre. She is a mean woman. You do not know her as I do." JC paused, changing his tone. "You are expected, amigo. Be here. There is also something she is not telling me. She has something up her sleeve and you have heard nothing from me."

"I do know her, and I love her for how she is helping me through this mess. The day is my anniversary. I will come. I will tell her myself when I speak with her this week. I am anxious to see both of you, and for the day when you and Carmelita will come to our home and be with us as a real family."

"That will happen, amigo, I promise you, and I am anxious to see you again. Now, forgive me, I must go. I hear the Mexican witch coming, searching for her broom and I prefer that she does not know of this conversation. Ciao, amigo, y cuídate."

Fifty-Seven

There were no purple and yellow foil-wrapped chocolate eggs with melt-in-your mouth creamy centers. There was no pretty pink dress with little-girl frills and no tiny black patent leather shoes with round toes and white ankle socks. There was no little hat or tiny white gloves for her. There had been no trip to the petting zoo, and she would have no little comb set. Nor would she see the Easter bunny. There would only be quiet and more darkness with her little white mommy and her little chocolate-brown daddy who asked her so often for love, never telling her what the words meant.

The situation had worsened and Richman never returned their calls. They doubted whether he even listened to their dozens of plaintive messages, let alone give reasonable consideration to their recently voice-mailed proposal, though they weren't giving up hope. They were desperate. What was to have been a beautiful adoption and the beginning of a happy family was a living nightmare. Their friends had begun phoning, questioning if everything was alright between them. None of them had been invited to the house in such a long time and they were wondering whether the Hillman's Traditional Beach Barbeque, the unofficial start to the Harbor Club's yachting season, was still on for Easter Sunday at the St. Augustine beach house.

The women from the yacht club seemed quite

concerned. The men more easily assumed between themselves that Roger Hillman was having an affair with some nubile, flexible thing that was still years away from the bitch phase that was invariably the precursor to the dreaded change of life, which was no reason to ignore them. That sort of thing happened all the time and who could say Marietta Hillman wasn't the one getting some on the side to offset her diminished hormone-related sense of self-worth and increased loathing of all things breathing. Particularly if those things sported penises.

Nothing of the sort was happening, he insisted to the men, and she to the women. They were as happy as ever and very much in love. Roger had simply been overworked since New Year's and Marietta had never expected to return to work. She had more traveling time and less time for herself. They were truly sorry. Time was going so quickly and, yes, of course, the beach barbeque was still on.

All was forgiven by the end of the day. The party was a great success, after a morning spent in St. Augustine buying groceries, beer, wine, prizes and working to make the beach house they hadn't been to in months look lived in. They arrived home late, cleaned and fed Anna Jane, and went to bed completely exhausted. Sunday morning they left early after giving her enough water for the day and a little meal that would hold her until evening. They were anxious to be with their good friends, anxious to re-ingratiate themselves into their private community, and they hurried out not thinking to check the phone in the study that had begun blinking red the previous afternoon.

All the rushing, the cost, the lying had been worthwhile and by dinnertime the destination for the Annual Harbor Club Flotilla had been decided and voted on. They would cruise the coastline to Miami, cross over to the North coast of Cuba and cruise east to the Dominican Republic. Weather permitting they would leave port August 18 and return September 03 for Labor Day celebrations. Roger and Marietta Hillman were elected as Chief Navigator and Secretary for the sixteen-day adventure and neither one thought to object.

The couple arrived home at the stroke of midnight, had a drink and went to bed too excited to sleep. Monday morning was when she remembered, when she saw the light flashing in his study and dialed into the message center, listening twice, scarcely believing what she was hearing.

She dropped the receiver and ran to her husband, crying happy tears. The many months of lies and subterfuge were over at long last and they hugged and kissed each other before remembering little Anna Jane. She left him to microwave a jar of oatmeal, pour a glass of milk and walk down the steps to the door that had become the portal to her own private hell.

She was anxious to call Richman and would after she fed the girl, changed her clothes and emptied the port-a-potty into the laundry room toilet. There would be no more mess, no more crying, no more of her ghastly speaking. Richman had called to tell them he had put them on a list of possible donors, explaining clearly that doing so would be very problematic for him and costly for them. The kid was Mexican, after all, practically a year older and more difficult to place. The ten thousand cash abandonment fee they had suggested was not acceptable. The applicable fee would be thirty thousand, which, he reminded them, was insignificant when compared to the impact of the estimated financial losses they would incur over the next twenty years and beyond if they kept the girl.

The kid would be placed on the list upon receipt of a one-third goodwill deposit, the balance to be paid at time of relinquishment and upon his receipt of all original documentation. Above all they would take him at his word and not call his office for any reason. When she phoned he made himself unavailable.

They both called in sick and by noon on Easter Monday the For Sale sign was posted at the entrance to the beachfront property with assurances from the eager realtor they would be celebrating a sale within a month. They didn't wait. As soon as she left they poured the sparkling wine and laughed gleefully for the first time in months.

Fifty-Eight

At the hotel Easter Sunday had no special significance. Monica spent day in her suite letting the warmth of Lucy's hands soothe her as she lay on her bed and cried incessantly into her folded arms.

Lucy didn't care about demerit points for missing dinner. She could afford the penalty, though Monica insisted she go to the dining room. Her obligation was coming to an end and Monica convinced her that her husband would not have remarried, that she would soon be with her family and nothing else mattered. He would understand, the same way her Manuel would understand and this was not the time to jeopardize her future.

As much as Monica wanted her to stay, she wanted Lucy to go, and she did with promises to come back as soon as she could with a plate. Besides, she would have to start weaning herself off the Sunday reefers so why not start now?

To Monica it seemed as though Lucy had never left when she returned without the plate. Genevieve hadn't allowed room service. She had, however, applied demerit points to Monica's account which she arbitrarily doubled in value before instructing Lucy to relate the news in lieu of room service. Monday morning she forced herself to eat and did an intense workout before going to the pool and spa alone. When she was done she casually strolled through the lobby with her straightened hair dripping water, snarling something in Spanish as she passed the Reception area where Genevieve waited hopefully for any sign of recognition. Instead she reached for the ledger and quadrupled Sunday's total demerit points, noting disrespect to a Prefect and the use of a foreign language. In two days Monica managed to accrue an eight-week add-on penalty to her obligation which she knew in her heart was a meaningless number.

What mattered more was one day very soon reminding Lucy that she was Mercedes Del Fuego. Lucy would know her phone number, she would know her address and Monica would whisper the information against Lucy's lips each night until she could drift into sleep hearing Lucy's soft echo.

William wasn't expected until five that afternoon and she spent the rest of the day in her suite making herself look special, for herself. She washed and treated her hair a second time, combed it the way she knew Manuel would like. Then she dressed for William who was always so easy to please. He never suggested what she might wear, which would mean what to wear, nor did he ever presume to tell her how to greet him. She never disappointed him and he was never disillusioned. During their time together she had learned what he liked, what he wanted and what he needed, which was usually determined by the hour of his arrival.

Later in the evening she would often let him find her lounging in the tub, or at the end of his day he might find her in heels, stockings, and either a bustier or bra and panty set. Most afternoon meetings might let him see her in satin tap pants and a camisole, curled into the sofa reading a book or pouring him a drink from the bar.

When he walked in this time he would see a loganberry stretch cami embroidered with midnight blue lace, a matching low-rise thong with ribbon-garters and sheer maroon stockings. She also knew how differently he acted towards her after long weekends. He was a man who never tired. He was always energized and vital, except after particularly long weekends when she suspected he missed being with her. Those were the times he became a changed man, a man driven by need as much as by guilt, a man tormented by memories as much as he was tortured by present love.

He had changed in other ways. They never shared love by any measure. Respect was his strongest emotion, his way of demonstrating she was something special to him. He did take part in Amanda's first experience, though soon after told Monica to advise Miss Divine he would excuse himself from future new girls.

He still enjoyed seeing her with Lucy, but her invitations to stay the night with them came to an end the night he roused himself by calling out the name she had heard so many times before as he slept by her side and she sat cross-legged thinking of another. His sleep was often disrupted and she thought of him differently from the one time she chanced to speak through his dreams, telling him without emotion that she loved him while pressing a warm palm gently against his cheek.

He had stirred without waking, speaking clearly that he loved her so very much and that he always would. He adored her, and Monica would never invade his dreams again. When he left her late that Monday evening she bathed, waited for Lucy, and prayed to her husband.

Fifty-Nine

Tuesday, April 24
Jacksonville, Florida

Richman hadn't called asking for his money, which was a good thing because they didn't have any to send. The realtor had visited the beach property with several interested prospects, but the Hillmans were holding out in the hope of balancing their need and urgency with the supply and demand of a slumping market and the twenty weeks remaining before the cruise.

They were nervous and excited, confident the sale would soon become a closed bid between the most interested parties, despite the agent's sage advice to counter the most recent and fair offer to purchase and close the deal. Each successive offer surpassed the previous one and was the sole topic of conversation at the dinner table. Caring for the girl had become even more of a chore since they'd become her guards and not her guardians. Her evening macaroni and tomato with milk was often delayed until convenient or remembered, and when they were rushed her morning pabulum or oatmeal with water was often forgotten until their return from work.

They soon understood a closed bid wasn't going to happen and, as good as the most recent offer might have been, accepting would mean losing their beach home and thirty thousand to Richman, with not enough left over for a minimal down payment on the most modest beach property. How would they explain that to the club?

That all changed Tuesday evening during dinner with an epiphany that would save their beach house or make them a substantial profit, give them freedom and, in the process, save them Richman's thirty thousand. The scheme was perfect and the decision not to accept anything less than the original asking price was an easy one. Phoning Richman to cancel the buyback and explain their decision to keep her was even easier.

They couldn't wait. What they needed to know was too important, too intriguing. And how could they sleep if they weren't certain their plan was failsafe or foolhardy? Hillman prompted his wife to make the call and she did so with an even calmness in her voice he should have found disturbing. An hour later they were on the second floor of Wolfson Children's Hospital and no one took notice. Nor did anyone notice four days later at the peak of Saturday's visiting hours when a three-year-old girl, sedated with red wine and dressed in a plain cotton night gown was left wrapped in a flannel blanket on the swivel chair of the deserted nurse's station.

Sixty

Monday, April 30
Miami, Florida

The police requested that the headline be worded as dramatically as possible in order to grab the attention of as many disinterested Monday morning commuters as possible, particularly because of the subject and not the subject matter. If all they got was one response, one clue that would be something, though no one believed they would.

ABUSED YOUNG GIRL FOUND ABANDONED AT WOLFSON
POLICE ASK FOR PUBLIC'S HELP AS STAFF AND SECURITY SEEK TO UNDERSTAND
LITTLE ANA JUANITA NEEDS YOUR HELP
DOCTORS SAY: PLEASE

Tucker Richman shook his head, stopping to aim at the wastepaper basket, blowing a brown spherical missile from his mouth. Roger and Marietta Hillman read the article separately, each feeling a sense of relief, each leaving a voice-mail message for the other that they should do dinner in town that evening. In Miami, Carmella read the headline and hurried through the restaurant to her cousin's office. She didn't bother knocking.

"Juanito, read this."

He was on the phone, his reaction telling her emphatically the interruption was ill-timed.

"Carmelita…"

"Read!" She threw the front page onto his desk. "We must go there now, and we must call Manuel to tell him of this."

"Cállate chica, if you want me to read." He uncovered the mouth piece saying "I will get back to you," and hung up.

She slapped his shoulder harder than she intended. She didn't like being told to be quiet, but it was nerves. She was agitated. "Call Manny, Juanito. Call him right now."

Juan Carlos read the article, slouching pensively into his seat. "No, Carmelita, we will not call him because we do not know. If we are wrong the false hope could make him worse than he is and that would not be wise." He looked at her with a wide grin, raising his hands in defense at seeing her black eyes widen incredibly. "Make arrangements to be away for a few days, chica. We will leave for Jacksonville as soon as you are ready. Driving will be faster and we will know within a few hours whether we should call him. But first you will call the hospital and the police to advise them we are coming, and you will not forget the photograph of Mercedes and the girl."

"Thank you, Juanito. That is why I love you. I did not mean to hurt you."

He kissed her hand. "You did not. Your lunch will do that, the one you will pack so that we waste no time. Ahora, ¡Vete!"

Sixty-One

The police were waiting with the hospital staff, none of them expecting the likes of Juan Carlos Martínez to walk through the doors, who would say nothing until he and his cousin saw the little girl. Yes, they had proof. Yes, they knew the parents if she was the right little girl. If she was not there would be nothing to discuss.

They acquiesced guardedly, the doctors ready to accuse, the female detectives ready to arrest. The girl was Sofia. There was no doubt. The girl was Sofia Del Fuego, not Ana Juanita Vaquero. When the doctors went to prevent Carmella from taking the little girl into her arms Juan Carlos did, and no one thought to stop him when he chuckled at the detective who had put a hand on the grip of her weapon.

He gave Sofia a gentle hug, smiled into her eyes and kissed her cheek. Then he passed her to Carmella and reached for his phone, ignoring the nurse who told him cell phones were prohibited. He spoke to them in Spanish, praising their big firm tits and tight round asses, and when they gawked at him with the dumb expressions he expected he pressed SEND.

"This is Manny."

"Chico, soy yo. Can you talk?"

"Sí, I can talk."

"Are you driving?"

293

"Yes, I am."

"Pull over. Tell me when you are parked."

The brief pause was an eternity to both men.

"I am stopped. I was not expecting your call, hombre. I told you that I would be there. Does Carmelita not believe me?"

"The plans have changed, Manny. The war has begun. I am at the Children's Hospital in Jacksonville with Carmelita who holds your precious Sofia in her arms as we speak. We have found her amigo and she needs you here. We expect you soon."

"JC, you have found her...really?"

"Carmelita found her."

"Sofia, you are certain?"

"You will see for yourself when you get here, amigo. Do not waste time talking with me. There is no doubt the girl is Sofia and she needs you."

He'd never heard his friend cry so openly. Yet, as much as the sound made him uncomfortable, he waited.

"Is this true, JC?"

"Yes, it is true, and hearing the words a fourth time will not change that. Take time to prepare yourself, amigo, and do not forget all your legal shit. You have to be prepared for all that DNA shit as well." He waited again until he thought the time was right. "And, Manny, you will stop often, before you must. You will do nothing stupid that will keep you from arriving safely and Carmelita is nagging at me about bringing some bear." He shrugged. "Get here as soon as you can, amigo, and be prepared to stay a while, at least a week. Believe me. She will need you very much. Be prepared, hombre." He looked at Sofia. "She is alright, but not entirely. Whoever had her has treated her badly. We will not leave her for one moment. I give you my word, and there is other good news."

"What is that?"

The Madam

"A week without Carmelita's cooking." There was no humor in his voice. "Just get here."

Sixty-Two

His passengers didn't know what to think about the lunatic in the front seat who was laughing and crying at once. The older couple held hands, perplexed. They wanted to get out, though they quickly relaxed when hearing Manuel call into the dispatcher requesting a backup driver as soon as possible to assist with his passengers. As he waited he explained to the couple what had happened, that they shouldn't be afraid. They weren't, not then. Not when seeing the photograph of the girl and her mother, feeling their own tears welling.

The offer of a free trip was refused. The man leaned forward to slap Manuel on the shoulder; the woman wished him good luck in finding his wife as soon as possible. She took the photograph as a souvenir and conversation piece as Manuel leaped out and into the second taxi.

By the time he arrived at the garage the dispatcher had broadcast the news over the intercom and the cacophony of cheering voices, applause and high-pitched horns was deafening as he hurried from the cab to his own car that was fueled and waiting for him. Manuel arrived at the hospital by 3:00 AM, met by Juan Carlos at the main entrance who wanted to fill him in on their way to the third floor where the earlier suspicious attitude had dwindled to the most basic levels required by medical and law enforcement officials for the sole purpose of saving face.

He ignored all but Carmella who wrapped her arms tightly around his neck as he lifted her from the floor. No one could have doubted who the father was, however cops are cops and witless questions are inherent to their close-minded and biased culture. Just as the words from the first one were being formed in her mouth JC raised a hand, slashing the air between them with his index, making his point. The man hadn't seen his daughter in more than a year.

Carmella told him to touch her as lightly as he could, and not to lift her. There would be time for that in the morning when she would be awake and stronger. He laid her favorite friend close by her side and called her name, telling her that her mamá and papá loved her, making even the hardened cops choke up as her uncovered arm slowly felt Poochie the Bear's soft coat and snuggled him against her cheek as though they'd never been apart.

Juan Carlos had answered many of their questions, telling them to verify all facts pertaining to the July kidnapping with the Atlanta Police, assuming they remembered the case or could locate the file. And any questions regarding Manuel Del Fuego's status with the Corps could be answered by Master Sergeant Bishops. They did both, well before Manuel had driven halfway to be with his daughter. Still, what was the use of having police and medical labs if they couldn't use them and by ten AM Tuesday Manuel was unequivocally her father. But what could he tell them?

He could only laugh along with JC as Carmella looked on, rocking Sofia in her arms and smiling at her men's quizzical expressions. He could tell them his daughter was found by his friends after almost ten months of being abused somewhere not far from the hospital because she was discovered by nurses, wearing only a nightie and a blanket. He knew she was abused because of the bruises and he could tell them she'd been shut in and badly nourished because her skin was pale and she weighed less than she should. He could tell them she had spent much of that time alone because she was shy and wasn't before. He could tell them she hadn't been loved for a quarter of her young life and he could tell them he expected them to do nothing about it. So, what could they tell him?

They didn't know, however they would contact him as soon as they had anything concrete to go on.

Sixty-Three

That afternoon JC reserved rooms at the Hilton for Manuel and Carmella, inviting them for a late dinner when the three were rested. He would return to his business concerns in Miami at sunrise. He hated sloppy goodbyes and Manny was in good hands.

Carmella would stay until Friday, or Monday if the common consensus was that Sofia should spend a few more days in the hospital. Then she would bring Manuel and Sofia to Miami. She had no intention of ruining her Saturday fiesta unless for Sofia, and there was more to hear as the men sat at the table nursing their vodka and tequila.

Downtown Atlanta was no place for a little girl. She should be with someone who loved her, not strangers. Sofia would stay with her where she could play with other little girls at the beach every day, where she would be perfectly safe. The other ladies at the restaurant were arranging their schedules, volunteering their free time to baby sit and her papá would be expected every weekend unless he was playing soldier.

JC let her speak. When she finished talking he signaled the waiter to order wine. Carmella took a sip of water and buried her face in the menu, ignoring Manuel who felt for some strange reason that he should argue. Then she ordered and Juan Carlos recited what he had selected. Neither one looked at Manuel who scanned the two lengths of parchment as though reading a menu in Braille.

When he was done Juan Carlos raised his glass, turning his attention to Carmella. "To our lovely Carmelita, Manny, whom we cannot do without it would seem. Thank you, cousin. Without you we might never have known." He turned to Manuel. "And to Mercedes who shall be with us soon. I feel it, amigo." The crystal goblets hummed. "A toast to the beautiful Mercedes who waits for us."

"Thank you, JC. Thank you, Carmelita." Manual sipped his wine with them, choosing his words. "Carmelita…"

JC interrupted. "Manny, the decision is made. Carmelita is right once again. Sofia will stay in Miami until we find Mercedes. Where else will you find one such angel to care for another?"

Carmella gave him the biggest smile. "Muchísimas gracias, Juanito. Te amo también."

The recovery came too late. "You see what crazy things you make me say and do, amigo. These words will be in her head forever." Juan Carlos took another sip of wine. "It is best, amigo, and what you must do. Do not waste your time thinking of excuses or kind words that are not necessary. What is necessary is that you find Sofia's mother."

Carmella ended the conversation. "Then we are agreed. I will be responsible for Sofia and love her as though she is my very own. And you will make certain that she will once again see love in her mother's eyes and hear her sweet voice."

Sixty-Four

Saturday, el Cinco de Mayo

Sofia hadn't been in the dark all week. Even the dimmed corridor lighting was bright to her. By Friday she hadn't spoken a single word taught to her by her plastic mommy and daddy who had been such a part of her life in the dark and kept her from being afraid.

Friday night when the lights went out in her own bedroom, when Manuel quietly closed the door behind him and Carmella, Sofia instinctively searched blindly for her mommy and daddy who were not there for her. Her scream made a man who had killed a hundred souls instantly freeze and wonder how the woman beside him had responded so quickly. Carmella had the girl in her arms within seconds, cooing and kissing her as she looked at Manuel with horror in her eyes, not knowing what to say or do.

"I love you, mommy. Please hug me. I'm hungry, mommy, please feed me. I'm a little girl. Please hug me, I'm crying. Tell me you love me," and they did until she fell asleep with Poochie the Bear to protect her and Carmella curled into the sofa beside her.

The next morning there was no sound of keys rattling or deadbolts sliding before a burst of harsh light, merely the warmth of diffused sunlight and loving smiles coming from the big people around her whose garbled noises meant nothing to her.

Sofia hadn't gone to the beach since Manuel and Mercedes had taken her to La Bahía de Campeche, when the bright blues of the ocean and the sky meant no more to her from behind her mesh window than the loud sound of crashing white waves. Now she was as excited as her father. The sky was overcast, but bright; the morning air was warm. By noon, when Carmella called them for lunch, Sofia had heard everything he could think to tell her about her mother. She liked looking at the young woman in the photograph when she wasn't touching him, or feeling the sand, or watching the crashing waves become white foam and disappear between her little toes. She hadn't eaten a midday meal since Christmas and surprised them all when she once again saw Mercedes' photograph and called out "mi mamá."

That evening Sofia was the sparkling centerpiece of Carmella's popular Cinco de Mayo celebration at the restaurant, a discreet celebration of Manuel's anniversary. She was a particular hit with those patrons who remembered JC's Christmas toast to his friend and by early-evening she buried her face into the curve of her father's neck, squeezing him as he carried her to bed amidst what must have sounded like thunder to her little ears.

Sixty-five

James Burton hated playing golf. He had little appreciation for those who lied about enjoying the mundane game as a ruse to get out of doing real work, when what they actually wanted was the nineteenth hole for boasting, flirting and drinking at his expense. He hated small talk and very few people knew him well enough to engage him in a discussion unless the topic was pertinent to another merger or take-over. That's why he had well-paid subordinates to stand in for him.

He hired and promoted each member of his executive staff, he enjoyed final approval of senior management staff changes and reserved the seldom-used right to terminate any of them at any time should their representation of him or the firm not be in keeping with his corporate philosophy. He seldom used his limo. He disliked people staring at him whenever he got in or out of the thing and he hated the pretense of nonchalance towards those who openly envied him. The car was another expensive business tool, a perk to his executives and certain few of the senior management team, equal in value to the proverbial and much sought after washroom key: deserved rewards for working longer hours than required to ruin their personal lives.

He preferred the escapism of walking and the anonymity of taxis. He walked to the office each morning unencumbered by briefcases or computer cases, carrying a cell phone that was permanently set to vibrate and often he would sit in the center of Olympic Park to watch the world hurry by. He wondered whether any of them realized what they were missing as they scurried along like automatons towards uncertain futures, fooled into believing all was well and wonderful because they already possessed the best of everything, which they paid for with credit that, like marriage, would be with them till death would they part.

They had once sat in the park together, a long time ago. Now she never went out. She had once been beautiful and still was, though she believed she wasn't and so she was not. Once they had laughed and would have thought nothing of dancing in the street, now they never laughed and would never dance. He was one of the wealthiest men in the Southeast, yet he was poor. He had everything and he had nothing, nothing he could do or buy to make her walk again. So who was worse off, the rushing automatons who lived for the day or a lonely man sitting on a park bench thinking of the past and regretting the future?

The argument with his wife was banal, harsh words spoken by both in lieu of what once would have been her inopportune candor parried with a quizzical expression or his frustrating smirk that would inevitably lead to his quiet conquest and her eventual return to normality. They once knew how to make up, and did with some frequency, now they were strangers with no apparent need for either to acquiesce to the other.

Saturday afternoon there was no park bench, no mindless horde. There was rain, a constant drizzle to wet the city streets and dampen the freshly scented springtime air. He enjoyed the rain: nature's way of bringing life and sadness at once, rejuvenating some while destroying or disappointing others. Being in the rain he could feel angry, or melancholy and pitiable. In the rain he could hide from what he had tried so hard at first not to become.

The air was warm and still. The drizzle was becoming a Southeastern downpour that might last a few minutes or long enough to transition city streets into impassable sluices of uncontrolled water. He loved each drop as he hailed the city cab at the edge of the park with his rolled-up newspaper waving in the air, keeping perfect time to his casual stride.

Climbing in, water dribbled from the brim of his fedora to between his knees as he removed his hat to shake off the stubborn droplets, not caring he had tossed the saturated and curled pages of his Saturday paper across the photocopied image of a young woman as he gave the driver instructions.

"Get onto Courtland and drive south, I'll tell you when to stop."

"South on Courtland, and then where?"

"And then I'll tell you when you can stop."

"That's a pretty short fare. Know what I mean?"

"Am I keeping you from something you would rather be doing?"

"Not what I meant."

"I know what you meant, yet we don't seem to be moving." He threw the man a twenty over the passenger seat. "Now you'll never know."

"What's that?"

"How much I would have tipped you. You might try working on your personality somewhat. You might be interested in knowing, or being reminded, that in the service industry a pleasant personality is directly related to your year-end net worth. Any chance you were ever a waiter in New York?"

"No, never been there."

"The question was rhetorical."

"Whatever."

Quiet moments later he said: "The next intersection is where you will stop, on this side."

"You need change?"

"No, I do not."

The tip was twelve dollars.

"Thanks, man. I mean it. Hey, let me ask you something." The cabbie twisted. "I got this picture here that I show to all my fares for this guy I know. His wife's…"

"Thank you, no. I have no time."

"Just a fast look, man, she's…"

The driver stayed twisted in his seat, holding out the photograph as James Burton climbed from the cab with his coat collar pulled up and the brim of his hat pulled down. He crossed the street from behind the cab, cushions of water at his feet, his coat thickly lined with a waterfall of torrential rain, walking unhurriedly until he disappeared into the dark weather.

The driver shrugged his shoulders. The man had no time. Rain was pissing down on a Saturday afternoon, he was walking along a deserted city street, and he had no time. As much as he never thought of himself as being remotely knowledgeable or worldly about anything, at least no one would ever call him a son of a bitch and mean it.

Sixty-Six

He should not have called to see her. He should have stayed away. He should have gone to a bar or the office. He knew the moment he walked through the door, the moment he saw her eyes. He was well aware that body language was the stuff of barstool analysts; he also believed the eyes never lied, his own included.

His first thought was of the cursed woman thing the average man has to deal with three hundred weeks of his life, and the female staff at the firm was no better. Their natural affliction created a major business expense and socially no different from blood-thirsty predators in the animal kingdom smelling the fear of their prey. Monica was no different. She was clearly and uncharacteristically on the offensive, albeit with an aberrant subtlety not commonly attached to her particular extraction.

Quite possibly, he thought. The time was about right. Or had he merely come at the wrong time, for the wrong reasons, and he was seeing his eyes reflected in hers? She was certainly as gorgeous as ever, sitting cross-legged on her settee, flipping through magazines, wearing a lily-pink deep V off the shoulder jersey that showed most of her steel-blue satin bra that was a perfect match for the day, the weather, and, he had no doubt, her mood. Not once before had he seen her so sullen and he didn't like the affect. Not that he particularly cared on an emotional level, as much as he did care for her. More importantly, he felt trapped inside a suite of rooms that seemed more like an inescapable lair.

He was the problem, he knew, not the status and prestige of his membership that afforded him the right to expect smiles, hugs and whatever other welcoming nicety was appropriate. He was no less sullen and realized he should not have come.

When she went to stand he stopped her silently with an open palm, walking to the bar where he poured a healthy measure of eighteen-year Glenmorangie he wouldn't stay long enough to finish. For the first time in many weeks he would be at home for Saturday dinner with a woman who had not loved him in years.

The Madam

Sixty-Seven

Sunday Manuel stayed as long as he could, waiting until Carmella helped put Sofia to bed for her afternoon nap before leaving with a slight smarting sensation at his upper arm for thinking he could politely refuse her food basket. When JC reminded Manuel in front of her with a sly grin that he hadn't mentioned to Carmella about not wanting to impose on her hospitality during his upcoming weekend visits, she pinched his arm again, giving him a key to her home. Then she walked away shaking her head, muttering to herself about stupid men.

His apartment was a lonely place. He was never in it long enough at any one time to feel the loneliness, now he did and he poured his first double vodka before dialing into his message service and preparing his file folder with a photo of Mercedes alone that he would have copied before work the next day.

The first message was from Bishops: "Del Fuego, congratulations on the success of your first phase. Understand we're still counting on you to complete your mission and bring your wife home, son. Permission is granted to be excused from your May weekend, just make sure you're here on base as scheduled for June. One more thing: apparently you should expect a package, which I know nothing about. Recent field reports indicate something's going on with the female contingent on base.

309

Good luck Marine."

He hadn't asked to be excused, though he knew not to acknowledge the kindness. Instead he made a mental note to have a photograph of him with Sofia ready for Mrs. Bishops in June. The second message was from Captain Peachtree, asking that he return her call. He penciled her cell number onto his folder and was neither surprised nor impressed when she picked up.

"Good evening, Corporal."

"Do you have information about my wife?"

"No, we don't, but the detective in charge is still working the case."

"Why did you call?"

"I called to congratulate you on finding your daughter. You said you would, and you did."

"No thanks to you, Detective, and make no mistake… I will find my wife."

"I believe you might very well do that Corporal, and as much as you think we're not doing our part, we are. Nothing would make me happier than finding your wife. If you manage to find her first, more power to you. I wish you luck, we all do. But I warn you: Don't do anything foolish or outside the law. Whenever you get something we should know about you make sure we do. Good night, Corporal."

He didn't bother to reply.

Sixty-Eight

Monica took the better part of the following week to recover from her deep-seated malaise, thankful for her Duty Week. She was approaching her tenth month and continued believing in him. She needed to believe, despite her dreams of him after William or Cynthia left her that had become graphic nightmares of a face she didn't recognize covered in blood.

Miss Divine hadn't forgiven her unprecedented confrontation and refusal to leave Lucy a month earlier, and since then Genevieve was openly caustic and belligerent towards her in front of the other girls who were all aware of the reason behind the ill-treatment, including Stephanie.

Lucy had made a commitment to refrain from the Sunday evening cannabis and Monica had committed to helping her, though rather than explaining why to the curious few they decided to put on as though they hadn't. They were two weeks clean.

Monica did her mandatory time in the gym and went to her suite to shower and wait for her scheduled meeting time with the new girl rather than spending time at the pool with the others. The concession was acceptable, a way of meeting them halfway: train Penelope or be with Cynthia. There was no difference. She hadn't seen William for over a week and was thankful Cynthia would be coming that evening, not him. They were practically girlfriends and being with her was less like work. At least she wouldn't have to pretend the previous week never happened or feel the need to explain her mood when he'd done nothing but sit quietly, finish his scotch while flipping through pages of a magazines, and leave with a faint thank-you and goodbye.

His mood was as dark as hers. She was there to satisfy the physical, not enquire after the psychological, though she was lost in her own time and space and had done neither. The repercussions would have been severe had he reported her, but no. He simply walked out, not saying anything to anyone, not even acknowledging the girls relaxing in the lounge before or between their confirmed reservations.

She knew she would see him again, and she hoped soon enough for her own well-being, for the continued success of her time-based stratagem, just not right away. The last thing she wanted was to become a Courtesan Girl. What she had accepted would be hard enough for him to accept, being a whore for anyone with fifteen hundred in his pocket would be impossible. But at the moment Penelope needed her.

Sixty-Nine

She knocked twice, not waiting for a response. The light was on; the woman was standing in disbelief by her newly acquired wardrobe. "My name is Monica. Good morning Penelope."

"No, my…"

"You are Penelope for the next three years. You already know much of what I will tell you, but there is more and you would be very smart to listen."

"Are you one of them, one of the kidnappers?"

"No, I am one of you. I also was kidnapped. I am in my tenth month. I have twenty-six remaining."

"It's not possible. How can it be no one knows about this place?"

"No one knows, not even the Prefects."

"Why me?"

"You are young, you are attractive, and I must think after he raped you the big man thought your body would be good for what you must do. Which I do not have to explain."

"What about my little boy?"

"I do not know. I am afraid for my own daughter. That is why I do what I must, and so will you or something bad will happen to your son and to you. This place has wires for sound and for video. There are no secrets, not one. When you talk in your sleep they will know if they want to listen, and they will until they are happy with you."

"They told me you'd be coming to train me."

"Yes… and later Dree will be here with us because sometimes they want two of us together. We are all women and being with women first is much easier. I did not believe so at first. Now I know."

She grimaced. "Train me for what?"

Monica smiled. She had neither the time nor the desire to be coy. "She did not tell you? We will train you to be with men, and with women, to have sex with them and make them feel good."

"I thought I was being kidnapped so that pig could rape me. Then she did me, too. I forget for how long. Now it's you and that other one?"

"Yes, but not for pleasure, not like her. We must train you, nothing more. What we will do means nothing to me, unless I am with Lucy."

"For how long? How long will I be here?"

"You will be here for three years."

Her face paled. "What about my husband? What will happen to him?"

"What is happening to you is more important. He will search for you or he will not. There will good times and bad, mostly bad at the beginning. Then everything will get better. You will see." Monica paused. "Tell me, have you known many men?"

Penelope hesitated, not expecting the question. "I've had a few before my husband, maybe fourteen or fifteen, mostly at frat parties or semester friends when I was at college. Nothing serious. Actually my husband was number fifteen. He's the one who got me pregnant before my last semester. I never graduated and since then all he wants is for me to pop out another one. We've been arguing about it ever since."

A year earlier Monica's chin would have plummeted to

her knees, now she didn't care about anyone's graduation. "Then this will not be so hard for you, I think, especially after the one they call Frankie found you." Monica paused, sitting on the bed, making a concerted effort to be pleasant. "And women?"

"That one the other night, which I don't remember, and a few kisses at school on a dare. Kissing some woman's tits doesn't do much for me."

"Then that is how we will start, very slowly, and when we are done we will go to the pool and I will present you to the other girls. We are ten including you. They are all nice, you will like them." She tapped the side of the bed. "Come, take off your slip."

"No. I can't. Shit, I should be doing my shopping for the week, not stripping for you."

"You are not stripping for me, Lucy does. You are stripping for yourself and for your son." Monica let her robe fall open and to the floor as she stood. "Soon it will be easy for you, like it is for all of us. Please, come here and take off your slip. I will try to make you feel good." She paused for a moment. "If we do not do this, I will go away and that will be very bad for you and for Dree. She is your Anchor Girl and what they will do to you they will also do to her. I think you will like her very much. She is very pretty, very kind, and I do not want her to be hurt." Penelope remained still. "In one week you will be with a man on your first night with Dree, or maybe a woman, so you must be prepared. After the first week you will be alone and begin as a Courtesan Girl with one man or one woman each day, sometimes two and you must be very good because what we do is expensive and if you are not good Miss Divine could bring your son here or do something bad to you." Monica lay on the bed. "Please take off your slip and sit beside me. I do not want to be here either, and I will not make you feel bad."

315

Penelope eased a spaghetti strap over one shoulder, then over the other. She caught the slip at her waist, holding it there until she felt foolish standing with her torso bare when she had just confessed her collegial sins to a hooker who seemed quite comfortable lying naked on the bed with a pillow tucked under her breasts. She let it drop, taking her first step without tears, trying hard to escape into a mind that was struggling to dispel images of Frankie hovering over her and the lingering sensation of his weight crashing hard into her hips and thighs.

Her two-year-old son had been in the front seat with Bobby, waiting for his mother to finish whatever she was doing with the man. She had kicked out at first, her strenuous groans muffled behind his gloved hand, stopping abruptly when the impact of his fist knocked her head into the side window.

As he went about undoing her laces and pulling off her runners he explained she could scream when and if she felt the need. However, he added with a grin, she would never again feel her real teeth and her nose and her jaw would require post-coital work. Then she wouldn't be screaming for anyone for at least six months. When he pulled away her spandex shorts he whistled, calling to Bobby that he had been right the past couple of days. She was a smoothie who didn't like panty lines, and when he saw that he forgot about her top. They had 400 miles ahead of them and suddenly he didn't think the drive would be very long at all.

They had spent two days on-site, agreeing they were wise to drop their maximum range to a more reasonable radius and better selection of slimmer and prettier packages. Miss Divine could screw off. The north was disappointing in the extreme and they were right to make the move.

They spotted her mid-afternoon Tuesday. She was twenty, max, lithe and athletic. They first noticed her as she was running the full length of Riverboat Row along the south shore of the Ohio River in Cincinnati behind a florescent yellow sports stroller for better than a mile before the binoculars lost her image. Bobby took the bet, insisting none but real Southern women would think to do such a thing and Ohio was Union, not Southern. Forty minutes later she came into view, gauging her pulse, bending, stretching and smoothing her skin-tight spandex shorts as she was being photographed for a home library in Atlanta. She was the one, and they spent the next two days designing a strategy as they followed her.

She was a stay-at-home mom with one kid, a husband whom she didn't meet at the door each night and she stayed dressed that way for working in the garden and going for the mail sans kid. Wednesday she ran late morning, did the groceries in the afternoon. Thursday she was at the path for a mid-afternoon run. Friday they were counting on a morning run, when they would take her at her vehicle while she was bending, stretching and wanting passers-by to see more of her than she would see of them, or at her home before hubby's return from work. The first strategy would be the more expedient with less risk involved and she didn't let them down.

The color was different each day, not the material, nor the finer details of her curves and crevices he was seeing in the parking lot as she went through her performance and strapped in the kid.

"Ma'am let me get that for ya'll."

She came up with nonchalant ease from the folded stroller, enjoying every millisecond of the attention. She knew she was Grade A. She could tell his mouth was salivating as she stood an arm's length with nothing left for him to imagine other than whether or not. The first question was answered as he came up behind her; seeing her from the front he knew Bobby would lose the bet.

"Thank you. That's very kind of you."

"Sincerely a pleasure, ma'am. Just here waiting on the wife is all."

"You're not from around here?"

He smiled as he bent at the knees. "No ma'am, I'm not. I got a home down south. Thing is, the wife likes the fresh air ya'll got up here."

"Let me help you." She volunteered. "It's pretty awkward."

She bent down, thinking to lift from her side at the precise moment Bobby used her momentum to lunge her into the rear of her SUV. He closed the gate as Frankie clambered in, pinning her to the floor. The Acquisition took less than ten seconds, Bobby climbing behind the wheel and emptying her purse beside the sleeping boy, checking his watch as he drove away smelling the chloroform.

He would let Frankie off at the entrance, then walk to their van and trail him beyond the city limits where they would stop to check on the girl. In any event, Bobby had a spare vial and would simply pull to the side of the road for a few moments to quiet her if she woke.

By the time hubby arrived home from work in Friday traffic they would be in Atlanta with enough time to transfer the girl into the van, dispose of the SUV the usual way and enjoy a good dinner before shopping for a new outfit to dress her in. The fact she hadn't left home with a suitcase was moot, though such wouldn't be the case with Miss Divine who insisted all Acquisitions arrive at the hotel properly dressed and Frankie was anxious to watch her slip into her new panties and dress after he was done with the inspection.

Miss Divine would be inspecting her by ten or eleven. By 12:00 Bobby would be at the bar and Frankie would be transferring the best of his photos to disc as her child slept on a blanket by the door, ready for transfer to Savannah the following morning. But Penelope had no way of knowing that and by midnight when she fell asleep in the dark quiet of the vault with the pungent taste of raspberry on her lips, she wouldn't care.

The following evening was fleeting moments later, and when she opened her eyes the clinical austerity of her surroundings was even starker against the woman staring at her. She remembered the woman who was now dressed in a rich ivory long sleeve satin gown open in the front to her waist and from her waist open to the floor. Her arms were akimbo, her feet wide apart making the elegant embroidery of her deep mocha tap pants the focal point of her body.

She stood there, saying nothing, smiling until Penelope felt a coolness cup one breast, then the other, pinching softly, making both nipples come alive, making her shiver. She knew they were nice, her whole body was nice. She studied herself, seeing her bare stomach tighten as the woman's hand pressed gently into the firm tanned flesh until coming to rest at her lower abdomen.

She had to be living a dream. She remembered the pain in her vagina, now a mild tingling sensation, though her head throbbed and her arms were sore. The woman in her dream was talking. She was naked and shivering, but she wasn't cold and the woman was holding out a beautiful black and gold silk robe that felt so good against her skin. She was free to move and was being hugged without knowing why. Something her husband had asked her to do again and again and she had always said no. So why would she be with a woman for him now and where was he?

Her mouth was dry and the wine tasted good. She wanted more but the woman took away the glass, then returned it. She wasn't dizzy, more as though her skin was coming alive, and her mind, yet she didn't want to think. She heard, yet she didn't want to listen. She saw, not wanting to see. She heard herself giggle and the woman laughed with her, giving her more wine and she felt the black and gold silk fall away from her. She had no sense of time, just the feeling of warmth and ardent sensual kisses. So where was he, and why did she care if he didn't?

Monica was right. The sensations and touching weren't bad at all, albeit strange, and, as anxious as she was, she was becoming undeniably aroused as the intellectual gave way to the corporeal. The real fear would invade her senses later, when her bracelet, her obligation to the hotel, the concealed cameras and the fact she would not see her family for three years, if they still wanted her, would become all the more real.

The Madam

Seventy

As much as Miss Divine had her code of conduct which was strictly adhered to, the girls had their own which was equally stringent: Never talk badly about one girl to another, and Monica reported to Genevieve that, in her opinion, Penelope would do very well and be an asset to the hotel, which she believed.

Penelope didn't cry a single tear. As much as Monica thought that peculiar, contrary to how all the other girls first reacted to their forced internment, Penelope either didn't believe her or didn't mind. Though she might have, had she had known her child had already been adopted. When Monica peered into her eyes for tears that never welled, what she saw was a woman weighing her options, deciding between staying and leaving, but not at the hotel, as though she had finally found a way out.

William didn't visit with her on the Tuesday or Wednesday, and she worried about the possible outcome, though Cynthia did book her for Thursday. She liked Cynthia, but without William she doubted Miss Divine would allow her Preferred Girl status to remain in effect. Despite female guests being a significant source of revenue for the hotel, male guests were the overwhelming mainstay.

No one doubted Monica's contribution would surpass the million dollar mark if ever stripped of her rank, neither did she, but then she'd be no more than a receptacle for the release of sick minds and torrid fantasies. She would be a whore in her own eyes, though William never treated her as one. She could not lose William. Losing him would mean never having Manuel.

Late Friday she lounged alone in her tub dreaming of what he was doing, how he looked, who he might be with at that very moment, wondering whether he was a sergeant or a lieutenant, or an important chemical engineer in a big firm, and if he cried for her at all. She knew their daughter wasn't with him, that he would rather die than stop searching for her and little Sofia. Still, they had been apart so long and he was so young and handsome.

She jerked forward at the invasive news blurting from the intercom telling her William had called reserving her for Saturday, asking that dinner be prepared for 7:00 PM room service and that she dress in whatever she deemed appropriate for the occasion.

She eased again into the warm scented water, her smile turning to tears. She told him how she missed him, how she thought of him every day and prayed for him every night, how she missed him and loved him, how very sorry she would always be for disappointing him, hurting him because she didn't listen.

He was coming for her. She still believed in him, wondering where he was at that very moment, what he was thinking and seeing as she was seeing the mirrored image of a glistening, tanned and lean body, wondering if he would still know her or love her.

She was relieved William was coming, relieved for herself and Manuel. She was happy William forgave her for treating him badly that awful Saturday. But she wanted only one man at the moment, who wasn't William, and she climbed into bed to be with him.

Seventy-One

William walked through the door with a dozen red carnations in his arm and a thin smile he fixed in place before putting his hand to the exquisitely designed dual knobs, nervous until he saw the exotic vision coming towards him. Monica was smiling the same way, no less nervous until she saw the flowers.

He was familiar with all the words, all the terms and all the fabrics. The girls liked him, they enjoyed his admiring glances. His compliments were sincere and they got into the habit of describing their ensembles to him in detail, quite amazed when he began telling them. She was wearing a black bubble dress that was décolleté to a velveteen bow and empire waist. Her nylons were dark, her shoes simple patent leather ankle strap sandals, and her hair was pulled into a tight Latin bun: a perfect entrée to a gourmet dinner and he was certain dessert would be equally delightful.

"You're absolutely heavenly, Monica." He proffered the long-stem flowers. "Ordinary flowers for an extraordinarily beautiful woman. I trust I have stayed away sufficiently long for you to forgive my appalling conduct of two weeks ago. I should not have come that day and you, I'm afraid, bore the brunt of my dark mood."

"Bill your gift is wonderful. What woman would not want such beautiful flowers? But you forget I am Mexican and my English is poor. You are speaking very funnily."

He threw his head back, laughing. "Then you forgive me."

"How do I know? You have used words I have not yet studied." She took the flowers. "But yes, I forgive you for whatever you said. You can tell me later. First, you must forgive me. Saturday I was not myself and I am very sorry, but now I am alright and I will not make you feel bad again."

He poured a scotch. "You never make me feel anything but wonderful."

"Yes, because you were not the same man."

He chortled. "Monica that man was me… is me. That is who I am. What you see before you is the man I want to be, the man you let me be; not the other person who so often haunts me throughout my days and nights."

"I know most of the words you are saying, but I have many to investigate in my dictionary tomorrow. If you want to be the man I see, then you must be that man. Who will stop you?"

He ignored the question. "You are simply beautiful this evening, a gift for my eyes and I thank you for being so lovely, so forgiving." He sipped his scotch. "I thought we would dine first this evening, before relaxing."

"Our dinner will arrive very soon, Bill, at seven, but if you want a bath first I can ask them to wait."

He studied her, smiling approvingly, telling her again how lovely she was. "No, though I believe that is precisely what the doctor ordered." Her brow furrowed, and he chuckled. "I meant to say I believe it's just what I need, not to mention I'm impatient to see what your charming cocktail dress is concealing from me, but that will come later. For the time being I'll enjoy you as you are and perhaps another of these, if I may."

The imagined ice wall between them had melted, the uninterrupted music she ordered permeated her suite and they danced, neither one feeling the need to speak. She was a perfect companion. She always was, always laying her head gently upon his chest as they danced. He was the consummate lead, guiding her every move as always across the floor with one hand opened lightly against the soft curve of her back, pressing her into him, the other letting her open palm rest upon it. He loved her, and she loved him, each one knowing in their separate worlds there was no pain in remembering. The pain was in remembering alone.

Kelly and Katrina knocked at the door discreetly at 7:00, and wheeled in dinner. Kelly uncorked the Grand Cru Classé and poured a probationary ounce into William's crystal goblet. Katrina arranged the intimate table setting as he lifted the ornate silver domes, inspecting the simple two-course delicacies as Kelly placed a decanter of Rémy Martin VSOP on the mantel of the electric fireplace.

He waited until Kelly placed the cork by the side of his bread plate, taking up the goblet to swirl it under the muted lighting. Both Duty Girls acknowledged Monica with secret winks and silent teasing kisses while William's eyes studied the color. His nose approved the bouquet, his tongue identified the complex relationship of acid levels, fullness and flavor until his smiling face nodded his contented approval.

He allowed the girls to serve the beef consommé garnished with parsley and sliced shallots before dismissing them. They left holding hands, swinging their arms as William raised his goblet to his hostess and commented on how difficult it was for a man to concentrate on requisite formalities when everyone about him was blinking out secret messages and blowing each other kisses, however tantalizing the scene might be.

She agreed, pouting. They were terrible. She would reprimand them in the morning, though she said she would 'schooled' them in the morning. Over the past months his ear had reluctantly acclimated to her idiomatic slant on the nation's already damaged language, though there were times when his eyebrows raised involuntarily to make her frown. This was one of those times and she told him instead that she would spank each of them very punishably.

He agreed, she should, chuckling as he moved his seat to clear away the soup bowls, suggesting she pour more wine. He admired the succulent filet mignons au jus and baby baked potatoes with glazed green and yellow beans adorning their plates, asking her to make certain she complimented the chef on his behalf. She promised she would as she dabbed the corners of her lips glossed in deep-prune.

He served her. She poured more wine. The entrée was delicious, truly superb, and melted in his mouth. The meal was heavenly; he was with a beautiful seraph from that exact location and life could be a good deal worse. There was no dessert served and none was needed. The dessert he wanted was on the mantel and under her dress, anxious for one and eagerly anticipating the other. After dinner she poured two cognacs, which was rare. Enjoying cocktails was allowed in moderation when Preferred Guests were in-house and she didn't want to provoke the Prefect who might be watching. She felt better about herself and she placed him comfortably onto her sofa before leaving him to run their bath. When she returned he was standing.

"I adore your accent, Monica. I do not intend to be rude when I sometimes show my surprise. Your English is excellent."

"Thank you, Bill. You are very kind. I suppose one day I will lose my accent and speak with a Southern drool also."

He caught himself. "I would hope not, Monica. How we speak is an important part of who we are, a link to our past and our culture." He sipped his cognac approvingly, "which should be very important to all of us. Without your accent you would not be the same person, and I suggest you would soon forget who you once were, which you should never allow to happen. There will be many occasions and opportunities in your life to lose what you love in ways you have no control over. Do not be so quick to volunteer the loss. Do not give up so readily that which is yours to cherish and preserve."

Madre de Dios, she thought, what was he saying? She attempted a smile. "What you say is true, Bill. I know what I have in my heart and it is secret. I will always preserve what is inside me, and I know in your heart you have secrets, also. Who does not?"

"Indeed, who does not?" He emptied his snifter.

"Maybe now I will teach you some Spanish words the way you help me with my English while you pretend that you are not. Why do we not start with su baño está listo?"

He chortled. "My bath is next on the list?"

She shrugged. The comprehension was close enough. "Yes."

She put her glass aside, stepping into the middle of the dimly lit suite, ignoring him as he sank into the plush recliner, and as she raised an arm to pull at the invisible side zipper of her dress that opened to her waist. She pushed one strap down, followed by the other, letting the top cascade over the bubble skirt and onto the floor around her two-inch suede pumps. She stepped to the side, letting him admire her.

She knew what he enjoyed, what he saw as natural beauty. She worked hard at countering the effects of a primarily sedentary lifestyle, keeping her body toned and feminine without becoming chiseled and hard. She was the epitome of sensuality and far from hard. She reached behind with one hand, unhooking her strapless black lace bra with cerise bows as she cupped her breasts with the other to prevent it from falling as she turned away from him and bent from the waist. She let it fall to the center of her crumpled dress and straightened as her fingers spread apart, their tips pressing into the taut flesh of her buttocks as their natural roundness returned. She raised one heel from the floor, releasing first the cerise ribbon from the front of her stockings, the second from the side. She raised the other heel until all four ribbons dangled against the soft bareness of her thighs as she toyed with the clasps of her garter, turning inches at a time as each tiny hook came undone and she let it fall away, watching his eyes unlock their gaze from her bare buttocks to take in the fullness of her exotically bare breasts.

She stared into space as she unleashed her hair into a lustrous explosion of chocolate brown curls. She smiled seductively at seeing his appreciation, feeling sadness for him as she brought her hands from the nape of her neck to her breasts where she lingered to titillate him, and from her breasts to the smooth curves of her hips.

Her matching satin bikini was tied at the sides with ribbons, William bracing himself for the exotic tug of war as she came towards him, his eyes lingering at her breasts. He wanted to pull her onto him. He wanted to fondle and kiss her perfect breasts, to savor the sensation of massaging and probing the roundness of her buttocks. He didn't, already hypnotized by her small hands playing with the ribbons that kept her from being completely naked beside him.

What was he doing with a girl half his age, a young woman who should be dancing with her friends or making love with someone who truly loved her, not stripping for him because he could afford the quarter-million each year? And what were the secrets in her heart, and why should he wonder? He would never know because he would never ask her. She had her own reasons for being there, as he did.

One of the delicate bows broke away, her fingers

quickly winding their way around the ribbon leading to the tiny front panel that barely covered the quintessential essence of femininity. His eyes went obediently to her other side, waiting as she stood there in complete control, the slender ribbons coming apart with cruel deliberateness as she paused with equally cruel delight before tugging her panties from side to side as the tiny V stayed precariously in place. He looked up at her and she acquiesced with a single nod, parting her legs for him to ease his forefinger behind the satin shield and pull it away.

She stood in front of him, naked, leaning forward, feeling the light pressure of his steady hands on her hips and the heat of his lips on her buttocks as she moved first one leg to the side then the other.

His hands moved, covering the apex of her inner thighs, enjoying her smoothness and her warmth. She was intoxicating, worth every penny, and he wondered who cared or worried that she was with him as he pushed one stocking to her ankles, then the other before letting her ease onto him to kick off her shoes and pull away each stocking by the cerise-on-black lacing.

He asked for another cognac, though more than his third digestif he wanted to see her walk away. He loved seeing her in the nude. She was perfect, a precious gem amongst women, albeit much more expensive, and if the thought of doing nothing more were not so perverse, seeing her would probably have been enough for him since whenever.

How many diamonds could he have bought her with the three million he'd spent over the past years, how many vacations and how many special evenings with dancing and gentle kisses from someone who once loved him so deeply?

He waited, letting Monica enjoy her time alone. She never called him and she never would. When he joined her she smiled. She tapped the water with her opened palms and he eased in behind her, holding her close.

When next he opened his eyes she was gone and he took his time to towel off and cloak himself in a freshly laundered robe before walking into the bedroom area of the suite where she was sleeping soundly. He wasn't driving, so why the hell not? He poured a fourth, two fingers deep, and sat on the bed beside her until he was tempted to pour a fifth.

Instead he dressed quietly and went home.

Seventy-Two

Sunday, June 10

"My skin is dancing Lucy, and pricking me. Thank you for a very perfect bath."

"Prickling, little girl, prickling; a prick is something else. Your skin is prickling."

Monica sighed. "One day I will understand all these words, Lucy. I am trying very hard, but I miss my own Spanish which is so beautiful, like you."

"We're all ugly ducklings beside you, little girl. I can't imagine not being with you each day."

"But this day will come, chica, and I will miss you very much. But you will also be with your family once again and you will be happy. Believe me, when you are in the hot arms of your husband you will not think of me... and you should not."

"That's stupid talk. I'll never forget you, not ever, and you mean warm arms, not hot arms."

"Latin arms are hot. Warm arms are not my fault, white girl."

"Bitch." She slipped her arms around Monica's waist and squeezed. "I love you."

"I know you do, but they will take you from me very soon. I want to be happy for you, and I am. Also I am sorry for myself at the same time because I will not have you to cry with and laugh with."

She squeezed Lucy just as hard, kissing her, inhaling the sweet air around her as their naked bodies fused. Their lips parted reluctantly, the pillow under them wet with melded and salted tears.

"I'm afraid for you, little girl. Miss Divine is angry with you because you refused to be with Genevieve until I left, and that bitch Prefect is being horrible towards you because she's tired of Stephanie and can't get her wrinkled hands on these perky things."

"I do not like her, and never will she touch me anywhere. I know she wants me very much. She is always following me with her eyes and I know she is watching me when I am with Cynthia, if Miss Divine is not here."

"It will be better after she invites you to her floor again, which won't be long. She likes you."

"Yes, and she wants to scare me while she is playing with Penelope. I do not like Penelope. I believe she is a real whore, not like the other Courtesan Girls. I believe it is fine with her that she is here."

"Dree seems to like her, but I can tell she's lonely. Penelope doesn't want to be with her this way. She says Penelope doesn't mind being with Miss Divine, but when she's with a woman guest she isn't very good."

"Dree will leave here after you, Lucy. She will not have long to wait and I know she still dreams of Daphne. She will be very fine without the whore until then. Also, if the whore is not good with women she must work very hard with more men so Miss Divine will not hurt her. Or she must be a Preferred Girl which is not possible. So very soon Miss Divine will want more than a long tongue to kiss her sad chica."

"So I guess I don't have to be jealous after I leave."

"She is always admiring herself and in the gym she is always touching herself like she is a shirt that is not ironed.

Also, when I had to kiss her, her lips were like stone. Men will like her because they will not see over her neck. The preferred men are different and the women will complain about her. I do not like her."

"Gee, take a breath." Lucy squeezed her. "I'll miss you, too. So take a pill."

"My head is not hurting."

"Little girl I will never forget you. I will dream of you, too, and I will remember you for the rest of my life. If he wants me, whoever he is, he will understand how I feel about you. Maybe one day we will see each other again."

"Your husband will want you, chica. He is not with another. Believe what I say and believe in him. Who would forget you, ever?"

"Kiss me again. I want to kiss you a lot because we will never know when, will we? We never do."

"No we will not." They kissed. "Please, Lucy, stay close to me and listen. If I make you afraid you will tell me, and I will stop."

Lucy giggled and whispered: "Stop what, little girl? Do you have another dirty little secret for me?"

"Yes, I do. Listen very well to what I will tell you now." Monica pulled the duvet to their eyes. "Lucy, I am Mercedes Del Fuego. My husband is Manuel Del Fuego and once we lived in East Point, Georgia. I believe my husband is not dead and his phone number is 706-555-0512."

"My God, Monica," Lucy whispered, "you're Mexican?" Monica tented the blankets over them enough to smack her bum, deciding to pinch the soft flesh instead until her confidante gave in with a kiss and more. "Mercedes is a beautiful name and I remember from the first time you told me. Manuel must be a strong man to deal with such a bitch. I promise you, if he is anywhere to be found in this world, little girl, I will find him for you and I will begin in East Point. Finding him will be the second thing I do, and if I no longer have a husband to love me the way Manuel loves you it will be the only thing I do."

"Thank you."

"Thank me one more time and I will hate you. What does Mercedes mean? It's so pretty."

"It means mercy and to give thanks. When my mother was pushing so hard to make me come out from her she was in much pain. She was screaming 'merced' so many times and so loud that my father called me Mercedes when he saw my little head. Never did they tell me if she was saying thank you to God or asking for his mercy." She sighed. "Now it means for me what I have so much trouble to believe."

"Would we have been friends, do you think, away from here?"

"Yes, Lucy, we would be good friends. And when we see ourselves outside, when I am free also, I will have a special name for you, but I do not know what it will be."

"Now you're the one talking funny."

Monica kissed her, not counting the times their lips lightly touched. "You call me little girl, I call you Lucy. That is what I mean. I have no special name for you."

Lucy stroked her hair, letting her fingers luxuriate in its fullness. "No one calls me Lucy the way you do. You make my name sound like music, sweet music, like no one else ever has. I love when you use my name, I love you and I love being with you. Believe me, Mercedes. If I don't find Manuel, it's because I'm dead."

"Do not speak in such a way or I will hate you."

There was a silence between them, each one luxuriating in the heat of the other's body.

"I'm sorry. Forgive me." Lucy brought a hand away from the bare warmth of Monica's back, covering her cheek. "We will never speak about this again, Monica. I know and will never forget. If I can bring him to you, I will.

I promise." She pinched and wriggled Monica's nose, "because I can never be without my best friend ever."

"I love you, Lucy, but not the same way as I love him. Do you think my Manuel will be angry with me for loving you?"

"He's a man. No, I do not think so."

"But he is a very proud man."

"He's a man, case closed. I loved Alice, Monica, or I thought I did, but not this way. Do you think she's alright?"

"Yes, I do. We must."

"I know, but I'm scared. I'm scared of what will happen to me when I leave. I'm afraid he won't want me because of what I've done and I'm afraid he really did marry someone else and won't want me at all."

"You are not listening to me, chica. He will be there for you, and if he is not, when I am free to leave here, I will find him and I will cut his neck."

Lucy giggled. Monica always made her giggle. "Throat, you will cut his throat, not his neck."

"What does it matter, chica, as long as he will suffer for not loving you? I am Latina. We can kill any man for very much less."

"Come closer, little girl. Promise me that for as long as I am here we will be together."

"You know it, girl."

And they giggled themselves into separate dreams.

Seventy-Three

July 04,
Atlanta, Georgia

The day would have been a bigger deal if he hadn't spent his first year in America as a third class citizen, if his wife hadn't cleaned toilets instead of working in an art gallery or design house. Or if he hadn't killed so many men in the name of oil only to come home to discover his wife had been raped and kidnapped. Now he had some drunken brain-dead fuck-up in his rear seat talking about how they should let Mexicans in to work, not the real dark-skinned ones because then who would know they were real Mexicans. Anyway, everyone knew Blacks refused perfectly good jobs every day that the Mexicans could do, and probably a whole lot better and cheaper.

Manuel stopped the meter and he pulled over. He stepped from the car and opened the door for the man who thought he had arrived at his destination. He left the car running, propping the man against the rear bumper rather than letting him possibly hurt himself by falling onto the sidewalk. He wished the man Happy July 04th, stabilized him before climbing in behind the wheel, and ever so slightly depressed the accelerator pedal as he took a few moments to fill in the details of his passenger report. No problema. He'd pay the fare himself. When he did drive away, what he saw through his rearview mirror was a man vomiting between his knees.

Neither was July 04th a big deal for Juan Carlos whose crowded workweek was seldom less than seven days and seldom allowed for holidays, unless his friend was in town. The day, however, was important for Carmella whose restaurant had been filled to capacity since dinnertime the previous evening and would be through to closing time on the fourth. She worked tirelessly, taking time to welcome each patron and drop-in alike whether American, Cuban, Mexican or anyone else. They all loved her and she took none of them for granted.

Juan Carlos had begun calling her mommy, which she ignored, and Sofia was calling her Lita, which she thought was perfectly fine. Each night before bed Lita would call Atlanta to let Sofia speak with the man she would call papá each time Lita pointed to his photograph by the bed. He would be with her in three days, but she didn't know that. All she knew was that Lita loved her and the really big one who threw her into the air made her feel good and she giggled each time Lita took her away from him. She liked playing at the beach, watching the water stop and sometimes being with others like her: small ones she could not understand any more than the big ones. She remembered the man she called papá each night before Lita took her into her arms, forgetting him as she went to sleep, remembering him when he came to see her, forgetting him when he went away without knowing she should care, so she didn't. But that would soon change.

Sofia still needed the light, she would for some time. However that night before she closed her eyes Carmella helped her to tell him what she had practiced so hard since Monday: a simple "tamo, papá" which meant nothing to anyone and everything to her papá. The first time Manuel heard her say that she loved him. But there was a shadow behind his happiness and Carmella put him on hold without saying more. The next voice he heard was Juan Carlos'.

"Amigo, ¿qué tal?"

"I have eight weeks left, amigo. I am thinking that I should tell Bishops I need more time, that maybe I should leave the Corps."

JC covered the phone, taking a deep breath. "Mercedes has not gone through this past year so that she can brag of her taxi-driver husband. You are a Marine, and a good one, the best one. If you let her down, you disappoint all of us. So what is all this bullshit?"

"It has been one year, JC. How can she have survived one year? Sometimes at night I wake up screaming because I see only the sorrow in her eyes. In my dreams she is dead and she asks me why I cannot come to her because I am so close…but I do not see her and she does not understand why. She asks me how I found our daughter, but that I cannot find her. She is afraid, JC. I know she is very afraid and I am useless to her."

"That is why you must not be afraid, amigo. You must be strong for her each day, more than ever, and you will not be useless to her until you stop."

"I know you are right… and Carmelita also. I know."

"I am not a religious man, Manny. Church doors flicker with sparks when I pass in front of them. But I do know that if Mercedes were as you see her each night in your dreams you would feel it also each day in your heart. She lives, amigo. She lives to see your daughter, and she waits for us."

Manuel cleared his throat. "I will see the three of you on Saturday. Thank you, JC."

"Manny."

"Sí."

He lowered his voice. "Tonight you will have one for me. I will tell the mother hen nothing."

"I will do that, amigo… for you."

"There is one more thing, Manny. I feel I should now be with you in Atlanta."

"No, amigo. The time will come when I need you here. The timing is not right. Tell Carmelita I thank her for caring, as usual."

"I will, amigo. Adios."

When Juan Carlos closed the line Carmella was in the doorway. He had nothing to say, no reason to smile. Instead he opened his arms to comfort her.

Seventy-Four

Thursday morning Manuel renewed the photo file for the drivers at the garage who continued to support him. He passed them out to motorists at red lights, squeegees and pedestrians at street corners, and asked businesses if he could replace either yellowed photos of Mercedes or place them in the windows of businesses which had previously refused him. This time no one refused him.

He drove his double shifts as usual, taking no breaks accept when he would stop at coffee shops to pass out even more photos. By Friday at noon he wondered whether he would have the energy for the drive to Miami. He would. In Sofia was Mercedes, and he needed both of them.

He didn't hear the rear door open. The door slamming shut ended his reverie. He never looked at a fare until the end. Not seeing their faces was easier than repeatedly judging his passengers by first impressions as to whether or not the person sitting behind him would be the one to help. He left that for the end of the fare when he would or wouldn't see her photograph and his business card lying at different angles on the seat.

"Good afternoon, sir. Where to, sir?"

"The Georgia World Congress Center, and please hurry. I'm already very late."

"Yes, sir," he answered.

Manuel felt compelled to see the man. He might well have imagined the man wearing a captain's or colonel's uniform, but he wasn't. Manuel's view of him in the rearview mirror was passport-size. The man was impeccably dressed, judging by the knot in his tie and the cut of his suit jacket around his shoulders; important, judging by the way he sat; and preoccupied, judging by the way he stared beyond the window without moving his eyes. He wouldn't appreciate having his concentration broken for a banal conversation with a common taxi driver. The man was somewhere else and the world around him was locked out.

He didn't care. At the first red light Manuel twisted in his seat. "Sir, beg your pardon, sir. Have you seen my wife?" He reached over the seat, dropping the 8 X 10 photo into the man's lap. "This photograph is two years old, sir. Her name is Mercedes. She doesn't speak English well, sir. Could be you've seen her somewhere, in a hotel or restaurant, maybe walking somewhere, and not just here in Atlanta. She could be anywhere, sir. I've been searching for a year, sir. I've got just got a couple of months left and I haven't done a very good job finding her so far, sir."

He turned at the sound of three horns behind him.

The man had ignored the photo throughout the entire emotive dissertation. "You say 'sir' quite a lot, young man. Have you recently left the military?"

"No, sir. I'm a United States Marine, sir."

"So, you're a week-end soldier?"

The eyes in the rearview mirror were piercing. "That's a negative, sir. I'm regular forces. I did nine months in Iraq as a sniper with a hundred hits on one hundred with zero misses, sir. When they shipped me home a year ago my wife was gone. I got compassionate leave so I could find her, that's why I'm driving. It's been a year now and I'm running out of time, sir. Like I said, I have a couple of

341

months left, but I won't stop till I find her. Right now I do a weekend a month, reservist stuff. But it's temporary. If I don't find her soon, I still have to report to finish my time, sir. Then I'll search for her on my time off."

"Why did she leave you? One year is a long time in our lives."

"She didn't leave me, sir. She was kidnapped from our home along with our little daughter, sir. They raped her before they took her. "

The voice was even, unperturbed. "Surely the police have told you the chances are very slim after such a long time."

"They have, sir, too many times. The good news is I got my little girl back last month. She doesn't know me right now, but that'll change pretty soon. She's with good friends, she's getting to know me a bit at a time, and the Corps's been real good about the whole ordeal. The ladies sent me a bunch of clothes and toys for my girl. I don't even know what half the stuff is, though I guess that doesn't matter."

"Your wife is very beautiful, young man. I hope she remains safe until you find her."

"Yes, sir, thank you. I won't stop searching for her." He pulled a card from his pocket, passing it to the man without turning. "Sir, keep the photo if you want. I've got hundreds. This is my card. Please call me if you see her."

The man accepted the card. "I certainly will, young man. Thank you, and good luck with your search."

"Thank you, sir. Thank you. Sorry the traffic's so bad. There's probably a cop somewhere up ahead directing."

"Indeed."

The one word sounded flustered. Reminded of his lateness, the man's eyes began alternating once again between his watch and the window. The Congress Center was three or four minutes on foot through the Centennial

The Madam

Olympic Park, at least ten in the heavier than usual noonday traffic. He dropped a crisp fifty over the front seat, not waiting for change or a full stop before jumping out and sprinting into the noonday crowd. By the time Manuel turned to argue the excessive tip the man had disappeared.

Seeing the photo in the middle of the seat Manuel shook his head, disappointed, though not surprised. The man did seem genuinely concerned, but most of them left the photo behind. What the others did with them he tried not to think about. He no longer swore or cursed them, doing so made him feel worse by day's end and did nothing to shake them up or make them more caring. He reached for the photo as he would a precious parchment, placing it onto the seat beside him so that she would see him and know that he hadn't given up hope. He was ready for the next passenger.

Nearing the end of his fourteen-hour day he was exhausted, ready for the bare walls of his tiny furnished apartment and what had become a sad nighttime ritual of training for two hours, a limit of two double vodkas, Carmelita's care package that now replaced his frozen dinners and the same sleepless dream.

She was the last fare, and then he was going home. Making certain the senior blue-haired lady was securely ensconced in the backseat he drove off, assuring her he would take the most direct route and drive safely, acknowledging again that she knew the city streets as well as he did.

He had no idea what he would say, or whether he should say anything. Usually the older ones sat held in place and talked to themselves, or when there was more than one they talked about someone who wasn't with them, dead or alive. This one sat quietly gazing at the city lights as though for the first time or the last, often disappearing from his mirror when he turned corners.

He had spent so many months asking people about

Mercedes, never telling them about her because he knew they would half-listen and forget. He did that evening because he wanted to hear about her, the old woman politely listening to the monologue as she rocked side to side, in and out of the mirror, occasionally interjecting an "oh my" or "oh dear", and he wondered what the hell he was doing to the point where he snorted. He was talking to himself, but he had given everyone else a picture of Mercedes, so why not the old lady?

When they arrived he twisted in his seat, smiling at the bent over diminutive body that was reciting a monologue of her own as she searched for the seatbelt release.

"Ma'am, don't worry. I'm coming to help you, but first I'd like to give a picture of my wife, and my card. If you see her, ma'am, maybe here or somewhere you go, could you call me?" He smiled widely, being sincere. "Yes, ma'am, I've shut off the meter."

He was such a polite young man. Wasn't it such a shame there were so few left? More's the pity, and she would prefer being dropped off over there instead of where they were, thanking him for such a pleasant drive as she put his card in her purse along with the folded semi-gloss print. She wished him a pleasant evening as he helped her out, telling him to go straight home and be with his family. Life passed us by too quickly not to be at home with one's family. His wife must be so lovely to have chosen such a nice young man and he should be with her instead of driving an old lady all over town. Money was not everything in life, didn't he know?

He agreed, forcing a smile, thanking her for rounding off the nine-eighty to ten dollars. Walking her to the door he asked if she would be alright, knowing full-well she'd be puzzled days later by the unfamiliar picture in her purse, trying to remember who else she had forgotten. He watched her walk away and he stayed a few moments longer to make sure he'd taken her to the right address. When no one brought her out he drove away, ready for a workout, a hot shower and his first double. He always ate dinner standing by the kitchen sink, his version of time and utility management, often eating straight from the pan or one of his two microwavable dishes.

He was on his second vodka, willing himself to stay awake a few moments longer when his cell phone chimed at five past midnight. The caller was unknown. He glanced at his watch and pressed SEND.

"This is Manny."

"Good evening, this is Miss Georgina Collins and I wish to speak with Mr. Manny, the taxi driver."

"This is Manny. Who am I speaking with?"

"Are you the nice cab driver from earlier this evening, the nice gentleman who brought me home and gave me the picture of the beautiful young Mexican lady who is lost?"

"Yes, ma'am, that's me."

There was a long pause, broken by muffled rustling sounds through the phone. "Then let me get my glasses. I'll be right back."

Manuel bolted upright, remembering her voice. He drained the glass, reaching for the nearby bottle, pouring a healthy shot. She was the old lady with blue hair.

"Hello?"

"Yes, ma'am, I'm here."

"Is this Mr. Manny, the taxi driver?"

"Yes, ma'am, it's me. Please, what is it?"

"Well, it's your picture, Mr. Manny, the one of the beautiful lady, or rather what is on the back of the picture. I don't know. I believe it might be important. I really don't know."

"Ma'am, please, what's on the picture? What are you're trying to tell me, Miss Collins?"

"There is writing, Mr. Manny, a note of sorts."

The vodka splashed loudly around his mouth. "What does the writing say, ma'am?"

"Please don't be impatient with me, Mr. Manny. Am I interrupting your dinner? Time doesn't mean very much to me anymore."

"No, ma'am, you're not. I'm not impatient with you and I thank you for calling. But, ma'am, please, the note. What does it say?"

"Let me sit down, Mr. Manny. The writing is quite poor, very poor indeed and certainly not the penmanship of my former students. My eyes aren't much better, I'm afraid. I haven't read much in years."

"Ma'am, Miss Collins, what does the note say?"

A slight pause followed before Georgina Collins began hesitantly. "I don't want to make a mistake, Mr. Manny. Please be patient with me. The note says: Yes, I have indeed seen your wife. I know her as Monica and she is well."

The empty glass dropped to the stained and threadbare carpet. It didn't matter. There was more.

Seventy-Five

Once he produced the four pieces of ID and told his story, the nursing staff at the senior's home let him stay. They offered him a cot in the infirmary and promised to wake him before Miss Georgina came down for the first breakfast sitting, but he couldn't sleep and spent the night in the lobby playing cards and drinking coffee with the security guard.

The cheerful guard had duly warned him, but his own parents whom he hadn't seen for so long were still in their fifties and light years from the world of Miss Georgina. When she finally came down, precisely at 06:59 AM, as promised, she was delighted to have such a handsome young guest for breakfast, after the nursing staff reminded her of the nice gentleman from the night before and the writing on the picture.

Their breakfast finished at 7:30. He waved to everyone in the restaurant she pointed out and graciously accepted an invitation to her room, fully understanding the need for the guard to accompany someone who was neither friend nor family.

The room was small, with a bathroom no bigger than a stall and not at all private. The linoleum floor was squared in black and white; the chipped walls were pale beige, liberally accented with smudges and fingerprints and decorated with rows of faded Christmas cards hanging from sagging bridges of once-white strings. Her bed resembled a theatre prop, part of a dungeon from the Middle Ages in a cell with one window, one ceiling fan, a blaring television and no balcony.

The motif was 50's shambles, yet to Miss Collins the little cubicle was home and what she thought of as an artistic nature morte on her coffee table was a wicker basket of yellow bananas with spotted bananas, and brown bananas with bananas that were once brown, now a textured shade of bluish green.

The guard had seen the same expression on so many faces. Being old was sad, he agreed, assuring Manuel in Spanish that she would soon forget him and that he shouldn't feel guilty leaving. The longer he stayed the more difficult leaving would be. She had a good life and good friends at the home. Just don't ever get old, hombre.

"Good-bye, Mr. Manny, and thank you for your lovely visit."

"Miss Georgina, I will never be able to repay you for this."

"Repay me for what, Mr. Manny? You were my guest. It is I who should thank you for coming to see me," she seemed puzzled, "though I would so enjoy meeting your wife, Mr. Manny. Perhaps you can come for coffee next week and bring her with you. That would be so lovely."

"Yes, ma'am, I will. When I find her, I will. You have helped me very much. Thank you. I would be proud to introduce her to you." He hugged her frail body. "One day I will."

Seventy-Six

He called Juan Carlos' cell at 08:10 Saturday with the news, with no idea of what he would say. He should have been driving to Miami and didn't want JC thinking he was calling again to whine or ask for help because his worthless antique had broken down. Juan Carlos listened calmly, watching Carmella and Sofia playing together at the foot of the stairs leading to their private beach entrance. When her peripheral vision caught him bolting from them, and the urgency of his step, she stood and swept the giggling little girl into her arms.

He would explain the news to Carmella, he promised Manuel, and he would arrive in Atlanta by late evening. He was set to go. Manuel could speak with her and Sofia by phone on Sunday, after the two of them had time to talk and formulate the next phase. Carmella had a disturbing way of making unwary men say things they didn't mean to say, he explained to Manuel, or what they didn't want to say. That's why she was still single, not her enviable beauty or her cooking, and at the moment he was no match for her skills at twisting and conniving to extract the truth.
*

"You are truly a mystical woman, Carmelita. Must you be everywhere at once? Can a man never have privacy from you?"

"That was Manny," she said.

"Yes."

"Something has happened, Juanito. He is not coming."

"No, Carmelita, he is not. Instead I will join him. I will be gone by noon. I do not know when I will see you next."

"What has happened, Juanito? Is he hurt?"

He faced away from her, reading from the leather-bound notebook he'd been unlocking when she walked in.

"No, he is not hurt. I would not lie to you about such a thing."

"Then what has happened?"

"Nothing I wish to discuss, cousin, not at this moment."

"He has found Mercedes. He knows where she is."

"No, he does not." JC looked up. "He will speak with you and Sofia tomorrow. By then we may know more. Right now you will help me by closing my door and asking the kitchen to prepare a light lunch for me. I have much to do, and do not interrupt me until I call you." She turned swiftly, furious with him, her black eyes flaring. "Carmelita, momentito." He came out from behind his desk. "Here is the key to my desk. Inside are instructions with what to do with another key. Do not use either unless you know without question that I will not return to annoy you."

Her expression was the one he remembered from the day he shipped out to Iraq. "He has found her, has he not, Juanito? He has found her."

"No, cousin, he has not, and I swear that what I say is the truth. Though Mercedes may have found him and not yet know."

She shook her head, not understanding.

"That is all you get from me, you black-eyed witch." He wiped his thumbs across her eyes. "Work your black magic to keep us safe, Carmelita. I do not want to miss any occasion to warn any of those nervous puppies who come wagging their tails around you about your sinister ways."

"So you do scare all of them away. I have always

ींकी,

known."

"Not just any man is a match for one such as you, chica. You will settle for nothing less than a stallion to mount, not some homeless dog with fleas to take for a walk along the beach. That is why you have me."

He whirled her around, smacking her hard on the tight seat of her cuffed trouser shorts, making her wince and flail, putting her three feet closer to the door.

"Because of you I will be an old spinster woman, you stupid man. It is good that you are going. I will be married before you come back to me."

He laughed heartily. "Then, cousin, before I leave I shall warn all the men in town who cannot see or hear."

She let herself go limp against the doorway, digging her hands into her pockets "Juanito…"

"I have no more time for you, Carmelita. Pray for us, that is all I ask. I will call you each night without fail. I promise you. Now leave me before I say something stupid like I will miss you until I return, or that I need you more than my own heart," he grinned, "albeit not as much as you need me."

"Return safely to me, Juanito, and bring me a new friend."

"I will always return safely to you, chica. You leave me no choice, until you have enough money saved from this failing diner to bribe a man of your own." He guided her gently through the portal. "I promise that I will come back to you…as soon as you let me leave."
*

The afternoon was bright, airless and humid. The mercury showed 95°F, the index a suffocating 118. The girls had done their gym time in the morning and were playing bumper floats in the pool. Even Stephanie decided to let her Prefect hair down and join them, from afar, spending most of her time talking with Penelope while the farthest cannonball was won by Amanda. The splashiest belly flop was Kelley's, Dree swimming away after the best reverse flip. Then they vied to win the best Women Warriors of the Tug, Pushing Piggyback Pussies and Wrap-Your-Thighs-Around-My-Neck Jousting, Penelope refusing to join in. So rather than Dree sitting out they formed four rotating teams of two.

Dree came through again with Katrina in the tug of war. Melanie and Jennifer took the PPP. And Lucy wrapped her thighs around Amanda tightly enough to win honors. The spectacle was enough to crash any helicopter passing overhead, if they could see, what teenage boys dreamed of through to their adult years, what adult men prayed to see once before death took them to a lesser heaven. They were beautiful, tanned, tight, and buck-ass naked except for Penelope and Stephanie who sat talking in tiny triangles as Genevieve remained at the reception desk with the video surveillance toggle lever in her hand.

At 3:00 the Duty Girls were called in, at 4:00 the others followed and by five they were either lounging completely relaxed in their suites or in the lounge. Monica stayed in her suite and not because she was the only one who hadn't won any of the challenges, though she maintained vigorously the girls had worded the instructions to confuse her and, in fact, she had probably won all of them, which did win her a serious dunking.

William arrived at 6:00, informing her immediately that he would not stay long. "Monica I have a few items of interest to share with you, good things. Firstly, I have made arrangements with the hotel to continue here as a Preferred Guest for the coming twelve months, and, of course, you are a requisite part of that extension. Secondly, over the next several weeks, I regret to say, as much as I enjoy your company, I will be a less frequent guest. In addition, and over the short term, I will be unable to appreciate you as I have thus far."

"What is wrong, Bill? Your voice is different. Are you well?"

"I am very well. In point of fact I have recently been advised that I should be a little kinder to myself, indulge in fewer of these wonderful Glenmorangies and a bit more soda. Also, I would probably be wise to reduce the number of fine meals from your kitchen, as much as I do enjoy them; though I do not intend to deprive myself entirely. The condition is nothing serious and I seriously doubt such precautions are necessary. Conversely, you can now attempt to teach me your beautiful language, which I will undoubtedly destroy."

"That would be nice, Bill. Of course I will, after you must speak with a Prefect or Miss Divine for permission."

"They will do as I say, have no doubt of that. In the meantime, as much as I love seeing you this way, would you mind putting on a long silk robe so that I might better recognize an angel, should I be required to meet one in the all too near future. And when, young lady, will you learn to stay out of the sun?"

Monica's camisole and tap pant set was the purest white, her long robe a rich Mediterranean blue, a combined affect far more appealing than expected and the pounding of his heart had nothing to do with red meat, scotch or red wine.

"I cannot stay long, Monica. I simply wanted to visit with you before your day away from the hotel." He held up his empty glass. "Would you mind?"

"You know I do not mind. Would you like to lie down, to rest?"

"I would love nothing more; however, I'm afraid I cannot. Pour yourself something and sit with me."

She did, curling onto the sofa, covering her legs when he regarded them in a way she had not seen before.

"Bill, are you certain you are very well? Never before have you not wanted to see my legs or my bum." She smiled. "Is it because someone has told you I did not win any of the games at the pool today?"

"Games at the pool... just you girls?" She nodded, grinning, raising her eyebrows. "God, no. Then it's for the better I've come late or I most certainly would have died and stayed in heaven." He sipped the scotch. "But heaven is for angels, not for the likes of me."

"Heaven is for everyone, Bill."

"What you mean, Monica, is everyone like you." He swirled the scotch pensively. "As privileged as I have been in this life, that is one club which I am certain will never accept me into its esteemed membership." He had no idea about the gateway he was passing through. He was pragmatic, results-driven, unyielding and commanding. He had no friends who didn't have or want their hands in his pockets, he had no love because he had let his one love escape him so many years earlier, and he hadn't laughed in thirteen years. "Monica, I'm a lonely man. I shouldn't be, yet I am. May I tell you why?"

"You are so handsome, Bill. How can you be lonely?"

"My question did not require an answer or false flattery, merely a nod." She nodded. "I know the rules, Monica. Have no fear, I will be discreet." He regarded her in a way she could not interpret. His eyes were distant; his body tense, in a way only a lover or a wife could understand and Monica was neither. "Years ago, Monica, I had a wife. I no longer have her because she was taken from me when I least expected, in a very violent and horrible car crash. And I believe in my heart I was to blame. We were on our way to an anniversary gala that evening. We were the guests of honor and the evening was so lovely I insisted we walk the short distance so everyone would see the beautiful woman on my arm. We had a limousine. Walking was the last thing we had to do. We did because I was so proud of her and I wanted the world to know." He took another sip. "I never heard the slightest sound, Monica. I never had the slightest idea what was about to befall us. All I remember is seeing her ripped from my arms, seeing her flying through the air. All I could do was stand frozen in time and watch her crash into the street and crumple like a broken doll. Though I do remember, when I did finally move, all I could think of doing was covering her with my coat."

Monica was sincerely horrified. "She is dead, Bill?"

"No, Monica, I am the one who is dead. She left me that evening, as she might have for another whose love for her was impossibly greater than my own. She hates me thoroughly, she has every day. I cannot tell you how many times I have prayed to relive the moment so that I might kill the drunk who so horrifically and irreversibly altered our lives together. I should have killed him. I was extremely wealthy, I had a high profile, I had just cause and the jury would certainly have forgiven me. Yet I did nothing. So now you know me in a very different light."

"What happened to the man?"

"They suspended his permit, gave him time served and let him go free after the trial to do 500 hours of community service. Go figure."

"Go where?"

He managed a smile. "To the bar young lady, if you would."

"Yes, you know I would. You are making me so sad. I wish so much I could hug your wife and tell her…"

"That you sleep with her husband after he made her a paraplegic?"

Monica didn't respond. She went to the bar, placed his empty old-fashioned on the serving table and held the decanter between trembling hands. When she rejoined him he took the glass, ignoring her stunned expression.

"We never had a daughter or son. Very often I wonder whether our lives would have been better had she been kidnapped, taken from me that way. At least then I would have had a chance to get her back to love her, and for her to love me. This way she will never love me again and we have no children. I am completely alone, facing possible death with no one to cry for me, not even my wife. And do you know what?" She shook her head. "I haven't felt this good about myself in years."

Monica stood and went to the intercom to ask for music. She padded back with a glass of watered-down Glenmorangie of her own.

"That is precisely why, Monica, you must begin dancing and being happy with your life. Often I wonder who you are with when you are not with me, about the man who would let you be here with me. You should have a husband, if you don't already, a handsome young man who would love you, give you a beautiful dark-haired daughter or son to love. I cannot even imagine how beautiful a little girl would be coming from you. "

Looking into her eyes was the hardest thing he'd done in years. He had always wondered at the dark pools that were her eyes, curious. Now he saw a distant and subdued image, compelling himself to disregard how she might feel. He was stoic, he was who he was and that would never change. She curled into him, crying softly, wanting him to hold her. Instead he stood, placed his glass on the table and walked out the door.

*

Once Juan Carlos saw the building he drove to the Hilton, parked the Corvette in the monitored interior parking and took a taxi to Manuel's, not solely motivated by his concern for the car. In the apartment he sat on the arm of the worn chair drinking his first neat ciento por ciento tequila, listening to Manuel recite every detail of his time with Miss

356

Collins. On the other side of town, James Burton paced the floor of his study telling himself he was acting prematurely and, as he dialed the number on the card, he was acting too late.

If what he now believed was indeed true, he had no doubt he would depart this world a better man, and that his departure was imminent. For the second time in his life he had no idea what to say or do, though he did rationalize that however badly his decision to act went for him, he would be doing good for Monica. He dressed quietly for a late-night walk and told the homecare nurse he would be gone for only few moments. He needed some air.

The cell number had been call forwarded. When the phone chimed Juan Carlos called out for Manuel to wait. Both phones connected simultaneously.

"This is Manny."

"Good evening, young man. Did you see my note on your wife's photo?"

"Yes, but her name is Mercedes, not Monica. Are you sure she's my wife?"

"For your sake I do fervently hope so. I truly do. I have spoken with her since my time in your cab yesterday and I have a very strong feeling such is the case, young man."

He remembered the voice. "You're the one who jumped out at the park, the fifty bucks."

"Yes, I am."

"Listen. I can get you money, anything you want. Just tell me she's alright and where we can meet. There won't be any cops, I promise you. I just want her back."

"The last thing I need in this life is money, young man, but, yes, she is well. I am not the one who kidnapped her or your daughter."

"But you know who did."

"Yes, I do. If we are talking about the same young woman that would indeed be true."

"Who are you? How do you know her?"

"A premature question at best, I'm afraid. I know her, let that suffice. At the moment nothing else is important."

"She's in Atlanta?"

"Yes, she is. She is safe and in no danger, especially from me. However, if the young woman in question is your wife, I must warn you...you will not like what you will eventually hear or see. You must be prepared for the absolute worst nightmare of your entire life young man."

"You're not telling me shit."

"I am telling you what I know. Believe me. She is safe, more so now than over the past year."

"Meet with me, anywhere. There won't be any cops, I swear."

"I am afraid that would be inappropriate at this time for reasons I will clarify when and if we do meet."

"When will that be?"

"As soon as possible, after I see your wife once more and confirm what I suspect is true. It would help me greatly, however, if I were to know something about you and your daughter in addition to what you told me yesterday."

"My name is Del Fuego, I'm from Veracruz. She wasn't just kidnapped, they also raped her. Our girl is Sofia. She's three and a half. Please tell my wife she's is safe, that she is now with me. Can you do that?"

"What color is your wife's hair?"

"Dark brown and she's five-two. Her English is very limited. She speaks almost nothing."

"Monica's English is fluent."

The line went dead.

"What the fuck, JC?"

Juan Carlos shook his head. "No, amigo. You mean, who the fuck? You know this man. You know where he got in and where he got out. Did you see him? Think."

"Yes, I did. He's white, tanned, well dressed, expensive

suits, conservative, fifty to fifty-five, in good shape for a civilian, silver hair, neat, the hundred-dollar haircut kind of neat and he wouldn't give a second thought to shit like me. He got in at Peachtree and Trinity, like a guy who'd never think of taking a taxi and dropped a fifty on a ten-dollar ride. He got out at the park, said he was late for a meeting at the Congress Center."

"So we know where to start and we know the target, amigo. But we will gain nothing by beginning the hunt before Monday. Until then we wait. Tonight we will drink and tomorrow you will phone Carmelita and Sofia before you take me to this dojo of yours so I can kick your ass, chica."

Seventy-Seven

James Burton stayed alone in his study all day Sunday, incapable of concentrating on any one thought before another bolt of guilt assailed his conscience. He felt a deep self-loathing, yet he felt strangely at peace. He felt elated and alive for what he knew would soon transpire, as much as he felt deep regret for the pain and suffering he had brought to the one he loved. He felt no redemption for what he was about to do. Nothing would ever be enough.

There was no doubt in his mind Monica was Mercedes Del Fuego. What he struggled to understand, was how she had come to The Hotel Le Chic, quite possibly of her own volition. Was she driven there by the shame of the rape, fearing her husband would beat her in a rage or reject her, blaming her for being so cruelly violated? She was always so happy, so pleased to see him, and the hotel had no bars on the doors or chains on her ankles keeping her from leaving. How many times had he waved to girls sitting in the lobby mere feet from those doors with no one in sight to stop them from running into the street?

The girls were young, beautiful, cashing in on a good thing, supply and demand and where would he be without them? Such places were needed by men of a certain reputation who were not free to come and go as others might. In his world privacy was of paramount importance. That's why he was there. Why was Monica? Her husband sounded exactly as he should have on the phone, which didn't mean she hadn't run from him or that she would be spared ill-treatment at his hands once reunited with him. He threw back his head and drained the glass.

He called his private assistant at 10:00 PM, telling her he would be unavailable for the coming week. She would cancel all his appointments and contact him strictly for extreme circumstances beyond her control. The limousine was off limits to all executive personnel effective immediately and the driver was on twenty-four hour call. Yes, he was fine, as was his wife, he answered without thanking her for the concern, reminding her she had no reason to answer to anyone but him.

Next he called the hotel, making a reservation for the following evening. He was a day too late and attitude by any guest at any time was not tolerated. Yes, he realized Preferred Girls were permitted to have two Preferred Guests if one of them was a woman. Genevieve assured him such was the case, booking him for a full stay on Tuesday after advising him Melanie would be free until nine and Katrina's guest for Monday might possibly cancel, if he was interested. He thanked her, refusing the offer. He would arrive by 4:00 PM Tuesday and, no, he would not require room service.

He hated the thought of being inactive for two days. He certainly couldn't be of any value to the firm and he couldn't risk being on the streets because Manuel Del Fuego would be searching for him between Trinity and the park. Nor could he think of Monica the way he had in the past, remembering his times with her. Monica was now Mercedes, a young wife who might have been raped, if not kidnapped, and, if so, he was aiding and abetting the perpetuation of a vile crime.

Whoever she was, the young woman called Monica was wrong in her youthful innocence. There was no heaven, and if there were some mythical gathering place for the pure and the innocent, he was certainly not one of them.

He had always known what to do next, or what he was supposed to do next, and when he didn't his private assistant was usually at his side. In any event, she was at home, probably in bed, and how the hell would he explain this one to her? He knew he wasn't being logical. He was letting himself get caught up in the emotions of a man he'd met once and a woman he wasn't even certain was the Mercedes the man was searching for. She might not be. Perhaps she simply enjoyed what she was doing, and she wasn't exactly working the streets. Christ, each of her outfits was four or five hundred dollars, paid for no doubt with her share of the quarter-million. Somebody was doing well.

By 3:00 AM he couldn't tell whether he was confused or drunk, until he gradually realized he was seeing two of everything in his study. He downed what remained of his scotch, brought his feet to his desktop, reclined and went to sleep, or somewhere he wouldn't be called upon to think.

By the time Burton woke Manuel was navigating downtown core traffic in search of the man on the phone; JC was walking those same streets with a near-perfect composite drawing of the man e-mailed to him on Sunday from a contact in Miami. When Manuel questioned him regarding the Miami contact the simple answer was that no one gets by on his own, JC adding with a smile that it was all about networking and very soon he would meet the man in person. His name was Pablo.

Men such as the one they were seeking never walked the streets after breakfast or before dinner. They hired flunkies to run daily errands. If he were to leave his mahogany office, the likely reason would be a martini lunch within a very small window of opportunity, small being a shitload bigger than nothing.

*

Monica left the pool by 4:00, her body glowing with SPF 30 and pool water. When Cynthia arrived at five, Monica was still undressed, wrapped in a towel and ready for more pool time with her guest.

She liked Cynthia, so did Lucy, which meant a lot. She would have been hurt to think Lucy was jealous. Cynthia was refreshing. All she wanted was the female companionship forbidden to her in the outside world by male and corporate narrow mindedness. She liked women, so what? As she had asked all the girls one day at the pool: "If men can like these little things, why can't we?"

She was nice, she was kind and liked doing girly things like combing hair, doing nails and playing with the newest make-up. All the things she was never allowed to do as a young girl. Often she would eat with the unscheduled girls in the restaurant or workout with them in the gym. She liked being at Le Chic and thought of Monica and the others as friends. When she left, very late Monday night, the two men were cleaning their weapons and formulating alternative plans as James Burton congratulated himself on coming to terms with himself and finding the man inside who had once escaped him.

Seventy-Eight

He arrived at 4:10, much to Monica's surprise.

She nodded, smiling approvingly. "Bill, never have I seen you looking like this."

"You don't like?"

"Yes, I do like very much. It is very you."

"I've taken a few days off work and selected them myself. I can't remember the last time I wore cords and a sweater. So, I'm presentable?"

"Yes, and if you ask me again I will be sure that you are asking me so that I will say nice things."

She was stunning in another long robe she borrowed from Lucy. Underneath were full micro-fiber panties and cami top because she didn't want to be the cause of his death.

"Again, I'm sorry about the other day, about walking out on you."

"No comprendo lo que dice."

His face creased, his brow furrowing into the uniquely American expression and universally accepted indication that he had no clue.

"It is alright for us to study Spanish together. Miss Divine did agree that it will be okay."

He smiled. "How wonderful. Perhaps a scotch might be in order to fortify the student."

"Sí señor. Por supuesto y con mucho gusto."

By eight he was done with linguistics. He hadn't cared about pronouns when he was in school and he didn't care about them now, and why was English the only language without bothersome accents. She answered that accents were the special flavor of a language and that English had no flavor other than the bad words she would not teach him because she did not know them.

He had no interest in knowing dogs were separated from cigars by one R, or that the Americas used ustedes and not vosotros. At some point he thought being killed by Del Fuego would be an appropriate punishment for what he had done to his own wife and Del Fuego's, if not a desirable alternative to the torture he was currently enduring with Monica.

Finally, the lesson came to an end not a moment too soon. They were both tired and ready for bed, though he wouldn't be staying. When he told her to stay dressed she understood why, dropping her robe and climbing under the covers in her panties and cami. When he joined her, he lay over the duvet fully dressed and put his face close to hers without touching her.

"Monica, thank you for my lesson and I hope we have many more of them. You are a wonderful teacher and I apologize to your countrymen for my linguistic inability."

"That will change, Bill. I will make you a good student."

"I believe you could."

"But you must also use books."

"I will arrange for books tomorrow." She snuggled into her pillow. "Monica, may we talk? I mean, may we discuss a serious matter?"

"Yes, of course, Bill. I am not a stupid girl."

"I have known few women as intelligent as you and you must be forthright with me. You must be honest with me. Saturday when I left you on the sofa I was goading you. I was searching for answers which were not forthcoming.

Now, Monica, I need those answers and you are the one person who might furnish them to me."

Monica pulled the duvet high around her shoulders. "Bill, on Saturday you made me very sad, now you are making me very afraid. And what is this goating and forthcoming?"

"I was trying to make you say something I still want to hear and need to hear. I need to know, Monica, what you are doing here and how you first came to the hotel. Tell me, and do not be afraid, be honest."

"Bill, I…"

"And I am not a stupid man, so do not lie to me. What you say will not go beyond this room, I promise you." He pressed his hand into the duvet covering her cheek. "I promise you on all that is decent and good, but I must know because I have every reason to believe I will die very soon and I must know the answers you alone can give me before that happens."

"You told me that you were well."

"I am well, as well as I can be. I merely believe with reasonable certainty that I might soon die, which has nothing to do with how well I am. We all die, Monica. In my particular case I get to choose when, if not how." He leaned into her. "I care for you, though not as much as I care for another, and for that I will be eternally condemned to remain in my own hell where I have dwelled for years. Tell me what I must know, Monica."

"Why must you know? Why at this moment after one year?"

"Because I have an opportunity to escape my private hell and quite possibly help you escape from yours. Do you understand me? Take a moment and think. Ask me nothing more, answer my questions, and believe in me. I would never do anything to hurt you."

Monica took a moment before twisting in her bed,

reaching toward the intercom to order music her guest hadn't requested. "Who are you, Bill? Who are you really?"

"I'm your best friend, Monica. Tell me your story. I will not forget one word, I promise you."

"She will kill me and she will kill Lucy."

His entire body shuddered from the single shock wave; the sensation of his blood freezing made him want to retch.

"Miss Divine?" he whispered.

"Yes, Miss Divine. She will kill us."

He crawled under the covers, still dressed, and simply said: "Tell me everything."

The next morning he smiled widely at Stephanie as he strode past the Reception to retrieve his cell phone on his way out. Then he went home, locked himself in his study and threw up.

Seventy-Nine

Monica wouldn't tell Lucy why she was crying. She simply asked one question with the music playing and Lucy repeated each unforgotten word, comforting her friend and confidante with gentle squeezes, kisses, and telling her somehow, no matter what, they would be together again. They would never be apart because they were buds. William had frightened her badly, yet he hadn't told her why, admonishing her not to say anything to anyone, including Lucy. When she fell into her restless sleep she had no idea Lucy's comforting arms were wrapped around her.

By the time the girls woke Manuel and Juan Carlos were on the streets processing each passing face of the breakfast crowd with an acuity that would make the best-trained and most astute TSA functionary at Hartsfield-Jackson appear unfocused and disinterested. By 1:00 PM they had been to dozens more restaurants and James Burton had left his high-rise condo without any explanation to his wife other than he would be home for dinner, suggesting she might join him for cocktails. When he returned early that evening a crystal old-fashioned was on the marble end table, filled two-fingers deep; Doris Burton sat in her wheelchair reading her favorite author. She glanced up without smiling, though not unkindly.

"Doris, you are very lovely this evening."

"It's been a very long time since you have invited me for cocktails, Jimmy, though I must say this morning you sounded as though you had more than a pleasant drink on your mind."

"That is quite so, my dear, and very astute of you, though I'm not surprised. I have a good deal on my mind and I am afraid not much of the content is very pleasant."

"Then sit and tell me about it all."

Burton swallowed most of what was in his glass without so much as a blink and sat beside her. "Doris I've been very mean towards you these past several years for purely selfish reasons."

"Jimmy, you have no reason to explain your actions. I understand."

"You may think you do, my dear. However, you do not. Apparently, for several years, I have unknowingly involved myself in something very tainted, something very diabolical, though entirely of my own volition, and the time has come to rectify a very unbelievable wrong. It's not the firm, which is very sound. It's me personally and something I shall never expunge from my memory in even the smallest way."

He stood to refill his glass.

"You're a good man, Jimmy. Nothing you could have done could possibly be so terrible."

"I'm afraid that's not quite the case, Doris. What's worse, I have no clear understanding of exactly how terrible, or how far reaching the ramifications."

"Can you be more specific?"

"Yes, though I ask you not to force the issue. I have no doubt you would hate me more than you have these past years for what I did to you."

She shook her head solemnly. "Jimmy, I told you in the hospital, as I told you so many times after you brought me home that I loved you, that what happened wasn't your fault or mine. We might both have been injured, or you, or worse, but I was." She smiled. "Luck of the draw, and I have always clung to the reason we were strolling that evening. That is what I hate, that you can never be proud of me again. Not like this, but I have never stopped loving you," she paused, bringing a smirk to her lips, "and I have never stopping missing you. I do understand, Jimmy."

"We were so young. You were only thirty."

"Would you have preferred that it happen today or tomorrow? There is no right time for what happened…and I survived, Jimmy. Our marriage is what died."

"I want that to change."

"This will never change, Jimmy. This is me from now on."

"It is not you who must change, Doris. I must, if I may." She said nothing. "This afternoon I went shopping, at a blue collar store of sorts. I bought jeans with holes in them, rather strange footwear, a sweatshirt, something called a denim hoodie of all things, and a baseball cap. I was very much a comical sight when I stood in front of the mirror, although what I saw wasn't comical, Doris: the real me without the thousand dollar suits and the hundred dollar ties. I even took a bus, with no particular destination in mind. I was contemplating my future actions and how those actions would affect us, you and me. Then I returned to the store and bought more clothes because I noticed no one on the bus ever paid me the slightest attention. I was no one special, except when I went to pay the driver with a fifty and he became rather difficult. I was a different man. No one cared whether I could buy the bus company. I know I can be a different man for you, Doris, starting right now. Though I must tell you before you answer, if you care to, that I will leave you this evening for a few moments and for the next few weeks I will be away from home for reasons you would be wrong to assume."

"What have you done, Jimmy? There's nothing you can't tell me and telling me may lighten your burden."

"Very much the opposite I'm afraid, my dear. What I require most from you over the coming weeks is your continued tolerance and to believe my motives are the best possible for everyone concerned, including you." He sipped his scotch. "When I come home to you I will never leave you alone again. In fact, I am considering resigning as CEO and president of the firm. We are still young, Doris. When I return I intend to rekindle the flame I allowed to expire, if you agree, and I suggest the Greek Islands would be the perfect venue, or anywhere else that pleases you."

"I believe, Jimmy, I might have a glass of wine if you would be so kind."

"Is that a yes?"

"I believe it is a yes... yes."

He walked away beaming. "Then you might also tell that frightful woman in white not to scream out tomorrow morning when she sees me in your bed. It's not as though she hasn't seen me in my robe once or twice."

Eighty

They were ready for him when the call came that evening.

"This is Manny."

"Good evening, Mr. Del Fuego."

"Tell me about her. How is she? Is Monica my wife? Is she safe?"

"First, young man, may I call you by your first name? This will not be our last conversation and I believe formality will be a foolish hindrance."

"Yes."

"Good. Yes, she is Mercedes. I have known all along. The root of my uncertainty was not knowing how she came to be where she is, or for what reason. I had to know you were not the reason and now I have the answers to those questions. She is very well, though she cries and dreams each night of you and your daughter. Above all she is safe."

"Who are you?"

"For the time being you may call me William."

"Where is she? What do you want from me?"

"She is very close to you at this very moment, Manny, and not metaphorically. Though she doesn't yet know and by now my intentions must be clear to you. I want very much to help her."

"Then meet with me, let me help you."

"Be assured that will happen, with a great deal of patience. I might also add, young man, that by helping you I am putting my life in extreme danger."

"From who?"

"From you, Manny."

"Where is she?" Manuel pleaded, raising his voice. "I won't hurt you, I swear. I only want my wife."

"Manny, believe me, I want very much to tell you, and I will. Until that time be satisfied that she is safe. We will do this a little at a time. You have no choice and neither do I, though I promise you she is safe and she will not be harmed. You will be with your wife very soon, young man. However you must be prepared for the very worst, as I have previously told you. Do not pretend to fool yourself. Be prepared to enter her worst nightmare. I must tell you she is very afraid. She is absolutely terrified."

"Terrified of what?"

"She is terrified of you, Manny, of what you will think. Until you see her you must remember how much she loves you and you must be strong for her. This is not about you. It's about her. You and I mean nothing in the scheme of things. Mercedes is the important one."

"I know that. Meet with me."

"Soon. In the meantime you must be patient. There is still much more for me to accomplish and discover before I meet with you. As much as I care for her, and as much as you love her, there is much more at stake here than Mercedes alone. Although I appreciate that is unimportant to you at the moment. Soon that will change and you will understand my reasoning. Some very influential people, some very important and dangerous people, will be seriously compromised by the fact you have found your wife. And the lives of other very innocent people are also at risk. What we will do together must be thoroughly thought out and meticulously planned, which will require more time. We will get her out, Manny, but you must be patient."

"Get her out from where?"

There was a slight pause. "From her incarceration in hell, young man. Very soon you will know everything. Be patient and wait for my call."

"Does she know I haven't stopped searching for her? Can you tell her how much I love her?

"She knows, Manny. No immediate need exists for me to reinforce her belief. She was told months ago you were dead, killed in Iraq after you abandoned her to reenlist. She believed the lie not for a moment. She believes steadfastly that you are coming for her and, to answer your second question, no, I cannot. Doing so would place her in grave danger and we cannot allow her the unfortunate and fatal mistake of betraying herself. Believe me when I tell you, Manny, we will not disappoint her. She believes you are coming for her and you will. We will not disappoint her and then you can tell her yourself how much you love her. Good evening."

The tumbler smashed into the wall spilling the vodka. He collapsed onto the floor, crying as Juan Carlos casually replaced the receiver, poured a fresh double vodka and knelt by his friend.

"Hombre, get up. She would not want to see you like this, and neither do I. It fucks with my brain. This is all good news, amigo. This gringo is helping us, and if he is fucking with us he will know his mistake soon enough. I swear to you. Mercedes is coming to you, hombre. She is coming and you will be the man she remembers. Get up, drink, and we will be ready for his next call. He has spoken with her. She loves you still. Think of her being here with us now, and she must not see you like this."

The Madam

Eighty-One

When James Burton walked through the door of his condo he was surprised at seeing the nurse preparing to leave for the evening. She was mumbling something under her breath about being long overdue and that she would be there early in morning to check on Doris who was waiting for him in her bedroom, if he remembered the way.

He hadn't disrobed in front of her in thirteen long years and doing so would be completely inappropriate in his mind. When he went to her, he wore a silk smoking jacket and matching pull-string pants. She had a drink in her hand and a double Glenmorangie neat waited on his bedside table.

She was beautiful and quite apparent to him that the female demon in white was kept busy during his absence helping Doris bathe and select the perfect negligée and peignoir, no doubt all the while making hissing noises and blowing flames from her flaring nostrils. He made a mental note to thank her in his inimitable way the following morning. Perhaps he would send flowers to her, or quite possibly a new personality.

He hadn't touched Doris romantically throughout those many years and both of them instantly felt as though he had never stopped touching her. The night of the accident was the last night he'd kissed her lips, now he could not stop kissing her. She was the same vital woman she had always been, she was beautiful, though she was unsure as he pushed and pulled away the overlapping lapels of her robe. He was not. Suddenly nothing mattered, as though they had just come home from their tenth wedding anniversary and he began not to despise himself.

He let her fall into a deep and peaceful sleep before he left her, weeping privately in his study for how he had misunderstood her all those past years. Thursday morning when Doris woke she was in his arms and she was the one who shrieked, until he kissed her once more. Then again and again, reminding her he would never leave her once his business was finished, but that he did have business to finish. At that moment she didn't care. She had her man back and as she watched him leave with several large bags filled with many of her clothes he had always hated seeing her in, she knew her dream was real and the memory of all those empty years disappeared. Exactly how much her life was about to change, she had no idea.

If she thought she knew her husband, she would soon learn that she did not, pondering the new James Burton as he sat a mere few blocks from Manuel and Juan Carlos, waiting to hear from his assistant as to who owned the building on whose steps he was sitting with his head lowered and his cap in hand. Apparently he did.

He wasn't humbled by the experience, despite appreciating how others must feel being regarded with disdain, scorned by those who avoided his eyes as though he was leprous. Certainly the experience did little to change his view of the world or many of those who took up space in it and he wondered about the consequences of an inopportune heart attack while in his current condition. Clothes did indeed make the man and riding the bus was a definite step above.

After a short while, when the concierge came out thinking to sweep another indigent from the steps, the unfortunate man learned the hard way that not all in life is as it seems. Rather than arguing with the man in vain, Burton simply arranged for him to receive a phone call on his own cell from corporate and the message was very clear: He was to allow Mr. Burton access to the building immediately and offer him every courtesy.

An hour later the office space was selected, high-end furnishings purchased by day's end with cash for delivery the following day. That night he went home to Doris who hadn't thought once to doubt his word as she busied herself shopping all day with the demon nurse. She was once again in the arms of her husband, her lover. She was ecstatic, falling asleep in his tender embrace.

The next morning, when he stood at the bedroom door, she knew something was amiss and she blanched. "Jimmy, you're an executive, not a spy or a commando or anything like that. Why are you dressed that way?"

"Doris, darling, as I have previously confessed, I am involved in something unquestionably horrific and unconscionable and my ignorance of certain events does not absolve me in the least. I alone am responsible for what I have done. More importantly, I now have an opportunity to reverse my complicity, if not the long-term effects of my conduct. I will never be able to completely right the wrong and I beg your forbearance. I am dressed this way so those who know me will not."

"Are you in danger?"

"No darling. Others are, and I must do all in my power to help them. Nor am I alone in my quest. I will come through these doors in a few weeks a different man, though I will not return home this evening." He forced a smile. "I have found a very beautiful woman whom I stupidly lost too long ago. I will not lose you again, Doris. I ask only that you believe in me with blind conviction, something I don't deserve, and that you believe I will not disappoint you again. I will call you every day and every night."

"From where, Jimmy?"

He leaned over her, hugging her. "From my heart, darling, from my heart."

Eighty-Two

He felt completely anonymous. The concierge thought he was an eccentric lunatic and the delivery men cared more about the fifty-dollar tips he was handing out. By noon on Friday his new office was ready. He did not imagine for a moment that Manuel Del Fuego was alone. The man was an active Marine, royally pissed, and he was the reason. Burton harbored no illusions. At some point over the next several hours he would admit to one very angry young man that he had spent the past year fucking his wife. It wasn't good.

By 6:00 AM Saturday he hadn't slept for two days and had spent the last twenty-four of those hours glued to the lenses of his Nikon Spotter scope and his Bushnell night vision binoculars. By 6:00 PM he'd spent an easy day reviewing the notes he'd begun compiling for each file classified by the names he knew, the faces he recognized and their times. Near 7:00 he left the building and circled the block, returning on the right side of Ellis Street and punched in his code.

He kissed Monica on the cheek. He never kissed her lips, an intimacy she never allowed and he never questioned.

"Good evening, Bill. May I serve you a drink?"

"Yes, thank you."

"Are you still well?"

"Yes, I am. Thank you. I expect a complete recovery

very soon and then you will know the real William."

"Do you like the music? Is it too loud?"

"It's perfect. Come, let's do our lessons."

William opened his workbook as Monica made room for it and the Glenmorangie on the table in front of the settee.

"You are very different once again, Bill."

He nodded, facing away from the mirror. "Yes, Monica, and I have you to thank for the change. I am very different. I have found my wife again, because of you, and I thank you profoundly."

"I am very happy for you."

He smiled, opening his book. "Where do we start?"

"We start with the truth."

He knew immediately. There was no subterfuge in her voice.

"What truth would that be, Monica? When is it that you believe me to have been dishonest with you?"

"What will you do with the truth that I have told you about me and this place?"

"I have every reason to believe things will turn out well for you, Monica. You must not give up hope. If your Manuel is as you say he is, then he will find you. You must not give up hope."

"Are you a bad man, Bill? I know that only a very bad person could come here after all that I have told you about me and this place."

"Yes, I believe I am bad, despite doing my best to resolve the situation and finding my wife has helped me greatly."

"It is good that you have found her, but my Manuel has not found me."

"You must believe he will, Monica, but for now I would prefer continuing with our lessons. It's what I need from you this evening, and after we have finished I would like to relax and listen to more of this wonderful music. Then I will leave you. Being here like this is strange. However, if I were not, you would certainly be with someone else eventually."

She lowered her eyes. "Yes, you are right."

"I promised I would let nothing happen to you and I intend to keep my promise for as long as you are here."

"Are you trying to find him?"

"No, Monica, I am not. What would I possibly tell him? Even if I did have the right words, which I do not, what could he do? Firstly, the people who come through these doors are very powerful people, your children would be placed in immediate danger and the other women here would certainly face uncertain futures."

She glared at him with such heat in her eyes that he recoiled.

"I see this conversation is upsetting you, which is not very conducive to your continued well-being should someone see you are unable to disguise your feelings." He paused, finishing his scotch. "Perhaps I should not have come. All I ask is that you believe in me. I would never lie to you. I thought coming here platonically and ostensibly to learn Spanish would be a good thing, a way to help you. Why don't we do that and change this dark mood."

She felt the same sickening fear she did in the vault the first night with Miss Divine, hearing she would be enslaved for three years. After a few hours William stood. He poured another scotch, appraising her.

"You know, I hated that when I was in school and I hate it even more now. I suppose some of us are simply destined to be linguistically challenged."

"It is the feelings in Spanish that you do not comprehend, William. You have no feelings." She stared at him wide-eyed in a way that would make a hardened Marine sniper take pause. "Are you saying that we will not do this anymore?"

"No, that is not what I'm saying. What other reason would I have for visiting with you until such time as I begin to feel myself again?"

"I do not understand. You told me that you are happy with your wife?"

He glanced at his watch. "It's late. I should go."

"You do not want to relax? Never have you left this early. It is not late. It is only hard for you to stay with me because you already know so much?"

"Do you hate me?"

"I do hate how you have changed."

He smirked with a sense of gratification, making her Latin eyes burn into his. "That is a good thing, Monica. You should hate me, for the rest of your life, for the part I have played in all this. The actual question being: can you delay your hatred until we part for the last time?"

"Now you are playing with me, and I do not know why. I cannot tell you to go, but I cannot tell you that I want you to stay."

"Then I will go. I have reserved for Tuesday and Thursday evenings of the week after next. Saturday, at this point, is up in the air, though I do intend being here that evening as well."

She took his hand, squeezing imploringly. "Bill, you could tell him that I love him, that I am sorry for what I have done to him and my daughter. That is what you could tell him when you find him. You know where this place is, we do not. Even when we leave here we do not know. Please do this for me, for us. Please."

He reached for the book. "Good night, Monica."

The Madam

Eighty-Three

Sunday when he woke to the not yet familiar sounds of horns and screeching brakes he phoned Doris to tell her how much he loved her. She asked if he would still be alive to call her that evening and he promised that, thus far, such was the case. He called her again at 8:00 PM, confirming his continued existence after spending the day reviewing more of his newly acquired data which included several seconds of footage he edited out, clearly showing him arriving at and leaving from the hotel the previous day. At 10:00 he called Manuel Del Fuego, by which time he knew most of what he needed to know and much more of what he needed not to know.

"This is Manny."

"Good evening, Manny."

"How is my wife?"

"She is fine, Manny, and the time has come for us to meet. I fear her current mood will soon betray her. We must come together and act as one without animosity or division."

"Where and when?"

"Twelve-thirty tomorrow on the east side of the Olympic Park."

"How will I know you?"

"You won't. I will know you. Be at the east side of the park at that time. I anxiously await our first encounter,

Manny. Good evening."

"Wait!"

"What is it?"

"Nothing… I don't know."

"Manny, let me tell you what I have recently told Mercedes and my wife. I told Mercedes to believe in me, which I hope she does because her life depends on it. I told my wife I would soon be with her, without telling her that whether I do or not depends entirely on you. Together we can do this. Good evening."

Eighty-Four

He watched the young man arrive and stand mere feet from him, facing east in a loose-fitting safari shirt, blue jeans and cowboy boots. He was 5'10", lean, hard as rock and carried himself with a very definite "do not fuck with me" look as he appeared completely unperturbed that someone he could not see could see him. Burton had no doubt as to what was under the shirt.

"Manny, are you alone?"

Manuel pivoted from the waist, not surprised by what he saw.

"No, I'm not." He studied the man with cool detachment. "Is this how you rich guys get your kicks, dressing for handouts?"

"Thank you for you honesty. Neither am I alone. Directly behind me you will notice a rather large limousine which is fully armored, completely impenetrable, and it's mine. My chauffeur is currently videotaping this meeting. If we are able to come to agreeable terms the tape will be destroyed at a later date."

Manuel chortled. "And if we don't?"

"The tape will be delivered to the authorities with a letter composed by me. Though I believe we have too much at stake for that to happen. We would each have too much to lose, not the least of which would be our wives." He moved over. "Sit with me, please, and might I suggest you have your associate either join us or leave us."

"He'll join us. Directly over your shoulder you will notice a rather large man who is leaning on the lamppost beside your rather large car. You got here at eleven. We got here at nine. If you want to play cloak and dagger, buy a cloak. Better yet, buy a dagger."

"I assure you, I did not dress this way to conceal myself from you. My disguise is intended to conceal myself from a dozen others who will be in this park over the next hour or so. Call your friend. We have a great deal to discuss."

"He's behind you."

Juan Carlos came around and sat on Burton's other side as he pulled out the earpiece, leaned forward with his forearms across his knees, clasped his hands and glanced sideways. He wasn't smiling.

"Do not fuck with us, hombre. You do and I'll snap your neck like a fucking chicken bone."

Burton had no doubt the man could kill him where he sat with little or no effort or remorse, then go for lunch and not think twice about what he had done.

"I assure you, I will not."

"That's good, William," said Manny. "Now, what is your real name?"

"William will do for now."

JC moved closer, nudging him as gently as a freighter colliding with a floating dock. "Then tell us about Quantum Communications? You the fucking office boy over there? Like my friend said, don't be something you're not. That armored tank of yours isn't worth yesterday's shit unless you're in it. Your vanity tag just fucked you up. So, once again, who are you?"

"James Burton. QC is my firm."

"Señor Burton, my friend has many questions for you. For your sake we hope you have as many answers. We don't care about your wife. She's safe. We care about his.

Understood?"

"I have much to tell you, Manny, none of which you will like. Your first inclination will be to kill me, which is the last thing you should do because I am the one person who can help you. Without me you will never find Mercedes, quite simply because where she is does not exist." He studied each of them in turn. "Your search is over. You have found her. All you need now is the key." James Burton stood. "Gentlemen, our task begins and, if all goes well, it will end on August 12ᵗʰ at the latest, the fifth if we are fortunate and I truly hope we are. What happens to me at that point is of no real consequence to anyone but my wife, though I do fervently hope she will not be disappointed by your decision."

"Where are we going?"

"Piedmont Park, gentlemen. A lunch of sandwiches and beer is in the limo, if that's alright with you. When we arrive my chauffeur will leave us, unless you would prefer walking with a cooler and basket."

"And the tape?" asked Juan Carlos.

"There is no tape, unless you kill me. I might also add the privacy shield and front seats are bullet proof. Whatever weapons you might have won't pierce them and my driver is very well trained."

They drove. When the driver popped the lid of the trunk at the park JC took one cooler, Manny the other. Burton took his notes, and the most unlikely threesome sat by the lake for a picnic lunch on a beautiful Atlanta afternoon.

"Talk seriously with us, Mr. Burton," said JC.

"James, please. We will be together for a long time, day and night. Call me James."

"Why we must wait for August 12ᵗʰ or the fifth, James? Why so long?" Manuel questioned. "That is a very long time to wait."

"That is the worst question you could have asked me,

Manny. Forgive me for the answer that will come later. Remember, I have much to tell you and I will start with what she told me the last time I saw her, which was Saturday. She loves you and she's sorry for what she has done to you and Sofia. She does not yet know your daughter is safe and she does not know we're talking."

Juan Carlos cut in. "Make it good, hombre… make it very good."

"I am afraid I cannot. There is no good in what you're about to hear, which I will recount to you as she told me."

"When did she tell you?"

"She told me ten days ago, the day after the taxi."

"That is not what I meant."

"I know what you meant. I have told you on previous occasions you must be prepared for the worst and that she is terrified of you. Did you listen? Did you hear and understand? Are you prepared to enter Mercedes' worst nightmare?"

"Yes, I am."

"Then understand I am a friend, despite what you may think at the moment. I desperately want to help her, to reunite you. The reason we can do nothing before the twelfth of next month will soon become clear and I chose this park so you might cry, scream or kill me. Trust me. You will want to do all three by the time we leave here. Forgive me for what you are about to hear. Remember above all else that she is very close to freedom." Burton downed half his beer. "July 18th of last year Mercedes was raped in your home and kidnapped by men whose names are Frankie and Bobby, men with whom I have no acquaintance. She was brutally raped many times by the one called Frankie while the other kept your girl in another part of your home. She was forced to shower with him and left the towels on the floor hoping you would form the proper conclusion. They then took her to where she has spent the past year. Your daughter was taken somewhere else, though she still does not know your daughter is safe. Manny, Mercedes is being held against her will in a bordello, she has been for a year, and you must remember she has never stopped loving you or thinking of you."

JC's hand shot out to both restrain and comfort his friend. James Burton jerked instinctively, commanding his mind and body with great effort not to leap backwards.

"You're telling me they made her into a whore?"

"No, she is not a whore, not by a long shot, and you must understand that at this very moment or all is lost to you, including Mercedes. She is saving your daughter's life, in her mind, and you must hold on to that truth. She was told terrible things would happen to the girl, the same way she was told you were killed. And, as difficult as this is for you, what she is living through is much worse. This is not the time to wallow in damaged egos."

JC crushed his first empty beer. "Is that how you know her, hombre? Have you been with her?"

"Yes, I have been with her." He looked directly at Manuel. "I am truly sorry, young man. All I can say is that I have always treated her with the greatest respect and have recently discovered that I was, in fact, part of her plan for you to find her."

"What plan?"

"That will come. What you must understand for the moment is that, since the day in your cab, I have duly modified my behaviour. I still have much more to tell you and it does not get any better. In fact, you have not heard the worst."

This time Juan Carlos let his friend cry without intervening as he sent Burton a very clear message with his eyes.

"There are ten girls, ten young women in their early twenties, and two so-called Prefects who monitor them.

They each have a private suite which is wired for sound and video in a building with no windows. They may only speak English, they all wear electronic bracelets, including the Prefects and they are responsible to and for each other as Anchor Girls, not to mention the threat of what will happen to their children."

"What threat?"

"Their children would be brought to the hotel to service the needs of particular clients if the women were ever less than cooperative. That has never happened to the best of my knowledge, although perhaps now you can understand more clearly why Mercedes never attempted to leave. The Anchor Girls are also their only support. The girls genuinely feel deep affection for one another. There is no strife amongst them, particularly between Anchor Girls who are special girlfriends, if you will, their only way to seek and find comfort." Manuel went to interrupt him. "I'm not finished, Manny. I have the Duty Girls, Preferred Girls, the doctor and hairdresser to tell you about. The girls work six days each week. Sunday is their day off. August the twelfth is a Sunday. The hotel is also self-sufficient. The Duty Girls prepare meals for the others, as well as the guests; they also do the housekeeping of the hotel and suites prior to the arrival of each new guest. Each girl performs as a Duty Girl throughout the week they are unavailable to their clientele for an obvious physical reason. Mercedes' next duty week begins August 13th, which is why the twelfth should be the latest date to get her and the others out, though the fifth would be preferable. We do, however, need time to prepare."

Juan Carlos saw the utter despair in Manuel's eyes as Burton continued, doing his best to control the inflections of his voice.

"There is so much more I must tell you, the most important aspect of the hotel being the Preferred Girl system, Manny. Mercedes is a Preferred Girl. She became one intentionally," he gulped his beer, "and that's a good thing. She knew what she was doing and she did it for you."

The unbelievable tale was becoming too much even for Juan Carlos. "Keep going, Señor Burton. I believe the longer you talk, the longer you will live."

"Thank you for your consideration, young man. Preferred Girls may have no more than two guests. Special Girls have no more than the same five, the Courtesan Girls, usually the newer girls, may have as many as ten or twelve in a week and not necessarily the same. The exception is when women guests are involved. Then a Preferred Girl may have one male and one female guest, no more. It's contractual. Mercedes understood from the very beginning that by being a Preferred Girl she would be with only one man, one man to explain to you and not ten or twelve. That is why she is afraid of you, even though from the very beginning she could do no more for you."

"You're the man."

"Yes, I am the man."

"You've been fucking her for a year?"

Burton's mouth dried. "Much more importantly, not since the day I wrote the note. Over the coming weeks you may learn more about me, about why I was there, not that my life story is relevant to you. Understand. Guests know nothing about the women and the women know absolutely nothing about the guests who are all very important, potentially dangerous people. They come and they go, and the girls remain with each other for companionship. They never leave."

JC's voice was flat. "They must leave at some point. Someone must know about this place."

"I did not. Guests are referred by other guests. Preferred Guests pay a quarter-million each year; the Special Guests, a hundred K; and the Courtesan Guests pay fifteen-hundred for each visit, of which the girls receive nothing. They work for points, what they call boutique points, which allow them to purchase various sundry items from their small store that is much like any other hotel store. There are also demerit points for misbehavior, which are applied to what is called their obligation, each point equaling one additional day of service beyond three years unless adjusted upward. Mercedes has found herself in the unfortunate position of accruing demerit points for the simple reason she refused to change her Anchor Girl for the convenience of a Prefect who has designs on her. Unfortunately, the Prefects, that one in particular, apply the points."

"Who is the other man?"

Burton finished his second beer before answering. "There is no other man, which was also part of her plan to spare you."

Manuel jumped up. "Where is this whorehouse?"

"You may use that term now, Manny. Do not use it in front of Mercedes. She has done everything her way this past year so that she might face you one day and believe she was truly not a whore. To say such a thing would alter your lives irrevocably. She knows what she's done. She doesn't need you reminding her."

"Sit down, amigo. My neck hurts staring up at you. Sit, and let him finish. Mercedes was right. One man and a woman are far better than dozens." JC turned to Burton, not sure he wouldn't ram the beer bottle down his throat. "Their enslavement lasts three years?"

"Yes. A new girl is brought in approximately every three months, at which time the most senior girl is taken away, always at night, so she might return to her family. They are almost always mothers of young children and singularly beautiful without exception. Each one of them has been raped by the one known as Frankie before their confinement, that's a constant, and there is an expectation one of the girls will be changed in a week or two. Her name is Lucy. She is Mercedes' Anchor Girl."

"Where is she?"

"The hotel is downtown. It's known as The hotel Le Chic and you will not find it in any phone book or travel brochure. You will see it for yourselves this afternoon."

"And you think we're going to wait three or four weeks to get her out." Manny retorted, not asking a question.

"Have you listened to nothing I have said? We must wait. This current week is her Duty Week, as is the thirteenth. I assure you she will be well throughout that time and untouched by me." Burton opened his third bottle. "But we must wait. My sole reason for being with her now is to assist you in protecting her, to perpetuate a falsehood. I have led her to believe I have a bad heart and that I am under strict instructions from my doctor."

"How does she look?"

"Very young and very beautiful. Her English is virtually perfect and you have every reason to be proud of her. All the girls admire her. They adore her completely, and maintaining our ruse over the next few weeks will be difficult in the extreme. However we must, gentlemen, if we are to succeed. I have initiated a plan which I believe is workable, though you will be the ones to decide. That will also come this afternoon."

"Señor Burton, why do you insist on saying we? You're an ivory tower executive with no experience in extraction or whatever else might take place. What we need from you is the address and for you to stay away from her."

James Burton smiled for the first time. "I'm afraid you do need me. There are three sets of mirrored doors, each one requiring a code which is changed daily for each guest, and each door is monitored with two concealed cameras. They would know immediately of any attempt to get through those doors. Don't forget the women all wear permanent electronic bracelets, which may or may not be problematic. Also, you must consider the Anchor Girls, so the dilemma is no longer one of getting one woman out safely, but ten, and doing so without any possible repercussion towards their children whose locations and well-being are unknown. So you see you cannot simply go crashing through the doors like a couple of Hollywood commandos. Neither have I told you the worst, though, as I have mentioned, I do have a plan." He paused, studying each man. "In truth, gentlemen, the plan is Mercedes'. She was very explicit in the details she gave me. What she also gave me was the basis of a plan she has no idea about."

"What is this plan?" JC asked.

Manuel put up a hand. "First let him tell us the worst."

"There are four floors. The fourth belongs entirely to the madam who calls herself Miss Divine. There is also a vault on that floor where the girls are taken and left alone throughout their first night. They spend twenty-four hours naked and shackled to a wooden chair in the dark, sometimes for as long as forty-eight hours. The second evening they are initiated by the madam before being assigned to their Anchor Girl for further training, normally of a week's duration." Manuel's eyes were difficult to avoid. "I told you it would not be easy, Manny. There is no other way. I am truly sorry." He cleared his throat. "After the initial week they are on their own."

"Continue Señor Burton. We are capable of listening as we think of whom we will kill for doing this. Do not fool yourself. This affair will end in someone's death. And before we leave this place, I will search you. Refusing me would be a mistake, though I would very much like you to."

"You may search me if you wish. I am not the one who is wired, you are."

"Finish your story so we can leave this place and begin formulating a real plan."

"I still don't know your name."

"JC will do very well. Finish your story."

"As one girl is brought to the hotel, another is sent away, as I have indicated. What I did not say is that both girls are drugged. With what, I don't know, however I suspect the one leaving does not go home to her family. I dread what might actually happen to them. It is not unusual for each new girl to witness the exchange before she is locked in the dark. Lucy is the next, in a very few weeks as I understand it. Lucy is Mercedes' Anchor Girl and if we let anything happen to Lucy that is preventable by our actions or caused by our impatience, Mercedes would never recover. They are that close and don't take their closeness lightly. All they have to cling to is each other. We must not fail either one."

Manuel stood. "Mr. Burton, James, I will not kill you this very moment because I need you to find my wife and I believe you are a brave man. That does not mean I will not have a change of heart at a later date and disappoint your wife."

"Thank you. I would appreciate any possible delay." Burton threw his last beer can into the cooler. "There is more to tell you, however, the worst has been told. Now let me show you where she is and explain how we might save her. I trust you will both be impressed."

Eighty-Five

Neither man showed exactly how impressed he was. James Burton had been very thorough from the folding cots, pillows and blankets, a mini fridge, three tripod-mounted 48X60 Nikon spotting scopes and three Bushnell night vision binoculars. A 70mm video scope with digital focus on the fourth tripod was attached to a 24-inch plasma screen and mounted on a fifth tripod was a Nikon digital with a 300mm telephoto lens. The five were aimed at The Hotel Le Chic and each photo taken could immediately be transferred to disc on the laptop or printed as quickly on the large format professional printer. There were boxes of latex gloves, disposable cell phones, three leather recliners and twin envelopes, each containing ten thousand dollars.

"Gentlemen, use that for what I may have neglected to foresee or for whatever you may need in the short-term for yourselves. When you need more you will ask me. There is no limit. I have also purchased two generic vans for the pending evacuation, one brown, one blue, and one green Land Rover which is at your disposal as of now. Also, I own a very private beach house at Wrightsville Beach in North Carolina which is being readied for the ten women as we speak. It will be a perfect short-term sanctuary for the ladies. From the shoreline the place is virtually hidden, access is barred with motion detectors and cameras located at strategic points. We would know immediately of any inadvertent trespass. I presumed you would want to be as far away as possible after we have them. Of course, what you see in this room was paid for in cash, I believe that was the most prudent form of payment. I have also booked three rooms at the Hilton for our comfort and personal maintenance. Your room packages are on the table and the billing of any and all expenses will be handled by QC, as we would for any number of corporate guests."

The two men adjusted the scopes to their respective heights. "That is where she is?"

"Yes, and I feel very peculiar knowing she is there and we are here," Burton volunteered. "She is beginning to hate me, Manny, and by the time we save her I suspect she will hate me a good bit more, which is my fervent wish. I have no doubt my next few visits will be extremely uncomfortable." Burton didn't misinterpret JC's expression. "Juan Carlos, that is what JC stands for, isn't it? We will be locked in here together for a month. It would behove you to accept me. We will never be friends, a loss which upsets me not in the least, but you need me and I need you. I did not have to write that note on the photograph, without which your chances of finding her would be severely diminished, dare I say royally fucked. So learn to live with it, at least until we get her out. Then you can do whatever the fuck you want. Do you understand?"

Juan Carlos' thin smile curved across his lips. "Understood Señor Burton, and anticipated. At least you have shown yourself to have balls, twice in fact. Just be sure you do not lose them before we free these ten women from their prison."

"I won't. I have too much to lose that I have just found. I won't let you down. More importantly, I will not let Mercedes down."

"She has come to hate you as you begin to help her," JC said.

"Yes."

He chuckled at the irony "Then she and I have something in common."

"I understand entirely."

"How well do you know inside the building?" Manuel asked.

"Very well."

"So tell me again why we don't cross the street and let them walk."

"There are many reasons. Firstly, guests may arrive any time after 3:00 PM and very likely some are in there as we speak. Some may stay for a few hours, others for a full fifteen. Secondly, more importantly, this is Mercedes' Duty Week. She could be anywhere in hotel, on any of the four floors, doing anything from housekeeping to delivering room service. The doors to each suite are double French doors, reinforced and locked electronically when guests are in the rooms to prevent possible inadvertent embarrassment and, again, the main doors require codes to enter as well as to leave. The latter is input by either the guest or the prefect with a one-digit change. You would never get them out, and if she's on the fourth floor that would be much worse. Access is normally restricted to Miss Divine, and when Duty Girl services are required during her absence they are monitored by remote video and timed. Remember also that the rooms are wired for audio and visual, and did I mention the children? I believe I did."

"What about the roof?"

"You can see for yourself there is no entry or exit point. There is a patio pool at the rear of the main floor, accessible strictly from the roof and how you would do that from the front and or the rear is equally problematic. The patio was designed to prohibit intruders and is invisible from the sky: traffic reporters, that kind of thing. A lattice gives the appearance of any other roof and also allows for ample sun bathing. And therein lays the real problem: while at the pool the women are all entirely naked. Imagine the reception."

"I would prefer you do not," Manuel answered.

"I have never been to the pool, as a matter of discretion. In fact, I am told such is the case for all gentlemen guests. The women do, however."

"What about neighbors?"

"Nine to five, five days a week."

"What about the madam?"

"I have seen her twice in eleven years or so that I can remember. The Prefects do everything for her and she keeps them on a tight leash. They only know at the last moment when she will arrive or leave, when she calls to advise which of the girls she wants for the evening or night."

"JC, tracking her would be easy enough. We take her out, then get the girls out."

Burton ignored the interruption. "I have no doubt, Manny. She goes somewhere and does something when she's not in the hotel, not to mention living somewhere. But when would you do it? It's been years since I last saw her. At best I'll have to see her through those things, or ID her in the videos. That could take a while, and what if a girl is locked in the vault, what if it's Lucy, and what about the rapists who'll be coming for her? I'm sure you are both very good at this tracking and killing business, and that any plan you formulate and perfect will be as effective as it will be lethal, but we are talking about a few weeks, four at most, with many more benefits. And we still have no idea about the children."

"We're listening, Señor Burton. Entertain us."

"I have given this a good deal of thought over the past ten days. I believe my plan is very workable."

"Just tell us."

"Mercedes' next duty week is the thirteenth, so our window of opportunity is between the 23rd, next Monday, and the twelfth. My next reservation at the hotel is for Tuesday, the 24th and the 26th with a tentative meeting on the Saturday, which I intend to keep. I will do the same through Saturday the 11th. They know my schedule. Doing so would not be out of the ordinary, whereas not being there would be unusual. This Miss Divine, whoever she is, and wherever she is, very seldom comes to the hotel on Sundays. It's the girls' day off, and she's not one of them. With rare exception she stays away. In any event, the guests are required to leave by six AM and most do between midnight and two or three. What I propose is spending the night with your wife and you contacting me by cell phone when you have determined the last guest has gone. They leave at specific intervals so that guests never see one another. Then I would simply be on the inside to open the doors for you. By the time the Prefect on duty understands what is going on the two of you will be inside. Then the girls, some of whom will be asleep, would have time to dress and we would have ample time to investigate the vault, destroy or take what is deemed necessary, and leave with the girls. In Sunday traffic we would arrive in Wrightsville by one PM at the latest, if we leave by eight. That would give us two hours to assist the girls and clean this place out, though we may be able to improve the timing by three hours, more if some of this can go during the day on the Saturday." Burton took a moment, catching his breath as he twisted the cap from his bottled water. "We could be back by seven that evening as a worst case scenario. She almost never calls the hotel on Sunday, though there is no doubt Miss Divine will be at the hotel on Monday when no one picks up. That is when you might have the opportunity to question her as to the whereabouts of the children and the kidnappers. Two of us could be in the hotel, waiting, and the third would be up here to alert the other two as to her arrival. There is also a distinct possibility we will see the kidnappers over the coming nights, in which case we also get to save Lucy and find the men who raped and kidnapped your wife. I presume you will take certain retributive action against them."

"What about these prefects? You have said nothing about them."

"I would suggest the girls would be very uncomfortable, were the prefects to travel to the coast, particularly Mercedes, if you recall my comment. They are, after all, the sentinels of the hotel. Though they are also being held against their will, in the sense they have no will. They were able to leave after their three-year term, so they either knew better or had no reason to expect their lives would improve. They enjoy a few more perks, they split twelve hour shifts, still required to wear bracelets, and they do not know the location of the hotel. None of the girls do. Escorting them to another location would be an easy matter, setting them free with sufficient funds so that they might care adequately for their future needs and let them go their way."

"You have been thinking about this."

"I believe the plan is workable?"

"Initially, but we will dissect each part and make changes as we see fit. Do you agree, amigo?"

Juan Carlos nodded noncommittally. "In the meantime, hombre, you must quit your taxi job. They will understand. They have known from the beginning that your termination would be announced without much notice or explanation, if any. Do so tonight. You have no reason to delay. Use the Marines as an excuse. Tell them that you need time to put yours affairs in order before reporting. Make it believable and do not forget to take all your photographs. If they ask why, amigo, tell them Mercedes was found in Mexico with amnesia, tell them whatever you want. They will be too happy for you not to believe that what you say may not be true and let us not forget those Marines. You will be gone from the twenty-seventh to Sunday the 29th. Do not screw with Bishops, hombre. He has been very good with you so far."

"Gentlemen," Burton interrupted, "I shall be maintaining my visits to the hotel under the unlikely pretense of learning Spanish, though you might want to remember I am not anywhere near your level at this juncture."

Eighty-Six

Tuesday, July 24ᵗʰ

The week was long, and even though the basis of Burton's plan was a good one, by the time JC and Manuel watched him climb the rose-colored steps of the hotel, every detail had been examined from every angle.

Juan Carlos spent hours at different times each day reconnoitring the vicinity, examining everything from the hotel entrance and possible municipal surveillance cameras to an aerial view with a pass over the midtown area in a helicopter with a camera and handheld GPS. Meanwhile, from their inside vantage, each guest and delivery was noted, photographed and timed.

James Burton surprised them. He stood at the window for hours at a time peering through his binoculars, identifying over twenty high-profile guests. Exactly how exclusive The Hotel Le Chic actually was soon became evident, though he hadn't identified the madam amongst the women entering the hotel, primarily due to their wide-brimmed summer hats. It was hard not to admire the man, despite his involvement. He surprised them with the depth of his answers to their questions and his intimate knowledge of Georgia's high-ranking elite who came and went through the hotel doors without compunction. He knew them all at some level, including Amy Pennington.

He surprised them even more when he suggested that, if Manuel could not speak with Mercedes, perhaps she might speak with him. However Manuel's reaction was very different when Burton insisted that visuals would not only be an indefensibly thoughtless action, but immediately self-destructive; that Manuel would not want to remember his wife that way for the rest of his ruined life. He was right, of course, but Juan Carlos was the one who convinced him with a firm refusal, not Burton.

James covered his mouth during his last few feet before the granite steps. "Do I pass inspection, gentlemen?" No response was given, though he could imagine JC's reaction from ten stories above. "Appearances are everything, are they not?" he offered with a smirk. "Whether on a bus or in a limo, our dress speaks to who we are for those too blind to see."

The next sound was a series of metallic pings.

"Good afternoon, William. How are you feeling?"

"I am much better, Stephanie. Thank you for your concern."

"That's good to hear. We would hate losing our favorite guest. Monica is in her suite. Good luck with your lessons and let me call the elevator for you."

Observing the house rule, William mechanically passed her his cell phone. "Thank you."

"Enjoy your evening."

"Thank you, Stephanie."

All they heard was his even breathing. His footfalls were silent along the carpeted hallway and when the doors closed behind him the faintest click was inaudible.

"Good afternoon, Monica."

"Good afternoon, William. I am glad to see that you are so improved since your last visit. I have not seen you for ten days."

"I am much better. Thank you."

"Would you like…"

"Thank you. I would like a Glenmorangie very much, and a double, if you would be so kind. Then I would like to get straight into my Spanish lesson."

"You would not…"

"A scotch will be fine, thank you. My subjection to medical orders continues, young lady. Actually, I believe the success of my Spanish is now directly linked to my health and longevity in the near future. You would be surprised to what extent, and" he added with a brightness in his eyes, "I shall be taking an extended trip with my wife in a few weeks. I hear August is a good time for Spain, or possibly Mexico, even though she has long had a thing for Greece. She'll be very impressed with me. Don't you think so, Monica?"

"I believe everyone is impressed with you, William" She passed him the glass. "But if Greece is where she wants to go, why do you learn Spanish? You should learn their language, not mine. Please sit down. Have you done your work from home?"

"Yes, though I am afraid time was not available to me the way I had hoped. I have done what I could, not quite having the spare time of a housewife."

"I do believe you will be a terrible student, William. You have forgotten what…"

"We cannot be good at all things, Monica, and I have not forgotten that you branded me as having no feelings, which I believe is an inappropriate evaluation. I do admit my immediate reaction was to say boohoo because feelings do get in the way at times, unquestionably, but I am very committed to learning your language properly. So why don't you demonstrate some of those linguistic emotions for me?"

He waited silently, before telling her to request appropriate music. He particularly liked the song about a black shirt.

"Emotion is not ordered for us like a meal from room service. Emotion comes from inside, from the heart, and for that you must have one. Also, you are not different from the others like you. To learn my language you must also forget your own and you cannot."

"Who am I like?"

"Like all the others who speak with a drool."

"Southern gentlemen are what I believe you mean."

"I did research the word, which means to leak from your mouth."

JC was bent over, hysterical, holding his sides. "Hombre, how I long to see this wild woman of yours. It seems we each have one."

"My mouth, señora, does not leak. I have had the best schooling, and might I suggest we get on with it."

Monica read his work, not disguising her surprise. "William this work is so perfect. You have not made one mistake."

"My point exactamente. You see how I am already forgetting my English."

"We will begin with pronouns and the present tense of simple verbs, which will seem like baby talk, but that is when we learn to speak."

"Not so. Before we learn to speak as babies, although I have had none, and at this stage I desire as many more, we feel our first emotions, not that we remember. Perhaps that is why the young master languages much more easily, like you." He sipped the Glenmorangie. "So why don't we start there? Show me an example of this youthful emotion you're talking about without trying to kill me with those dark eyes for being a bad man. I have not forgotten your criticism, young lady."

"I am sorry for that. I was wrong to say such things to you."

"Our exchange went no further, nor will it."

"And never will the words I shared with you be told to anyone. This I do know."

He looked at her in a way she had never seen. "We do not yet know that. Do we?"

"Do you know anything about my husband to tell me, or my little girl?"

"I fear not. No more than you already know or suspect, and perhaps we would be best to concentrate on Spanish and emotion. Why don't I pour another drink, and one for you? Eyes are something I believe would help me understand. In business body language means nothing... quite circa seventies thinking and completely without merit. Eyes, however, tell us everything. So speak to me with your eyes and please remember my aging heart. Convince me in Spanish about this emotion. Say anything that comes to mind. I merely want to see your eyes."

She lowered her head, her hands in her lap. "Querido, mi cariño, how I love you so much."

Juan Carlos eased off his headset as she began and walked away from Manuel.

"Not for one moment have I ever stopped loving you, not for one breath have I ever stopped thinking of you, or dreaming of you, or talking with you before I sleep. I know in my heart that you are not dead, cariño, that you will come for me one day because you still love me so much, even though I am the one who has caused you such sorrow. I am so sorry for what I have done, because I did not listen to you. Because of me our daughter was taken from us and is afraid. What I have done and what I will do in this horrible place I have done for you and for our little Sofia. Though I know you will hate me for what I have done, I would rather that you hate me than be without you and our little girl. When you find me, I will spend the rest of my life trying to make you love me again and asking our daughter to forgive me. Te amo, mi amour, te amo. Forgive me.”

“I understood Sofia and amo. You were taking about your child.”

“Yes, I was, and also my husband.”

“I was thinking of something a little more mundane, along the lines of poetry.”

“Love is poetry.”

“And very often both are sad. Now, why don’t we get to pronouns and some beach words?”

“That is what we should do, William. I am sorry.”

“I preferred when you called me Bill. William sounds so severe coming from you.”

“Lo arrepiento, William.”

“Does that mean you will?”

“No. It means that I am sorry that I cannot.”

“I have made you sad once more. It is I who should be sorry, not you. May I pour you another?”

“No, thank you.”

“Monica, let me ask you a question. Was Cynthia here yesterday,” he glanced at his watch, “around three-thirty or so?”

“I am not allowed to say. You know I am not.”

“Was she wearing a red dress with black accessories and does she have blonde hair?” he continued, his gaze fixed.

“There was such a woman in the hotel.”

“Was she with you?”

“Yes.”

“How long has she been coming here?”

“Not as long as you. She likes to swim with the girls and enjoy the sun with us. In the winter we do what all girls like to do.”

“Like what?”

“Our hair and our nails. She is very nice.”

“Thank you.”

"Why does she matter to you?"

"Perhaps I want to know who my competition is, or maybe it's a turn-on."

"I know, but never can you be with us together. Guests are not allowed with guests, only the girls."

"That's not what I meant to say." He tapped a finger against his chest. "I am truly sorry for that." He wasn't talking to her. "I believe this is getting away from me."

He sat facing her, away from the mirror. Manuel struggled to hear.

"You have no reason to be sorry, William." She whispered. "There is no competition. You both pay the same for me, only she has never hurt me the way that you have since two weeks." She stared into her lap. "It does not matter. Lucy will be gone from here very soon. She will help me and if he does not find me first I will find him. Then we will find our daughter."

"Suddenly, Monica, I don't believe my lessons are a very good idea."

"Then why do I not order dinner for us and you can leave here with some Spanish dinner words for your vacation in Greece with your wife?"

"Actually, Monica, I would like to sit here, have another drink and leave. I'm not feeling very much myself. I don't expect you to understand." He tried his best to chuckle. "It's like the female hormonal condition that converts most men to cowards."

"You are not a coward, William. You have only forgotten how to be brave. That is why I am disappointed with you. You know that I am here without my permission and you are doing nothing to help me when you know I cannot help myself or the other girls."

"Monica, none but an absolute fool would enter into a confrontation of any dimension without having at his disposal the most complete and confirmed details of what has led up to that confrontation, good or bad."

"You have said too much for me to understand, but I know you are not a fool."

"No, certainly not. What I am is suddenly very hungry. I have changed my mind. Please order a meal while I read. I must be able to speak at least a little bit of this language very soon. Those who wait for me can wait longer."

He tapped his chest.

Eighty-Seven

James Burton made his way to the Hilton. Refreshed, he arrived at the tenth-floor office by 9:30 as Juan Carlos was in the middle of his three nightly kata rituals. Judo was the first, karate the second; Marine killing techniques required a third half-hour. Over the first weekend together he witnessed each man performing kata with impressive precision and a remarkable smoothness, a graceful ballet, though when both men had donned protective gear and bowed to each other he understood precisely how lethal they were and how vulnerable he was. The fear he felt was cold.

"Amy Pennington is confirmed as being the woman Mercedes knows as Cynthia."

"She's Mercedes' other visitor, the lesbian?"

"Yes, and you know the reason why. So let's leave it there, shall we? She's also QC's leading client. I never knew. I never had a clue. The world is small indeed, which is not necessarily unwelcome news."

"How so?"

"She's almost as wealthy as me and has tendencies which are more acceptable to the less wealthy or the less well-placed, not to sound superior. In other words, gentlemen, she can be easily embarrassed, if not severely damaged by what is soon to transpire and she does not deserve such harsh treatment. She is as beautiful a woman inside as out. You may have interpreted that for yourselves, if you were listening. If not, you will accept my word. She is very kind and very generous. We live in a world with double standards, a world she knows well. She is constantly surrounded by those who want something from her, to be close to her for gain, though never to share closeness with her. I won't throw stones, gentlemen, and I blame her not at all for her way of escaping. Her very conservative corporation would be unduly embarrassed by this and I won't allow that to happen. Despite what you might believe, she will want to help us.

"She's not invited to the party," insisted Juan Carlos.

"I understand your concern, and for the same reason you won't be invited to mine." He glanced at Manuel. "When you are enhancing your killing skills this weekend, Manny, I shall be entertaining Miss Pennington privately."

"That is not a real good idea."

"On the contrary, and I'll tell you why, though I had not planned to until later. You see, I have only given you the first part of my plan. We still have much to talk about. Once the ladies are safely sheltered in North Carolina they will need a good deal of assistance." He put up his hand. "Manny, you recently paid off a large debt to the bank in one lump sum, which means you now owe someone else, presumably him, and you are living in what would, in another life, be unacceptable to you and Mercedes. I commend you for your integrity. You may also have noticed the Rover is registered in your name. Don't bother to thank me. You see, I know more than a little about you. I also know why you're in debt and I presume the other ladies and their families are experiencing the same predicament. Right now they have no clothes beyond a few cocktail dresses and a wardrobe full of lingerie. Granted, all very high-end, though not very appropriate for crowded bus terminals or airports. They have no credit and no money. I intend to resolve that issue and I know Amy Pennington will assist me without any coercion on my part."

"That's very generous of you, to a fault, a serious fault. How will you explain to her what is about to happen here, Señor Burton?"

"I won't have to, JC. You already know much more about many of these people than they would ever want you to, and they don't yet know. Although as a group they are formidable, divided they are not, unless confronted from behind their tiered HR departments. I assure you, the reservations at the hotel will drop to zero immediately. They have too much to lose from this association and won't sacrifice any of it for something they can have delivered to private offices anytime they wish. Being discovered with someone's wife or an escort is one thing, being found paying for services with barely legal girls who were all previously raped and kidnapped along with their children is entirely another matter and irreversibly destructive."

"Your point?"

"Once Miss Pennington is warned, I have no doubt she will stay away. Bear in mind, what I am doing is for the benefit of the girls and Amy."

"What about Mercedes, James. When your Miss Pennington stops coming after your dinner together, and you're with her only for Spanish, what happens to Mercedes?"

"Mercedes is a Preferred Girl, nothing will happen. Miss Pennington will simply be on vacation for two weeks after calling to tentatively reserve for the week of the 13th or 20th. Preferred Guests are normally acquainted with availability restrictions. However Cynthia is apparently not restricted that way and continues to enjoy the pool and the spa."

"Do you have other friends we should know about?"

"No, Miss Pennington is the one to whom I feel any

obligation. I will give you full details of our meeting, which will certainly be a picnic after my Saturday Spanish lesson with Mercedes."

The Madam

Eighty-Eight

As he had done over the past twelve days, James Burton phoned his wife once each morning and he never forgot call her before her early bedtime, which he noticed was considerably later than prior to his departure. They spoke in giggles and whispers about everything and nothing, sometimes not speaking at all, not wanting to disconnect from what was renewed and vital. Fleeting minutes had become long, precious moments and she wanted him home.

He was halfway through his commitment, he promised. He was in good hands, good company to do what he knew was noble and right, if not praiseworthy. If she wanted, he would explain everything upon his return. Until then she must believe he was doing good for the first time in a very long time. She believed him.

He had hoped Thursday evening with Mercedes would be a pleasant precursor to a longer visit on Saturday. Not so, and began with his refusal to once again wear a camera with JC's firm support. Manuel spent most of Friday grumbling in Spanish as he worked on Thursday's sound track, separating Mercedes' voice from her conversation with Burton and transferring her to tape so that she alone would be with him for his weekend at Fort Bennings.

Saturday, when Burton arrived from the hotel, Juan Carlos was in front of the plasma screen reviewing eighteen hours of videos, freezing all images and converting them to prints. He had done all but the three who had left the hotel between five and 7:00. The imagery was crystal clear despite the swirling winds and violent rain. The person caught leaving at seven was a woman. She was tall, slim, blonde, and her eyes emitted the same sparkling ice blue of North Atlantic icebergs JC had once seen on a postcard. She wore no hat, nor did she carry an umbrella. She wore low-rise blue jeans, a sheer white blouse and something underneath that was either black or blue.

"Jaime, ven aquí." JC's way of telling Burton he might not die in a week or two, though nothing in life was guaranteed. They had had too much time together the night before and James Burton needed very much for someone other than Manuel to understand the torment of his past thirteen years, what had driven him to the hotel and to Mercedes. By the end of the evening he was Jaime.

"Is this another shy lesbo? She left at seven on the nose, an hour late."

Burton answered after peering into the screen for long moments. "No, JC. That is the head lesbo herself. That, my friend, is the infamous and reclusive Miss Divine."

"I believe she would easily eat my balls for lunch, and not choke. How come you still have yours after so long?"

Burton snorted. "They were packed away. I have just recently taken them out of storage."

JC nodded, chortling. "I will be ready to track her next time, in case our plans change. Will we see her again tonight?"

"Possibly, though by her leaving this late your guess is as good as mine."

"She's not bad on the eyes in a tough shit kind of way, but I'm thinking she must be fucking cold to the touch, hombre."

"You'll have to ask the girls. No one else would know. She's strictly business and strictly into girls, or so I'm told."

JC swiveled, facing him. "You did right by refusing Manny's request on Thursday. Neither do I want him to see her as she is or where she is. He'll get over you refusing him. I will see that he does. He would never get over seeing her that way, though that will not be the case tonight, Jaime. Tonight you'll be wired like a fucking fence in Laredo. We need to know what to expect when we get inside and precisely what to expect."

"I understand."

"What we need…"

"You will have the fullest and most complete coverage possible, of all but the fourth floor. It's been a long time since I've toured the facility."

"We need what comes after the entrance, precisely and slowly, a full scan of the reception, the stairs, the corridors, and the suites. Whatever you take of Mercedes I will edit out on Sunday before Manny returns. Above all, do not hurry unless you must. What will you wear?"

"Loafers, linen slacks and a light-weight summer sweater."

"That's no good. Wear a dark suit or a dark suit jacket that you will not take off unless you can put your sunglasses in the open pocket of a dark cotton shirt. I'll wire you before you go and test you before you go in."

"I understand."

"I will need you here on Sunday, before your dinner meeting, to detail the video footage and stills for me, so I can figure out our timing. We can extrapolate distances, but try to count the distance from the doors to the reception, from there to the elevator, and from there to her suite. What suite is she in?"

"She's at the very end of the third floor, the Southwest corner. Each floor houses six suites and each Prefect has a suite adjacent to the elevator. The doors are staggered as an additional privacy measure for the guests. They lead into a salon; off the salon are a full bathroom and bedroom. No windows."

Juan Carlos chuckled. "That's very good, Jaime, but if you don't mind I need to catch some zs. Don't let me go past noon. We need time to get you ready and go over a few more details."

Eighty-Nine

James Burton was in much better spirits knowing how proud his Doris would be of him penetrating deep into enemy territory to lay the footwork for a difficult and dangerous extraction of a dozen innocents. He was equally exhilarated by the thought of his confirmed dinner with Amy Pennington the next evening, understandably curious about how she would react to his information. He inhaled deeply.

"How do I look?"

He felt a strange pride when a single the tenth-floor light flicked on and off imperceptibly. JC approved. He was going in.

"Good evening, Miss Genevieve. Miss Kelly, Miss Melanie, you are both ravishing this evening as usual."

Genevieve smiled because she had to. She didn't like him being there in the least; she hadn't since Christmas. Kelly skipped over, helping him with his damp raincoat and Melanie pirouetted, asking how he liked her costume of white cotton panties with pastel pink ruffles and matching three-quarter push-up bra with white knee socks and a lollypop that would last a year.

His reaction was sincere. "Melanie anyone seeing you would fall from his chair, I harbor no doubt. To say you are lovely is to say nothing, and you. Kelly, you are so," he seemed perplexed, "so exquisite in that, that..." He furrowed his brow.

"You know exactly what it is, Bill. Come, now. It's not like you don't know all this stuff."

"Well, if I must. I suppose my fine scotch might wait a moment longer." He nodded thoughtfully, turning to appraise her. "I suppose your delightful little ensemble might be considered a whimsical floor-length gown of sheer white chiffon with satin spaghetti straps, flowing front and back panels to accent the nude female form, a bra top featuring open lace details and matching sheer chiffon panties with delicate satin side ties. And I love your four-inch sandals...a perfect accent. If you were model on television I would jump through the screen to be with you this very moment."

"What about me, Bill."

"You're a naughty little girl, Melanie, and you should be severely spanked. Now, take my phone. I abhor when people are late, especially me."

Juan Carlos hadn't noted the increase in his heart rate. When he first saw the drop-dead gorgeous Kelly appear from behind the dark curtain of Burton's coat he did come close to falling from his chair, when he saw Melanie he reached for the zoom and tried his hardest not to blink. James Burton did a full turn, slowly, following Genevieve to the sliding doors. Thirty steps from the main doors to the reception and another twenty to the elevator, from where another hundred steps along the third-floor corridor to the southwest corner brought him to Monica.

"Buenas tardes, William. Bienvenido."

"Gracias, Mónica."

"Me parece que estés enfermo."

"I apologize for being late. I was in the lobby speaking with Melanie and Kelly. They are beautiful girls, very nice. I felt I could not be rude."

Only her eyes looked up at him. "I said that I think you

are not well. You are very tired. Are you sick once again?"

"No, gracias. No enfermo, sino bueno. Yo digo gracias por usted."

She shook her head. "No William, décimos: te doy las gracias. Te doy las gracias."

"De nada, Mónica."

Monica's head was level with the thick-rimmed black sunglasses. Juan Carlos had seen all her photographs Manuel had taken of her since their beginning as lovers in Veracruz, not one of them preparing him for the live image he was seeing. She wasn't the same woman at all. He understood, when seeing her and hearing her voice, the emotions Manuel suffered over the past twelve months. He also understood the hardship wasn't over, that a different woman was coming home to his friend, and something would have to be done to lessen the devastating shock. What he also understood for the first time, though he would never admit the revelation, was James Burton.

"William, come in and give me your jacket. Let us do the book work first. After that we can work on more simple verbs."

"A drink first, I would hope."

"It is on the table. But you should not because your health is not good."

"Will you join me?"

"Yes, please, with much water."

"You are especially beautiful this evening, though I would feel that much better seeing your pearly whites."

She frowned. "William, I do not wear las perlas. I do not like them. They are for old women."

JC laughed aloud with a sudden burst. He harbored no doubt that Carmella would love this woman and he would phone his cousin to tell her so as soon as Burton left the suite.

"Sometimes we refer to teeth as pearly whites. It's an

expression. Would you excuse me for a moment? I won't be long," and he left the salon to walk as slowly as he reasonably could through her bedroom and into the bathroom.

He whispered the numbers in Spanish and from behind Monica thought at least he was trying.

Juan Carlos peered into the screen, hardly believing what he was seeing. Burton's description of the suite was extremely accurate and he certainly wouldn't be showing Manuel. In fact, he would go one step better and destroy the video of the three-rooms lavishly decorated with high-end simplicity. Mercedes had William's drink in her hand when he walked from the elegant bathroom where he provided Juan Carlos with a 360° scan and whispered commentary.

"Monica the music is perfect. I'm beginning to enjoy the Latin sound. Perhaps one day you'll teach me to dance a few steps."

"I would like that, perhaps for your trip to Greece, William."

"Will they serve dinner soon, do you think?"

"Yes, very soon. I told the kitchen that you wanted to eat early."

"Perfect. I seem to have much more of an appetite these days."

"You do not seem very well to me."

"I'm fine. Thank you."

"You are very tired, maybe because you are never at home. Do you eat there also?"

"Not always, but with the upcoming trip I really must work harder at maintaining my appearance."

"Would you like that I prepare…"

"Only dinner will be prepared tonight, and for a while longer, I'm afraid." He poured another scotch. "Also, thank you for not dressing to give me a heart attack. Melanie and Kelly were sufficient visual delights for one night."

"They are very pretty."

"So are you. Now can we begin?"

Sitting and bearing witness to Burton's abysmal effort was excruciating for Juan Carlos. He would never be a linguist and not because he had waited too long. JC had also spent the time studying Mercedes as she filled the plasma screen to the accompaniment of Burton swallowing food and drink before processing the intake past a very sensitive mike.

After Carol and Dree wheeled out the serving cart loaded with dishes and glasses, William commented on what efficient Duty Girls they were, causing Mercedes' eyes to brighten with disgust the way only a Latina's eyes could. JC recognized the glare all too well and knew beyond any doubt Carmelita and Mercedes would be best friends very soon.

"Again, I apologize. I did not mean to imply anything of a derogatory nature, Monica. The meal was superb. Please tell them again for me when you see them."

"Why do you not tell them yourself? They are the ones who did prepare your meal, not me, or the fine chef in our kitchen. Telling them would make them happy. They will be in the kitchen when you leave, cooking, or in the lounge, cleaning."

"Thank you for the suggestion." He checked his watch.

"Your wife is waiting for you?"

"No, not right now, but she will be in a little while." He sipped his Rémy Martin. "We are worlds apart, Monica, and I don't mean to speak disparagingly, however I would have liked for you to meet my wife under more appropriate circumstances. She would have liked you, as I do. I believe she would have loved you and treated you like the daughter she never had."

"And what would she think about what you have done for one year with the daughter she never had, William?

Would she feel love for me then?"

"Yes, I know she would. Of course, she would be disappointed in me. She would be sad, yet she would forgive me because she knows I am a man of my word."

Monica missed the message. "And what words have you told her?"

"That I love her; that I always have and always will."

"But you are here with me and not with her."

"Yes, because I am a man of my word."

He checked his watch again.

"You are not speaking very well in Spanish, William. You need many more lessons. I believe at least ten thousand. Will you come to be with me after your trip to Greece?"

"I believe I have answered that question. I will be here for as long as it takes for you to leave. If that means two more years, I will be with you for two more years and my wife will know why. Should you leave earlier, I will cease being a guest here forthwith." He sipped. "Why are you staring at me like that?"

"You are laughing at me. You know I do not understand when you talk funnily."

"You should ever talk as well."

She glared. "¡Ten cuidado, abuelo!"

"I believe I have just witnessed more of your Mexican emotion. Might you be so kind as to afford me a translation?"

"I said that you should take care of yourself because you are not as young as before and I worry about you."

He nodded, smirking. "A very concise language, this Spanish. It mustn't take any of you very long to read a book."

She fumed. "Would you like me …?"

"To call the desk? Yes, I would. My energy level seems to be waning, possibly due to my medication. Please tell

Genevieve as well that I would like to thank Dree and Carol." He kissed her cheek. "I will be here with you on Tuesday, Thursday, and Saturday. I think I should feel somewhat jealous of your time with Cynthia."

"Do you know her, William? Do you know Cynthia?"

He pinched her chin gently. "No, I do not Monica, and she is never to know me. Do you understand?"

Ninety

Once outside James Burton put his hand to his mouth, glancing upward; an hour later he was at the tenth-floor office. "You've been here thirty-six hours. Nothing more will happen tonight and I'm not unfamiliar with this equipment should more photos be required. We can prepare a schematic of the building tomorrow before I leave for my dinner with Miss Pennington."

"She hates you, hombre, because she feels you have let her down. She counted on you because of your soft-hearted exchange after the taxi ride, now she believes you have failed her."

"The more she does the better. An expression exists in business, which I first heard during a rather ridiculous conference in New Orleans in the mid-nineties, one I've always considered as pure corporate bullshit. Its adoption is strictly forbidden in my corporation's culture and goes like this: Short-term pain for long-term gain. It's short, to the point, and pure unadulterated bullshit because in the business world those who most often tolerate the pain, the minions, are not those who see the gain. So the feeble corporate maxim is reversed for the many. Mercedes' short-term pain will last a lifetime, not to mention my pretended ill-treatment of her. Those who gain will be her family, which is why he must be all that he can be to her and forget totally about himself once he walks through those doors."

"He knows, Jaime, and I know him. By now he has listened to her voice a hundred times. He will not fail her, if we do not."

"Do you believe she is strong enough not to betray herself, were she to know?"

"I do not know her well enough to say, though I see how she has changed. I also see she has not hardened. She still feels love and I hear warmth in her voice."

"Perhaps we should tell her, rather than continuing this hurtful ruse. She's a very smart girl. That's why I didn't ask her those other questions. This cursed dark-eyed Latina emotion business might be cute with me, not so if it should suddenly appear for the benefit of Miss Divine."

"We will need those answers on Tuesday. It is imperative that we know."

Burton shook his head in agreement.

Ninety-One

Sunday, July 29

"Amy you are a vision to behold. I took particular care dressing myself this evening so that I might be seen as equal to the loveliest lady in Atlanta. I see now how miserably I failed."

"James, sit down. And be good. You already have my business. You are still incorrigible and your compliments are still outrageous."

Burton pushed in her chair. "True, nonetheless."

"What a charming corner table." She raised an eyebrow, grinning. "Are we starting an affair?"

"No, Amy, though only my advanced age prevents me from any attempt."

"How is Doris, James? Will I ever see her again? It's been so very long. I miss her so much."

He beamed. "On that note I have the best news to report. Yes, you will, and very shortly. Something happened recently that has transported us to where we were before the accident, Amy. In fact, she's planning a month-long trip somewhere overseas as we speak. It's been so long since I've traveled I have no doubt it will cost me a fortune for a new wardrobe, and hers will certainly bankrupt me. I'm even taking Spanish lessons in the event we end up in Spain, though my bets are on the Greek Isles."

"That is so delightful, James. Might I assume the once-famous Doris Burton soirées will once again be the envy and talk of the town?"

"Yes, you may indeed, and you will be the first one invited. Until then I would ask for your complete discretion. One never knows, does one?"

"I'm happy for her, and for you."

"Thank you. Although there is an unfortunate downside Amy, which is why I have asked you here this evening." He paused as the waiter brought the vodka and soda for the lady, the Glenmorangie neat for the gentleman. He raised his glass. "To your health, Amy, and your happiness in all things."

The glasses clinked softly.

"Thank you, James. I wish the same for you and Doris. You deserve so much happiness. The years have been so difficult for both of you." Burton took a sip. What he wanted was to empty the glass. Amy Pennington's vodka and soda barely moistened her lips. "So what is this downside, James? You have me intrigued, as well as honored that you're telling me this."

"Three and a half weeks ago, Amy, completely by happenstance unless one believes in God, which I don't, I met a very nice young man. A year ago he came home from Iraq to discover his wife and daughter were missing. He's searched for them tirelessly since that moment. He's a chemical engineer, yet he labors as a taxi driver, putting in double shifts as they say in the business, all in the hope of finding her. To-date he has not."

"James that is so terribly sad. What about the police? What are they doing?"

"They are of absolutely no help or consequence, I'm afraid." He swallowed half the remaining scotch. "Amy I met this young man by the most incredible circumstance, by virtue of being late for a meeting with the Peterson Group.

What is even more unbelievable is that I am the one person in this entire world who is able to help him. You see, by the hand of fate, the young lady who is burdened with teaching me Spanish at the moment is the young man's wife."

"James that's absolutely wonderful. And why haven't you brought them together?"

"Amy, my Spanish teacher has only become my teacher since I met the young man in his cab. Prior to that she was, we can say, a friend, the one description that seems fitting. She's adorable in the extreme and very kind. Her name is Mercedes."

Amy Pennington ventured innocently from the reality, smiling with understanding. "And you love her, James, but now that you and Doris have found each other again, it's complicated."

"Complicated is an understatement and, no, I do not love her. Though I do see her on a regular basis when she is not with another, a woman she knows as Cynthia. Amy, we are talking about a young woman we both know as Monica. She and her daughter were kidnapped a year ago by Miss Divine's senseless thugs and brought to Le Chic after repeatedly raping her." Burton signaled the waiter to bring the wine, excusing himself to Amy Pennington for having taken the liberty of earlier ordering for her. He had not been wrong in assuming she would understand his intention. She was in another world, devastated, unable to move. "Amy, what is said at this table stays at this table, not even Doris will know. You have my word as a friend and a gentleman. I will do nothing to offend or embarrass you. I know Cynthia's visits to the hotel were completely without the knowledge of what I am about to tell you. You will be shocked and horrified to say the least, but as I told her young husband, this is not about any of us. This is about freeing her and the other girls as soon as possible, and why you must never return there. What you must do, however, is call the hotel tomorrow to cancel your existing reservations. Tell them you will call during the week of the thirteenth when you return from vacation, or the twentieth. Then, Amy, you will go on that vacation and be somewhere far away from here. Do not return until then."

Her hands were cupped over her mouth, real tears flooding over them. "Monica was kidnapped, James?" She buried her face. "I truly thought she was there…"

"As did I, Amy, as did I."

"James, please let me explain."

"Explain what, Amy? You owe me no explanation. I enjoyed working with your father, as tough as he was, and I am equally proud to work with you. I cannot think of anyone who is lovelier or kinder and I am honored to have you as a friend. You have helped me through some difficult times, if you remember, and I am anxious to once again receive you into our home when we return from our respective vacations. Do not be concerned about what I think or, for that matter, Doris. We think nothing but good and wonderful things of you. You should know that."

She grabbed at his hand. "Does Monica know any of this? Does she know anything about her husband?"

"No, she does not, though she is the one who told me the entire story in whispered details a few days after I met her husband. Now she dislikes me immensely because she believes I'm doing nothing to reverse her situation. It's very difficult, more so for her than me."

"James, did she speak with you about Cynthia as well?"

"Wipe your tears away. You are far too beautiful for anyone to see you this way. I won't allow it." He pulled a silk hanky from his pocket. "She told me Cynthia is a beautiful person inside and out, that you like each other as girlfriends, not one word more."

"I'm so embarrassed."

"Why, Amy? Were you embarrassed before you

discovered I knew? Do I appear shocked or horrified? Do you think I will become less of a friend," he grinned, "or raise your fees?"

"No to the first three." She sipped her wine nervously. "A definite I hope not to the fourth. James," she squeezed his hand, "what will we do to help her, to get her and the other girls out of there?"

Unexpected tears welled in his eyes and he felt no need to explain as he brought the palm of his free hand to his face. "Thank you, I knew to expect as much and much has already been done. We are in the final phase, Amy. There is absolutely no way she or the others can be hurt. While you're on vacation I shall be learning Spanish with her, nothing more."

"I'm stunned. All this time, I never suspected. I never even thought about it."

"I intend to assist these girls financially, Amy. May I count on your assistance?"

"Yes, you can, of course. Any amount. What were you thinking?"

"I've been too preoccupied with planning over the last while to consider the details, as you can appreciate. However, my initial thoughts are of creating a foundation of sorts, which in my case will equal four times the annual hotel fee. I also intend to give each of the ten girls, as well as Stephanie and Genevieve, fifty thousand in cash. I'm proposing twenty the day they are set free and thirty at a later date, through the foundation, when we have established they are safely reunited with their families. If such is not the case, for a number of possible reasons, we will not permit them to endure the slightest hardship. I intend to interview and track each one very closely through the foundation, with the utmost discretion. Amy, the story worsens. Most of them, like Mercedes, were kidnapped with their children. The children must also be found and reunited, though I daresay the earlier victims pose a very dark problem. The horror has existed for several years and that could be very problematic. Amy, the need for secrecy and discretion is absolute. The girls must never know who is setting them free, or assisting them. They do not know the location of the hotel and their lack of knowledge must be maintained for reasons I am not at liberty to discuss."

"Let's make that one-hundred thousand cash, James, and I'll meet you equally on the million. If that's not enough, you need only ask. There's no limit for me. None whatsoever. Those ladies are my only friends, especially Mercedes. I will arrange for the transfers from my personal account the very moment you're ready. Is tomorrow too soon? And I will play an active role in the foundation as soon as possible. It's a fabulous idea and I won't take no for an answer."

"Thank you, Amy. I suspect very strongly that several dozen very worthwhile charitable donations will come our way from some of Georgia's leading citizens. I daresay several million dollars. Let me tell you why, and let me tell you all I know about Le Chic, Miss Divine, and as much as I deem prudent about the rescue. There is nothing to gain by telling you everything. But first, let me correct you. Those wonderful ladies are not your only friends. Old friends, who are now reacquainted with you, are anxious to meet and embrace anyone you would care to introduce to us."

Burton added a discreet amount of wine to her glass, and much more to his that was empty.

Ninety-Two

"Good evening, gentlemen. How was your training, Manny?"

"My time in Iraq did not seem as long. JC filled me in about yesterday. How is she?"

"She's distraught, of course, not at all the same woman I knew three weeks ago. She clearly wants to push me for information, but she's afraid. Remember the suites are monitored randomly for conversation and activity and she knows all too well that frowns and tears don't come with the package."

"We need that information on Tuesday. It's critical."

"I understand, and you will have it without fail. I believe I have the perfect way." He looked first at Juan Carlos. Neither man knew. "Manny, how strong is Mercedes. Will she be able to pretend not knowing you are only feet away from her? Be certain."

"I don't know. On the other hand, I'm afraid she will do something foolish if she does not. You did what you had to, questioning her that day. I understand, but you sure stirred up a hurricane of shit."

"What's in your gut?" Burton raised an open palm, preventing the answer. "Let me say this first. My presumption is, whether true or not, that you don't want the police involved because you would prefer that Miss Divine and her goons not get out in five to ten years. Quite frankly,

I have no qualms about what happens to her or her cronies. I mean that. I also believe that when we get to the fourth floor we will learn much more than what drugs she uses. I believe we will learn more about the girls and their children. I say we let her know. However, let us be certain she is never alone since Miss Cynthia will no longer be visiting."

"Amigo, do you agree with this?"

"It could be the right thing to do, Manny, in a way not to shock her." JC turned to Burton. "Remember, Jaime, all you are doing is learning Spanish."

"Precisely, gentlemen, and I still require a great deal of tutelage. Manny, will she recognize your writing?"

"Yes, she will."

"Then you will ask her what we must know in your own hand, warning her that discretion is of paramount importance. That is how she will know. Say what else you wish. Also tell her our lives will be endangered, should her emotions betray us. Cruel and unfair, I grant you, but let us put the onus on her. I believe doing so will infuse her with the strength she will require. She may surprise us; though tell her nothing of your daughter. Let's play that one by ear. It's your call."

"Let me think about it. How was your date?"

"The company was excellent and our time spent together was productive in the extreme. Though the fine meal was wasted and the wine might as well have been grocery grade swill. Miss Pennington did not let us down, gentlemen, as I earlier expressed. She is giving one-point-six-million dollars to match my contribution towards helping the girls. She will transfer the money tomorrow morning. I will give you the details later. Suffice it to say she will vacation for a few weeks and will not require the services of the hotel."

"You trust her, knowing what she does?"

"Yes, I do implicitly. We enjoy a long history. Her father and I were well acquainted in business and now that we have even more in common she would do nothing to jeopardize the girls, herself or our friendship. I believe she has proven that in a very tangible way. Don't you?"

Manuel nodded. "Yes, I do."

"That emotive eye thing is not exclusively Latin property, Manny. She cried copious tears throughout the entire evening, to the point where I had to discard a very wet and very expensive pocket hanky." They acknowledged the attempt at levity. "If she could, Amy Pennington would kill Miss Divine herself, whoever she is. Mercedes is not alone in her anguish at this moment, gentlemen."

"What about this Miss Divine? Do we have anything on her?"

"A clear photo, taken yesterday morning, hombre," Juan Carlos answered.

"Show me."

Juan Carlos raised the screen of the laptop. "You will love this, amigo. I made her the wallpaper. Not the prettiest cow in the pasture, but she's good enough for practice."

"She's a lesbian, JC."

"It's not what I meant, Jaime. Examine what you see more closely. See my artwork."

Manuel stood still, frozen. "That is her, James? You are certain of that?"

"Yes, that is her."

"You have no doubt? You said it's been several years… you are one hundred percent certain?"

"Yes, that is her… my final answer."

Manuel's eyes were glued to the screen. "Hombres, we attack in one week, when I will replace this red dot on her forehead with my own that will go through it and blow her into hell. James, I will write our questions in Spanish and you will deliver them tomorrow, not Tuesday. From now on, hombres, Mercedes will not be alone, not for one moment, and James, be sure you do nothing that will make me kill you after I send this lesbiana puta piece of shit to hell. Juan Carlos, call your friends who stand ready to help us."

Until that point Burton only imagined what might happen. The guesswork was now removed and he put a hand discreetly to his chest to calm his heart. There was no longer a need to dream or think about the outcome. Manuel Del Fuego's eyes were not black with Latin emotion. They were ruby red and focused on the screen with pure hatred and the intense need to kill.

Ninety-Three

The Week of Monday, July 30

"Stephanie you are a shining seraph of the highest order in an otherwise horrible and dreary world." He handed her the vase. "For you, Stephanie my dear, and for the other little angels who surround you. Thank you so much for taking my last minute reservation. You were very kind to accommodate me."

"Thank you, Bill. It's a little unusual, but the girls will love you for them. Those are for Monica, I suppose."

"Yes, if I may." Stephanie shrugged, more interested in her flowers. "I haven't been myself lately, but I'm feeling much better," he smiled half-heartedly; "despite the fact my wife has left me. She's thrown me out actually, which leaves me free to concentrate on not having a heart attack as well as my Spanish."

"We won't let anything happen to you, Bill, and it's not the first time you've brought her flowers." Stephanie inhaled the sweet scent. "I suppose you'll want dinner served this evening?"

"Yes, thank you. And I will keep my reservation for tomorrow as well."

"You can have the whole week if you want. Monica's agenda is open except for you."

"That would indeed be excellent, Stephanie. Then I'll

have all week to make proper arrangements. Even the best hotels soon become tedious. Thank you."

"Consider it done. I believe Monica is waiting for you."
*

"He is not too bad for a gringo, hombre." Manuel offered, "In another life he could be as good as us."

"Jaime has big balls, Manny. He should be with his wife, or signing checks instead of fucking with the lesbian bitch."

"What is with this 'Jaime' thing?"

"What the hell. Would you want to go through life being called James? I did not think so, chico. So shut up and listen or I will kick your ass another time."
*

"Hola, Señorita Mónica. Me llamo Jaime y tengo floras para usted."

"Muchísimas gracias, William, son muy bonitas. Gracias, entre por favor."

"It is my insignificant way of apologizing to you for treating you so badly over the last little while."

"You have not treated me badly, William."

"Yes, I have, and I beg your forgiveness."

"I do forgive you."

"I will not be going to Greece or Spain, Monica. My wife has left me. However, I do want to continue with my Spanish until my health returns. Who knows? Maybe I'll meet a sexy Latina lady. By the way, I believe the music is a little low for the required ambiance and I could use a boost."

"I will serve you one."

Manuel gave Juan Carlos a punch to the shoulder, both men guffawing at Burton's expense.

"Boost, Monica, not booze. It means a pick-me-up, not a drink." He saw the eyes.

She shrugged, inhaling the aroma of a dozen yellow

carnations. "I am sorry for you. I know you did love your wife."

"Life must go on. Arrange your flowers, and I need that drink. I believe you will be pleased with my homework. I have worked very hard since Saturday."

"Good, William. Until now I am not very impressed with you."

"May I pour you a drink?"

"Yes, please, with much water. Thank you."

"Please sit, I'm very anxious to hear your review of my work." He brought the glass to his lips, keeping his hand over the workbook. "My work is in the form of questions. I thought you might help me with the answers, though I believe I began with a statement. Go ahead, but take a sip first. I made it quite strong. Forgive me." Mercedes was instantly curious as she read the first line. When she glanced at him, his eyes were cold, his expression grave, and his voice strangely commanding. "Feel free to make any corrections, Monica, or additions, and please do keep your head lowered as you read."

Cariño, we are coming for you. Do not betray us with watery eyes. I heard your voice and the silly words you spoke to me. You must believe that I have never stopped loving you. But we need your help, cariño, and know that none of this would be possible without the man who sits by your side. First: Are the girls always in their suites after the guests leave? Yes or no. Second: How many cameras are on each floor? Write the answer. Leave nothing out. Third: Write the physical details of the men who raped you in our home. Challenge your memory, mi cariño. The memory is painful, but you must if they are to pay for what they have done to you and the others.

440

William leaned closer to her, facing away from the mirror. "Monica," he whispered, running a firm finger across the page, tapping for affect, "please read the first line again. It is critical that you remain strong for us. Please do not raise your head until your tears have dried. Please continue."

Fourth: William is with you to help, cariño, since the night you told him everything. Deceiving you has been painful for us; do not defeat us with your tears. Our lives and your freedom depend on your strength. He is a brave man, risking his life to help us. I love you. Be ready, and do everything that William tells you without question. We are not far from you.

Her hand was trembling, the ink on the pages becoming blurred stains before she turned to Burton.

"I believe the third question is the most difficult, Monica. However, the first and second are causing me a good deal of difficulty. Perhaps if you were to speak all three very clearly, and quietly, as you write, I would have a better and more immediate understanding."

"How close is he?"

Burton stood, hiding her from the camera. He drained his glass and stretched as he widened the space between the center buttons of his shirt, revealing the thin wire. "I will understand whatever answer you give me, if you speak clearly enough. I'm really working very hard at this."

"Bill, I was very wrong. Forgive me," she whispered, her face streaked with make-up.

"Don't be silly. I told you my Spanish would improve with time. But that's English and not why I am here this evening. Or have you forgotten so quickly?"

"You will understand everything that I say? Are you certain?"

"Yes, Monica. I will understand every word." He sat beside her, running a finger over the same page. "With the flowers you will not be alone. Let no one touch them. We will hear every word, every sound, every minute, and do not go to the fourth floor for any reason, Monica. If you feel in danger when I am gone simply call my name as loudly as you can, or Manuel's. Scream if you must, but only if you must. You will not be alone, even when you are." He smiled brightly. "And I forgot to tell you, Stephanie has arranged for me to visit every night through Saturday, regular hours, of course. Spending more time with you will be a great help for what I must accomplish over the next few days." Monica went to the bar. She poured a straight Glenmorangie away from the mirror. "Young lady, unless you poured that for me, you have sufficient liquor in your hands to put you to sleep for the night. I can't have you dozing during my lessons."

"Where will you go when you leave here if you do not have a home?" Her tone was plaintive, her face damp with tears.

"My office for the time being, I suppose. Though I do have friends a few moments from here who understand what is happening."

"So close?"

"Yes, so close."

"Thank you for doing so well on your Spanish. I feel so good in my heart to know that you are working hard and so bad in my heart that I did not believe in you."

"That's very nice, thank you. But I have a wonderful idea, Monica. This is a perfect song for dancing at my speed. Why don't we do that? You might also increase my pathetic vocabulary at the same time." He took one small hand in his, pressing the other against the middle of her back. "Just don't wet my shirt."

She spoke softly, so that he could hear. "What is he

wearing right now? Do you know?"

"Dress boots, black I believe, leather pants, also black I believe, and a black sweater. Not quite my style, though I suppose it's a suitable fashion."

"Does he have long beautiful hair?"

"No, he does not, and you know why."

"Is he handsome, as I remember him?"

"He's a very fine representation of the specie and he hears every word you speak, Monica, as though he were here with you." He narrowed the gap between them. "The song won't last forever, young lady. He hears every word clearly."

She spoke to him through two songs. When Amanda came in with Jennifer to serve the meal William thanked them graciously without missing a step. He would serve the dinner himself, after the third dance.

William understood not a word of what she said and after dinner he fell asleep with stains on his shirt.
*

Tuesday, July 31.

"Good evening, Bill."

"Hello, Monica. It's been a busy day, indeed. I hope dinner is already here."

"Yes, but you do have time for a scotch first. Do you have any homework for me?"

"Yes, I do. There is so much more I must learn. And since you're such a fine teacher. I'm sure you will have the answers."

"I do hope so. Did you speak with your friends? Will they help you to be okay?"

"I left my friends a few moments ago, before coming here. Apparently my plans are working in my favor."

"I have adored my lovely flowers all day. I spoke to them to tell them how I do love them so much."

He chuckled, pouring two fingers. "Yes, indeed. The flowers enjoyed each word. I can't say I ever saw flowers water themselves so frequently heretofore."

"Thank you, Bill, for my flowers. Thank you for bringing them to me. It has been so long since the last time. I, too, will water them each day."

"Perhaps we should dine, listen to this beautiful music, and then get down to business".
*

Lucy sat stretched out in the lounge, enjoying a rare evening off with a bag of chips, a soda and Nicholas Cage.

"Lucy."

"Yes, Genevieve?"

"Miss Divine will be here at ten. She wants you in her suite at ten-thirty. Wear anything you wish."

"Thank you. I'll be ready." What time is it now?"

"Eight."

"Would you call me in my suite at nine-thirty?"

"Yes."

The plasma screen went black and Lucy spent the ninety minutes sitting in the dark calculating, remembering, wondering why her, why tonight. Most of the girls had lost track of time, but Monica hadn't let her. She knew exactly how the night would end. She was going home. Wherever that would be, she knew it wouldn't be Charleston.

At nine-thirty she stood in the shower, watching her skin transition to red, the only way to stop herself from trembling. She stepped out at ten. At ten-thirty the elevator doors opened onto the fourth floor.

"Good evening, Lucy."

"Good evening, Divine."

"Come in, darling. I've been anxious to see you all day."

"I only heard a little while ago you wanted me here. Thank you."

"You're lovely. Is that new?"

"Yes, you bought it for me in the spring."

"Did I buy you panties for it?"

"Yes, you did."

"I've poured you a glass of wine. It's on the bar. Why don't you bring us a couple of reefers at the same time and take them off for me. I've run a bath for us, but there's no hurry."

Lucy beamed. She wasn't going home, not that she had a home, a husband or a child. Alone in the dark she had thought to ask Divine if she could stay on at the hotel, to become a Prefect. That way she could stay with Monica two more years and they could leave together, even live together, but that was no longer necessary. She still had time.

"Thank you, Divine. I'd like that," Lucy giggled, "and what girl really likes panties?"

"Not me."

Divine let her crocheted shawl drop to the floor, waiting for Lucy to face her before pushing her satin side-vent boy shorts to her ankles. "What a bitch of a week. Why don't we have our wine, a couple of tokes and finish off in the tub?" The words were neither a question nor a command. "Lucy, show me the rest of you. I can't believe it's only been a few weeks since our last time together."

At twenty-five Lucy could easily pass for eighteen. Her unblemished, unlined skin glowed pale amber from measured time in the sun, her breasts and buttocks were perfectly proportioned to the slimness of her body and her straight mahogany hair draped over her shoulders. She eased into the steaming water first, waiting for Miss Divine who was bringing more wine, and all she could think of was how delighted Monica would be in the morning. She was so frightened sitting in the dark of her suite, wondering. Now all she felt was warmth and titillation until the madam slid in behind her, framing Lucy with her open legs and cupping her breasts, pulling her against her own. She blinked away her reverie. She lay motionless; her head cradled into Divine's neck, enjoying the soothing heat, the soft cushion of water between their bodies and the rhythmic massaging of her breasts.

She knew when to ask, when Divine would be the most amenable, and she would do her best to make that happen. She could have been there for hours or days, floating. Her long wet hair cold against her back as she stood with her legs apart, her eyes closed, letting Divine dry her and cover her in warm silk. Then she was floating, falling onto clouds of soft cushions.

She purred with the trail of scented kisses from one breast to the other, her legs responding obediently to the gentle probe of Divine's warm fingertips, lost in time and euphoria. As the probing intensified so did her need for more, arching her hips over the cushions, moistening her lips with each urgent thrust, her entire body jerking violently, racked with electric intensity. She was staying. She wasn't going home. Monica would be so happy for her, for both of them. She buried her faced into soft flesh, muffling her scream.
*
Wednesday, August 01.

Wednesday morning was 85° and sunny in St. Louis, Missouri. She had spent the week with him, mostly at night. She liked him. He liked her. They had met Thursday night while she worked the end of her shift on the River Boat Cruise as a barmaid. She lived in the dilapidated North End tenements where he'd gone twice with her, neither one caring they were worlds apart. They were each other's dream come true.

He was a Florida businessman, alone on the cruise for dinner, spending most of the evening leaning over the bar.

The Madam

He was everything she thought she would never have. He was wealthy, he owned a pied à terre on the edge of Forest Park in the ritzy Central West End, even though she had no idea what that was. He wore a Rolex, a gold one he'd bought for fifty bucks at a pawn shop during his last trip to New Orleans, one with the famous four-pronged crown, but she wasn't stupid. She knew any Rolex sold for at least hundreds, if not twice that much. Above all he was single, which was the real added value.

Apart from a body to die for that she didn't mind him admiring, or ogling, she was twenty-five, divorced with no children, currently unattached, worked twelve-hour shifts from Thursday to Tuesday and most of her days were taken up with home-study courses. She wanted to become something or other.

He was expected in Tampa late Sunday evening, but their time together was too special for both of them and she had no difficulty convincing him to stay longer. Likewise, he had no trouble convincing her to put aside her studies for the week. She loved the Marriott, their walks in the park and she hadn't shared a bed with a man who cared about her for years. He said all the right things; he did all the right things. He wasn't the best of her many one-night attempts at love, and far the best in looks, but at least he knew her name.

Bobby delayed the start to his day until 1:00 PM, when she left him to begin her day. He and Frankie had no luck whatsoever thus far and Miss Divine was on the phone with them every day asking when. She was also very specific: If it wasn't from at least 500 miles away, she didn't want it. Though most of the women they'd spotted to-date were undeniably unacceptable, the few likely candidates either inconvenient or potentially labor intensive.

Tuesday evening, as he had done for the past five nights, Bobby met her at the bar and drove her to the hotel. An

447

hour later she collapsed on top of him, each one naked and wet from exertion. She had the whole day off, and yes, she would go to Chicago with him. They would leave right after breakfast. They would drop by her home for her clothes and they would be in the windy city by 11:00. He knew the finest restaurants and wanted to outfit her perfectly for a special dinner he had planned, once they arrived. He was well-acquainted with the Golden Mile and she would love the shops. He couldn't help kissing her. They would stay in Chicago and they would dance the night away under the twinkling stars and perhaps by dessert she would consider coming to Florida with him.

Yes! Arching her back and gyrating her raised hips in response, lowering herself onto him with a long sensuous groan. She had known all day what her answer would be, so did he. Finally, after all those years on the Mississippi river boat dealing with drunk or stupid tourists her ship had come in.

Officially she was a No-Line. She was also every bit a Ti-Fi. Best of all for Bobby, she was the only woman Frankie hadn't fucked and morning came too soon for both of them. They hadn't slept; Dorothy was in a living dream and sleeping would mean waking to a reality she had lived for too long.

They left the hotel by 7:00, arriving at her home at 8:30. At 9:00 they slowed to a stop in front of a pale green van with its emergency lights flashing. Bobby spoke briefly with the other driver, seemingly upset. Three minutes later Dorothy was sprawled unconscious in the van. By 10:00 the rental car was returned and Bobby was driving towards Atlanta, blocking out the whimpering pleas behind him.

They stopped in Nashville for a leisurely lunch of sandwiches and wine. Frankie loved his wine. Nashville was halfway and Frankie knew the perfect place, the Elm Hill Public Use Area, and he was anxious to make the best use of it for as long as he could. Though Bobby wouldn't see her face until 10:00 that evening, no matter how many times she cried out his name in the park.

*

"Buenas noches, Señorita Mónica."

"Buenas noches, Señor Bill. Come in. I must talk with you."

"We will all evening, Monica." He paused for a moment, visibly appreciative. "Where are you finding all this wonderful music?"

"Later. Please, Bill." Her expression was urgent.

"I have my books. I must tell you they are becoming somewhat awkward to carry. Even Stephanie has commented on my dilemma. I believe they are all laughing at me."

"No, they are not. Here is your drink. Please, sit and give me a book. Let me see how well you are learning from me. But first sit close to me. I have something to tell you."

His smile was thin. "First check my work."

She sat, visibly frustrated with him, parting the pages at the bookmark:

Cariño, we know about Lucy. We heard you. Do not discuss her for any reason. We are prepared to act immediately. We will let nothing happen to her.

William moved his forefinger across the page as he sat closer. "As you already know, Monica, we are very close indeed. As he wrote, you must believe in us. We will not let you down. He knows how you and Lucy feel about each other. He's good with it. He understands."

He stood.

"Dime cuándo, Bill. ¿Cuándo?"

William pursed his lips, seemingly giving the question some thought. "Muy pronto," he spoke slowly and well, causing her eyes to open wide. "En tres días, Mónica," he paused, "Domingo por la mañana y muy temprano."

"¿En tres días?"

"Yes, in three days." He smiled at her, moving in closer to conceal her tears from the mirror. "I will be here with you throughout."

"Bill, tienes otro profesor, yo creo."

He held up five fingers. "They are all very good teachers, very determined to succeed and not a one of them is as impatient as another teacher I may know." He paused long enough to pour a second Glenmorangie. "He gave me a message to deliver. We all agreed you are strong enough, if you feel you are. Are you strong, Monica? You must be sure of yourself, and assure me without question that you are strong. I must hear the words and I must believe them."

"Yes, I am so strong. What is the message?"

"You are certain."

"Yes."

"Then open at the second bookmark and please keep your head down. Keep your head down."

The glossy 5 X 7 was of a beautiful young woman she didn't know, helping a gleeful little dark-haired girl sitting by the sandcastle she had just built to wave at the camera, dated that morning and William admonished her with a gentle pressure to the nape of her neck.
*

"Hombres, get over here. Shit is going down."

Manuel saw the van before it pulled in alongside the hotel's yellow-line reserved parking for the third time in ten minutes. The vehicle's windows were heavily tinted, but when the driver stepped out they recognized him immediately. Juan Carlos was gone from the office with no hesitation, trailed by the three men who had arrived from Miami. When the passenger stepped out his face filled the plasma screen until the van's raised tailgate blocked out both of them. Moments later, when they dragged her out, the woman's writs were bound; she was blindfolded and wasn't struggling. They took less than thirty seconds to carry her into the hotel.

Manuel spoke calmly into his headset. "JC, go. Good luck, hombres, to all of you."

JC bolted across the street, barely stopping to stoop behind the van, instantly igniting a blip in the center of the Rover's GPS screen as the three men waited for him by the side lane.

"It is done, amigo."

"I see you. Join our friends. Vayan con Dios, amigos."

*

"Welcome, Nicole."

Dorothy was crying, thrown over Frankie's shoulders, absolutely terrified, struggling in her mind to search for Bobby, though her limp body wouldn't allow it and all she could see was the carpeted floor.

"Put her in the chair."

Frankie dropped her rudely against the wood and forgot her, letting Bobby shackle her. He should have known the Disposal was Lucy and he was suddenly anxious to leave. Just seeing her stirred him. She was in a white mesh micro skirt and halter top with red panties and bra and white stiletto shoes, making him wonder whether the madam purposely dressed her girls intending for him to rape each girl again as an appropriate prelude to their new lives.

Lucy glanced up, her eyes dulled. She remembered him, the one called Frankie. They all did. She remembered his smell of cigars and sweat. She remembered the matted hair on his back, how he hurt her, and how he laughed as she tried to scream with his hand over her mouth. Her head sank. She wasn't going home and she would never see her Monica again.

She saw the new woman trying to resist, crying to

451

Bobby as though she knew him, and she saw Miss Divine's hand sweeping down hard against her face. She didn't care. She knew the rest. She was the one being blindfolded, unshackled, yanked from the chair and heaved over his shoulders. He smelled. She jerked once, twice; the third time her body settled onto his and his hand pushed under her cheap skirt and panties to probe uncaringly into the warm cleft of her buttocks. The deal was done. Lucy's new home would be Mobile, Alabama.

*

"Hombres, they are out. They are throwing the girl into the van like garbage. The big one will be the driver. Wait for my word."

"My blood runs hot, amigo, like our past times together. You are with me in my heart."

"And you with me, hermano. Go hombres."

*

JC's eyes never left the screen. The driver's eyes never left the vehicle a half-mile ahead of him. Ninety minutes later when the van exited into Valley, Alabama he slowed and did the same, the chilling darkness broken by the glare of a solitary hotel's bright yellow sign and a 24/7 convenience store.

Frankie went directly into the store without scanning the parking lot. Bobby changed from passenger to driver, paying no attention to the SUV pulling in four spaces over and one car length behind, or the four somber passengers who stepped out.

Juan Carlos' timing was perfect as Bobby raised his window after taking the two coffees from Frankie who then went to the rear doors and Bobby had no idea the man beside him wasn't Frankie. When he twisted at the touch of the Beretta pushing into his side, seeing Ramón's deadly serious face, he spilled the two cups into his lap completely oblivious to the scalding pain and to Frankie whose mind was racing.

"Leave them closed, asshole."

"What the fuck."

Juan Carlos stood behind him with his arms relaxed at his side

"Check your chest, asshole." The red dot was steady. "Now, walk into the beam and open the tailgate. Before you get there I want your wallet."

"Take it now."

"I said move, and pull it out real slow."

JC turned on his heels as Frankie passed him.

"There's no cash, just cards. You're wasting your time."

"I don't want your cash. I want your permit. We're going home together, asshole, after we take care of the girl. Now lean in and put both hands behind you." He didn't, JC slamming a rigid hand into his ribs. "Lean in. Put both hands behind you."

Frankie never thought he could be moved so effortlessly. He wasn't pushed in with his hands cuffed behind him. He was picked up and hurled. He lay still as his feet were strapped together. The second man climbed in behind Bobby, checking on Lucy. Seeing what he did, Pablo slammed a clenched fist into the side of Bobby's head and crawled over the backseats to cradle her under his jacket as JC climbed into the front passenger seat of the Rover, talking to Fernando, the third man, as he loaded Frankie's address into the GPS. ETA: one hour.

*

Thursday, August 02.

Lucy was at the midtown office thirty minutes later, carried easily in the arms of the man who hadn't stopped stroking her hair and reassuring her throughout the ride. After he laid her onto the cot and covered her with blankets Pablo crossed himself.

*

Frankie and Bobby sat back to back, tied to vinyl and chrome kitchen chairs as JC and Fernando searched every inch of the middle-income bungalow. They knew what they were searching for, following the phone call from Ramón who had returned to the indoor parking of the office building to clean out Frank Randolph's van before driving to the long-term parking at Hartsfield-Jackson. He found forty thousand dollars and a digital camera with a number of girls in various short-skirt positions and at least fifty random shots of one particular woman, taken in the nude from inside the van. The woman was Dorothy.

When they finished they went through each room again, tossing beds, checking for false walls and loose floorboards as both Frankie and Bobby denied they had ever kidnapped or raped. They were told to take the girl out of town and they didn't know anything else.

When the men came into the kitchen for the last time carrying a laptop, labeled CDs, and dozens of dated file folders, each one containing multiple 8 X 10 prints of a naked woman, Bobby blocked it all out. He began reciting the Lord's Prayer in a choking whisper while Frankie steadfastly denied ownership, insisting he had pulled them off the web.

The file Juan Carlos opened first read: Combo/Ti-Fi, East Point: July 18. The first of several photos showed a young mother and daughter laughing and dancing on the way home, the last was one of Mercedes Del Fuego lying naked on her bed, her face drenched with tears. He didn't have to see another, erasing the images from his mind.

JC shrugged after Frankie insisted he knew nothing of the files. He asked once again if he was certain. Frankie said he was and JC left the house matter-of-factly, saying something they didn't understand to Fernando. An hour later he returned. He walked directly into the kitchen, nonchalantly shoved a dishtowel into Frank Randolph's mouth and both he and Fernando casually suited themselves into one-piece disposable overalls. Just as casually he put Randolph's thumb into the bolt cutters and brought the three-foot long handles together, watching the severed digit fall with a dull thud to the floor before asking the question again. The question was simple: Where were the children?

Muted by the towel the answer was the same. There were no children, Randolph insisted, and the forefinger fell beside the thumb. JC walked away and when he returned he was apologetic in a monotone voice. His face was expressionless. Certainly, if Mr. Frank Randolph hadn't said anything at this point there was nothing for him to say, the victim of a terrible misunderstanding and the least he could do was staunch the bleeding.

Randolph's face purpled with strain long before the triple blue flames of the titanium butane sizzled and sparked against the open wounds. His body convulsed, his head twisting in all directions, smashing into Bobby's as he tried in vain to escape what he could not. Blood trickled from his nose, soaking into the dishtowel, and what began as a slight dribble from the knuckle stumps was now hectic squirting.

Juan Carlos stepped back, Bobby still strapped to his chair when Fernando dragged him away by the front of his shirt before positioning himself behind Frank Randolph, gripping his head in a suffocating lock, lifting him from the floor. Bobby raised his voice louder in prayer, forcing away the muffled screams as the stench of smoldering flesh enveloped him. He stopped abruptly when his need to vomit became greater than his need to be forgiven. The mismatched digits were dropped into his lap and the same question was asked of him. The man's name was Tucker Richman, he lived in Savannah. He was the one they wanted, not him or Frankie. He was the one who bought and sold the kids.

Bobby was allowed a beer to calm himself. They could be in Savannah in five hours and Robert Baker very willingly phoned Richman with the good news of an unexpected Acquisition. He would drive them, he agreed, as though given a choice, and he didn't object when hearing from Fernando that he would dispose of the bolt cutters before JC closed-up the house.

JC replaced Baker's chair, he checked the window locks, the backdoor, lowered the air conditioning and increased the fan speed. At first Randolph's transition to consciousness was slow, until the cold of the ice penetrated his delirium and he awoke to incredible pain and the stench of his seared flesh.

"I have killed ninety-five men, hombre, as I witnessed the disbelief in their eyes. You are the first I will enjoy, but a bullet is too quick for you, too quick to appease the women you have raped and to satisfy their desperate husbands." He took up the bolt cutters, opening and closing the handles with a wide smile, suddenly laughing at Randolph's expression. "No, asshole, these are way too big for that, or that is way too small for these."

Frank Randolph screamed hysterical groans no one could hear as he watched the jaws of the bolt cutter close across his forearm before snapping through the radius and ulna bones to sever the mutilated limb. JC stepped away, leaning against the counter for a moment with a smile to watch the body convulse and twitch as Randolph seemed uncertain whether he should look at the man who had just killed him or the twitching halves of his mutilated right arm.

"Adiós, hombre, I don't think we'll be seeing each other again. I believe in my heart I will go to heaven for what I have just done."
*

"What has happened to the men who took her?" James

456

asked.

"One is driving with them to an appointment that may be helpful to us. The other is talking face to face with the devil. Juan Carlos will be with us this evening." Manuel studied Lucy asleep on the cot. "This is not how you described them, James. Is this what I must expect when I see her?"

"I would not have known she's the same girl. The last time I saw her she was so beautiful. The answer is no, but we certainly know what would have eventually happened to her had we not met one another."

Manuel knelt beside her, inches from Pablo's knees. "She will be beautiful again James, when she's clean, but she will not have an easy time. She's in for a rough couple of days. It would help to know what she was injected with."

"The poor thing needs clothing. I'll take care of that." He sighed deeply. "She can't stay here and she certainly can't leave in that condition. But where do we take her. There's no one at the beach house to care for her at the moment and we can't book her into the hotel without staying with her."

"She must stay here for now. When she's properly dressed, Pablo will take her to his hotel room where she can rest properly and bathe herself. He will bring her back when it's dark. Nothing will happen to her. It's a matter of two days, James. She knows you. She'll trust what you say and she will soon understand that Pablo has appointed himself as her sole protector and nothing else."

"And she'll see across the street unless we keep her blindfolded, which would be a very cruel gesture on our part. We have already decided they should never know, even though none of these women will ever return to Atlanta." He was right. The complication was welcome, yet one they didn't need. "If Pablo can be trusted to take her into a hotel room for bathing and to watch her sleeping,

why can he not be trusted with her at the beach house, Manny? If she hears reassuring words from me she will go willingly. I have no doubt he will treat her honorably and she will do nothing to jeopardize Mercedes or the other girls. You will understand that for yourself when she wakes."
*

They searched Robert Baker's apartment thoroughly, finding nothing, though when they left the bolt cutters remained behind under the sofa and by the time they arrived in Savannah Juan Carlos had bartered Robert Baker's life. He knew about Daphne in Memphis, Valerie Templeton's murder, the precise definition of Combo/Ti-Fi relating to Mercedes and the difference between Acquisitions and Disposals.

Bobby linked many of the disposals with cities and locations, crying as he heard himself say that after so many years on the street most of them wouldn't be worth saving, if they were even alive. He explained how the girls were all given Rohypnol, injected with crack cocaine at least twice in twenty-four hours, dressed for street work, given over to them for relocation and that Frankie was always the girls' first pro bono. But he hadn't done anything to Lucy. He didn't have time.

JC's timing was perfect once again, calling Manuel as Pablo was leaving the city limits with Lucy who was dressed in blue jeans, bobby socks and a cotton blouse for the first time in three years, already deciding she liked the big man beside her who was pulling off the highway.

He would stay where he was until contacted. Lucy wasn't going to the ocean. She was going to a private rehab center for tests and treatment and soon after Pablo's cell phone buzzed again. He listened intently, nodding with words she didn't know until he passed her the phone. He wanted to give her a tight hug and tell her everything would

be alright, but he thought he would frighten her. Instead, when she passed the phone to him, after listening at length to what William had to say, she leaned over and hugged him, crying something that sounded very much like "gracias."
*

Tucker Richman's office closed early, though Bobby knew the door was unlocked.

"Frankie's staying at the car for a change?"

"Yeah, he's with the girl. She's real quiet and won't be any trouble at all for you. You got the ten grand?"

"Seems like business is picking up for the two of you." Richman reached into his attaché case for the bundle and threw it across the desk. He dropped a single file folder into the case as he stood. "Let's go. It's Thursday. Traffic's going to be the mother of all bitches."

Juan Carlos walked in casually with Fernando behind him, as though they were expected. Even Tucker Richman took a moment before speaking to them.

"Baker, why don't you tell this smoking piece of shit to sit down?"

"Friends of yours, Bobby?"

"They want the files, the kids' files, all of them, from the very beginning."

"Who are they Bobby? They're not cops. They're too well-dressed and much too flavorful for these parts."

"Tell him, Baker."

"They killed Frankie, Tucker. Do not fuck with them. They mean business. They cut off his fucking fingers. Then they cut his fucking arm in half."

He showed no surprise. "So there's no girl?"

"Let's stop fucking the dog here gents. Step away from the desk, face the wall, and put your hands behind your back. You too, Baker, right now." JC went behind the desk; Fernando went to lock the door, the ten-inch stainless steel blade of his throwing knife extending from his cupped palm. "Now, gentlemen, squat a foot from the wall and lean forward. I want your heads on the wall, your knees apart and your butts off the floor."

There were two filing cabinets, a mass of papers on his desk mixed with ashes and rows of books on his wall. JC went through the papers and files sheet by sheet, missing nothing as Fernando did each book with the same thoroughness. At the end of four hours the men on the floor had fallen a half-dozen times, JC had the files they'd come for and Fernando had well over sixty thousand dollars including Baker's ten.

"Hombre, how do you get to be that way?" JC asked. "This place smells like shit."

"From hard work. That money was honestly earned, supply and demand. The smell comes from people who walk in off the street who know shit about hard work."

"Fuck you. Your hard work is stealing and selling children. Tell me about the Hillmans in Jacksonville, and tell me about the Del Fuego girl from last July."

"There's nothing to tell. They needed a kid, I had one. And they had the money to pay for it. Then they wanted to return it because it was a little off color."

Richman crashed into Baker, certain his ribs were crushed. He'd never in his life felt as many litres of air leave his lungs at one time, his spastic coughing leaving a wide patch of yellow and brown spittle across Baker's front."

JC waved the file. "Is this information current, the address is good?"

"As far as I know," Richman coughed.

"What time does the restaurant downstairs close?"

"Eleven."

He spoke to Fernando. They had three hours to transfer the files to the Rover before the streets emptied. Fernando asked a question of Juan Carlos, pleased as the immediate response came as an indifferent shrug and neither man on the floor thought to be afraid.

At 11:00 Juan Carlos pulled Richman to his feet by the handcuffs, grateful he was wearing gloves. He asked the lawyer for his wallet, his billfold, his car keys, his cellular, and told him to face the door with his back against the wall and to remain still until they were gone. Richman didn't speak. They'd be gone in a few seconds and then he wouldn't need a glass.

Bobby walked out first, followed by Juan Carlos. Fernando remained, his expression serene, eyeing Richman as he reached under his jacket for the smooth stainless steel handle. He held it shoulder-high with practiced skill, smirking, shrugging at the loud explosion from Richman's bowels. Such things happened. He'd seen men die badly many times before.

There was no reason to be embarrassed, and suddenly shame was forgotten. Neither was there fear, simply the knowledge his death was surprisingly painless, not bad at all. The worst was over. Richman stared from the handle protruding from his chest to the towering Mexican walking towards him, wondering why as he felt the steel twist and slide from his chest. What hc didn't feel was falling away from the wall and crashing into his desk.

*

"She is well, Monica, or she will be very soon. She is being cared for by the very best."

"I will see her in two days."

"No, you will not. She needs special attention."

"When will I see her?"

"Be content that she's safe. She's thinking of you. She wanted me to tell you."

"She was hurt in the vault?"

"Yes, by Miss Divine. She was hurt very badly. But the

461

pain is over Monica, for her and for all of you. You will soon know the reasons for our seemingly long delay which we regret each minute of the day. For now we must change the subject." He patted her knee. "Only hours remain."

She put an open hand to his cheek. "I do not like you with this thing on your face. You are so old to me now. It is silver like the moon."

"I would have preferred sophisticated, or gentlemanly."

She shook her head. "Old."

"Then prepare yourself for a surprise, young lady. I am not the only one." Her mouth formed a perfect O and her eyes widened. "Or would you prefer that we wear itchy wool ski masks?"

She pondered the question. "Ski masks, I think."

"I would as well... much more dramatic. However, for once, I am not the boss."

"Bill, you are much better. Next time you are born you could be Mexican."

The honesty caught him off guard. "After more dance lessons, yo creo and, yes, I am quite proud of my progress. I believe my wife will be as well." He leaned closer to her. "She hasn't left me."

She whispered. "I did not believe so, but I was so terrible to say what I did about your vacation."

"No, you were speaking with emotion. ¿No es verdad?"

"Can I know about her?"

"No, you cannot, as much as I would like to tell you."

"Manny knows her?"

"He knows about her through a friend. And I must insist we change the subject, in lieu of which you might tell me all the ways to order a scotch from inattentive hotel staff."
*

The three men were in Richman's Abercorn home a full two hours verifying the existence of any additional information that might link the dead lawyer to the selling of children while Robert Baker spent the time with his face to the floor and his hands cuffed, pleased he would be released once at home in Atlanta. There was nothing more to confiscate. They had it all.

There was nothing worth touching, though Fernando thought the mattress might be worth slicing open. He was right, to the tune of several bundles of hundreds and Juan Carlos suggested it would be his for the keeping if he wanted to remove the bundles himself. He declined.

Richman's Mercedes was parked at the Savannah airport by 2:00; they stopped for gas, burgers and fries midway to Jacksonville where they arrived at 5:00. By 6:00 all three men were having coffees as they sat in front of the red Corvette and the new silver Saab parked in the Hillman's carport. The Hillmans came out at 6:30.

Part Four

Friday, August 03

The width of the property was entirely cloaked under the far-reaching branches of two reddish brown Live Oaks, sloppily dressed with Spanish moss, and the neighboring properties were hidden by six-foot latticed fences draped with thick, untrimmed climbing ferns.

Robert Baker sat between the two men knowing his friend was dead. Nothing was said about Richman, though he had witnessed the telling nod earlier, now he was certain they were there to kill the Hillmans. He felt dwarfed sitting on the ground between them, completely vulnerable even though they assured him his cooperation would be rewarded. They instructed him not to say one word, and he didn't. When they spoke, they whispered in Spanish. He didn't care.

With his eyes squeezed tightly closed and his knees pulled to his chest, he was silently reciting the Lord's Prayer for the fiftieth or hundredth time when Marietta Hillman came out alone. He didn't even realize JC had jerked him to his feet.

"Good morning, Mrs. Hillman." Juan Carlos showed the Beretta. "Come towards me, right here, right now. Believe me, no one will hear the shot if you don't. No. Do not think to run."

"Here, take the keys." She extended an unsteady hand.

"I don't want your keys, Mrs. Hillman. I prefer the car I have. Is your front door unlocked?"

"Yes."

"We're going inside." He took her by the arm. "Do not resist me. This will not take long and then we will leave you and your husband."

She was first through the door, following his instructions. "Roger, come here quickly. I need you."

Roger Hillman hurried into the living room. He saw the gun, the three men, and simply said: "Take the car keys. We don't keep cash in the house."

"Sit down, Mr. Hillman, Mrs. Hillman." Fernando pushed Baker into a chair and watched the street from behind half-closed blinds. "Meet Robert Baker. You have much in common: the reason we are here."

"I don't understand," said Hillman, ignoring his wife, "this isn't an invasion?"

"I suppose so, since we weren't invited, but not for what you might think."

"So what do you want?"

"I want an answer, and I intend leaving here with it. You tell me what I want to hear and you'll live, you don't, and you're both very dead. Now tell me, have I said anything you don't understand?"

"We haven't done anything to you or anyone else. We don't even know you."

"This man in your chair kidnapped a young woman a year ago. Then he watched as someone else repeatedly raped her, before selling her into prostitution and her daughter to you."

"We've never seen him before."

"But you have seen Tucker Richman who told us you don't like certain colors of the spectrum. In fact, you dislike them so much you wanted to return the little girl you bought from him for thirty grand. Then you thought of a way to save the thirty and still get rid of her. We found her the same night. Now we have found you."

"We gave her up in a way we thought was the best for her," answered Marietta Hillman, her trembling hands pinched between equally nervous knees.

He ignored her. "Here's the thing, people. The little girl's all fucked up and your answer as to why that is will help your day or spoil your day. So you see, what happens next is all up to you."

"She's right. We thought we were doing the right thing, the best way to avoid questions. We knew whatever Richman did wasn't legal, but we had no idea she was kidnapped. Richman told us the parents were killed in a car crash or something and we wanted a girl badly enough to believe him."

"Until you saw she was naturally tanned. Show me her room. Show me where she slept."

"We did the room over a little while ago."

Juan Carlos took Mrs. Hillman by the arm, pulling her up as easily as he would a cushion. When her husband went to stand Fernando pushed him down just as easily. The house was a single-level ranch style with a basement, nothing in the existing rooms was new and none of the paint scrapings on the blade of JC's stiletto from any of the rooms was fresh.

She led him to the basement that was semi-finished, sealed off from the rest of the house by a door at the bottom of the stairs. The utility room and laundry rooms were separate; a cedar closest held countless forgotten clothes, a larger open area was Hillman's private workshop and open storage area for nautical equipment. The only other door was locked, closing off an eight by eight unfinished room of drywall and two by fours.

The door crashed in like cardboard under his foot. The

only light came from outside the room, the marine port-a-potty was in one corner, a small two-inch mat wrapped in blankets was in another, and half a dozen pink pajamas hung from protruding nails.

Marietta Hillman was too petrified to cry when he peered behind the door. Juan Carlos reached for the brown doll and pulled at the string. "I love you mommy." He pulled again. "Please hug me," and again, "I'm hungry, mommy, please feed me," and a fourth, "I'm a little girl. Please hug me, I'm crying." JC pulled the string one last time, mouthing the words as he stared at the panic-stricken woman and the doll said: "Tell me you love me."

Marietta Hillman shook her head and whimpered into a cupped hand as he dragged her up the stairs faster than she'd ever climbed them herself.

"Hillman, do you have a gun?"

"No, I don't."

"You live in fucking Florida, you own a fucking boat, and you don't have a gun." JC pulled out his 92FS, pressing the barrel against the woman's ear. "Do you have a gun in the house, Mr. Hillman? Before the count of two, for her sake."

"Yes."

"Loaded?"

"Yes."

"Amigo, go with him. Mrs. Hillman, go into the bedroom. Baker, go with her." With the .357 Magnum held firmly in a gloved hand Fernando was in the bedroom within moments attached to Richard Hillman who was having difficulty walking. "Amigo, hold him securely," JC said in Spanish and Fernando's grip all but lifted his charge from the floor. "Mrs. Hillman, take off your clothes, everything... now."

"Marietta, don't." Hillman shouted. His eyes pleaded with an uncaring JC. "We can talk about this. We were going to pay Richman thousands for taking the girl. We can pay you the money instead."

"We will watch her, amigo, all of us, at her, and so will you. Baker's career was not as physically rewarding as that of his dead partner. Your wife is going to undress and you're going to bring me any and all documents relating to Ana Juanita Vaquero unless you want to stay and watch her strip for us. I would suggest you get back before she's finished, with everything. Go." He gave his attention to Baker. "This is your lucky day, amigo. Mrs. Hillman, I told you to remove your clothes. Do it, right now. Or he'll do it for you."

Marietta Hillman supported herself on her dresser, kicking off her shoes, forcing them from her mind as autonomous hands began unbuttoning her blouse, clumsily tugging it from her shoulders. She unzipped her skirt, hesitating, pushing the waistband to her knees and letting it free-fall to the floor. She unclasped her bra, shrugging one shoulder free, then the other, baring one breast, then other, crying as she pushed her white cotton briefs to her ankles. JC ignored her for the first five minutes as she stood naked by the bed, Robert Baker somewhat more eager.

When Richard Hillman finally came in with the Richman file, which Fernando confirmed was complete and that no other reference to the once Ana Juanita remained, his wife was naked by the bed with her shoulders drooping and her arms dangling by her side. She glared at him, wanting the bravado he constantly displayed at the club, always seeking to be the center of attention. He couldn't, not seeing her completely naked in their bedroom with strange men after all the times he had asked her to go nude during their weekend evening anchorages at the sandbar with their friends.

JC spoke in Spanish and Fernando pulled Hillman across the room, pushing him into a chair.

"Mrs. Hillman, remember the mother of the girl you abused has spent the past year doing what you have just done and what you will do with Baker. Please get under the covers and pull them to your shoulders. Take your time." He spoke to Baker. "Get in, hombre, and we will watch, the way you watched the girl's mother. Enjoy, and don't worry about the husband. He won't bother you."

"Roger, please do something."

Hillman could do or say nothing. He sat staring at her, hoping his wife was all they wanted, thinking he would survive if she didn't do anything stupid. Marietta Hillman's eyes were fixed on Baker who wasn't sure himself what he would do with her. He was naked in a room with a fairly attractive, naked woman and three men, certain what would happen if he did nothing.

He looked at Juan Carlos. "Now... like this. You're staying?"

"Do her, and do her fast. Mrs. Hillman, help him out. Start him off with a nice hard kiss on his mouth with those big red lips." JC turned to Fernando as Baker crawled in beside the woman. The exchange of guns was smooth, the Beretta now digging into Hillman's temple. "Baker...one more thing before you start on her."

Baker brought his smudged mouth away from her, twisting from the waist. The gloved hand clamped over his mouth, his eyes bulging as the high-calibre cartridge ripped through his covered chest, his final reward. Half a breath later Mrs. Hillman was dead, Baker's silver crucifix was ripped from his neck and the limp hands of a stunned Roger Hillman were easily manoeuvred around his own gun, pointing inward. The murder-suicide took fifteen seconds with the blood-stained cross laying at Hillman's feet.

The red Corvette drove away 7:15. Later in the day its nearby location would become a no parking zone and by dinnertime the entire neighborhood would be in agreement about the always-suspected Hillman love triangle.

*

"Good morning, Nicole. My name is Monica."

Nicole stood facing her empty closet. "What is this place?"

"You are in a bordello."

"Bobby and this other guy kidnapped me and brought me here. Why?"

"They are very bad men."

"You have to show me how to get out of here. Where are my clothes?"

"They are gone." Monica put up her hand, knowing what was coming next. "I am here to train you. First you will learn to be with a woman, then with a man, but I think you already know very much about men."

"And I've already been with a woman, the first one and the last one, the blonde whore last night after he left me here. She made me sick."

"Two nights have passed since he left. She can see and hear you in your bedroom, in your bathroom and your sitting room. Your only privacy is when you are at the toilet. Say nothing bad again. At first they will watch you, and her, then not so much unless you are with a woman. She likes that very much." Nicole started for the door. "Escape is not possible. And if you do escape they will punish me. Sit here and listen. I will not touch you today and maybe not tomorrow. I will begin to train you on Monday. Before then you will have nice clothes to wear, you will know the girls and you will feel better."

Nicole's head sank into her chest. She wept uncontrollably. "I was going to Chicago, then Florida, and now this."

"I will make changes to the routine for you. First we will go to the pool where you will meet the girls. You will like them. They will have much to tell you. Tonight you will stay in your suite while I am here with my guest. He stays very late, but if you want I will bring you to my suite after he leaves so that you will not be alone. I am your Anchor Girl." She paused as she stood. "I have a bikini you can have for the pool, but I think you will soon not like it. I do not wear one, no one does."

*

JC and Fernando did the return trip in six hours, staying under the Georgia Police radar. They went to their Hilton hotel rooms where they removed their clothing, carefully placing each article into green garbage bags, including their shoes and socks, the 19.95 watches and pharmacy sunglasses, their gloves and belts. They woke in darkness, met for dinner in the restaurant, left the hotel on foot and by the time they arrived at the tenth-floor office they had disposed of the plastic bags over several city blocks.

"Hombre, we have much to tell you. We are ninety-nine to one hundred, you and I, thanks to the rapists and those who abused Sofia. Fernando took out the lawyer who supplied him with a generous bonus for doing so, which would have evened our scores, unfortunately he asked so nicely I could not refuse him."

"Gentlemen, might there be an English version of this gleeful dialogue."

JC smiled. "Yes, Jaime. The women of Atlanta and other cities are much safer this evening, as are the children."

James Burton nodded grimly. "And the local Mexican male population is also safe from harm?"

"Sí, amigo, very safe." He tossed Fernando a beer, and Burton a large bundle of cash. "Our soft heart here wants you to have this for the girls your foundation will help. Here is sixty thousand more for them."

"Thank you, Fernando. Your generosity is overwhelming."

Fernando shrugged. Manny opened his beer. "Hombres,

James, can I say something. Fernando, can I ask something of you?"

They nodded in unison. "Hombres, when James first called to ask if I had read his note on the photograph, I said yes, but I did not read the message in my cab. My last fare of the evening was a very old lady who cannot have many years left. She phoned me after midnight and read James' note to me. I went immediately to her home, a home for old people, and I waited for her until morning. Her name is Miss Georgina Collins. She invited me to breakfast and then to her room. Hombres, what I saw was terrible. Fernando... James and Miss Pennington are already being so generous to our ladies across the street. Can you find room in your heart to help this old woman live better in her final years?"

"Young or old, amigo, they are all lost without us," Fernando answered. "Is that not so, compadres? My answer is yes, Manny, if Jaime allows me to withdraw my offer to him."

Burton chuckled. "I have much to learn, gentlemen. I should have met you in another life. I'm sure if I had I would be a much better man in this one as a result of this entirely bewildering and emotional Latino thing. I never realized emotion could be so contagious." He addressed Fernando. "My friend, your offer is too generous for me to return, for which reason I refuse." Manuel was next. "Thinking of an elderly woman at such a difficult time is unquestionably commendable, Manny. I did intend to save this announcement for a later date when others could share the news with us, though I believe the current mood makes the moment propitious. Gentlemen, the Search Foundation is a reality as of early this morning. Miss Pennington vehemently refused to vacation while all this is happening to people she cares for so deeply and called me this morning with the news. She is a remarkable young woman and I can tell you she has worked tirelessly to achieve these amazing results in so short a time. As for Miss Georgina Collins, caballeros, you have my word. Tomorrow she will wake up to a very lovely and kind visitor to begin a much better life. She will live in comfort for the rest of her days, Manny. She will lack for nothing and enjoy the best of everything. Caballeros, please raise your bottles in a toast to Miss Collins."

*

The first phone call was between James Burton and his long-time college buddy who was the Chief Physician and owner of the best and least publicized rehab center in the Southeastern US. Good news that made Pablo purse his lips like a relieved parent. Later in the evening Manuel called a man he didn't know, someone he would never see, and Pablo was by the phone.

"Mr. Grainger."

"This is Grainger."

"Mr. Grainger, I hope I am not calling at a bad time. I'm calling about your wife, Tracey."

The line went silent.

"Who is this? Is this some kind of sick joke?"

"No, sir. This is no joke. Mr. Grainger, I need you to listen and I need you to answer a few simple questions. Then I will tell you as much as I can over the phone. My voice is distorted for my protection, nothing more."

"Do you have her? Are you the one who took her? Are you calling for money?"

"No. My call is not about money. I am one of those who recently found her through fate," Manuel paused, "as I was searching for my wife who was taken from me. Tracey is free, Mr. Grainger. My wife will also be very soon. Do we talk?"

"Free from what, and where is she now? Is she alright? Can you tell me about her?"

"She is receiving excellent care, the very best. And I

must ask you some questions."

"Go ahead."

"She believes you have remarried. Did you?"

"No. I never gave up hope of finding her and our son."

"Do you want Tracy to come home?"

The man's voice was tremulous with excitement and Manny remembered when Miss Collins first read him the words. "Yes I want her to come home. Tell me where she is. I'll leave right now."

"She's being cared for. She is very sick, Mr. Grainger, although she is getting better. She will be well in a few days. I am told by a friend she is thinking of you and your son. She knows we are talking."

"My son is still missing."

"I know, possibly not for much longer, Mr. Grainger."

"They're not together."

"No. They are not."

"But you know where he is?"

"Yes, I do."

"And my wife, where is she?"

Manuel ignored the question. "Mr. Grainger, do you love her? Do you love her very much?"

"She's my wife, of course I do."

"That is not an answer, sir. It's a reason. I need to know if you will want her after what I am about to tell you, and if you can help her. Sit down, Mr. Grainger. You will not like what you are about to hear." Manuel paused, moistening his lips. "For three years, since she was taken from you, Tracey has been forced to work in a bordello." All the men in the room reacted the same way to the scream; only Burton did not cross himself. "Remember, she is safe and I can bring her to you. She was with me briefly yesterday before a good friend took her to a place where she is being cared for. If I were you, I would not refuse her. I will call you later. Think about what I have said. Good night."

The five men surrounding him slapped his shoulders and walked away. What could anyone say?

*

"Yes."

"Mr. Grainger." The synthesized voice was assertive.

"Yes. Yes, I want Tracy to come home. Please, I want her home. I want her so badly and I want our son. I've never given up hope they would be found. I did my best to find her until I didn't know where to go or what to do. She's my wife. Tell her I want her, that I need her. I want my family."

"She lived in hell, Mr. Grainger. You won't see the same woman. Be aware of that. None of us will, and we are many. Also be aware that, if you hurt her or reject her, I will act against you very quickly. So tell me again. You and Tracy have many months, possibly years ahead of you before you are both healed. Are you certain? This is your time to say yes or no, without reprisal."

"Yes, I am very sure. When will she come?"

"Very soon. Until then she will be safe and unharmed. She is with people who care about her. She is protected and will call you herself in a few days. Tracey will be the one who believes what you say or not, although I believe she will. Good night."

Manuel snapped the phone closed and crossed the office to hear the conversation between his wife and James Burton.

*

Apart from Halloween the previous October, Monica rarely made use of the costume selection the few times over the year when William thought he might require private nursing or a lecture and frisking by an aggressive Mexican policewoman. No one did the naughty schoolgirl better than Melanie. Though one time Cynthia did think wrestling with a cowgirl in chaps might be fun.

She had run out of clothes to wear. Knowing Manuel

was as close as the flowers and Williams chest, she could no longer wear her lingerie, despite William's perfectly fine heart. Other than the night he fell asleep on the sofa, he slept on the edge of the bed each night, not in it. She was, after all, his Spanish teacher.

There was one costume that would fit her perfectly: a form-fitting blazer buttoned at the waist that came with a tie and short skirt with detachable stockings that would leave her thighs bare. Panties were optional. A man-killer outfit, the girls all agreed, and with a few alterations she was certain William would survive and Manuel would approve. She added a bra and panties, she detached the stockings in favor of unfamiliar pantyhose and she wore low-heeled pumps, not stilettos. She was the quintessential and Titillating Tutor from every man's dream.

"I must say, my teacher is exceptionally beautiful this evening."

"Thank you."

His scotch was poured and sitting on the table.

"The old leather-skinned ones I had back in the day were never nearly as stunning, not in their best dreams." He tapped the mike. "Though if they had been, their sense of propriety would have been as complete as what I see before me. My heart is beating this quickly strictly by virtue of having climbed the stairs, not amorous intention."

"Have you done your homework, Billy, which I did assign?" She pushed the fake horn-rimmed glasses down over her nose. "Or I will be very crossed with you."

"Cross? Billy?"

She nodded, beaming. "Yes, Billy. Amanda taught me to speak this way. She told me this name. You are a little Bill, like –ito in Spanish."

Juan Carlos roared, grabbing Manuel by the shoulders, shaking him as Ramón laughed hysterically with them. "I cannot wait to meet her, hombre."

"Thank you for that." William sat, patting the cushion beside him. "Shall we proceed?"

She sat straight, crossing her legs for affect and pushing up her glasses. He hadn't seen that much of her legs in three weeks and suddenly Billy wanted to raise his hand to leave the room. She was a teacher he would never forget; then realizing he would not see her again after Sunday.

"Why are you so sad, Bill?"

"I wouldn't say sad. I believe happy would be a more appropriate designation. Sometimes the distinction is indistinguishable."

"Do you have something for me to read?"

William opened his Level I Spanish course book as he passed her the workbook.

"You have done well, Bill. Do you have any questions?"

"No, thank you. Do you?"

"No, I am very happy that you are coming to the end of the book. I cannot believe how fast, and sometimes how long."

"It's complete. With minor accents and nuances to consider. I'll soon be ready for Level II." He stood, topping off his drink and pouring a generously watered-down version for Monica who was slouching slightly into the sofa and seeming completely uncomfortable. "Why don't we put our lessons aside for tonight and simply enjoy the music?"

"I will call the reception, Bill, for something happier."

When she returned the outfit was gone, replaced with a knee-length honey-colored silk chemise, telling him simply the teaching was finished as she tied the pantyhose into a knot and threw them into the corner. By midnight the suite was dark, the music was turned down low and William lay with his arms crossed at the edge of the bed wishing he'd never given Stephanie the hard luck story about his breakup. But, then, the ruse was about the girl lying beside him with a yellow carnation gripped tightly in her hands, not him.

*

Saturday, August 04.

When Monica woke at 7:00 he was gone, drinking coffee with Manuel until he left for the Hilton to sleep, shower and call his wife twice before rejoining the five men whose day had come. The girls would be free in twelve hours.

He loved her. He would be with her in less than two days and did his best to sound as though he believed he would see her again. She loved him. She had a big surprise for him, and not the thirty-day Mediterranean cruise she had booked for them. Something much better was waiting for him and he promised to call before coming home. He had a surprise for her as well, one that would make her happy and long overdue.

*

Everything and anything he had worn to the tenth-floor office and The Hotel Le Chic was put into suitcases for disposal in North Carolina. Whatever he wore on his body before and after he stepped from the shower Saturday afternoon was intended for the garbage or the suitcases, without exception. Everyone did the same, as they would immediately upon arriving in Wrightsville Beach Sunday afternoon with everything worn during the operation.

*

Manuel was waiting for him in the Rover outside the Hilton with the tailgate open.

"James, are you so perfect for your last date with my wife? Perhaps too perfect?"

"You're pretty slick yourself. I believe the term is 'no contest'."

"Let's not be late, James. We have much to talk about and review. Throw in your stuff."

James Burton climbed into the passenger side, too excited and tense to feel comfortable. "Manny, I have one question if you don't mind."

"Sure."

"I'm curious. How many men have you injured in battle?"

Manuel smirked. "Not a single one, James." He turned the ignition, "But I have killed one hundred. Sometimes dying is the best solution."

"And Juan Carlos?"

"Ninety-nine, I believe."

"I've never even punched anyone in the nose."

"You will very soon, amigo."

"I'm sorry, Manny, for everything."

"At first I wanted to make you 101, but without you and Miss Collins this would not have been happening today. One hundred and one will happen very soon, hombre. It just won't be you who sees the red dot. When that does happen, however, you will be home with Doris. We will make sure you are… and so will you. What is done is done. Now we will all live again, the four of us."

"Thank you for using my wife's name…thank you for returning me to her."

Nothing more as said. When they arrived, the equipment and necessary amenities were taken out except for two sets of binoculars and the three-week long glove rule still applied.

"No one so far, amigos," said Juan Carlos. "We have a couple of hours before Jaime crosses into enemy territory for the last time." He spoke to James, deadly serious. "Show us one last time, Jaime. If you are not finished before the fifth snap of my finger, you have eaten too much for lunch."

"I had no lunch. Who the hell can eat at a time like this?"

The five men raised their hands, Pablo with a sandwich in his.

"Remember, Jaime: One shot, one kill. Aim, kill, reload, aim and kill, before the fifth snap of my fingers."

The shoulder holster he'd worn every moment he wasn't with Mercedes felt good, exciting. He'd practiced each of the last several days and all day Sunday until his forefinger began to fail him. His final test had come, running a gauntlet of five men who had no need whatsoever to prove their skills.

One, he drew, bringing up the weapon, aiming. Two, he fired the single shot. Three and four, he reloaded and hit the second target without ever lowering the gun. He was ready.

JC went to Ramón's and Pablo's spilled coffee cups. "Fantástico, Jaime... worthy of a silver star."

"James, I did as you advised," said Manny, pleased. "Come. Give me your opinion, and bring your school bag."

Burton ignored the chuckles. Manuel opened each wrapping separately, waiting anxiously for the appreciative whistles and nods of approval. Laid out before of them would be his first gift to Mercedes in almost two years. He pursed his lips, his head lowered. "I bought no jewelry."

"Why would you, when she will wear a priceless gift from another. You have done well."

"Hombres," called JC, "one more review before we send our learned student to attend his graduation ceremony, and I do not think one beer will hurt." He turned to Burton. "Jaime, no scotch tonight, and your dinner will be with water. You will let Mercedes have a glass of wine to calm her nerves, not a drop more. We will have time enough tomorrow for good wine and the best homemade Mexican cooking that has ever burnt your tongue."
*

"Genevieve you are a gift to my eyes, as usual."

"Thank you, Bill. By the way, tomorrow's Sunday, have

you found a place to live until you reconcile with your wife."

"Yes, and thank you for your kind thought. There are so few people who care these days."

"You know we do." She skimmed the pages of the register. "Next week is open, if you would like to book now."

"Yes, thank you. Monday, Wednesday, and Saturday would be wonderful with another fine dinner on Saturday. I suppose I should learn to cook for myself."

Genevieve saw the leather shoulder bag. "You're studying on the weekend, Bill?"

"I intend seeing the project through. I'm beginning a new level this evening. Is Monica in her suite, or with the new girl? I told her before leaving this morning that I wasn't certain what time I would arrive."

"She's waiting for you. Enjoy your evening."

He tilted his head in a genteel Southern bow and disappeared into the elevator, feeling strongly he should blow Genevieve a kiss through the lens.

"Good evening, young lady, and what are you wearing for my pleasure on this wonderfully warm and bright Saturday evening." He closed the doors behind him.

"I did not know what to wear. You did not tell me what to wear." Monica's expression was distant with worry as she stepped back, anxious for his comment and approval. "I did not want to dress like a whore for him."

"Stop such talk this very moment." His voice was sharp and commanding. "You are radiant. I cannot remember when I saw you so heavenly, and I certainly cannot remember you as anything less than a heavenly angel, you silly girl."

"Will I be beautiful enough, do you think?"

"Yes, you will… for him, the world and everyone else including your best friend if she were here to see for herself… little girl." He winked as her eyes opened wide. "Come. Let's dance as we wait for the evening's wonderful feast." He took her hands in his, holding them to his chest. "Lucy's instruction was very clear. She insisted I that I use her intimate appellation for you and made me promise. She is well, Monica. I spoke with her for a very long time this morning. She will be home with her husband by Tuesday if all goes well when they speak with one another tomorrow. She wants you to know how much she loves you. She's reverting to a cherry blonde and I feel like a gossiping old woman talking this way."

"Does she know that soon I will be free with the other girls?"

"Yes, she does. She said one day she will find you, which I hope does not imply what I somehow believe."

"Thank you for helping her. I do miss her so much."

"Don't thank me. Thank another who anxiously waits to see you. He's pacing the floor like a nervous schoolboy on his first date." He stroked her hair. "No tears, young lady. You have no reason. Lucy is happy, as you should be."

"You are so handsome, Bill. Never have I seen you like this. It is so different to see you this way."

"Indeed. I'm undecided as to what bothers me more, the collar or the beard, or whether I appear like a gangster or a fisherman going to church. Monica, put your hands under my jacket and around my waist, slowly." Anyone would know what she was feeling. He ignored the worry etched into her face. His smirk was real. "I'm very good, or so I'm told by my teachers. However, you will understand if my water glass is a little unsteady this evening."

"What will happen, Bill, and when?"

"You will know in time and events will happen very quickly, Monica, which is why I am here with you. One reason I am here. When the time is right I will tell you what you must do, and we expect you not to fail."

"Will it be very bad?"

"No, quite the contrary, and you should already know they are the very best." The door opened discreetly. "Jennifer, Amanda, come in ladies." He walked towards them, savoring the aromas as Monica went into her bathroom. "You are both the epitome of youthful beauty, ladies. Which one of you has cooked this heavenly delight? Which one of you must I praise?"

"Bill you know very well who." Jennifer pouted. "Can we pour your wine?"

"Yes, you may, and then you can leave me to impress another young lady with my recently acquired Spanish waiter phrases."

He stood with his arms crossed, watching.

"Would you care to approve the wine, Bill?" Amanda asked.

"No, thank you. My mouth remains tainted with fine scotch, Amanda. You do the honors. And Jennifer, perhaps you would confirm her findings with a glass of your own." The two girls exchanged curious glances, giggling as they poured the wine and raised the crystal goblets to their lips. "Once more ladies; we must be certain of the quality. Then you may be excused. My lady awaits me."

When Monica came in he pulled her chair from under the small dining room ensemble, moving his crystal goblet in front of her setting and her tumbler of imported water in front of his. "I would like to propose a toast, which I believe you will understand, and please forgive my simple Spanish, "al hombre el más insolente de Veracruz que conocemos."

"Gracias a ti, mi amigo. Your Spanish is not excellent, but not very poor. As a teacher I am pleased with my student."

"And I am very pleased with a young woman who entirely changed my life." William put a hand over Monica's. "Estamos a solas. No hay nadie aquí y las flores

son muertos desde poco." He chuckled at her expression.
"Y el joven de Veracruz lo sabe."

"Bill, are you laughing at me? Do you already speak
better than you are making me believe?"

"No...not at all. It's all I've listened to this week and I
practiced the lines several times. Enjoy some wine, young
lady, and then we shall dance. He is still very close, even if
the flowers are not."

When Amanda and Jennifer came in to clear the table
the couple was still dancing. William was one of those guys
everyone seemed to like, including the girls, and no one
understood why his wife had thrown him out. By midnight
the Duty Girls were asleep in their respective beds and Bill
was sitting on the dresser, leaning against the mirror with
yet another empty glass of water in his surprisingly steady
hands.

William noted the hour. "The time is near." he said
firmly. "Monica, may I have one last dance with one of the
three prettiest women I have ever had the pleasure to be
with?"

"Claro, Bill, con mucho gusto."

He put a finger to her lips. "Without words, Mercedes,
please. Nothing I can say will adequately apologize to you
or your young man. Believe in your heart that I will spend
what is left of my life happily making up for what I have
done to you and the other girls."

"We all like you, Bill, all the girls do. I am afraid for
them."

"Don't be. There is no reason. Nothing but good will
come to them. Much is being done to ensure their futures."
He leaned forward to whisper. "Soon you will all be at the
ocean with a few surprises. Now, young lady, take another
bath and change your clothes. Take my bag. Prepare
yourself for your eager young man. All you need is in the
bag, Mercedes, gifts from Manuel. He is quite excited about

his selections. I must also say I am not responsible and accept no blame. I did my best to describe how you might have changed without getting killed for having such intimate knowledge in the first place."

Monica hugged him, grabbed for the bag and glided into the bathroom on a cushion of air. Thirty minutes later Mercedes emerged and the French braid had gone. Manuel had done well indeed, Burton thought as she pirouetted for him, waiting nervously for his nods of approval before losing her composure. She burst into tears and he opened his arms to her, thinking of her as a daughter for the first time.

"He will be very proud of you. You are an angel from heaven, an absolute delight to see."

"I am very afraid. All this week he has written how he does love me, never that he does forgive me. It is my fault that I am here, Bill. I did what he told me never to do."

"He knows, and he doesn't care. He has nothing to forgive." Burton stroked her long flowing hair. "That is in your mind alone, though I hope the lesson is learned."

She nodded into his chest. "Never did I doubt that he would come for me."

"He never doubted he would find you. He is a very brave man, a fearful enemy to confront. Be prepared, Mercedes, you will be shocked by what you see. These are very powerful men coming to save you, very dangerous men who have lately become very angry. Be prepared. Saving the girls is but one reason they are here."

"I am glad that he will not kill you. I would be angry with him for that."

He chuckled. "Let that be our secret, Mercedes, lest he change his mind."

He held her at arm's length, admiringly. The deep blue low-heeled pumps wrapped once around her ankles, her skirt was Mediterranean blue, mid-thigh and slightly flared, and her midnight blue summer-weight sweater with a scowl neckline had three-quarter sleeves and a deep V bare back with faux-buttons along each edge.

"He always did like my breasts and my legs, my bum also. My panties are blue under my skirt, and backless. Also, I am not wearing a bra."

He took a deep breath, blowing a dry whistle. "Because he's not going to kill me, young lady, does not mean you can." She touched her neck. "No, Mercedes, your accessories will be delivered to you personally, something very special indeed." Burton paused. "Later this afternoon is the last time I will see you, Mercedes. I will miss you and always remember you. You, on the other hand, will forget the past year as quickly as possible. You must. This place holds no good memory for you."

She put her hand to her throat, gasping for air. "Bill, I am not ready."

"Yes, you are... and so is he. He knows everything, Mercedes. You do not. He has much to tell you. All he wants is his wife, you. You have no reason to fear his reaction. Let others fear him."

Burton excused himself. He went into the bathroom, dimmed the lights and stayed for twenty minutes. When he emerged he called her into the bedroom where he was once again leaning against the dresser, blocking the hidden lens, signaling her closer. He was no longer the man she knew. His hair and beard were black, the woolen skullcap was pulled over his forehead and ears. Thick dark-rimmed sunglasses completed a threatening result.

At that moment her new reality became real and she understood why they had waited so long.

"Mercedes, this is what you will do." She jumped at the sound of his voice, tumbling onto the bed. "First you will dim the lights, then you will pack everything in the salon and bedroom, everything. Leave the men's clothes and your bedside drawers, do not worry about the camera, and do as I say. Forget nothing. When you are finished you will do the bathroom. Forget nothing, not even a bottle of soap. Take your time, be sure."

She worked silently and methodically. He went into the salon, first tossing the flowers into the wicker wastebasket, putting the dislodged bug into his pocket, carrying the full decanter of Glenmorangie into the bathroom where he emptied the contents into the sink. The decanter and two glasses went into her suitcase.

"Mercedes, my phone will buzz any moment now, confirming the last guest has departed the hotel, though the moments will seem like hours. We will leave together. I don't believe you want him to see you in these rooms. He will have enough to deal with without seeing you in here. I believe the lounge is a more appropriate venue for the happy occasion and, don't worry, he'll know where to go." She nodded, vigorously, choking. "Now you must listen carefully." Mercedes hung on his every word. "Do you understand what is expected of you?"

"Yes, Bill, I do."

"Tell me."

"We will go to the reception. You will occupy Genevieve and I will go into the lounge and close the doors. When I am told, I will speak to Stephanie first, then to all the girls to tell them you are not bad men. I must not use your name or show them my love for my husband. They must empty all their rooms, the way that I did. The men will check what we do and we have one hour to do all this."

"Good girl."

"Bill?"

"What is it, Mercedes?"

"I thank you for being a good man. You have done this. Gracias, amigo."

"Your husband has done this, not me. Do you have any

final questions?"

"Yes, I do. What is your real name?"

"William. My real name is William." His smile was wide, surprised by his own stoicism. He put gloved hands to her cheeks. "Please stop your tears. I told him you were a gorgeous little thing and now he will think I lied to him. You will have plenty of time for crying happy tears when you are walking with him this afternoon by the ocean, alone."

James Burton flipped his phone open at 3:15 Sunday morning.

*

Sunday morning, August 05.

Genevieve sat at the reception waiting for the call from Monica to say William was ready to leave. She hadn't bothered checking Monica's rooms since he began using her as a language instructor. She was anxious for him to leave, when she could tune into Monica's suite to watch her favorite girl bathe, shower or be with Nicole, anxious to see whether there would be a Nicole. If not, Genevieve would be beside Monica and neither woman would be disappointed. All she needed was one chance.

Then Genevieve blinked incredulously into another time and place. No one ever exited the elevator unexpectedly, yet the man came out walking quickly, straight toward her. Nothing made sense. He held a gun, and wasn't who he was supposed to be. The man wasn't William, she knew, yet Monica was following quickly behind him, dressed so differently. But why was he pointing the gun at her, why did she not care, and why was she falling and feeling so blissful?

Burton holstered the gun, dragged the prefect from behind the desk, plucked the dart from her chest and guided Mercedes into the lounge, assuring her repeatedly that

Genevieve was not dead.

He held her close one last time before bringing the French doors together. He flipped open his cell and the cold voice said "on the count of five." Five seconds later five men rushed up the granite steps and through unlocked doors like a determined death squad. The second man carried thirteen large silver and gold embossed shopping bags. If there was humor in the scene it went unnoticed.

Inside the lounge Mercedes stood frozen in a corner, too afraid to tremble. She heard more frightening voices, a mere second passing before the lounge doors flung open framing a figure dressed entirely in black and masked identically to the man who seconds earlier anaesthetized a stunned Genevieve. He stood with his legs together, fierce and dangerous with dark glasses and black beard covering his face as one hand pulled at his jacket and the other holstered his weapon that seemed part of him. He was a Manuel she would never have known.

He stood there, seeing her quiver and unable to move. Burton was right. She wasn't the same woman. She was more beautiful than he remembered or what he had dreamed. When he spoke her eyes widened with shock and she burst into tears, terrified. Then he understood. He came towards her, putting a warning finger to his lips as he tugged off his gloves, absorbing every inch of her as he pulled at the neckband of the digital voice modulator.

"Cariño, soy yo. Do not be afraid of me. You will very soon see me the way you remember." They were crying, Mercedes cowering into the wall, biting hard onto her quivering fist. "Mercedes, I am here, as in a dream. But I am no dream. The dream is over, and our daughter is safe." He raised his hands to his collar. "I made a promise to a special friend who waits anxiously to meet you for the first time, only hours from now. She is the woman in the photo at the beach. She has helped me beyond words. This is her gift to you with her love. She is awake and praying for us at this very moment. I have worn this for many months knowing this day would come." He draped Carmella's gold cross around Mercedes' neck, clasping the hook and cupping her wet face in his hands. "Kiss me, chica. Then we must go and you do not know me. Think of nothing but our success and your instructions. Kiss me, and believe I will never stop loving you."

She shook her head in a daze, talking in a whisper with tears streaming down her face. "I can never be the woman you once loved. I can never be your cariño."

"You will always be my cariño, and I will never stop loving you. That will never change." He pushed up his left sleeve, raising his arm. "You see, I have come. I have never stopped searching for you."

Without warning he was in a death grip of constricting arms and legs and a flood of more heated tears, Juan Carlos calling them to real time. Manuel replaced the band and gloves; he took her hand and ran from the room.

"Gentlemen, please meet the reason we are here," Juan Carlos announced.

The five men faced her, hardened faces unsmiling as a dull thunder emanated from gloved hands. William was lost amongst the others. He was one of them, equally fearsome, and she would not let them down.

She didn't falter. "Stephanie, please come to the desk. I do believe that Genevieve is not very well. Stephanie, wake up and come to the desk. I do not believe that Genevieve is very well."

Within moments Stephanie came running down the stairs, with the unexpected. By the count of four she and Penelope lay crumpled on the carpeted floor, Mercedes once again knowing Bill as he knelt between the girls to extract both darts.

"Everybody, this is Monica. Come to the lobby.

Amanda, Carol, Jennifer, Melanie, Dree, Katrina, Kelly, Nicole, come right away to the lobby. Amanda, date prisa, es muy importante. Partimos de aquí, chica. Do not be afraid. Come quickly. We are leaving from this place."

A flurry of silk and satin chemises, robes, barely covered breasts and bare legs flooded into the lobby. The men were as surprised to see such an erotic array of colored silk and skin as the women were to see six ferocious men in black with only the hollows of their open mouths lending them color. The women instinctively huddled together near the stairwell; the men stood several feet away in the center of the lobby, forming a semi-circle behind Mercedes.

"Amanda, come here to stand beside me. Girls, listen to me. These are very good men. They are here to help us. They do seem very bad, and do sound very horrible, but they are good. Please believe me. They are good men. They are the men who did save Lucy from dying. You must believe what they tell you and you must do what they say."

They couldn't fathom seeing three women propped against the wall behind six frightening men dressed in black. They wanted to be terrified, not understanding how Amanda went to Monica and was holding her hands, listening as though she understood every foreign word.

"Girls," Amanda began, "listen to Monica. Listen to these men. They have come to help us, not hurt us. Listen to them. They are taking us to our families."

Juan Carlos checked his watch and stepped forward. "Good morning, ladies. You must listen very closely to what I say. Do not be afraid. How we appear to you and how we sound is not real, done for our protection as much as your own. The women you see behind us are sleeping. They will be awake in ten or fifteen minutes, although they won't feel very well for a while. You will be treated with every respect and courtesy, but you must never discover who we are. We are here to help you, but secrecy is very important to our success. You have one hour to clean out your suites of everything you possess, and I do mean everything. All you will leave are the personal items we believe are kept in your bedside tables and the men's clothing. Take everything else. When you are done you will reassemble in the lounge. These men will then check each of your rooms for anything you have forgotten, so please save us all that time. Put your suitcases outside your doors. These men will do the rest. You are free ladies. You are going home. In one hour you will be taken to a safe place where you will see the sun, the ocean and speak with your families very soon after. So do not waste time. Unless you decide otherwise, you will be with your families within a few days. This we promise you. We also promise you will no longer wear those monitors. Ladies, form a line quickly so we can remove them for you. Your children will not be harmed in any way as a result of your escape and, when we have you settled, we will work at reuniting them with you. We know where they are. Each of you will be given new clothes more appropriate to our destination. Each of these bags is labeled with one of your names. Change into those clothes and put what you are wearing in your suitcases along with these shopping bags. The bag without a name has a special purpose. You are no longer in danger from the one you call Miss Divine and the men who brought you here. You will never see them or her again. Ladies, we will travel for six hours, non-stop. Do you understand? We will not stop for any reason. Once your bracelets are removed you will each do as instructed so we can get you out of here as quickly as possible. You will hear more once we arrive. You now have fifty-five minutes to change and evacuate. Shower if you must, and do so within the timeframe." He checked his watch and pointed to Mercedes. "Hold out your wrist."

Ramón and Fernando stood by the main doors, waiting

for the three women to regain consciousness. Pablo was the computer and vault expert. The fourth floor was expansive and smelled of raspberries. The four men searched meticulously through every drawer, every crevice and corner of the suite that was both feminine and sexually decadent. The wardrobe was filled with gowns and lingerie of every description in silk, satin, latex and open mesh with leather trim. When JC clicked the remote to the plasma screen by the cushion-laden bed they saw Dree hurrying through her room, then a close-up of Kelly holding her new dress against herself in front of the lens, another channel showed Amanda reaching for a towel and they hadn't yet seen the vault.

"Pablo, can you do it?"

Pablo sneered at the challenge, nodding confidently. "Perhaps if I had finished my coffee I would have worked faster, but, yes." He rubbed his gloved hands together. "It is done."

Burton was the first in, fumbling for the light switch. Manuel, Juan Carlos and Pablo followed, standing in awe of what lay before them. The vault was a fifteen-by-fifteen panic room housing wooden chairs with restraining hardware, counters and cabinets filled with vials, syringes and bags of a white substance JC recognized immediately as the date rape drug roofies. Behind the chairs was an extensive library of DVDs and VHS tapes classified by guest and girl, a player for each format, a desk, a laptop and a digital safe Pablo assured them was child's play. Juan Carlos tapped into the computer as Manuel and Burton went through the files.

Burton spoke first. "With the names in these files, the photos and those videos, the plan to assist these ladies will be well-funded by several dozen contributors who will be extremely anxious to right a wrong. We must take everything and be sure to make copies. I would estimate twenty to thirty million. These are the titans of industry and politics, both local and offshore."

"That could become very dangerous for you, once they discover who you are."

"They won't know. I intend hiring the best. Nothing less will do for what must be done. In any event, I assure you there isn't one amongst them who isn't familiar with monetary solutions to most of life's difficulties. I thank you for your concern, though I assure you, both I and the Foundation will be fine"

"It's a lot to carry. We have no boxes."

"There's a laundry room with ample pillow cases. We'll make do." Burton faced Manuel, standing straight. "I would ask one favor."

Manuel nodded. "Take yours and hers. We won't need copies."

"Thank you. She'll be grateful."

Manuel examined the wall of DVDs, hesitantly reaching out for a particular grouping.

Burton's curt command stunned them. "No! Do not do that. What will you prove? Are you so anxious to witness her misery that will bring you deep pain until your dying day?"

"He is right." JC took over. "Touch a single one and I will crush your pathetic head and take your woman for myself. What you are thinking is not worthy of you, or her. Both of you get down there and tell her you need pillow cases." When Manuel and Burton returned Mercedes was not with them. "I have good news," JC said.

"How good?"

"Everything in those files is in this computer, which we will take as well. That's not all." He looked at Burton. "We hit pay dirt, sixteen million in an island account which I have transferred to my offshore account with Pablo's help. She is now a peasant. She's completely broke. We also

494

found a hundred grand or more in the safe." He passed Burton the bundles. "When you are ready, amigo, every cent will be transferred from my account to wherever you say."

Burton wrapped an arm halfway around each of his massive companions in turn. He was speechless and thirty minutes after they began the vault was empty of everything save the drugs, the desk, the safe and the chairs. Before they left Pablo reset the combination to zero, requiring several trial openings and closings before the others believed him, and each mirror on the floor was smashed to reveal four cameras, two of which were in the bedroom.

Each of the eight women showered, becoming flustered schoolgirls in their summer dresses and low-heeled sandals. They were different women, crying with confusion and excitement, not believing what was happening to them.

JC spoke. "Ladies, you are all glowing more than the sun that will soon rise. Not much time is left to us. Please go into the lounge and remain standing. We will join you in a moment and forgive us for closing the door behind you." When they were closed in he spoke to Genevieve, Stephanie and Penelope. "Ladies, let me tell you what you missed during your sleep. You are free to leave this place. We apologize for the manner in which we subdued you. We had little choice. You are, after all, the guardians of this hell. We have new clothes for each of you, and a new beginning, whether you choose to come with us or relocate on your own. The choice is yours. If it's the latter you will be taken away immediately with sufficient funds to start over."

"How much?" Penelope asked.

The question took them by surprise.

"We can help you find your families and the lives you lost. What does it matter how much?"

"Or you can condemn us to lives we never asked for or wanted." She took Stephanie's hand. "So how much?"

"We will lose track of you and, for that reason, fifty thousand each."

"And the others, what do they get?"

"They are not your concern, Penelope." He pointed to the bags. "Go to your suite with this man and change your clothes. He will not harm you." Then: "Stephanie, do you agree with her?" She did. "Then stand and do the same, with this man. And you, Genevieve?"

"Is all this true?"

"Yes."

"My husband was killed years ago."

"Possibly, or he may be waiting for you."

Genevieve's face glistened with tears. "I want my life back. I want my daughter. You told them you can help. How will you do that?"

"We can and we will. You have been gone seven or eight years if my information is correct. You might be too late for your husband, only time will tell. I don't know, but certainly you will never be too late for your daughter. We will succeed for you. The choice is yours." Her lips were quivering, uncertain as time was becoming more precious. "Why would you forfeit future happiness because of past doubts?"

She nodded, wiping away a steady stream of tears. "I do want you to help me. Please."

He helped her to her feet. "Go to your room with this man and change your clothes. He will tell you what you must do, and please hurry. He will not harm you. We are not here to hurt you more." JC, Burton and Manuel joined the others in the lounge. "Ladies, time is against us. Stephanie and Penelope will not join us. They made a different choice and will be taken away in a few minutes to begin whatever life they see for themselves. Genevieve, however, will come with us. She will be here momentarily. We are aware of some discord between her and the rest of you and I cannot say too strongly that what is done is done."

Burton walked in and around the women with the open shopping bag in his hands.

"Ladies, we are simple men and we apologize for our poor taste. In the bag is a purse for each of you. Take one. If you do not like the one you select feel free to exchange yours with a friend. What you will find inside one is inside the others: fifty thousand dollars in denominations of fifties and hundreds, half of what you will receive to help you regain your lives. Please," the laugh sounded freakish through the modulator, "do not lose them. The rest of what you will experience in the coming days you will hear about this afternoon, by the ocean, with champagne in your hands."

The purses were Gucci and the girls giggled and swapped with one another to match their shoes.

"Ladies," Juan Carlos continued, "now that you seem no longer afraid of our artificial voices and faces we will blindfold you and help you into two vans. Blindfolds because you must never know where you are at this moment or where you are going. Should you somehow learn of this location later on, so be it. However, no longer is there anyone to punish for what has happened to you or your children and do not ask questions we will not answer. We will travel for six hours with food and water. Then you will feel sand under your feet, free to sing and dance as much as you want. You will remain there for as long as three or four days and there is much more for you to discover. This is not over for any of you. What lies ahead will possibly be very long and painful for you. More importantly, you will not be alone, but that is for later. Good luck."

Stephanie and Penelope were given purses, blindfolded and driven to the suburbs by Fernando and Ramón. Burton and Juan Carlos went to each suite to do a final inspection

and smash the mirrors as Pablo dismantled the control panel of the exterior surveillance system, removed the current tape and reset the codes for the doors so any combination of numbers would open them. Manuel confiscated the computer and register from the reception as the girls followed his every move in quiet awe, one in particular who was too happy or nervous to speak.
*

Pablo blindfolded Genevieve first. Monica was the last to leave. The vans were windowless with a dark curtain behind the drivers to prevent road signs from being sequentially remembered. Once inside the blindfolds were removed and eventually the chatter and tears of uncertainty stopped and the women slept under warm blankets. When they awoke, for the first time in long months and years, they saw blinding light and heard the sound of crashing waves, not silent darkness. James Burton and Manuel arrived an hour later. During their time together Manuel drove and Burton read aloud.

In the afternoon the girls cried, hearing what had happened to past Anchor Girls, as much for themselves and the eventual horror they had each been spared. Mercedes was first to hug the six men, squeezing two harder than the others. The other girls followed.

The women didn't learn of Cassandra or how she was brutally killed, though they did learn how a growing team of specialists was being hired, some already diligently searching for the most recently abandoned girls. They hugged each other tightly, pressing their wet faces together when they heard Daphne's, Brenda's and Alice's current locations were already known. The men asked for nothing in return, other than they be forgotten.

The girls were allowed on the beach three at a time for one hour, each one accompanied by a man who kept his distance. Monica went first with the man who had spoken the least, and when the beach house disappeared behind them she nestled herself into his side. She was the last to return and no one seemed to mind.

When they reunited, one of the six men explained an organization that was available to them whenever they needed help and for whatever reason. The keyword to type in or speak into the 888 number would be First Search and their PIN. The Foundation would know immediately where to send help.

By early evening the girls were asleep, two to a room, though Genevieve slept with her face to the wall, her back to Nicole. She didn't care how they felt about her. She wanted her promised phone call and cried herself to sleep believing he wouldn't want her.

Mercedes spent the entire evening watching DVDs of Sofia at the beach, Sofia at the park, Sofia with a huge man Mercedes wasn't supposed to know, and Sofia with all those who had been her friends and protectors for so many weeks. Carmella obeyed her cousin's instructions implicitly and didn't treat Mercedes any differently than the others. She thought ignoring Mercedes would be difficult, and she was right, diminishing her quandary by fussing over each girl equally. Now she was with her new friend. She could be Carmelita and spend the evening telling Mercedes how perfect Manuel was, how perfect both men were, assuring her that both men would return to them.

As they lay together by the open window Mercedes heard the ocean and felt the warm evening breeze as she listened to Carmella tell her everything Manuel had been through and how relentless he had been in his search. They fell asleep wiping each other's tears.

Seven hundred miles away, secure in the warm amber glow of a single light and the soft humming of their favorite lullaby, little Sofia and Poochie the Bear shared their own dreams, and new memories of a young mother's sweet voice.

Ninety-Five

Away from the women and with a tempered anger Burton threatened each of them with the immediate infliction of excruciating pain not yet known to mankind, and he was serious, although he had no idea what exactly the torture would be or how he would begin.

None of them laughed at him. They respected him, each for their own reasons. Finally the five agreed. He had proven himself. He would go with them, with the proviso that Fernando would accompany him. He agreed, and they shook gloved hands.

JC, Manuel, Fernando and Jaime arrived in Atlanta as the girls slept peacefully in North Carolina. The evening sky was black with torrential rain and would be for twenty-four hours. The four men drank to the health of the women they left behind with a double shot of tequila before separating. They had hours left before the final kill shot, according to what they knew. They acted according to what they did not know.

JC and Manuel shook hands with Burton. They would not see each other again. When the job was done he would return home to his wife and his newly chosen career while Fernando kept impromptu appointments with an unfortunate Christopher Brandon and a soon-to-be defunct Warner Stevens. Any future communication would be through an intermediary of the Search Foundation. Watching them cross the street James Burton knew he would never understand how he felt at that precise moment seeing the young men walk so calmly towards killing someone.

Ninety-Six

Monday, August 06

Fernando and Burton maintained their vigil sleeplessly for fifteen hours as JC and Manuel assured themselves nothing had been neglected or forgotten in the hotel. They didn't think to occupy the reserved parking spot, the last thing they needed was a zealous cop calling it in or, worse, braving the violent rain to meet a weekly quota.

By early morning the street was alive with wildly flailing coats intended for show, drenched office workers rushing towards personalized boredoms and furious windshield wipers animating stalled traffic. By 9:00 the street was deserted with rivers of rushing water swirling into curbside gutters.

Moments before noon Fernando spoke into his headset. The street was filled with a fleet of delivery vans and cars, flashing lights, scurrying delivery boys, and the same black Chrysler had already made two passes, slowing in front of the hotel each time. This time it parallel parked. Burton confirmed her identity through his headset. She was going through the first set of doors.

What she saw at the reception told her all she had to know. The eerie silence engulfed her and she gripped the 10mm Glock 20 firmly in both hands. With her back to the wall the lounge was first, then the store through the glass partitions, the restaurant, the kitchen, the spa and the gym. There was no need to call out for Genevieve. She was alone and how that had happened was not important. The fourth floor was all that mattered.

Her suite was black, lit by a wide path of dim light spreading from the elevator that stretched her shadow to the far wall of the salon. When she stepped out she flipped the wall switch with her shoulder. Nothing. She stopped breathing.

The carpeted floor was covered with shards of mercury-coated glass; a chain-mail skirt and halter top with leather trim were draped over her settee. The twin French doors to the vault and her bedroom were closed. She chose the bedroom, easing down on the curved handles, pushing one door inward with her foot, then the other. Going in was pointless. She could see the smashed mirrors and bared lenses from where she stood and the room was dark. Were there someone inside she would be the disadvantaged one. She pivoted slowly, keeping the open doors in sight as she inched her way to the vault, swinging open the French doors and punching in her code.

Manuel flipped up the lens of his night vision goggles as the door eased open, letting the beam of his laser-guided Berretta draw a perfect red line from the desk to the door. On the other side the voice behind her was barely audible.

"Drop your weapon, now, and turn to your immediate left. You'll see a red dot on the wall. And now you don't because it's centered at the back of your head. Go in, slowly, and flip the switch."

She did. Her disbelief was genuine and absolute. "Del Fuego."

"Captain Peachtree." She stood immobilized. "I told you I would find her, Peachtree, though I didn't think I would also find an offshore bank account worth sixteen million and eleven other women turned into whores by one of

Atlanta's finest. Come in. Sit down. You're in for quite an afternoon, chica. Enjoy. This is your last one."

"I have no idea what you're talking about. I told you to call me as soon as you found out something. I'm here responding to a call from someone at this address."

"Then where's your backup?" He moved towards her. "They're all dead, Peachtree: Robert Baker and Frank Randolph, Tucker Richman the lawyer and the two fuck-ups who bought my daughter. We have the lawyer's files, every name of every child and the ones who bought them. It's been a busy few days. The doctor and the hairdresser will join them at the gates of hell within a few hours and now there's only one person left." He chuckled. "Wanna guess who."

"I'm not guessing fuck all."

"We saved you for last out of necessity, not preference."

"I'm walking."

"No, you're dying, but first you'll strip completely. We still have a bit of time, so if you want to make it special for us, go ahead, and don't worry about your millions. It's all gone, so are the files of your clients and the women. By the way, we have Lucy. Now strip."

"Go fuck yourself."

The voice behind said: "Do it, or I'll hang you by your feet while he does it for you."

Manuel tilted his head as though asking her what she was waiting for. Her coat dropped to the floor followed by her holster; her silk blouse came off one button at a time before she tugged her camisole out from her slacks and pulled it over her head in one fluid motion. When she was finished she stood with her arms crossed.

JC stayed behind her. He slid an open hand into her linen slacks, made a fist, and jerked her from the floor as anyone would a bag of groceries, dropping her on all fours, telling her to remove her pants or he would.

She used one of the chairs for support as she kicked off her shoes. She undid her belt mechanically, tugging at the zipper, unfolding the front panels. She bent forward, pushing them to her ankles, making certain the man behind her was staring at her bare buttocks.

The violence of JC's knee crashing into those buttocks hurled her comically forward against one of her own restraining chairs, her flailing arms unable to soften the impact against her bare breasts. One huge hand pushed hard into the small of her back as the other first tore her pants from her ankles, then the backup weapon strapped to the inside of her left ankle. When he finished he helped her stand, ripping away her thong with a single tug before spinning her and pushing her into the chair. When he was done he closed the door and both men lowered their goggles as he closed the light.

Manuel continued filling the syringes from the vials. "Is it dark enough for you, captain? Have you ever done this for kicks, lock yourself into the dark to feel the terror those girls felt when you locked them in here without light? How do you feel being terrorized in the dark, being naked and not knowing what will come next? Are you afraid yet, Captain?" All she could hear were muffled footsteps, all she could see were the red beams of laser trackers. "You have a choice, Peachtree, before we strap you in. You can wear the outfit we selected for you or you can stay naked. Personally, I don't see much difference between the two."

She said nothing, her body reacting with a jolt to JC's invisible grip when he knelt in front of her to shackle her ankles. When she was secured he pulled her forward by the nape of her neck, maneuvering her holster around her rigid arms and shoulders before shackling her wrists and her elbows. He finished by roughly pushing apart her knees, fixing them in place to the sides of the chair before strapping her empty ankle holster in place.

Both men stood in front of the naked woman whose hair dripped rainwater with streaks of dark mascara scarring her emotionless face, all the more ghoulish in the green of their goggles. Her eyes were blinking rapidly, her chest heaving in rhythm to the sound of her labored breathing as her pale skin reacted to the chill of the air-conditioned room.

"There's a reason for everything, Peachtree. You could have let her go so easily. I believe the reason you didn't is that we were intended to find the other girls, as painful as that was for my wife." Samantha Peachtree stared straight ahead. "Why didn't you let her go when you knew I would not stop my hunt?" She said nothing. "Captain, the more you say the longer you will live, but if you prefer my monologue we won't be here very long at all, despite the pleasure we and the women would gain. And don't forget, we'll also be searching your two apartments in the city." He chortled at her reaction." Yes, I've known for a while. So why did you not let her go?"

"She wanted me right away, from our first night together. She was hot. I liked the way she felt when she was on top of me and she liked everything I did to her." She gulped trying to moisten her mouth. "If you don't believe me, check the tapes."

"Your library is destroyed, with the exception of one tape, and we have copies to leave in your apartments. So why don't you tell us about Cassandra, Mrs. Valerie Templeton? The mother you murdered so horribly. What could she have done that was worth cutting her throat and throwing her body onto the middle lane of a highway?"

"Guess she didn't like the way I taste. She didn't work out."

"And all the others?" he questioned. "Why didn't you let the girls go free after their three-year sentence?"

"That should be obvious to such a smart man. I had no way of knowing how they talked together when their heads shared one pillow, when they weren't kissing or doing whatever. Eventually they would have known they were in Atlanta. I'm in charge of Missing Persons." She manufactured a caustic smile. "How stressful would that have been? Figure out the rest yourself.

"As stressful as being strapped naked to a chair with your legs wide open and men you can't see preparing to kill you?" He reached into a pocket, a faint purple glow showing no more than the gloved fist holding it. "Imagine the surprise of your compadres when they see proud Captain Peachtree strapped naked to that same chair with her legs wide open to greet them, a purple glow-in–dark rubber dick stuck in her mouth, her weapons holstered, and a bullet hole in her forehead." He passed the dildo to JC, both men smiling as he rammed the dildo into her mouth, securing it in place with duct tape as Manuel continued speaking. "There is nothing more I need to hear, nothing more I wish to say. You humiliated dozens of women and we assume you are responsible for many untimely deaths. This is how we will humiliate you. You fucked with the wrong guy and there's an irony to all this, Peachtree, which I'm sure is not lost on you, so to speak: You are now a missing person." Manuel slipped a note between her thighs, protected in one of her own plastic bags as JC slid both her useless weapons into the respective holsters. "This is a note explaining that you murdered Valerie Templeton. I'm putting it here because it's what your men will gawk at the longest after they find you, their boss' bare pussy, although," he paused, twisting the end of the dildo to activate the motor, "you'll probably be a little too mummified by the time they find you for it to be a sexual thing." He grinned. "If all your bills are paid up you might not be found for months, so by the time they come you won't exactly be pretty, not to mention the stink of your lost fluids and decayed flesh." Her chest was pounding, her nostrils flaring to compensate for her taped mouth. When he spoke in Spanish to Juan Carlos who agreed to whatever was said, her streaked face glistened with fresh tears against her purple mask. "When they see the drugs, the marijuana and the hypos on your fourth floor with your DNA all over it, and the video of you and Valerie Templeton in the bathroom the night you killed her, they'll know everything, including how Valerie ran from you for her life. Nothing else is left, except the toys and condoms in the girls' bedrooms and your file on Valerie Templeton that I have left on your desk with photos of her first night in this chair you are now warming with your charms." He stayed silent for long moments, letting the darkness take over. "By the way, her children will soon be reunited with their family."

She whimpered involuntarily at the dual pricks, wanting desperately to struggle free of her tight shackles as JC injected one forearm and Manuel the other with liquefied cocaine that felt cold and frightening as it melded with her blood. The third and fourth went into her thighs, neither man bothering about a vein.

They left the syringes firmly embedded under her skin, stepping aside indifferently, invisible, watching her eyes glaze over as Manuel brought the sleek 92FS from under his jacket. Her eyes focused instantly on the weapon's red laser beam becoming a translucent red dot at the juncture of her thighs, the only thing she could see beyond her luminescent death veil.

Samantha Peachtree twisted her head sideways, contorting her face downward past the whirring dildo to see the tiny beam illuminating the open folds of her lips as a gush of warm water sprayed out from between them with a loud hiss.

The voice was indifferent as the dot traveled upward to her abdomen. "Don't be embarrassed, Captain. We have seen better men than you piss themselves at the time of their deaths. When they find you they will close your file faster than you want to close your legs, puta, and one day I will spit on your infested grave."

The dot rose with terrifying slowness, disappearing under her chin. Miss Divine inhaled her final breath and died at the very moment James Burton walked in to the biggest and happiest surprise of his life.

*

Not so for Doris who'd been sitting comfortably alone on a down-filled futon since his call, and not appearing very much at all like his Doris. Her auburn hair was streaked with blonde, swept into a young and current updo style, her skin was lightly tanned for the first time in thirteen years and two hand-widths of very attractive legs showed scandalously above her knees. Her skirt was pleated, nicely short and her blouse was décolleté and sheer with a silk and lace camisole showing provocatively between the lapels.

When he came into view she shrieked and the white wine in her glass which had threatened to cascade over the rim of her crystal goblet did, in a hectic splash that reached her knees and the carpet under her feet. He spun around, puzzled, looking for the devil woman who had gone; instead seeing his image in the gold embossed full-length mirror for the first time since preparing himself in another young lady's bathroom. He swaggered towards her, his face a mystery of changing expressions as he sank beside Doris on one knee, not knowing whether to laugh or cry, thankful Fernando had taken the gun.

She had a gift for him, and he had a gift for her; however ladies always came first in the South. She was so beautiful, their lost years already forgotten. The gift was small, she explained, very small, and came after the tickets and her modest boast about a smaller dress size. The best was yet to come, and when he opened the tiny box his eyes sparkled, thinking how beautiful and sexy she would be wearing the tiny triangles on the beaches of their thirty-day Mediterranean cruise.

He apologized profusely for his appearance, for scaring her and for not thinking to bring flowers for such a beautiful woman, causing Doris to look at him curiously. He did send her flowers, twelve beautiful yellow carnations, she reminded him, delivered a few hours earlier, though she didn't understand why 'thank you' was written on the card. Thank you for what, she asked?

He followed her gaze, sighing deeply and wiping his eyes, Doris believing she understood. He was ominous and scary and he begged her not to ask questions. As much as he wanted to laugh when she said how much she liked the new and dashing him, how much his new virility turned her on, he couldn't. He wasn't like the others. They were a special breed of men who hadn't disparaged him. He admired them. He had come to like them, but he wasn't one of them.

Doris sat patiently, sensing she would never know the real reason for his leaving home, or what had inexplicably turned a CEO of a respected firm into such a fearful and brave man whose gift to her was simple: At month's end he would walk away from Quantum Communications and take the chair of a special foundation recently begun by him and Amy Pennington to help special young women who, along with their children, had suffered greatly. She absorbed him for the longest time in his black turtleneck and dark beard, his black jacket and his beleaguered face, telling him to bathe and come to her. Nothing would stop her from loving him, unless he tried to stop her from working by his side and seeing Amy once again.

Ninety-Seven

October 31

Platoon Commander Billings and Master Sergeant Dwayne Bishops had concurred. Manuel Del Fuego had acted meritoriously, above and beyond, and Sergeant Del Fuego of Parris Island, South Carolina now stood in dress blues on the patio of his new home with the two men who had done so much to shape his life.

Earlier Juan Carlos took Dwayne Bishops aside to explain his presence and the sergeant's response was to stop JC the way men of a kind do when their assumptions are proven correct. Del Fuego hadn't lied. He had protected one of his own and that's what the Corps was all about.

The three men raised their glasses. Juan Carlos understood Bishops, understanding the man who saved his life even more. The two would forever be closer than brothers and when JC went to leave, to give the Marines space to talk, Bishops put a hand on his arm to stop him. He had something important to say, something he was certain Juan Carlos would want to hear firsthand. Manny's new rank was temporary, he confessed somberly, grinning at Manuel's furrowed brow and JC's visible uncertainty as to where all this was going.

Bishops sipped his wine, enjoying every second. Temporary, he continued, because Commander Billings and he fully expected Del Fuego, Manuel, Sergeant, would soon become Lieutenant Del Fuego. He put up his hand, prohibiting any response, and for that reason Mrs. Del Fuego, Mercedes, and Sofia were expected at the state capital building on the coming second of November where they would be sworn in as the state's newest US citizens, a strict formality for any commissioned officer in US Marines.

Billings had signed the papers, pulled some strings and Dwayne Bishops saluted as he handed Manuel the envelope sealed with the official USMC insignia. Juan Carlos took up his friend in a bear hug, dropping him to shake hands with Bishops and step into the house.

Three Miami business associates were heatedly arguing sports in the living room, their wives, Miss Collins and Mrs. Bishops were cooing over Sofia, and Mercedes still wanted to know from an evasive Carmella who else was coming. Manuel had no way to thank Bishops for what he had done. They were now Dwayne and Manny and no words were necessary. That was for pissy-eyed civilians. He had done the US Marines proud and they both remembered his first full day back on base. No questions had been asked, nor would there ever be.

Dwayne left to join his wife and ask Mercedes to join Manuel on the patio, warning Manny with a salute between equals not to fuck up the Marine protocol of always being cool in the heat of battle. The couple was the center of attention through the sliding doors, including Miss Georgina's who wasn't at all certain why as she waited for the shrieks and hugs that came on cue. When the couple eventually came in to loud applause Mercedes' face was streaked with color, Sergeant Del Fuego's uniform was no longer parade approved and he begged a few moments away from his guests to correct the indignity.

When he returned Mercedes called her guests to the

table, but first there were birthday gifts to open and what would a birthday party be without a special surprise for the birthday girl. They all knew, everyone except Mercedes and Miss Georgina.

Standing at the head of the table Manuel toasted an elegant and coiffed Miss Georgina who had come with the Bishops, all the other ladies, Sergeant Bishops, Colonel Billings in absentia, JC, whom he called his brother, Pablo, Fernando, Ramón and those who could not be with them. Then he toasted his wife and the men stood, everyone waiting with bated breath except Miss Georgina who thought everything was so wonderful.

Mercedes had endured much, yet she hadn't changed, he said, even though she'd spent the past weeks hovering between tears of joy and tears of sadness for lost friends. He added with a sheepish shrug that, after so much time apart he couldn't think of anything more original for her birthday than a cell phone, adding that, of course, that particular model came equipped with built-in GPS.

He laughed off the obvious implication as she hugged him around the waist, her face glowing with tears. She listened to each word, visibly startled when the phone chimed from inside the box. The room fell quiet, Manuel gulping the rest of his wine to the accompaniment of wide grins from his guests as she looked up at him, seeing him dumbly shrugging his shoulders. She knew her man. He was playing a stupid joke. She tore at the paper, fumbling at the box and styro wrapping as the phone continued ringing, knowing full-well he had done something silly to embarrass her.

"Yes, hello, who is it?"

"Happy Birthday, Mercedes. It's Tracy."

"I am sorry. Who is it?" She didn't understand, and Manny was focused on Pablo who was already walking to the front door.

The voice giggled. "It's Tracy, Mercedes. I'm your birthday surprise from Manny. You once told me you would always love me, little girl, and that you would never leave me. That night, the night I spanked your little Latina ass, you were already sleeping when I told you I would never let you leave me." A completely new Tracey Grainger stepped through the portal, squeezing Pablo like the big brother he'd become. She closed her phone with a loud snap. "So why don't you hang up and come to meet my family, chica?"

Juan Carlos barely managed to reach out for Mercedes' falling chair at the very moment a youthful Doris Burton hung in her lover's arms, their lips pressed together between a dark sky sprinkled with twinkling stars and the black midnight waters of the warm Mediterranean Sea.

The Madam

Other Mystery – Suspense - Thriller Novels

By Doug Booth:

Split Verdict

The 4th Man

The Madam

Family Lies

Mother of Pearl

From Inside Her Bedroom

The Feast of Tombola

Deferred Prejudice

The Hunt for Gilligan Rose

The Fatal Diners' Club

Silent Conviction

A Christmas Killer, Comfort and Joy

Pariah In the Mirror

***

No One to Tell (Creative Non-fiction)